Show Me How

A OAK POINT NOVEL

HANNAH COWAN

First Edition

ISBN: 978-1-990804-84-7

Edited and proofed by: Sandra @oneloveediting

Cover design by: Mary @booksnmoods

Interior chapter heading illustrations designed by: Riley Nevels @roobee.doodles

Oak Map designed by: Ink And Velvet Designs @inkandvelvetdesigns

SHIMMER LAKE
PAINTED SKY STABLES
SHIMMER PINES
Twice Treasured
TWICE TREASURED
POST OFFICE
Maggie's DINNER
INTO THE SHADE
TATTOO SHOP
MAGGIE'S DINNER
INTO THE SHADE
GAS
FIRE STATION
GAS STATION
welcome to
Oak Point
COMMUNITY CENTER

For those of us who have lost ourselves somewhere along the crazy journey that is life. It's never too late to find those forgotten pieces again, or to complete the puzzle with new ones.

You might even find a tattooed playboy who barks for you like a fucking dog along the way.

1

Millie

I FLINCH WHEN MY MOTHER TUGS TIGHTER THE TIES OF MY corset, nearly sending me toppling backward. She yanks like her life depends on it, and I'm genuinely concerned that I'm only five minutes away from losing consciousness.

Palming my stomach, I gasp when she pulls again, this time grunting at the effort. She sighs and digs a finger between the silk ties.

"Have you gained weight, Millicent? I don't remember having to work this much at your last fitting."

I ignore the dig. "You weren't the one pulling."

And yes, I probably have gained weight. The idea of making myself appear in the best shape of my life just to marry a man whom I don't love wasn't even slightly appealing. I've ignored the meal plan she had created for me and have ordered in every day for the last two weeks. The only thing I regret is not trying harder to get food poisoning last night.

"Either way. I'm sorry, but it has to be like this. You won't have to do much moving once we've finished with photos and the ceremony starts. I recommend standing until it's time to go," she snips, the apology lacking feeling.

"When do we have to go?"

"An hour. Your makeup needs touching up. Meredith!" Fingers rub at my face and poke at the backs of my arms before the makeup artist appears. "You forgot the lashes."

"I don't need them, Mom," I say, lightly pushing away the artist's hand when I spot the thick black eyelashes in her fingers.

"You forget how many cameras will be out there. Do you really want to be caught with a flat, bare lash? Don't be ridiculous." She pushes forward and takes the lashes from the artist before jabbing them onto my eyelids.

The tip of her nail glides across my eye, and I wince, blinking past the burn.

"Don't cry! You'll smudge the rest of your makeup!"

Looking up, I try to keep the tears from falling. "I'm trying."

"You're being ridiculous today. First, it was the sulking, and now you're just trying to sabotage the entire day. Are you not happy with the arrangement? There are a thousand other women in this country who would be jumping at the opportunity to marry Chadwick today. You're being ungrateful. Do you have any idea how lucky you are?"

If he's so amazing, why don't you marry him, then?

I keep staring at the ceiling. It's high, with skylights covering the entire thing and diamond-encrusted chandeliers that glimmer in the sunlight. There's nothing subtle about this venue, and that's exactly how my mother wanted it. It's supposed to be the wedding of the year, but it feels nothing like it to me.

"You've never been happy with anything we've given you, Millicent. I don't know what else you want from us. All I hope is that after today, you'll be able to let this bitterness go and enjoy your time with Chadwick. The jet leaves tonight at ten on the dot, and I expect you to treat your new husband with the respect he deserves on your honeymoon. He spent quite a pretty penny on it."

I keep my lips sealed, trapping the scream that's trying to escape.

My mother doesn't wait for a reply before huffing and stepping away. The makeup artist takes her place and begins to pat a powder puff beneath my eyes. The pity written all over her isn't surprising.

The room is so large that I don't hear the knock on the door before Mom's there, pulling it open with a star-studded smile. It's hard to grow stiff in a dress this time, but my muscles still try.

"Oh, Chadwick! You look phenomenal! What are you doing here? Don't you know it's bad luck to see your bride before the wedding?"

"Thank you, Celeste. Your beauty puts mine to shame," he drawls, his voice sounding just as putrid as it was during his speech at dinner last night. "I had to risk coming. My bride and I haven't had a moment alone since the rehearsal, and I'd just really love to get one before we're at the altar."

The awe in my mother's voice is disgustingly expected. Her adoration for powerful men knows no bounds.

"That's so romantic. Who am I to keep two people in love apart? Please, come in. I'll just step out for a few moments, then."

With a snap of her fingers, she has both the makeup artist and hairstylist rushing after her. They follow her out of the suite, and I turn away, trying to suck in a full breath before he reaches me.

The hot touch of his hand on my bare back is enough to have me considering ripping my dress off and running from the room. I think I'd prefer everyone outside seeing me naked than being stuck alone with Chadwick.

It's bad enough when we're somewhere surrounded by people far more interested in him than me. They're a much-appreciated buffer. But alone, there's no one to save me from his endless business babble and arrogant demeanour. The thought of having to spend three weeks alone with him wherever it is he booked our honeymoon . . .

"You've never looked more beautiful, Millicent," he says into my ear.

I stomp down my true feelings and slip on the mask I've grown used to wearing over the last twenty-six years. Smiling, I let him take my hand without smacking him away.

"Thank you."

He turns me to face him fully before grabbing a long look at my body. I swallow, keeping my chin up as his eyes linger on my breasts. It's no surprise that's where he's gotten lost. Not when my mother's tightening of my corset has them one wrong move from spilling out of my dress. I'm still surprised she didn't choose a dress more modest for me, considering how much she's always complaining about my heavy chest. It makes shopping for me that much harder, she says.

The only reasoning I have for her choice of dress is that Chadwick had something positive to say about it when she showed him the options. Which, I knew she did.

Chadwick brings his knuckles to my shoulder, tracing the curve of it as he meets my gaze and smirks. "The dress looks better on you than I imagined it would."

Bingo.

"It's beautiful," I say.

"And one of a kind. I had the designer change a few things, and I'm pleased to see they paid off."

"Did you want to speak about anything specific?"

His eyes flare at my tone, and the gross smirk on his lips stretches. "No, Millicent. I just wanted a moment alone with you."

Dread rains down on me. "Well, we've had that. We don't want to risk bad luck with us being together so long before the ceremony, do we?"

"Not so quick."

It was only a matter of time before he did this. He never

approved of our parents' decision for us to wait until our sham of a wedding night for the physical aspect of a marriage to begin. Besides a kiss on the cheek, I've gotten away without feeling his lips on mine or his hands drifting anywhere lower than my shoulders for ten years now.

Ever since we were introduced at sixteen, he's been too desperate for my father's approval to risk a quick peck or grope. That's the only reason I've been okay with being alone with him thus far. But today, it seems he believes he's waited long enough. We'll be husband and wife in only a few hours, after all.

"My father could come in any minute," I warn him, beginning to fidget.

"No, he won't. He's too busy with mine. Their lawyer is here preparing the paperwork for the merger. That's where their heads are at today. We've got a few more minutes. Don't make me beg you, Millicent," he groans.

My stomach swirls, the thought of kissing this man entirely unappealing. "Chadwick——"

He cuts me off with his mouth. His lips push against mine with a rough pressure that makes them throb. The hand he uses to paw at my waist is overly hot, but it's nothing compared to the one he uses to claw at the hair at my nape.

I clamp my teeth together when he tries to slip his tongue into my mouth and push a hand against his chest. He curls his fingers in my hair, effectively pulling them from the intricate updo that took hours for the stylist to complete this morning. My lipstick smears across my mouth, and the thick foundation rubs off my nose.

"Chadwick," I say, giving him a firm but restrained shove. "My makeup."

He pulls back, brows slanted together to expose his frustration before he looks at my ruined mouth, nodding. "Right. You need that fixed immediately."

"Yes, I should get on that. My mom will bring everyone back in."

"I'll be thinking about this all today, Millicent. Once we're alone, you're mine. You'll finally be my wife," he says excitedly, as if any of this should be celebrated. With hooded eyes, he steps back and looks me over once more. "Soon."

My lungs constrict to the point of pain as I avoid rubbing my lips together. "Yes."

"I also hope you've thought about what I proposed last night. There's no reason to wait once we're married. You don't have anything to lose, and I would hate for you to grow bored in our home when we return. At least you could keep busy with doctor appointments and preparing a nursery. Without a career, you'll need something to keep yourself busy, and a baby is the perfect thing for that. The last thing I'd want is for you to become needy for my attention while I'm busy with your father's company."

My breath catches on the massive stone in my throat. Chadwick doesn't wait for me to collect myself and respond before turning on the heels of his expensive shoes. He stalks through the suite and lets my mother back inside. She immediately stares at his mouth, no doubt catching the nude lipstick left there before shooting me a furious look. It's there and gone in a blink, because when she gazes back at Chadwick, she's smiling and offering him a silk handkerchief from her clutch. The words she whispers don't reach me, but I can only imagine what they were.

She ushers the team of women she brought with us this morning past her and toward me once he's gone. I prepare for the lash of her voice yet still flinch when it reaches me.

"You just couldn't help yourself! You know your father's rules, and now look at you. You're a mess. We don't have time for this, but here we are. You'll keep your hands to yourself at the ceremony until they've declared you husband and wife.

And when you see your father, you won't mention this. It never happened."

I simply nod, taking it on the chin because there's no point in telling her it wasn't me that initiated what happened. She'd never believe me, and even if she did, she both fears and admires Chadwick too much to mention it to him.

The makeup artist gets to work with fixing me up, and I close my eyes, falling into the endless halls of my mind. Where I can be alone.

THE PANIC SETS in after I take my first step down the aisle.

My father keeps a strong hold on my arm, keeping me locked beside him. It's like he can sense what I want to do and isn't going to allow it. I dart my eyes through the rows of people, searching for even one familiar face amongst them, but there isn't one. Not a single person who I could hope to free me from this prison cell I'm about to be locked into.

My palm shakes at my side, fear tasting sour in my mouth. Chadwick is at the end of the aisle, his posture perfect and face chiselled to perfection. It's hot in here, and I can't help but stare through the windows behind him. The mountain ranges and their promise of freedom tease me and beckon me closer, their call hitting deep in my chest.

I've always wanted freedom. To run away and cleanse my soul of the poison fed to me every day of my life. But I've never chased it. This is all I've ever known. My life has been planned out for me since I was a child, and I've been stuck here, too afraid to leave. All I've ever known are expensive homes, designer bags, and lacklustre conversation with those who couldn't care less about me.

I've let too many years slip by. Chadwick won't ever let me

go. The moment I say I do, I'll be trapped forever in this endless cycle, yet somehow, with even fewer choices.

My father removes my arm from around his, and I wobble onto the altar on a pair of heels I didn't have time to break in. Sweat drips down my spine as I look at Chadwick, my mind racing. He reaches for my hands, but I keep them at my sides. The prick of my ID and bank cards in my bra reminds me that I'm running out of time if I want to do this.

I'm frozen, panic becoming the only feeling in my body.

I glance at the mountains, and they scream for me to run.

"Millicent," my father hisses beneath his breath.

Chadwick chuckles tightly, eyeing the rows of attendees. He tries to play this off, but I'm already stumbling backward. My mother's voice rips through the air, and I grip the gauzy material of my dress in both hands and start to run.

"Millicent!"

I shake my head, stumbling slightly on the thin heels as I pick up speed. No one chases me. They wouldn't risk the way that would look. Still, I keep running. Without looking back, I dive out of the venue doors and gasp in the crisp October air.

Behind me, I swear I can hear the mountains clapping for me. A breeze licks my back, and I kick off my shoes before snagging them from the pavement.

My car is still parked at the front of the ski lodge parking lot, and I quickly get into the driver's seat. I've never left the doors unlocked before. Not until today. It's like I knew before I even went inside that I'd be here, doing this.

I find the spare key where I hid it in the console and turn the car on. The engine roars, and I roll down every window before peeling out of the parking lot.

The highway I turn onto is unfamiliar, and that's why I decide to keep going. I need to go somewhere new. Somewhere I've never heard of before and where my family won't be able to find me.

I'll keep driving until I find the place that calls to me the way the mountains do, wherever that is.

2

Shade

The buzz from the tattoo machine travels up my arm as I start on the final patch of skin I've been working on shading for the last three hours. Besides a couple of short breaks, the guy slung over the back of the chair has been pretty fucking solid for me today.

I resist the urge to stretch my fingers out until I need to wipe the ink away from his skin. Back pieces aren't always as smooth to maneuver as today's has been, and I owe that all to my client. Sitting in that position can be a pain in the ass, and he hasn't complained about it.

"We're just about done," I tell him, rolling my stool to the left.

My elbow rests beside his spine as I lean in and press the needle back into his skin. Moving in small sweeping motions, I bring the teal to the shark's fin, watching as the sketch turns into a piece of art. This is my favourite part of the job. The journey of turning an idea into something beautiful.

My client, a beefy dude in his early forties named Owen, nods and asks, "You got a mirror for me to take a look?"

Across the shop, I hear a low laugh come from the only other artist I'll ever work with. My closest friend is a tidal wave of a woman who gives me a run for my money every day here. She's almost as talented as I am with a tattoo machine, and that's why she's here, sketching up a design for a client at her station.

"You got something to say, Bryce?" I call, using my paper towel to dab away the extra blue ink.

"Nope."

"Did I say something funny?" Owen asks.

I shake my head, even though I know he can't see me. "I don't take breaks to show incomplete work."

"Right. You mentioned that."

"It's distracting for both of us, that's all," I clarify.

Bryce ventures over and hovers, her brutally honest gaze dragging over my work. "He just doesn't want to risk you telling him something looks like shit."

Owen tenses, and I pull the needle back before finishing the tail.

"She's just fucking around," I tell him before elbowing Bryce's thigh. "And now, she's going to take the garbage out back for me."

Bryce rolls her eyes. "It looks good, Owen. You came to the best."

"Bye, Bryce," I say before getting back to work.

Her boots clack against the floor while I put the last sweep of blue on the piece and push away. The instant relief in my wrist when I set the machine down is almost as euphoric as my first full look at my latest design. The burst of pride in my chest never gets old.

"Alright, give me a minute to clean you up here before I bring the mirror over. You can stretch out a bit."

I've been setting up my station the same way for the last thirteen years, so reaching for the proper supplies is instinct. I get Owen cleaned up quickly and then spread my favourite healing gel across it, making the colours appear brighter. With the mirror in my hand, I angle it just right and tell him to look back. The approval that floods his expression is a high unlike anything else I've ever felt.

"Holy shit, Shade. You're insane!"

With a chuckle, I move around on my stool and grab the camera from my table. "I'll bring you over to the wall of mirrors once I grab a photo of this."

"You got it."

The lighting in the shop has already been tweaked to my preferred brightness, so snapping a good picture is easy. Once I've finished and helped him up from the chair, I stay back while he checks himself out in the backlit mirrors. The ache in my fingers is almost comforting as I get to work on cleaning the chair and tossing the used needle.

"I'm almost too scared to ask what your availability looks like for me to get another piece done," Owen says on his way back.

I smirk. "Depends on what you want to do. A full piece like this . . . you're looking at about a year. Something smaller, I can cut that in half and squeeze you in somewhere."

"Christ."

"Or I could hand you over to Bryce. She's *almost* as good as me, just a lot less handsome."

"Thanks for that," Bryce calls from the back.

"She's not as friendly either, but if you're after skill, she's got it in spades," I say, quieter this time.

Owen nods thoughtfully, glancing down at his bare bicep. "She's good?"

"All that ink on her skin may be from me, but a little less than half of mine is from her." To prove my point, I yank the hem of my shirt up to under my pec, exposing the scorpion piece on my ribs. "This baby is all her."

"I'm in," he agrees instantly.

Chuckling, I slap his hand and guide him back to my station to finish with the aftercare.

"I'm going to wrap this for you, but you can take it off in a couple of days. This bitch is going to ooze for a bit here, so just make sure you keep it clean once the wrap comes off. Unscented soap, unscented lotion, all that shit. If anything starts looking funky, just give the shop a call."

"You got it."

Bryce comes over and hands him the debit machine. She snags the camera and starts looking through the photos.

"Got you a new client, Bryce," I say.

"Oh yeah?" She looks him over, searching for skin bare enough for her to work on. "Bicep?"

"I was thinking that, yeah. You're up for it?"

She stares at him, expression flat and giving nothing away. "Do you have an idea for the piece or just interested in me coming up with something?"

Owen looks to me for help, but I just wink, printing his receipt off.

"How about you come up with something? I'm sure you have quite a few ideas in your head already," he says, inspecting her ink now.

There's a fuck ton of it to look at, and once again, it's a head rush.

Bryce tips her chin. "Yeah, alright. Shade has your contact info?"

"I do," I answer for him.

"Okay. I'll reach out with more info once I have a look at my schedule."

"Thank you. It's been a blast today, guys," he says after taking his receipt and starting for the door.

"My pleasure, man. See you."

Bryce leans back against the front desk, her head slightly cocked at me once he's gone. "You didn't have to do that."

"Do what?"

"Hand him off to me."

"I didn't hand him off. Not like that. He wanted another

piece, and you know how far I'm booked. Why not let him get something done by the second best?"

Her nod is stiff, but it doesn't worry me. Bryce is . . . Bryce. She's not much for talking, even if you're one of the lucky ones she's let into her so-called frozen heart. Her circle is small, and I'm just grateful to be included in it. Her fiancée, Daisy, is the only one who has the ability to really pry her voice box open.

"Owen was my last appointment today, so you should head out," I say.

"You don't want me to close up tonight?"

"Why would I?"

She blinks slowly. "Don't you have plans tonight?"

"Oh, that. Yeah, but I'm not in a rush."

"What time is your date?"

"It's not a date. But we're meeting at nine." After tucking the card reader away, I lock its drawer.

"And why are you so curious?"

She jostles a shoulder, eyeing me curiously. "I'm not."

"Yeah, right. You have a worse poker face than you think you do."

I'm a naturally tidy person when I'm working, so cleanup is quick. Everything has its proper place, and I'm incredibly anal with making sure I keep organized. After so many years in this industry and getting as busy as I am, not knowing where something is leads to delays that I can't usually afford when I'm in the middle of an appointment.

I spray disinfectant on my chair and table before starting to wipe it away.

"You can't just not answer me and think that changes anything," I tell her.

Bryce huffs and stands beside me, hovering. "You've been extra busy after work lately."

"Are you worried about me?" I tease.

"Worried about you catching something from all of these women you're seeing, yeah."

"I haven't had sex in months, actually. But I appreciate your worry."

She grits her teeth, struggling to get her next words out. "If you're chasing something, I could . . . help. Get you on a real date."

"Oh, Bryce, you're sweet, but I'd rather poke my eyes out with a dirty needle. I'm doing just fine."

"You're not twenty anymore."

My smile is tight, lips touching. "Don't piss me off when I've had a good day, Bryce."

"Fine. I'm going home."

With her hands up, she turns away and heads to her station. With her bag over her shoulder, she walks past me on her way to the door.

"Tell my little devil that I miss her. She can come here any day," I say.

I can hear the eye roll in her voice. "She's not your little anything."

"See you tomorrow."

"Condoms, Shade. Don't forget them tonight."

"You've got my word."

She leaves without another word, and I let out a breath. Slowly, the high from having a tattoo machine in my hand is settling, leaving me antsy. That's why I'm going out again tonight. To help soothe the boredom that's started to grow like a fungus in my brain. I can't stay here day and night, so I keep myself busy during the day and find someone to help entertain me at night. Not having sex is a choice I didn't consciously make but wound up doing automatically without a real reason.

I don't need Bryce's approval on my life choices. I've been single for damn near my entire life, and I plan on keeping it that way. Unlike her, I haven't met anyone who's made me consider changing that, and I've grown to accept that if there was, I'd never find her.

Not going to make it! Please let me make it up to you another time! xxxx

I STARE DOWN at the text for a second longer before locking my phone and slipping it into my hoodie pocket. The same beer I've been nursing since I got here tonight is growing warm, the dew evaporating from the bottle.

I'm never the first one here, so maybe I should have pieced it together myself that she was going to bail. Peakside isn't busy outside of Saturday nights, so I knew it would be a safe place to grab a drink. It's usually my number one place to take a girl out, but I won't lie and say it isn't a pain having to drive the half hour to Cherry Peak.

Oak Point is too small a town for a bar, so this is our only alternative for a night out. The town's residents have been coming to the town over for as long as I can remember, and it almost feels like home at this point. To Bryce and her group of friends, Cherry Peak is home. I'm the lone wolf, having been born and raised in Oak Point.

Swiping a hand through my hair, I spread my knees and lean forward on the bar. I tap the bottom of the bottle against the wood surface and debate heading out already. It's dead in here tonight.

Decided, I pull my wallet out and drop a twenty for the bartender. I'm nearly off the stool when the door flies open.

I debate blaming the wind for it when nobody comes inside. It wasn't bad when I got here, but—

Not the fucking wind.

She's more like a tropical storm, all soft curves and bright colours, like she doesn't belong anywhere near a place like this.

Strands of blonde hair slip free from whatever careful style they were in, her gauzy white dress is wrinkled, mud clinging to the bottom of it, and the high-top sneakers beneath it match. Her lips are slightly parted like she's trying to catch her breath, and the energy coming off her is restless. She's trouble, but the sweet kind you almost want to let wreck you.

Caught in the net she's cast, I slowly lift two fingers and signal the bartender to send me another beer. I've got no fucking clue if she likes beer—not looking like that—but I'm up to the challenge of figuring out what she is into.

That's why I keep my stare open as I focus on her and wait for those pretty eyes to find me. And once they do, I wait for her to come over, another kind of buzz replacing the one from earlier.

3

Millie

I think I've officially crashed out.

After more than eleven hours in the car after a ruined morning wedding, there's stiffness in muscles that I never knew existed, and my ass feels flatter than a pancake. Driving in the rain has never been one of my favourite things, especially not today. But at least when I pulled onto the side of the road and stood in the rain as I sobbed, I couldn't tell what were tears and what was rain. That made me a little less embarrassed.

Until now.

The gauzy material of my wedding dress hasn't dried properly since my whole crying-in-the-rain incident, and I may have been a bit too upset to realize that I'd been dragging the hem through mud. The cream-coloured leather in my car is ruined, pools of water left in the print of my butt as I stand outside of some old bar. I cringe, not bothering to look down at myself again.

What I need is a bathroom and somewhere to sleep tonight. Unfortunately for me, only one of those things is available to me as of right now.

I shut the car door with my hip and lock it twice, taking a

long look around the neighbourhood. *Cherry Peak.* I've never heard of it.

As if realizing that I've gotten out of the car again, the skies open up and scream along with me. The rain pelts harder and faster than it has the entire drive here. I jog toward the bar, hating the squelching sound of my wet socks in my shoes.

They were the only spare pair I had in my car, and now, they're ruined.

The wind tries ripping the door off its hinges when I give it a slight tug and freeze in the doorway. My stomach pinches at the rustic aesthetic, this irrational sense of discomfort only making my frustration grow. I've been taught to hate places like this at first glance. It looks dirty and smells like cigarettes and the kind of warm beer you find being tossed around at a sports game.

I try to catch my breath while stepping inside, water dripping onto the floor beneath me. There's nobody in here besides a straight-faced bartender who clearly isn't impressed by the mess I'm making, and . . .

My cheeks burst into flames.

It would be my luck. Truly, there could not be a more fitting outcome to the day I've had than to stumble into a bar to find the most ridiculously good-looking guy in the entire world nursing a beer. And, of course, he's looking right at me.

How could he not when I look like some woman straight out of a horror film? Splash some fake blood on my chest, and I'm sure I could pull it off.

He's quite literally everything my parents told me to stay away from. Dressed in full black, he keeps his long hair swept back out of his face and down to the centre of his neck, and the *tattoos*—every inch of his neck is covered in them. Some are black, but others have pops of colour. And his hands match. He grips his beer—the bottled kind, of course—and taps the base to the bar as he flexes his fingers.

I snap my eyes back up and regret it the moment they connect with his. They're so dark, a rich brown that matches the leather stool beneath him. Unlike the men I'm used to seeing with their perfectly sculpted facial hair, he doesn't have even one patch of it over his thick, sharp jaw.

Sucking my lips into my mouth, I catch the shine of the tiny black hoop in his nose. A piercing . . . he has a nose piercing?

Completely aware of my staring, he curls the corner of his mouth into a smirk, and I freeze. Mortification swells inside of every inch of me as I choke on a swallow and dive out of sight. My sneakers squeak on the old wood floors with every step I take toward where the bathroom sign leads.

I'm panting by the time I slip through the door and find two empty stalls. I head into the first one and pee for the first time since some filthy rest stop. When I finish up and leave the stall, I realize that the low I've hit outside of this bar wasn't truly the bottom. This is.

"Ah!" I shriek when I find my reflection in the mirror.

I look like a drowned rat.

My hair is ruined, the bun at my nape sagging and coming apart, and the makeup that I sat for hours having done is smeared and crusted. My lips look as dry as they feel. And my dress is simply ruined. Although that doesn't make me all that upset. I never cared for it in the first place.

I lean over the counter and turn the taps on before grabbing fistfuls of paper towel. Once I've soaked them in water, I try and scrub away my makeup, hating the sore, red skin revealed beneath it. The fake lashes are already discarded on the floor mat in my car, but that doesn't seem to help how raw my eyes feel.

After dumping the wet paper towels, I grab dry ones and start to pat my face. Then, I do the same to my arms and beneath the chest of my dress. The corset is still tight, and as hard as I try, I can't untie the laces myself. That realization has me growing more anxious.

I don't know why I stopped here or know where I'm going next, but if I can't get myself out of this dress, I'm going to freak out. The spare clothes in my trunk are nothing special, but at least they're dry, and . . . *I didn't grab them.*

Gripping onto the counter, I hang my head and sigh.

What am I doing?

Three confident knocks hit the bathroom door. I swipe the back of my hand beneath my eyes and straighten, expecting someone to come inside. Instead, another set of knocks comes a beat later.

I stiffen and keep quiet, waiting.

"I don't make it a habit of barging into the women's bathroom, but I will if you don't let me know you haven't passed out or something."

The low, very male voice shocks me. I suck in a breath and lean against the counter, my eyes fixed on the closed door.

"I'm conscious," I call out, hating how shaky I sound.

"That's a good sign. You need anything?"

Furrowing my brows, I answer, "No."

"Are you sure? You looked like you were running from something."

I almost laugh at how right he is. Only, I'm pretty sure nobody is chasing after me. I'm running from my life, not necessarily one person, although Chadwick isn't someone I'm interested in keeping around.

"I'm fine," I say.

The mystery man taps the door. "Alright."

I assume he's left when I don't reply and he doesn't try forcing me to. Facing the mirror again, I focus on my dress. The fabric is soaking wet when I take the skirt into my hands and wring it out over the sink. Mud stains my fingers, and I let it.

After what feels like forever, I let the skirt fall back to cover my legs. It's not perfect, but the dripping has stopped. I wiggle my toes in my wet socks and pull my hair free of the bun. With a shake of my head, I let the damp strands fall to my shoulders. It's not perfect, but after a bit of touching up, it looks better than it did.

I have to make peace with this. It won't get any better until I find somewhere to stay tonight.

Breathing deeply, I grip the door handle and pull.

"You weren't lying."

I jump into the air and whip my head in the direction of the voice. The man from the bar is leaning against the wall, his hands in his hoodie pocket and that dark gaze latched onto me without a single ounce of hesitation. I feel pinned in place, unable to do anything other than stand here and try not to gape at the perfection of his features.

He's so intimidating. The urge to shrink inside myself is there, and if I weren't so dead to every emotion I'm feeling, I'd probably give in. Tonight, I'm not who I've been for the last twenty-six years. I'm someone else, a sliver of the person I wonder I could be if given the chance.

"What?" I ask, almost breathlessly.

"You didn't pass out."

Blinking repeatedly, I nod and grip the side of my dress. "No. I didn't pass out."

"You don't sound very relieved by that," he notes, reading too much into what I've said.

"How would you know what I sound like? I didn't want to pass out. Not here."

Intrigue flickers across his face. "Not here? What exactly is it about this place that you don't trust?"

"I didn't say that I don't trust it."

"So, what is it, then? It's just not up to your standards?"

I narrow my gaze. "What does that mean?"

"What should it mean?"

"I'm leaving," I state briskly.

He nods, waving me past him. I'm a step down the hall when my stomach grumbles. I grow warm, too busy wondering if he's heard it to catch the shift of his body.

Without touching me, he manages to catch my attention with a wave of his fingers. I twist to see him behind me, so close that I have to crane my head back to find his eyes. "Let me get you something to eat first."

"There's food here?" I ask, unable to deny how hungry I am.

His mouth turns down slightly. "Yeah, there's food here. Do you not have places like this where you're from?"

"If there are, I haven't been to one," I admit, more to myself than him.

"Well, it's your lucky day, then. Peakside has the best poutine I've ever had."

My stomach grumbles again, and the grin that spreads his lips threatens to send me into a spiral. It's so pure yet somehow has this sinful twist to it. This is the kind of smile only a man who knows how good-looking he is can pull off.

I hesitate to accept his offer, regardless of how badly I could use a good meal after the day I've had.

He watches me closely before adding, "Text whoever you need to and let them know where you are. Give them my name if it will make you feel more comfortable."

"Can I give them your name when I don't have it?" I blurt out, ignoring the realization that not only do I not have my phone, but even if I did, there wouldn't be anyone I'd want to text.

"You can tell them you're with Shade at Peakside in Cherry Peak. They'll be able to find me if you mysteriously go missing, which you won't."

"Shade? That's your real name?"

His chuckle is deep, almost a purr. "No, princess. But it's the only name anyone here knows, and that includes you."

The pet name grates. I narrow my eyes and snap, "Don't label me."

"Isn't that what you did the moment you spotted me?"

"No," I say, but it's a weak attempt at a lie.

I deduced exactly what type of guy this Shade was from the moment I spotted him, and he damn well knows it too. Maybe I just didn't expect him to do the same to me, or realized that I'd made it so obvious where I came from.

"Eat with me, and I'll let you convince me you're not who I expect you to be," he suggests.

"And if I don't care about what you think about me?"

"Then I'll convince you to let me get some food into you another way."

Pressing my lips together, I hold in a laugh. Really, what do I have to lose? At this point, the answer is not a damn thing.

"Okay. Fine, yeah. I could eat."

4

Shade

A princess . . . yeah, that's what this woman is.

It wouldn't be so easy to recognize it had she not been so obvious in her judgmental examination of the bar. The slight twitch of her nose, tightening of her eyes, and flattening of her lips as she gave the place a once-over gave her away. I've seen Bryce's parents give my studio looks just like that, and considering they come from old money, I'm betting this woman does too.

Or I could be wrong. I'd love for that to be the case.

"You haven't told me your name yet," I murmur as I wait for her to hop onto the bar stool.

She stares at the bar, her fingers hovering over the edge of it as if she's nervous it's going to be sticky or something. Chomping down on my tongue, I guide her hand to it and pat the stool.

Her eyes flick between my hand and up to stare at me as her fingers curl around the rounded edge of the bar. "It's Millie."

"Millie," I repeat, letting the two syllables dangle on the tip of my tongue.

With a slight inhale, she pulls herself onto the stool and twists away, her hands falling to her lap.

"Well, do you approve of it?" she asks tightly.

"It's fitting."

"Millie isn't a princess name."

"Are you agreeing with me, then?" I tease, taking the seat beside her. My beer is still there, but it's warm. Hers, though, looks just fine, so I slide it over. "I ordered this for you when you got here. Got him to leave the cap on so you could take it off yourself."

"No, I'm not agreeing with you. And I don't like beer."

I crook a brow. "Have you tried it?"

"I don't need to. It stinks."

My laugh falls out, encouraging her to narrow her eyes at me. "Just try it, Millie. You might surprise yourself."

Hesitating for a moment, she reaches behind her to tug at the ribbons looped through the back of her dress. I watch curiously, piecing together that it's a corset. With a sigh, she sets her hand back on the bar and stretches her upper body.

"If I try it, you'll let it go?" she asks.

"Absolutely. I'll order you a glass of the fanciest wine they have here instead."

"You're stereotyping me again."

I shove my sleeves up to my elbows before resting one on the bar and turning to face her fully. I'm aware of how intimidating I can look, especially when I want something, so I try to keep my expression light. If I spook her now, she'll take off before I can get to know a damn thing about her besides her name.

And I wanna learn a few things about this woman, even if it's obvious that she'll be long gone tomorrow morning.

"Prove me wrong, princess. Just one sip."

"This is peer pressure," she argues, but it's weak.

I hide my grin when she takes the bottle into her small hand and holds it in front of her face. It's unnecessary to push her any harder because in a blink, she has the bottle in her hands. In a move that yanks a disbelieving laugh from my chest, she slams the cap against the bar and sends it sliding down past me. Then, she brings her lips to the bottle and takes more of a gulp than a sip.

Even the simple rise and fall of her throat as she swallows is just as dainty as she is, and that's more than enough to convince me to keep my ass seated right now. I'm intrigued, and I've been chasing this exact feeling for a while now. The rapid pulse in my veins and excitement stirring in my chest that only comes when I meet someone who I know will keep me on my toes. I crave the rush that comes with having to put work in to grab a woman's attention, and Millie's giving me more than that already.

Her eyes flicker, and then she's staring at me. Slowly, she lowers the bottle to the bar and shifts on the stool. We're facing each other now, and I let my grin free.

"You liked it, didn't you?"

Her cheeks turn pink. "It wasn't so bad."

"You looked good drinking it."

"Don't flirt with me," she warns lightly.

I let loose a laugh. "Is that a hard rule for you?"

"It is for men who look old enough to be my dad, daddy."

"We both know that isn't true, but if you're into a bit of daddy play, I could be too," I rasp, focusing on not getting a goddamn hard-on at the idea of that.

Her eyes flare wide as she yanks her beer back to her mouth. I chuckle, extending my leg to rest my foot on the bar beneath her stool.

She swallows loudly. "That's not what I meant."

"I know."

"Do you always flirt like this with women you don't know?"

"Are you trying to see if I'll tell you how special you are, Millie?"

This time, instead of blushing, she grows a bit fiercer, her posture straightening further.

"No. I'm just trying to see if I was right about my judgment."

After taking a sip of my beer, I ask, "What judgment was that?"

"That you're a playboy," she snips, reaching behind her to claw at the ribbons again.

Her frustration is obvious when she can't seem to do what she wants to. She huffs, squeezing her eyes shut for a moment before inhaling deeply.

Concern digs between my ribs. "What's wrong?"

"My corset is too tight. I've been tied into it since this morning, and it's starting to really hurt."

"Can I help?"

She freezes, a genuine glimmer of appreciation appearing in her eyes. "Would you?"

I'm already off my stool and standing behind her. The gauze from the front of the dress isn't on the back piece. I stare at the red skin appearing just slightly above the corset and frown.

"How do I undo this?"

"I don't know," she says, voice wavering.

The only idea I have might piss her off, so I tread carefully. "Do you want to tell me why you're in a wedding dress, Millie?"

"I was supposed to get married today."

The air stills around us. "But?"

She shakes her head before taking long swigs of her beer. When she's drained it dry, she says, "But I didn't. I ran from the aisle, got in my car, and now I'm here."

"So, it's safe to say you're not going to be getting married in this dress again?" I ask, still waiting for my brain to catch up with what she's said and what that means for her.

Her laugh is almost sad. "Yeah, I guess that's exactly what I'm saying."

"Give me one second," I say before moving from our seats to the opening in the bar that leads behind it. It takes me a bit to find what I'm looking for, but then I'm clutching the scissors and going back to Millie.

She watches cautiously, staring at the scissors like I'm going to toss them at her instead of what I'm planning on using them for.

Stepping back into the spot behind her, I trace the length of the top ribbon. She sucks in a breath, and then I risk touching the red skin that's hiding beneath the corset. It looks sore, like it's been rubbed raw all day.

"Stay still for me, Millie," I mutter.

She doesn't so much as breathe when I bring the scissors to the ribbons and cut them one by one. I pinch the side of the dress in case the entire thing gives, but when it doesn't, I relax my hold. Instead of falling off, the top of the dress simply slouches slightly, the tension in the material disappearing.

"Oh, my God," she half moans, half gasps while pressing the front of her dress against her chest. "Thank you."

Without answering, I drop the scissors on the bar and tug my hoodie off. Millie tries to look over her shoulder at me, but I'm already starting to lower the heavy black fabric over her head. She doesn't fight me on it and works her arms into the sleeves instead.

"You don't have to hold it up now. Not unless you think the dress is going to fall right off onto the floor," I say, returning to my stool.

Without my hoodie on, I'm instantly cooler. It's not that it's hot in here, but I'd be lying if I said being this close to Millie hasn't cranked my body temperature up a few degrees.

Her blue eyes soften when they find mine, holding there. She looks so ridiculously tiny now, with the sleeves of my hoodie hanging a few inches past her fingers and the bottom hem passing the seat of the stool. I'm a smug bastard, though, and I like looking at her in it.

"Maybe you're not just a playboy," she admits, smirking slightly.

"Yeah? That's the best compliment I've ever gotten, princess."

Returning my foot to her stool, I add my other one and lean forward. She watches me trap her in place, not saying a word. It's a testing gaze, almost like she's trying to see just how far I'll go before she has to set a boundary.

If she were anyone else, I'd love to find those boundaries. But for some reason I can't pinpoint yet, I'm having more than enough fun staying right where I am.

"You haven't gotten very good compliments before, then," she tosses back.

"Maybe I've just been getting the wrong ones."

Millie lets that go when her attention shifts to my newly exposed skin. The surprise that morphs her entire demeanour is something I'm used to. It's the typical reaction from someone who hasn't had a lot of experience around vibrant pieces like mine. Considering nearly every inch of skin on my body is covered with some sort of ink, I've grown immune to other people's reactions.

Or so I'd thought.

My blood hums beneath Millie's attention. Everywhere her eyes fall, my skin tingles. Instead of going into detail about every piece, I sit in silence and let her look. From the hooded reaper on my bicep to the teal riverbank with the Rockies in the background running along my forearm and the five chunky letters on my fingers, she stares, examining.

There are too many pieces to show her in this place, and I'm one second away from asking her to come back to my place so I can show them off properly when the bartender slips back behind the bar from wherever it was he'd gone off to.

I grit my jaw and search her face for any sign of her wanting to leave before waving him over when I don't find one. It was both the worst and best timing he could have had to interrupt.

"Water for me," I say and then point at Millie. "Another beer or something else?"

"Are you trying to get me drunk?"

"No, princess. Just trying to make sure I can drive you somewhere safe tonight. You're more than welcome to get a water, but I'm driving you either way. There's a campground just out of town with decent cabins. It's the best place there is around here."

She rolls her lips, thinking. "I'll take a beer, then."

"You heard her, Matty," I tell the guy staring at us.

"You have ID?" he asks her.

Millie reaches a hand into the hoodie drowning her and pulls a thin card out. When she flashes it at Matty, I try to catch a look at it but only catch a glimpse of the British Columbia written on it before she's tucking it away.

Settled, Matty leaves to get the beer and then slides it across the bar to her. This time, the cap is already off, and she takes it without needing encouragement.

"So, you're not from Alberta," I say.

"You're a snoop."

"Can you blame me? You come here in a wedding dress, diamonds in your ears that have got to cost more than my car, and pretty eyes that demand my attention, and I'm not supposed to wonder?"

She shrugs. "I didn't come here on purpose."

"So, you just chose a road and took it?"

"Yes. I've never done anything like this before."

I get more comfortable on the stool, spreading my knees wide. "Why Cherry Peak?"

"I'm hoping it's a place nobody will think to look for me in," she answers honestly.

"And that's important to you? Not being found?"

She takes a long drink of her beer. "You ask a lot of questions."

"I'm curious, Millie."

"You also seem to be pretty confident in yourself, considering you've decided you're driving my car tonight without asking me first."

The surprise that travels across her features after she says that intrigues me. Fuck, everything about her does.

"Cherry Peak is a quiet town, princess, but it's not private. You're better off hiding somewhere else."

"And I suppose you know where that is?"

I grin. "Yeah, I've got a good idea."

"Well, do tell."

"Oak Point's about a half hour from here. It's quiet, and unless you've driven through it, you don't know it exists. Cherry Peak's home to one of the biggest names in country music, and since he's moved back home and gotten married, the world knows this town."

Her throat jumps with a thick swallow. "Maybe I should just keep driving."

"You could, but you stopped here for a reason, and I don't think it was solely for the one you've told me."

"Why do you have so many tattoos?" she asks, completely swapping topics.

I let her obvious attempt at avoiding that conversation go and drop a look to my exposed arm. "They're my passion."

"Don't you worry about whether you'll like them in twenty years from now?"

"No, because right now, I love them. I don't plan on hating my art ever, but if I do, at least I loved it once."

She nods. "That makes sense."

"Haven't you ever had anything that you've loved so much that you wouldn't be able to go without it?"

"No. I don't think I have."

My stomach pinches at that. "Well, I'm sorry, Millie. Everyone should experience a love like that at least once in their life."

"There's still time," she says.

"How much time?"

She quirks a brow, finding humour in my question. "Is that your way of asking how old I am?"

"Yeah, it is."

"I'm twenty-six. And you?"

"Thirty-three."

Yeah, I'm too fucking old for her. She's seven years my junior and absolutely not a woman I should want to get involved with.

It's too bad that I still can't seem to get up and leave.

5

Millie

My cheeks burn from the smile I've been wearing for hours now.

Shade's funnier than I expected, and I'm sure once I've slept off the three beers I've had tonight, I'll feel guilty for assuming he wouldn't be. It wasn't a cruel judgment, but it was almost automatic. Maybe that does make me a cruel person.

"Do you dance?" he asks, the crinkles beside his eyes letting me know that I'm not the only one enjoying myself.

"With how many charity events I've attended, yes, I do."

"I don't mean that type of dancing, princess."

Jabbing my wooden fork into the bowl of fries, gravy, and cheese curds, I say, "Then, no. I don't dance."

"Wanna try?"

"You're the dancing type?"

I slide the poutine-heavy fork into my mouth and conceal a moan at how good it is. He wasn't lying when he claimed this place had the best. I've eaten more than three-quarters of it myself while Shade's watched with a smirk.

He keeps his hand over mine in the place it's been for a

while now, his thumb stroking my knuckles. I've let him touch me, not hating the steady weight of it.

"Not typically, but tonight isn't a typical night for me."

"I'd be shocked if runaway brides are constantly flocking to this place."

"You never know with Cherry Peak," he retorts.

"You're here often, then?"

"A few times a month. The drive is a pain in the ass if you want to have a night out. I'll only stay if Bryce lets me crash at her place."

The prick at my side is hot and sharp. "She's someone special to you?"

"Yeah, you could say that," he replies casually.

Nodding, I glance down at our hands. The letters on his knuckles still make me want to laugh. I imagine it takes confidence to tattoo your name on your body, but to do it somewhere so obvious? The letters spelling SHADE are thick, bold, and downright impossible to miss unless his hands are tucked away.

"Do you forget your name sometimes?" I tease, cocking my head.

He chuckles deeply and taps his fingers to the back of my hand. "Nah, but you'll remember me once you're gone, won't you?"

"I don't think that would have anything to do with your finger tattoos."

"I hope you're right. I'd like you to remember me, Millie."

I bite down on my lip, a restless sensation continuing to flutter in my stomach. "And what about you?"

"What about me?" he asks, a knowing smirk tugging at the corner of his mouth.

My cheeks have been pink for so long I've forgotten what they feel like when they're not warm.

"Will you remember me?"

His fingers slip beneath mine, the soft touch growing firmer. I swallow, our eyes holding.

"I'll remember you, and this night, Millie."

What if I chose to say screw it to the plans that have been made for me and stay?

I could hide out in the town he mentioned for a few weeks. I'd grab my bearings and try to figure out what I'm going to do next without the pressure of my mother's disappointment or my father's anger with me for leaving the way I did.

But, if I did stay, there's no telling that Shade would even care. Despite the fun I've had tonight, we're strangers, and I'm not naïve enough to believe this man cares much about more than one night with someone.

I'm not the woman for a man like that.

"What are you thinking about?" he asks, voice low and calm.

Blinking, I try to shake my feelings off. "I think I need to sleep."

"Yeah, I bet you do. Want to leave?"

"If you don't mind."

He frowns, already standing beside me. I try not to think too much about the fact that he hasn't let go of my hand.

"It's okay to be tired. You've had one hell of a fucking day, princess."

"You can stop calling me that any minute now."

His wink is answer enough. The bartender slides a receipt across the bar to Shade, and he snags it before I can.

"I can buy my own beers," I mutter.

"Don't give me a hard time. I'm trying to be a gentleman."

I laugh, the beer doing a number on me, considering how little I drink in my real life. "Fine."

It's almost comical how he not only grabs his wallet with one hand but insists on using his card to pay the same way, all so he doesn't have to let go of me. There's this natural comfortability that I feel with him, and clearly, he feels it with me too.

"Have a good night," the bartender calls when Shade leads me away from the bar.

I give him a wave and hurry my pace to keep up with the long strides of Shade's legs. He holds the door open for me, and I stare at the rain still falling before following him outside.

"Which car is yours?" he yells, the downpour swallowing his voice.

Considering there are only three cars in the parking lot, he has to already know, but I point to the white one anyway. When I first got here, I didn't pay much attention to the vehicles already in the lot, but as we jog through the rain, I take a look.

There's a dark grey, rusted pickup truck and a sleek, black two-door car parked in front of the bar, and I know without a doubt which is Shade's without needing to ask. He confirms my guess when he waits for me to pull my key from inside my bra and unlock my car before taking a detour to the black one.

I quickly get into the car. Water drips into my eyes as I try to look out the window and see what he's doing. It's raining too hard, so I sit in silence and shiver, pouting despite myself.

When the driver's door finally whips open, my shivers disappear. I watch as he slips inside the car and knocks his knees against the steering wheel before tossing a ball of fabric at me.

I drop the key in the console and wait for him to start the car. The immediate heat that comes flowing out of the vents makes my toes curl in my socks.

"Jesus, you're small," he mutters, fiddling with the seat settings.

"You're just unusually large," I shoot back.

"Most women find that a good thing."

I roll my eyes and then stare at what he dropped in my lap. "What's all this?"

"Clothes. They're clean. I wasn't sure if you brought anything here with you, and you can't be driving home all day tomorrow in that dress, even with the hoodie over it."

When I lift my gaze, he's too busy adjusting all of my car settings to notice the intensity in it. I take in his wet, dishevelled appearance and immediately want to do something I've never wanted to before. He's so completely unaware of how attractive he looks right now, his long hair wet and messy and water running down the length of his tattoo-covered neck. The T-shirt he's wearing is soaked and sticks to his body, only making it harder to keep my thoughts from dipping into uncharted waters.

My breath thins as I keep myself frozen in my seat. It could be so easy to lean over the console and grab his face . . . but then what would I do? The only person I've kissed was just as inexperienced as I was, and the entire experience was horrible.

If I lunged at him and kissed him the way I want to right now, I'd only embarrass myself.

"Thank you," I murmur instead.

"It's no big deal." Finally settled, he looks at me and grins. "They won't fit you, but I figure you won't mind that once you're out of that damn dress."

"Do you have something against my dress, Shade?"

"Other than the fact you seem to hate it, nah, princess. It's just a dress to me."

"I don't hate it," I mumble, dropping my eyes to my lap.

"You don't have to put on a front with me right now. If you hate the dress, say that. I'm not going to tell on you."

"So, you're not going to judge me for agreeing to wear it, even if I do think it's one of the ugliest dresses I've ever seen?"

He drops his hand to my thigh and backs out of the parking spot. The ease of his movements as he spins the steering wheel with the heel of his palm threatens to bring back all of the desires I just pushed down. Still, he keeps my thigh in his grip and shifts the gears with the same hand he used to steer the car before returning it to the wheel.

"No. I don't know enough about your life back home to judge you for why you didn't tell them to burn it instead," he says.

My throat feels drier than it's ever been. "I appreciate that."

"How often do the people in your life offer you the same kindness, Millie?"

"I'm sure you can come to that conclusion on your own."

He pauses, his jaw working as we turn onto the main street. The windshield wipers swish at a quick pace, but the rain is still falling too hard for them to do much.

"Why did you run?"

I swallow. "Because for my entire life, I've been forced to live a certain way, and I guess I finally found a backbone when I was being married off to someone who I didn't love."

A subtle jerk of his chin is the only answer he offers me, and I sit in the silence, marinating in it. I'm not sure what I was hoping to hear him say, but maybe it's better he didn't say anything.

It will be easier to say goodbye tonight this way.

"IF YOU TELL the woman in the office that you know me, she'll put you up in one of the better cabins. This place isn't one of the fancy resorts that I'm sure you're used to, but it's run by good people, and for tonight, you'll be safe and warm."

I nod along to his words, my stomach clenching painfully as the reality of staying in an unfamiliar place alone has started to set in. The rain is nothing more than a sprinkle in Oak Point, and I know I need to get inside the office . . . but I can't seem to.

"There's a second-hand shop in town that might have something more your size if you didn't want to wear the clothes I gave you. And Maggie's is open at five in the morning for breakfast. She makes the best coffee—if you like coffee," he adds, sliding his hands awkwardly into the pockets of his jeans.

"I do like coffee," I blurt out.

Shade turns to look at the cabin that's used as the camp office. "Do you want me to come in with you? I could talk her into giving you a better deal. The last week of September is shit for tourists, so you shouldn't have any problem getting a good cabin."

"No, I'll be okay." Pulling the soft clothes into my chest, I take a step closer to him, drawing his attention back to me. "I guess I just don't know the right way to say goodbye."

"Yeah, me neither. Usually, I avoid having to do that."

"Should we hug?" I ask, immediately wanting to smack myself in the face.

The laugh that escapes him takes away from my embarrassment. He takes a single step forward and pulls me into his body. With his arms wrapped tightly around me, I press my cheek to his chest and palm his back with my free hand, the muscles thick and warm despite the cool fall night.

"It was nice meeting you, Millie."

"Yeah, it was nice meeting you too, Shade. Thank you for tonight." I pull back first and force myself to smile before nodding to the camp office. "I should head inside."

He nods, the action clunky. "Yeah, you'll get sick standing outside in wet clothes."

"Are you going to walk back?"

"I'll find a ride. Don't worry your pretty little head about it."

"Alright."

I start toward the office, every step feeling like I'm wading through tar. Shade lifts two fingers into the air and waves.

"Goodbye, princess."

"Goodbye," I whisper, knowing he won't be able to hear me.

Then, I'm turning forward and rushing out of the rain, this night turning into a memory that I hope I never forget.

6

Millie

THE ROCK-HARD MATTRESS BENEATH ME DOESN'T SO MUCH AS creak when I sit up. There's no give to it, and I'm feeling painfully sore after two nights in these scratchy sheets.

I stare at the small TV on the dresser in front of the bed and hesitate to get up. I'm exhausted despite having done nothing but venture to the gas station for food. My hopes weren't high the first time I left the campground to find something to eat, but when I spotted the prepaid phones tucked behind the register, I felt a sprinkle of relief.

Of course, the moment I got back to my cabin with my armfuls of junk food and set up the phone . . . I quickly realized there wasn't any reason for me to have it in the first place. Besides my parents, I don't have any other numbers memorized, and I wasn't about to call either of them.

It's that thought that's kept me in this cabin longer than I was expecting.

For the first time in my entire life, I'm somewhere I shouldn't be. I'm in a place completely different from where I've spent my last twenty-six years, and I don't think I want to leave yet. Not without at least learning a bit about this tiny town first.

My accommodations could be better, though. There's hardly any hot water in the pipes, and considering I don't know how to start a fire in the fireplace, it's been cold at night. At least it's clean enough. And quiet.

I force myself out of bed and across the freezing floor to the bathroom. The yellow light burns my eyes when I flick it on and strip out of the black hoodie I haven't kicked aside yet. Even after grabbing my spare clothes from the car my first morning here, I opted out of wearing my cinched top and kept the hoodie on instead. Paired with my tight-legged leather pants and stained sneakers, I know that I was walking through the gas station looking like some wannabe biker chick or something along those lines.

It was that or nothing, though. I've even run out of clean underwear, which has thrown a bit of a wrench into my whole sticking-around plan. From what I've seen, there isn't anywhere to do any shopping around here other than the second-hand shop Shade mentioned, but I certainly won't be getting any underwear from there.

My skin itches at the thought of going there at all, but I'm truly out of options here unless I want to continue wearing my dirty clothes every day. The townspeople will send me packing because of my stench.

Decided, I turn the shower on and wait the five minutes for the water to heat up before scrubbing myself with cheap body wash. My hair feels dry and underconditioned when I step out and wrap it up on the top of my head. I've never in my life used complimentary shampoo and conditioner before, and I'm already unimpressed.

Half an hour later, I'm standing naked in front of the bed, my clothes laid out neatly over the duvet. My hair is dry and almost crunchy as I pull it behind my shoulders and dart my eyes to the black hoodie and sweat shorts near the pillow.

I sigh, reaching for the proper clothes. The pants are tight around the waist, but I wiggle into them anyway and then slip the top over my head. The cinched material at the stomach is uncomfortable, but I ignore it while slipping my feet into the wedding heels once again. Yesterday, it was so cold out that I worried it would snow already, and from my view out the window, it looks like it's the same temperature.

With my keys and phone in hand, I slip out of the cabin and to the gravel drive where my car is parked. The wind is bitter this morning as I slide into my car and start the drive into town.

To get anywhere in Oak Point takes all of two minutes, but to get there from the campground is about triple that. I park in front of the thrift shop and take a deep, reassuring breath before stepping out on the curb.

Twice Treasured is what's written on the sign and drawn across the front window of the shop. It's a cute name.

I pull the door open, and a bell twinkles from above it. At first glance, I get overwhelmed. There's a stale smell and terrible lighting that exposes the rows of white tubs full of clothes and toys. Without labels pointing me where to go, I just stand inside the shop, my hands held at my middle.

A loud bang from the left has me shifting. Another sound follows, like something's fallen off a shelf.

"Oh! Welcome! Is there anything I can help you with?"

I search for the woman who's spoken but can't see her. "Hi. I'm not sure, actually."

"Give me one second! I'm just—" she grunts. "Sorry, we just got a few boxes of things in from a couple over in Calgary, and it's been a long time since these many things have been dropped at the door."

"No rush," I call back, moving out of the doorway.

There are a few bookshelves beneath the large window, and I browse over the titles, not recognizing any of them. Most of the shelves are children's books, and neither of my parents was big on reading. I've always navigated more to romance. Even in my early teen years when I had to sneak them home in my backpack.

"Okay, I'm free. I'm so sorry about that," the woman rambles, drawing my attention away from the shelves.

I try to hide my surprise when I come face to face with her for the first time. She's not what I was expecting in the slightest. The complete opposite, actually.

"I'm Lacey. I don't think we've met before, have we? Are you here for a drop-off?"

I jerk myself out of my thoughts. "Uh, no, I'm not. I'm Millie. I've been staying at the campground for the past couple of nights."

Lacey can't be much older than me. Her brown hair is chopped into a bob with bangs to match, and they actually fit her face perfectly. There's a genuine, welcoming smile on her face as she stares at me, her hands rubbing over her denim-clad thighs, leaving dust behind.

"How are you liking it? Have you had a chance to check out the lake? It's mountain water, so I wouldn't recommend swimming in it this time of year, but if you're into ice baths, you might enjoy it!"

"It was more of an unintentional trip, so I haven't had much of a chance to see it. That's kind of why I'm here, actually."

Her eyes glow with intrigue. "Really? Well, I'm here to help with whatever you need."

"I need some clothes. And maybe some recommendations on where I could go to find some more intimate items," I say, fighting past my immediate embarrassment.

"Sure. What are you looking for exactly? We have a pretty big selection." She presses her lips together, dropping a look at my shoes. "I don't think we have anything like those here, though."

I pinch my brows together. "Like high heels? That's okay, I can make do."

"I mean, we don't really get many luxury brands here. One time, we got a vintage purse from an older woman passing through, and there was a fight in the corner over who saw it first, but that hasn't happened since. Are the bottom of those . . . red?"

"They're old. Knock-offs, probably," I blurt, knowing that I'm lying.

They were purchased by my mother only last week for my wedding day, and considering I wasn't offered the time to break them in, today has been the longest I've ever worn them. Luxury shoes might look beautiful, but they aren't crafted for comfort. I'd take my sneakers over this pair any day, but it seems I still can't shake the habit of what I should and shouldn't be wearing in public.

"If you're okay with something a little simpler, we did just get a great pair of heels in the other week. They're a bit shorter than the ones you have on, but I'd bet they're more comfortable," Lacey says, keeping the judgment I know she has to be thinking out of her words. "They're just over here, if you want to come with me."

"Sure, yeah. And if you have anything a bit warmer, I wouldn't complain. I don't think I'll be able to walk all that well in heels once the snow falls."

We head a few rows over, and she begins digging through the white bins for the shoes, laughing. "Of course. Are you planning on staying for a while, then?"

"I'm not sure. I just figure I could be prepared in case. My selection of clothes right now is very slim."

"I sense that there's a story there somewhere."

I huff in agreement. "The horror kind."

"Well, if you do choose to stick around for a bit, I'd love to grab a coffee or something. Have you been to Maggie's?"

"No, but I was told how good the coffee is there."

With a whoop, Lacey pulls the heels free of the pile of sandals and boots they were under. There's no rhyme or reason to where things are put, and the disorganization feels like nails on a chalkboard to me. But it's not my place and not my mess . . .

"Here they are! I'm just guessing that these are your size, so I hope I'm right. Try them on!"

I take the shoes when she shoves them toward me and take a step back. The heels are a simple nude colour, and despite the worn soles, they look in fairly good condition. I notice the size stamped onto the heel.

"You were right."

She smirks. "I have a pretty good sense of feet size. You were absolutely a six."

An odd skill.

I drop to a crouch and trade my wedding heels for the second-hand pair. The difference between them is instant, and I bite my tongue before I start cussing out the designer ones for being so uncomfortable when they could have been like these.

"They're really nice," I admit.

"Yes! Okay, now, let's find you some clothes. You're going to freeze wearing that once the snow falls. Though you do still have a few weeks. We don't usually get any until later on in October," she says while leading us a couple of aisles over.

"How cold does it get here?"

"Oh, that depends on the time of year and how cruel Mother Nature wants to be. Last year, we got to about negative forty with the wind chill, but it was only for a couple of days."

I trip over my feet and bump into her back. "What?"

"Where are you from? Is that out of the ordinary?" she asks, glancing at me over her shoulder.

"I'm not used to more than negative ten at the coldest."

"BC? You don't sound like you're from out East."

I snort a laugh. "Whistler, yeah."

"I've never been."

"It's beautiful."

Lacey stops in front of a rack of clothes and starts flicking through the hangers. "I've seen photos, so I'd have to agree. I can imagine it's better in person, though. Are you a skier?"

"I've done it a few times."

It's a massive understatement, considering I had my first pair of ski boots custom made for me when I was four and was forced to skip the bunny hill entirely before being dropped on the rabbit.

"I think I'd prefer snowboarding," Lacey says, pausing her search.

The knit sweater she's staring at is a pretty peach colour that I've always avoided because I was told it washed me out. I've always loved it, though.

"I'll take that one," I rush out before she can move past it.

"You sure? It's not really—"

"It's just fine. Looks warm."

She grins and takes it off the rack. "Then it's yours. Now, for pants. Do you like leather? What about dresses?"

"Please, no leather. And I don't shy from dresses and skirts."

"You got it. Jeans?"

"Maybe not."

A few minutes later, there's a stack of things in my arms, and she still shows no sign of stopping. I don't say anything as she drops article after article of clothing onto the pile and tells me all about herself and this shop.

"Okay, let me take some of this over to the register before your arms break," she says.

"I don't know if I'll get a chance to wear all of this."

"So, take it all home with you. If you don't, all of this will just sit here and collect dust. I'll never be able to sell most of this to anyone else. Skirts and tights aren't really a big fad here."

"Most of them still had the tags on."

"Exactly. You'll find more cowboy boots and jeans here than stilettos and dresses. But that's working out in your favour today. And mine!"

I try to smile and stand at the register, my eyes on the clothes but not focused. "I'll stand out, then."

"Do you want a pair of boots? The entire back wall is dedicated to them, and I'm sure we could find you a pair."

"No. I think that would be worse, actually," I mutter.

Lacey starts inputting all of the prices of my items into her old machine as I glance out the window. Across the road, Maggie's is open, a consistent rush of people entering and exiting. I could really use a shot of espresso right about now.

"If you're interested, I wouldn't mind closing down the shop for a couple of hours and taking you into Cherry Peak. There's a new boutique there that carries the cutest panties."

My heart lurches with excitement. "Really?"

"Yes! I've only been there on the grand opening and have been wanting to stop in again. It's a bit expensive, but the owner handcrafts everything in the back of the shop."

"I'd love that, actually."

"Okay, great. I'll finish getting you rung up, and then we can head out. Do you want me to store these things in the back while we're gone?"

"That would be nice of you. All of this is, really. I wasn't expecting it," I admit, almost hesitantly.

Lacey's eyes are soft as they focus on me. "Consider this a warm welcome to Oak Point, Millie."

I'll take it.

Sure, it isn't my first welcome . . . but Shade's a guy of the past. I doubt I'll ever see him again, and this girl could be someone I do see in the future. And even if it's only today, I'll still be glad I met her.

I've been offered more kindness in this town by two strangers than I have ever before, and that's something I'm going to be thinking about for a long time after this.

7

Millie

LACEY'S CHOICE OF VEHICLE SHOULDN'T HAVE SURPRISED ME.

After being shown bits and pieces of her personality while having her as my personal shopper, it should have been obvious that she was a bit out of the box. The purple Volkswagen van she drives down Cherry Peak's Main Street draws eyes, and I sink into the seat a bit, wishing I had some sunglasses to hide beneath.

The itch on my scalp has me scratching at it again until it feels too raw. I bite down on my cheek and sigh.

"Does your head hurt?" she asks, glancing my way before pulling into an angled parking stall.

"It was the shampoo I used at the campground. I'm not used to it."

"Want to stop at the salon before we hit the boutique?"

My jaw nearly unhinges. "There's a salon here? In this town?"

"Yes." Lacey laughs, turning off the van. "Thistle and Thorn comes highly recommended. I'm not sure Anna will have a spot open for an appointment, but she does have shampoos and things like that there."

I get out of the van in super speed, already up on the sidewalk by the time she's opened her door. My new shoes are far more comfortable than they look like they should be, and I'm taking full advantage of that with my quick pace. The wooden sign for the salon is just up the street, swaying in the breeze.

"You really move in those shoes," Lacey calls, rushing behind me. "How can you walk in those so well?"

"These are lower than I'm used to."

"That makes a difference when the heels are that thin?"

"A little. I've just worn them a lot and gotten used to having to work on my balance."

She hums. "Makes sense. Maybe you can give me some lessons sometime."

"Do you have a special occasion coming up?" I ask with a quick look down at her fuzzy-booted feet.

"No. There aren't really many special occasions that pop up in Oak Point for me to attend. I just figured I could give them a whirl and see what it is about fancy footwear that you seem to enjoy."

"You could always use going to Peakside as a special occasion. That's what you do around here for fun, right?"

"I guess so. Have you been there?"

I flash a subtle smile and let the question go before opening the salon door. I'm not sure I want others to know about my first and only experience at that bar yet. Shade could be completely unknown in Oak Point, or he could be their biggest celebrity. I don't know yet, and the uncertainty of whether I'm even ever going to see him again has me deciding to keep him to myself for the foreseeable future.

Stepping into the salon, the immediate smell of luxury shampoos and hairsprays is more than welcome. I breathe it in greedily, the itch in my scalp disappearing long enough for me to concentrate on what's going on in front of me.

It's busy but not to the point that it's uncomfortable. There are two women sitting in big black chairs parked in front of tall mirrors, and rows upon rows of hair care products along the opposite wall. Bright and open, the space feels very cute. With its checkered floors, light pink paint, and tons of gold fixtures, it's unique and welcoming.

"I'll be right with you, Lacey," the woman behind the first chair says.

She's concentrating on the brush between her fingers as she coats the hair in what I know to be bleach before tucking it away in a foil. I watch in fascination, never getting to be on this side of the process.

"No worries, Anna. We're just going to browse a bit," Lacey says.

The low beat of the music in here is soothing as I start looking over the various hair care products on the shelves. I bounce in place when I spot my shampoo and conditioner right in front of me.

"I owe you a thousand cups of coffee, Lacey," I cheer while snagging a bottle of each.

"I'll take you up on that."

"Have you always had short hair?" I ask, gripping onto my products like I'm scared someone is going to come rip them away.

Lacey fiddles with her bangs. "Yep! I don't have the desire to spend that much time on it or the money to keep up with the maintenance."

"It looks good on you."

"Thanks! Are you a natural blonde?"

"I'm going to bet yes, but if you didn't get it lifted, it would be a bit darker, right?" Anna, the stylist, asks, coming up to us. There's a towel in her hands that she's using to wipe her fingers before offering me a hand. "I'm Anna Steele. I don't think I've seen you here before?"

"No, this is my first time," I reply, shaking her extended hand.

Lacey grins. "She's staying at Shimmer Lake."

"I'm jealous. I've been here for a few years now and haven't gone," Anna says.

"I haven't been to the lake yet. Just staying in the cabins there. I'm afraid I missed the proper time of year for a swim."

"Maybe that'll entice you to come back sometime," Lacey suggests, a hopeful rise in her voice.

I nod, shifting awkwardly. "Yeah, maybe."

"Have you used those before?" Anna's focused on the bottles in my hands, a spark in her eyes that reminds me of my hairdresser back home.

"They're my usual ones, actually. I had to use the complimentary brand in my cabin this morning, and I'm sure you can see how that went," I explain with a wince.

Anna laughs softly and nods, taking in the dry strands. "I've got a couple of good leave-in conditioners, too, if you wanted to grab one. I can give you a sample."

"I'll take the whole thing! Load me up," I ramble.

"You got it."

I'm overeager but can't find it in myself to care right now. The more help I get, the longer I can stay without needing to go back home. If I'm lucky, I'll be able to extend my stay for a few weeks. It's not like my parents would have sent out a search party for me.

They probably think that I'll be back before they could even get one situated. I've never been able to get them to take me seriously, and this won't be any different. I'm just throwing a tantrum. Surely, I'll just get over it.

They're wrong.

By the time Lacey and I are pulling back into Oak Point, my stomach is grumbling. A diet of snack food and gas station sandwiches has had a bit of an ugly effect on my body, and I'm in desperate need of something that won't make me want to curl into a ball all night.

"Want to grab something to eat at Maggie's?" Lacey asks, having heard the grumbling.

"You don't mind?"

"Not at all. I'm sure my mom's found her way over to the shop by now."

"You two run it together?"

"Well, it's technically my grandmother's, but we've taken over for her now that she's gotten too old," she says.

We pull into a spot in front of the diner as I say, "That's nice of you."

"Yeah, it's what you do for family, right?"

An ache grows in my chest. "Right."

"Well, come on. I'll point out all the best things on the menu for you."

"You have to let me buy you lunch, then," I counter.

"Hook, line, and sinker, baby, you got me."

My laugh is genuine, so much so that it takes me by surprise. We get out of the van, and I focus too hard on that. On how truly unhappy I've been that I've forgotten what it feels like to enjoy myself. I'm twenty-six and have never had as much fun as I've had today with a woman I only met a few hours ago. How is that possible when all we've done is buy hair care products and handmade panties?

Lacey takes my hand and leads me through the doors and into a booth tucked in the corner of the diner. It's . . . dramatically orange in here, and I think that helps pull me out of the hole my thoughts have crawled into.

"You're going to love this place. Do you like lemonade? Maggie makes the best strawberry lemonade. I swear I could drink it every single day."

I swallow, lowering my eyes to the menu Lacey's already opened in front of me. "I'll try it."

"The bacon burger is good, but so are the chicken strips. Are you a chicken strip girl?"

"I don't know."

She pauses for a brief second, curiosity drifting across her face. "You could try a bit of everything?"

"How about you order for me? I trust in your taste of food."

"Okay, I can do that. We're going on a bit of an adventure, then, are we?"

I crook a smile. "Yeah."

"Oh! What about mozza sticks? You've had to have had those."

"Once or twice. I don't really remember if I liked them."

"We're ordering them, then," she exclaims, her finger running down the menu, poking all of the potential options.

I sit back in the booth and run my eyes over the place, trying to piece together why it seems to be so popular. Is it because it's the only restaurant here, or is it really that good? The busy atmosphere somehow manages not to be overwhelming, and that's new for me. Everywhere I've gone for dinner before has had music too loud to hear a conversation properly or so many waitstaff that you're constantly interrupted.

Similar to the second-hand shop, there's a bell above the door that chimes as it's opened. There's a slight flurry that carries to our table, ruffling my hair. I turn in my seat and go hot in a flash.

The head of black hair is familiar, but it's nothing compared to the smirk crooked in the direction of the woman behind the worn, orange bar. I try to steady my breathing when Shade strides straight to her and leans his arms against the bar, tattooed fingers tapping.

She's older, maybe in her fifties. The silver streaks in her long hair match the makeup she's spread on her eyelids. I don't know how I missed it when we first got here, but there's a name on her yellow apron that tells me she's the famous Maggie.

Shade's in another black shirt today, but it's long-sleeved this time, hiding the art that I had a first-class seat to explore the other night. His jeans are a dark blue, and he's in a black pair of boots that eat the hem of them. I swallow tightly and clamp my legs together when I get a spark between them that's too familiar to the ones he ignited the last time we were together. It's dirty, and I feel like a creep when I remind myself that he's not even aware that I'm looking at him.

Straightening, I spin forward and gasp when I catch the grin on Lacey's face.

"He's hot, right?"

"What?"

"Shade. You think he's good-looking," she states bluntly.

I tuck my hair behind my ear and stare at the menu. "What made you think that? I was just looking at him."

"Yeah, like you wanted to call him over and take a seat on his lap instead of the booth."

"Lacey," I scold, keeping my voice down as my cheeks burn. "Don't say that so loudly."

She covers her mouth with her hand. "Sorry, sorry. I'm not the best at being discreet."

"Is he gone?"

"Not yet. Maggie's in the back getting his order, I bet."

I try to sink into the corner of the booth. "Tell me when he is."

"Maggie has the food. What do you think he ordered?"

"A guy like that? Beef, probably," I mutter.

"I've always thought he'd be the type of guy to really toss a girl around. You know?"

I squeeze my eyes shut and cover my face with my hands. They're wet, sweaty beyond belief, and I drop them right away. Lacey's right. I have thought about that these last couple of days. Shade's been a focus for my brain quite a few times, actually. And not one single thought has been innocent.

"I'm such a creep," I groan.

Lacey sucks in a breath. "He's leaving."

"For sure?"

"Yeah, he's crossing the street to the studio now."

When I open my eyes, Lacey's almost climbing onto the table to get a look out the window. I puff my cheeks out to hide a laugh.

"I'd consider getting a tattoo if he was the one doing it," she adds.

"Because of how many he has?"

"Well, that, but also because of his talent. Have you seen his studio yet?"

I blink. "What studio?"

"Into The Shade. It's right across the street. I'm surprised you didn't see it when you came to my place earlier."

"I wasn't really in an exploring mood," I say slowly, twisting to follow her gaze.

The brick building sticks out like a sore thumb, and the bright sign on the front makes me feel incredibly unaware. How *did* I not notice it before?

I relax my legs beneath the table. "That's his studio? A tattoo studio? Here?"

"It's out of the ordinary, for sure. But yeah, he's that good. People come from all over the country to see him. He's actually been looking for someone to work the front desk if you're interested. I could come in with you to pick up an application today if you wanted."

"That's not necessary. I don't know if I'll be staying that long. And I'm fine on funds," I rush out, waving my hand.

My stomach drops. *Am I?*

Growing still, I run through the numbers in my mind, adding up everything I've spent in the last few days. The sum in my personal account was already low, but I couldn't exactly use the cards attached to my father's accounts without him learning where I am. All of the money I have is his, besides what I have with me here. Everything I've spent after getting here has been what I've slowly transferred from their accounts to mine over the last few months.

It was a spur-of-the-moment decision that I made once

they announced the official wedding date for me and Chadwick. Maybe it was fear or a gut feeling that the future ahead
of me was all wrong. I was so afraid that they'd notice and
start asking questions I didn't have answers to that I kept the
transfers small.

Now, I wish I hadn't cared if they'd seen.

Dread drips down my spine. I'm so underprepared for
this. I've relied on my parents for too long, allowing them to
convince me that working was unnecessary and that I wasn't
going to have time to find a career I'd enjoy. Shade was right
to call me a princess. That's exactly what I am, and now more
than ever, I'm embarrassed by that.

I only have two options now, but only one looks appealing,
and it involves the man I thought I'd never see again.

8

Shade

I've been closed for a few hours now. The buzz of the neon sign hung above me should be the perfect kind of white noise for what I'm doing.

The sketch in front of me is rough—beyond it, really. I haven't set my pencil down for hours, and I've got a hand coated in graphite to prove it. Bryce has tried to get me onto the whole iPad thing, but I was shit at it the first time I tried. Paper and pencil are what I'm comfortable with.

Only today, I'm drawing like someone who's never held a pencil before.

I rip the page off my sketchbook and crumble it into a ball before tossing it across the shop. It hits the outside of the garbage can and falls to the ground to join the six prior ones.

Maybe I just need a break. The client I'm drawing this for isn't scheduled in for a couple of days now, so I'm not behind. I've just got to kick this mind block before it gets me in trouble. My confidence can afford the hit, but the business can't.

A headache blooms behind my eyes, and I break the pencil in half before abandoning the pieces on my desk. The new piece on my thigh itches like a motherfucker, and I palm it through my jeans, seeking some sort of relief.

After flicking off the neon sign shaping my name, I nudge my stool out of the way and growl under my breath when I find Bryce's iPad on the edge of her desk with a sticky note on it.

Give it a second chance before we both end up jobless.

There's no reason to try it a second time because I'm fine. It's just a lack of inspiration. I'll get past it.

My patience has been dwindling all afternoon, and I'm so close to flipping my lid when the studio door opens behind me. I hear the cautious steps of feet on my floor and tense. Forgetting to lock the door has never been an issue before, so I guess it's fitting that after the day I've had, someone can't seem to read a fucking sign—

"Oh! You're closed. I'm so sorry! God, I should have been paying more attention. I'll come back tomorrow."

The speed at which I spin around is terrifying. Jesus, I'm going to end up making a fool of myself with this girl.

"You can stay," I drawl, fixing my eyes on Millie. "I wasn't expecting to see you here, princess."

Her stare brightens. "Still haven't forgotten about that nickname."

"It's only been two days."

"Can't blame a girl for hoping."

I abandon the mess of pencils and the open sketchbook still on the desk and let myself get drawn closer to her. Millie darts her eyes to the side, focusing on something in the studio.

"You stayed longer than I thought you were going to," I state.

She twists her lips and brings her hands to rest at the low of her back. "I couldn't get myself to leave just yet, I guess."

"And you were giving yourself a tour that led you here?"

"You could say that. I've seen more of the town today than I did my first day here."

"Did you like it?" I ask, unable to help myself.

Similar to the way I felt the night we met, Millie seems to

bring out a natural curiosity inside of me that I've only experienced a few times in my life. All of which involved my best friend and her soon-to-be wife. There's a difference, though, because I never got aroused around either of them but can't seem to shake it with Millie.

It's typical for me to be flirty and outgoing, but to really dig in . . . yeah, I'll usually pass.

"It's small," Millie says, slightly awkward.

"Smaller than where you're from, I assume."

"I didn't grow up in a big city, but it does have more to it than Oak Point."

When her eyes meet mine, I try my hardest to keep them there. The slight part of her lips is undeniably sexy, and I know without a fucking doubt that she has no idea. There's such an innocent energy to her that I can't tell if I love or want to push.

"Are you going to tell me where exactly you grew up, or should I start begging?" I tease.

Her cheeks deepen to a soft pink. "I didn't come here to play twenty-one questions."

"Do people still do that?"

"I don't know! You're doing this on purpose now," she says with a huff.

Chuckling, I slip my hands into my pockets. "You're right. Tell me why you really came here."

The immediate nerves that swallow that glimmer in her eyes pique my interest. I keep my mouth shut, though, before I piss her off to the point she abandons this and disappears.

"I met a girl today, and she was telling me that you were looking for someone to work at the front desk. Honestly, I don't have a lot of experience with office work, but I like to think I'm a quick learner. You don't have to say yes either. I won't be offended or anything."

What?

I clear my throat, attempting to keep a straight face. "You came here to ask for a job?"

"Yes," she replies cautiously.

"Sorry, I'm just trying to catch up here." I run a hand over my head, my fingers slipping through hair that's getting a bit too long. "You're not going home?"

"Not right now. I'm thinking of staying for a bit. But if I do that, I need a way to make money."

Sweeping my eyes up and down her body, I try to piece this all together. Her wedding dress is long gone, replaced with a knee-length pink skirt, a pair of nude tights, and a long-sleeved blouse that pinches beneath the bust. Fuck, the heels on her feet make her legs look a million miles long despite being so much shorter than mine.

She doesn't look short of money now, and she didn't in Peakside either. Her car was a luxury brand that I've never seen in person before, and I nearly offered to clean it that night because of how filthy it was, just so she didn't have to do it herself. There's nothing about this woman that screams strapped for cash.

"Like I said, you don't need to say yes. I can't guarantee how long I'll be here, so I know I'd be a liability that way," she adds tightly, her muscles growing tight like she's preparing to abandon her offer and leave.

Before she can make a run for it, I reach out and touch her elbow. She sucks in a breath, and her eyes blow wide, so I drop my touch, unable to read the reason behind that reaction.

"The job is yours if you want it, princess. There's no question there. I'm just surprised to see you again, let alone here, wanting to work for me."

"It's not that I *want* to work for you," she clarifies.

My grin is instant, my skin buzzing. "Jeez, way to cut a guy down at the knees."

"I meant that I didn't stay here just so I could work for you. I'm not ready to leave yet, and you'd be helping me out."

"I know, Millie. You're more than welcome to snag the job."

She lets out a breath and nods, the hint of a smile tilting her mouth. "Thank you."

"You're welcome."

"I guess I should leave you to it, then. You seemed like you were doing something before I interrupted."

I lift a taunting brow. "Were you watching me in the window, Millie?"

"Don't get a big head about it. I was just making sure you were actually inside."

"My head's already big, so I'm afraid it's too late for me."

"I'm leaving now."

She's still wearing that playful smile when she turns away from me and starts for the door. An invisible hand finds my back and gives me a push after her.

"Have you eaten dinner?"

Pausing her exit, Millie offers me a surprised look over her shoulder. "No."

"Do you want to?'

"With you?"

"Yeah, with me."

"Are you sure? Is that something you do?"

I bark a laugh. "Have dinner with a friend? I tend to from time to time."

"Then yes, I'd like to have dinner with you, Shade."

I should have spent some time cleaning earlier.

It's been years since I've had a woman in my space like this, and even then, I didn't have half the shit I do now. The two-bedroom apartment above my studio was a blessing when I bought the place, but over the years, I've outgrown it. I'm too old for the whole bachelor pad thing, and now I'm struggling with the prospect of ditching it and finding a real place to live. Somewhere with a space to have friends over and a shower that I don't have to duck to get into every day.

"So, this is where you live?" Millie asks, taking a seat on the couch beside me.

"It's usually more organized than this."

"You don't have to lie. I think it's nice. Lived-in and cozy."

"You mean small and messy, but I'll take the compliment."

I've already ordered from Maggie's today, but when Millie wasn't picky about what we had tonight, I figured it was a safe bet. The weight rack in my living room is there for a reason.

I start pulling our food out of the brown bag it came in and pop the top of her container before sliding it over. The chicken strips she asked for smell up my entire apartment, and for some goddamn reason, I like that.

She scoots to the edge of the couch and reaches for a fry, her smile infectious. "Thank you for dinner."

"Anytime, princess. All I ask in return is that you keep smiling like that."

"You're helpless."

"I've been called worse," I joke before digging into my burger.

"Is this your usual order, or was it something different earlier?"

I almost choke on the beef in my throat. Swallowing, I look at her. "How do you know I ordered from Maggie's already today?"

"I was there with the girl I met. You were just picking up your food, but I did see you."

"Well, there goes my hope of you thinking of me as this big, beefy Hulk man."

She cracks up, using the back of her hand to cover her mouth. "I never once thought of you as that."

"Do tell what you did think, then," I encourage, keeping my voice low, intimate.

"Didn't you already warn me about your big head?"

I jostle her knee with mine. "Want to hear what I think about you instead?"

"Kind of, but I'm a little scared."

"I'll be gentle, princess," I purr.

Her throat pulls tightly. "Go for it."

"I think you're far too beautiful to be so sad."

A long, heavy pause. "What makes you think that I'm sad?"

"People don't run from lives they're happy with. None that I've met, at least. Your eyes give you away, Millie."

"Is that why you invited me to dinner?" The doubt in her voice cuts at me.

"No. I did that because I wanted to spend time with you. I've wanted that since the night we met. Besides, I'm not really the guy women call when they want their broken heart mended."

"So you just avoid all the sad people you see?"

I leave my food in its container and wipe my hands on a napkin. The restlessness that's swarming me right now makes it hard to sit still. Spreading my legs, I scratch at my jaw.

"That's not what I meant."

"I don't understand," she murmurs.

There's a ball of fire rolling through my groin, sparked by the innocence in her tone. The confusion that hints once again at an inexperience that should have me crawling back into myself. I don't mess around with women who don't know what they want, and I damn well don't entertain the idea of it with one who seems blind to the sexual chemistry that's been throbbing between us since the night we met.

Sipping on a long inhale, I bend over my lap and turn my

head so I'm staring directly at her. Guarded, almost shy blue eyes pierce into me, watching and waiting.

"I'm someone women seek out when they want their memory fucked away, princess."

She squeaks. The prettiest pink crawls up her throat and to her ears. I drop a hand to my knee and squeeze to keep from doing something so fucking stupid and reaching for the thighs she snaps together. Her chest rises with uneven breaths.

"Oh."

My chuckle is rough, grated. "Yeah."

"Is that . . . what you like?"

"Sex with no strings is the only kind I have. It's more passionate that way. Raw."

She jerks her head in a nod and reaches for the collar of her shirt, plucking it away where it cups the base of her throat. I fidget again, the crotch of my jeans growing a size tighter.

"I'm not feeling well. I think—I'm going to go," she rambles, her cheeks growing a deeper shade of red.

Alarm shoots through me. "Are you sure? What's wrong?"

"Can I come by the studio to talk about the job tomorrow? I'll—I'll leave my number."

"Yeah, of course you can. Are you alright to drive?"

Snagging a pencil from the bowl of them on the kitchen counter, she scribbles on a scrap of paper. "Yep!"

I get to my feet and follow her when she collects her things and rushes around the couch and to the door. Not wanting to overwhelm her, I keep a few paces back, hovering as close as I can.

"Do you want to take your dinner for later?"

"No, thank you. I'll see you!" she rushes out, already halfway out the door.

I keep my feet anchored to the floor and let her go with a reminder that I don't chase women. Not like that, and not in any other way. It's not who I am.

Yet here I am, wishing like hell I was.

9

Millie

I'm sweating. It has to be dripping from my skin like water at this point.

My heart is hammering so loudly that I can't hear myself think as I rush down the stairs and out the door. The cool temperature of the night doesn't help. The wind sticks to my slick skin, making it feel all the more sensitive.

"Oh, God," I groan.

The heat from Shade's gaze lingers, even once I've made it to the street in front of the studio. His rasped, rough voice replays in my ears, and I try to shake it free. My breasts feel tight, constricted in my bra and blouse that I've been debating ripping clean off.

This is new. I'm not used to having such a raw reaction to someone like this.

It's like he's picked the lock on some hidden, lustful part of me that I've kept tucked away. Only he didn't even have to try to pick it. I handed him the key and begged to be broken free.

Licking my dry lips, I touch my hot cheeks and suck in a long breath. I've got to slow down. He's not beside me anymore, which I'm as grateful for as I am annoyed. The sooner I got out of there, the less of a chance there was that I was going to make an even bigger fool of myself and try to what? Get on his lap and maul him?

Another low noise escapes me before I unlock my car and follow the glow of the headlights. My heels clap against the sidewalk, and I ignore how fast my pace is.

It's fine. I'm fine. Everything is *sooooo* fine.

"Were you just with Shade?"

I nearly jump out of my skin. Wild eyes searching through the dark, I spot a woman a few steps away. The scowl on her face is a big enough giveaway that I should not be answering her with the truth.

With a hand on the sliver of bare waist exposed from her cropped shirt, she asks her question again. "Were you just upstairs with him?"

"Upstairs? No. I was just, uh, getting a tattoo consult," I ramble, growing more uncomfortable by the second.

"This late? He's never open past seven."

I glance at my car, preparing an escape route in case I'm the one about to get mauled. "Are you meeting him tonight? I'm sorry if I caused a delay."

"No. I was just . . . stopping by." She squares her shoulders, eyes rolling with annoyance. "You're leaving now?"

"Yeah. That's my car," I say, jabbing my thumb behind me.

She pulls her lip into her mouth before pushing it back out. "And he's inside? He wasn't answering my texts."

At least I'm not warm anymore. Suddenly, my temperature chills.

"Yeah, he's inside," I mutter.

"Thanks."

I force a smile and abandon the studio. Once I'm in my car, I crank the heat and get the hell out of here before my confidence can dive any further than it already has.

The cabin is freezing.

I stand and stare at the fireplace, willing the wood that's been placed inside of it to magically light. There's no thermostat in here, and I expect that these places are too old to have a furnace or air conditioner for the summer heat. This may be as bad as camping in a tent, which . . . I've never done. But that's not the point.

For the cost of this place per night, I didn't exactly expect to have to freeze half to death every night. The blankets that were folded on the bed when I arrived are scratchy and thin and have done nothing to keep me warm at night. It's only going to get colder too, and unless I plan on turning into an icicle while I sleep, I need to figure out what to do.

First, I want to shower.

The clothes I purchased today are still scattered where I dropped them on the couch earlier, and right now, I'm glad I took Lacey up on her offer to give them a wash before I came back here. I grab the hair care products still in their bag and make my way to the bathroom. The tiny space has a slightly musky scent, but it's clean. Unfortunately, that's not enough to keep me from missing my bathroom from home.

The Jacuzzi tub and glass shower with the three waterfall heads and the bench in the corner feel more luxurious today than they ever have. I miss my electric toothbrush and the heated tile floor. If I could go back and change one thing, it would have been stopping at home and packing before setting out on this journey.

After stripping out of my new clothes, I stand in front of the vanity mirror, staring at myself.

I'm beautiful, I think. I've never hated the way I look, and at one point, I was confident enough to easily snag the eyes of men whom I'd meet at various functions. Their attention didn't last, though. Not when I couldn't manage to hold a conversation with them or lean in for a kiss when they did. I've always been terrible at reading men and situations where I should have done one thing or another.

I'm not a virgin by definition, but I may as well be.

Darting my eyes away from my reflection, I run my hands over my hair and haul my shampoo and conditioner to the shower. With the water running as hot as it can be, I spend a long time massaging the products into my hair before moving on to my body.

The soap runs down my torso, and I watch it pool at my feet. Inhaling deeply, I stare at the rivulets cascading over my peaked nipples. They're a deeper pink in this lighting, or maybe it has nothing to do with the lighting at all. I swallow and bring a finger to it, slowly tracing the soft tip.

My toes curl in the soapy water as my breath thins, reminding me of being on the couch with Shade. Hearing his blunt, dirty words . . . I've never felt that intense of a pulse between my thighs. It was like he had slid his huge hand between them and stroked me there.

My belly blooms with warmth as I bring my thumb to meet my nipple, pinching it. A breath explodes from me, and I press my thighs together, searching for a friction that I know I won't find like this.

The water turning ice-cold above me turns my arousal to panic. I gasp and slap my hand back to turn it off. Chilled, I hop out of the tub and wrap myself in a towel as fast as I can. My teeth chatter as I rush out of the bathroom and snag the black hoodie from the bed. It doesn't matter that I'm still wet because once I have the heavy material over my head and falling to cover the majority of my body, I can breathe normally again.

A few minutes later, I'm slipping beneath the scratchy blanket and curling up in bed. With the hood up over my wet, unbrushed hair, I grab my phone and unlock it. The one and only message waiting for me is from a number I don't recognize.

> Hey. It's Shade. Just wanted to make sure you got home okay.

I squeeze the phone tight and stretch my legs out along the cold sheets before I text back.

> I did. Then a shower tried to kill me off.

The lag in his reply has me tossing over in bed, unease creeping into my mind. Maybe he didn't want to start a conversation and really only wanted to check up on me.

> Oh yeah? How?

> There's not much hot water. I enjoyed it while it lasted.

The message goes through quickly, and I hate that this phone doesn't let me see once he's read it. Sighing, I lie on my back and stare at the ceiling, my toes close to turning into ice cubes.

> I remember it being the same way when I'd stay there as a kid. They haven't upgraded that place in years.

> Do you know if there are heaters in the cabins by chance?

> Only fireplaces.

Of course. So, I'll either need to ask someone for help or try to figure it out on my own.

> Did you find the woman who was looking for you?

I did.

> And?

And what?

I tap my fingers to my hip, contemplating asking what I really want to know. If I do, he's going to tease me about it. But honestly, that wouldn't even be the worst thing.

> Did you invite her inside?

No. I didn't.

> Aw, I'm sorry.

If I did, we wouldn't be talking right now. Is that what you'd prefer? She didn't have an invite to my place.

> I'm tired.

The quirk of my lips is unstoppable as I send my message and stare at the screen, waiting. I make sure my hair is tucked fully into the hood and lift my knee beneath the blankets.

Well, how do I keep you awake?

> I remember something about 21 questions.

Shall I go first?

Something about this feels dangerous. Like I'm poking the bear and waiting for the swipe of his paw. Typing out my reply, I wiggle against the mattress and try to relax.

Only if you have a good question.

Why did you really run out earlier?

My mouth goes dry as I stare at the message, rereading it. The heat crawling up my body is welcomed, even if I'm now too hot beneath the blanket.

I already told you why.

That was an obvious lie. I just didn't want to push you too hard by demanding a real answer.

How generous of you.

Princess . . .

Playboy.

The hoodie doesn't smell like him anymore after Lacey washed it with my other clothes. But as I zone in on the rapid rise and fall of my chest, I swear I can smell the manly cologne still lingering on the fabric. The heavy weight of it feels uncomfortable on my breasts, and I swallow thickly when my nipples rub beneath it.

The game is about answering the questions you're asked, not ignoring them.

Fine. I was overwhelmed.

Did I do something wrong?

No. Not wrong. I'm just not used to hearing things like what you said.

It's an understatement, but still the truth.

What exactly was it I said that freaked you out?

You know what I'm talking about.

I need you to say it just in case I'm wrong.

It was about you sleeping with women.

What about it?

Stop trying to rile me up.

Is it working?

I blink at the screen and then look down at where the hoodie has risen up my stomach. I've unconsciously kicked the blankets down my ankles, and my panties are exposed, the pale pink lace soft instead of rough. I palm my abdomen and follow the warm skin up beneath the heavy fabric. My breast is large despite my smaller stature and overflows in my hold.

Replying with only one hand is complicated, but I can't get myself to bring the other one back.

Is that the only time you do it?

The only time I do what, princess?

Sleep with someone.

Usually.

But not always?

My fingers dance over my nipple, resuming their soft tug from the shower. I clench between my legs before pressing them together, rubbing lightly.

There are always exceptions to every rule.

> Like what?

> Is that your question?

> Yes.

> It would depend on who the exception is for.

A moan slips free of me when I pull a bit harder on my nipple. The pleasure zips down my body to swirl at my centre.

> I see.

> That was answer enough for you?

> I only get one question at a time.

> Alright.

His first text barely arrives before a second follows.

> Would you want to be the woman in question?

My vision grows blurry. I move my hand from my breast to the waistband of my panties, hovering there. This isn't what I expected for tonight. It's not polite or respectful. I shouldn't do this. If I did, I'd surely regret it.

How would I look at him at the studio tomorrow, knowing that I'd pleasured myself to nothing more than the thought of him here and a few somewhat innocent messages shared between us?

My fingers move on their own. I feel the soft, waxed skin beneath my panties and keep going lower. The slickness waiting there shocks me.

> That depends on what your exceptions are.
> My heart isn't broken.

I can always hear his chuckle in the room with me when his message appears, and I dip my touch between my hot flesh, searching for the only spot that I know brings me pleasure.

> Tell me what you like and we'll go from there.

> I don't know what I like.

There it goes. The complete truth.

> What do you mean?

> The next question is mine.

> Ask then.

> Have you ever been with anyone who didn't have a lot of . . . experience?

> How little are you talking?

> Only once.

I bite down on my lip to hide the noises that try to escape when I circle the ball of nerves between my legs. My thighs grow tight with the effort it takes not to allow them to close. Maybe I'll actually be able to come like this.

> No.

> Oh.

> Would you like me to make that exception?

> Shade . . .

The pleasure swells, an orgasm hovering and exciting my pulse. I abandon my phone on my chest and bring my other hand to my breast, rolling my nipple quickly while giving the same treatment to my core. I'm nearly there. Closer than I've gotten—

The rush drops. My pleasure morphs into a frustration so sharp I can nearly smell it.

My phone buzzes twice, and the drop continues. A wave of embarrassment and disappointment in myself hits me so hard that when I grab my phone again, it's with shaky hands. Two messages wait for me.

> Answer the question, Millie.

> I already know my answer.

It won't be one that I'd like. A man like Shade isn't interested in teaching me about sex. The only reason I let myself go along with this was because of what I was doing, and that's wrong on so many levels. Hearing his answer would have only hurt my feelings.

Maybe my body working against me was a blessing in disguise.

Before he can send through another message, I turn my phone off and toss it onto the small side table. I'm never turning it on again. Especially not before heading into the studio tomorrow. At least this way, I won't have to pretend not to be upset in front of him. Instead, I can live in ignorance.

I'm good at that by now.

10

Shade

"Who pissed in your cereal this morning?" Bryce asks.

I glare at her from where I've started setting up my station. She pretends not to notice, focusing on the roll of cling wrap in her hands instead of me.

"You didn't have to be here this early. Isn't your first appointment after lunch?"

"Shit, grumpy ass. If you wanted the day to yourself, you could have called in sick."

I scrape a hand over my hair. "Sorry. Late night."

"Oh, pray tell."

"Daisy's turned you into a gossiper."

Her shoulder jostles with a shrug, the loose fabric of her cropped tee shifting with the movement. "Could be worse."

"I just couldn't sleep," I tell her.

"Too many women blowing up your phone all night?"

"Yeah, that's it."

Or more like the lack of.

After Millie disappeared on me, I spent the following two hours constantly checking to see if she'd returned. Spoiler: she didn't.

I woke in the shittiest mood this morning, and it's safe to

say it hasn't gotten any better since. I'm not used to being ghosted like that, especially in the middle of a conversation that had my attention in a death grip. Yeah, my dick was hard, but I was more intrigued than I was horny. There's something about that goddamn woman that entices me more than warns me away.

The admission of her lacking sexual life was only another alarm shrieking for me to turn back before it's too late.

Yet, here I am, in a piss-poor mood because I wasn't done speaking with her. I'm still not done.

"If you stop taking your blue balls out on me, I'll run across the street and grab us coffee," Bryce offers.

"My balls aren't blue, Brycie. They're purple."

Her nose scrunches before she walks right past me, her middle finger flicking up. "Fuck off."

"I love the way you flirt with me!" I call as she steps outside.

Ignoring that, Bryce heads across the street, leaving me here alone. I clear my throat and try to shake the tension from my muscles. With my legs spread wide, I lean over my small leather table and fidget with the order of my supplies again.

I've always hated wearing rubber gloves, so I'm glad when I finish and can snap them off. They fall silently into the garbage before I stand and head to the front desk.

My appointment book is somewhere under the mess of invoices and receipts that I haven't been assed to sort the last couple of weeks. Recently, Daisy has started taking it upon herself to organize them for me, and I'm a bit nervous to mess up her system. Her fiancée might be a rottweiler, but Daisy isn't always a golden retriever. On a rare occasion, I've watched them switch roles.

My head snaps up immediately at the sound of the door opening. Half expecting Bryce already, I'm pleasantly surprised to glance up and see a blonde, bright-eyed princess instead.

"Good morning, Millie," I say, unable to help the rasp that drips from my tone.

Her spine snaps straight as she stares at me, a blush already tinting her cheeks. She shifts on her heels and pulls one leg in front of the other, crossing them.

I follow the movement, having to grit my jaw to avoid blurting out my thoughts. Despite the early October chill, this girl is still in a skirt. Even with the thin beige tights beneath them, I know she has to be cold. The long coat she's wearing over a white blouse with a bow between her tits matches the colour of her tights, and Jesus Christ—I keep looking at her legs.

I've never seen legs like hers. Or maybe I have but never noticed them. I've got no idea why I've become so fascinated with the long, lean shape of them, but here I am. If I thought getting a stiffy from a few innocent texts was bad, I should be embarrassed by the one I'm sporting now.

"Good morning," she replies coolly, her eyes focusing on everything in here but me.

I'm no fool. Her cheeks are pink because of last night, and just like I have been, she's still thinking about it. If she wasn't, why isn't she looking at me the way she was yesterday?

"I wasn't sure when to expect you today, considering you never told me before you . . . Oh, what was it that you got up to last night?"

"What?"

"What did you get so busy with last night that you couldn't tell me when you were coming in today?" I ask.

"I fell asleep."

"Oh, did you? That's nice, then. I'm sure you needed a good night's sleep," I drawl, keeping an unbothered front.

Her gaze snags on the wall behind me, and I turn to see what she's grown distracted by. The photo of one of my favourite pieces is a newer one and has been moved from further in the studio to front and centre. A flaming dragon on the back of a woman whom I've been tattooing for the last five years.

"She let you take that photo of her?" she asks, surprising me.

"What do you mean?"

Her hand lifts, a finger pointed at the photo as if I don't know which one she's talking about.

"It's—She's . . . it's hung up on the wall."

"Her name is Ruby, and the pose was her idea," I say, keeping a cautious eye on Millie's reaction.

"She was okay with being photographed naked?"

"She's not naked, princess. But, yes, she was very okay with being photographed in only her panties. To keep the entirety of the piece unobjected, she couldn't wear anything above the waist, and she chose to be without pants. There wasn't anything sexual about the pose. The focus was on the dragon."

It's obvious she doesn't believe me. Her eyes are busy, providing me with an insight into her mind. It's not surprising that she doesn't understand. We don't know each other well yet, and I have a feeling she knows nothing about this type of art.

"The confidence that must take is incredible," she reveals a moment later.

"It is. Everyone has it in them, though."

Her smile is weak. "I wouldn't say everyone."

I round the desk and come to stand in front of her. She follows my every move, holding herself perfectly still. Slowly, her eyes lift to hold mine.

"Feeling confident is a skill that takes time to master. Little by little, you can grow it until you're a cocky motherfucker like me," I tease.

The smile that breaks through her small frown is danger- ous. "I don't think I want to be that confident."

"If you're going to insult me, maybe wait until you're off shift," I say with a wink.

Her eyes widen. "Oh, right. I guess I should ask what you want me to do for you."

Oh, I'm *so* screwed here. My groin tightens, and I wet my dry lips before shaking my head. The way she truly has no idea what she's doing to me should be studied because it's got me aching.

"How good are you at organizing paperwork?" I ask tightly.

Some of the colour leaches from her face. "Um, I'm not sure."

"You can figure it out today, then. I've got stacks of shit on the desk that I haven't had a chance to get to in a while. When Bryce gets back, I'll have her give you a rundown of Daisy's system."

"Who's Daisy?"

"Right. She's Bryce's fiancée. Bryce is my best friend and the only other person who works here besides myself, and now, you. There will be calls for both of us on the phone, and she has her own appointment book, so you'll need to run any potential appointments past her before confirming anything," I say.

She nods quickly, still pale and almost overwhelmed already. "And for your appointments?"

"My book is on the desk and somewhat on the computer. I'm shit with transferring appointments from paper to the computer, so I'd go off of the book. Just take a look at what day I'm booked till and go from there. I'm about six months out right now for small to medium pieces and a year out for large. Oh, and I don't work Sundays. I'll take occasional Saturdays but prefer them off too. If you aren't sure where to schedule someone in, just let me know."

"Okay. Anything else?"

"Let's just start there for today," I suggest, taking in the worry written all over her face. "We've got time to get you working on other things."

She nods and releases a long breath. "Sounds good."

"I've got someone coming in at ten, so if you need anything after that, Bryce will be your girl. She's free until noon today. All of the log-in information for the computer is on a sticky note on the desk. Probably under all of the papers."

"That's a terrible place for it."

I hold back a grin. "Find somewhere else for it, then."

She keeps her gaze on me until the door opens again. Turning, she focuses on Bryce, her jaw loosening slightly. I laugh under my breath.

"Is that your car out front?" my best friend asks, her sharp blue eyes piercing into Millie.

I expected some sort of examination from Bryce, so I'm not shocked when she gives Millie a quick up-and-down look. She's reacting the exact way I thought she would. Like she's gone back in time.

Bryce might be a tattooed, dark-haired force of nature now, but there was a time where she was playing dress-up in her parents' mansion, wearing handmade clothes and debating throwing her diamond earrings into the rose garden. As she stares at Millie, I know she's thinking things that I'm grateful I can't hear.

Millie recovers quickly, ignoring the eyes on her. "That is my car, yes."

"What's it doing here?"

"This is Millie, Bryce. She's taking the front desk position," I say, flashing her a pointed look.

Bryce blinks and darts her eyes over to me. "She is? Since when?"

"Since yesterday. And because you're here early, you're going to show her how Daisy started organizing things."

"I can try it on my own," Millie puts in, the nervous vibrations in her voice giving away how she's feeling as obviously as the tap of her toes does.

"It will be easier if Bryce helps."

Bryce slowly looks back at Millie. "What experience do you have?"

"I've already hired her," I say sharply.

"Have you filled out the proper paperwork?"

Millie takes the questions on the chin without crumbling. She's growing less nervous as the questions come, until suddenly, she's uncrossing her legs and straightening.

"I've been here for all of five minutes, so no."

I swallow slowly, revelling in the sharp lash of her tongue. The switch between nervous and smart-mouthed keeps my mind running as I watch the both of them, waiting.

Bryce lifts two black brows and cocks her head just slightly. Then, the scowl on her lips begins to transform into a crooked grin.

"Alright. I'll get it for you before we start," she tells her.

Millie stares at my friend, confused at the switch up. I'm not. Bryce respects a backbone, and after nothing more than a first impression of a rich girl with an expensive car, she was waiting to see if there was one hiding beneath the fancy clothes and perfect hair.

After spending the time I have with Millie, I had a feeling there was one just waiting to introduce itself to Oak Point, but I'm pleased to have seen it so soon.

Millie nods at Bryce. "Thank you. I'd appreciate that."

"How do you take your coffee?" Bryce asks her, lifting the two cups she brought from the diner.

"I'm not big on more than an espresso shot."

"Try this."

She hands one of the cups to Millie, and I watch as she takes it and sniffs the small hole in the lid. "What is it?"

"Shade's."

"Mine?" I guffaw.

Bryce stares at me, deadpan. "Did you think I was going to give her mine?"

"I was hoping, yeah."

"Get your own, asshole."

Millie's giggle snags my attention, drawing my eyes. I focus on her, watching as she lifts the cup to her lips and takes a small sip, staring at the both of us. Warmth fills her face before she takes another one, this one longer, making her throat move harder.

"Look at that. You both like mochas," Bryce states, reading me like a fucking book.

I chuckle, crossing my arms. "I'll keep that in mind."

"You do that."

Millie takes another drink of my—*her*—coffee before lowering the cup. "I'll pay you back for it."

"You won't. Coffee comes with the job, even if I need to go get myself another one. I'll be back before my client gets here," I say, already pushing past Bryce to the door.

Bryce's smirk is devilish, and I'm already prepared for the comment before it comes, quiet enough for only me to hear.

"Don't worry too much while you're gone. I'll take care of her for you."

11

Millie

LANDING MY FIRST JOB AT TWENTY-SIX IS EMBARRASSING.

I could have done anything in the world, and I chose to be tugged around by my sleek ponytail instead, living naively in my privilege. Being born into the world of business meant that I picked up on things here and there, but I never really thought I'd ever need to put that information to good use. I wasn't invited into my father's board meetings, but I was always the one trying and sometimes failing to shmooze the men my father wanted to invest in the lodges or join him in another venture that would lead to another few million in the family trust.

My lack of real experience in the hands-on aspect of business has been made obvious today. Popping a bottle of champagne for Bryce when she began running through the online calendar wouldn't have helped me remember the right buttons to push, and offering a special tour of the studio to the woman who came in for her appointment with Shade wouldn't have done anything but make me look as out of water as I feel.

I've always been a fast learner, but today has reminded me that there is only so much I can improve on in a few hours' time.

But hey, at least I knew how to use a stapler correctly.

Taking that hit on the chin, I finish with the newly organized stack of receipts and slip them into their proper folder. Bryce left an hour ago, leaving me on my own for the rest of the day while Shade works on the thigh tattoo he's been doing for what feels like forever now.

I should have done far more today, and I would have . . . if it weren't for him.

From the moment the woman got here and Shade got to work prepping her thigh, I've been utterly distracted. For a huge guy, he moves with a precision that seems unnatural. He got her skin shaved and a blue sketch of the design she wanted placed down with a confident ease that held my attention for way too long. I couldn't hear the ring of the studio phone until he looked up from where he was working and saw me watching him.

I ignored him for an hour.

The continuous buzz of the tattoo gun has filled the studio for so long that I'm positive I'll hear it in my dreams. I don't know how he can hold it in his hand for this entire time. It must be uncomfortable.

"Want to take a break? You're almost done," he says to the woman, lifting the needle off her skin and wiping it clean.

She pulls her long pink hair over her shoulder and pants slightly. There's a quiver in her arm from holding herself up on the table for so long.

"No. Let's just finish it."

Shade grins proudly at her, and I swallow, ignoring the nip of envy in my side. It's so ridiculous to be jealous of that and this woman at all. I blame how out of the ordinary today has been for that. It has to be acceptable to be all out of whack after the week I've had.

Sitting behind the desk, I cross my legs and start flipping through the brown leather book that I've gotten quite familiar with today. Month by month, I move through the pages and take another mental note of when exactly he's open for more small bookings. March seems like years rather than months away from now, and yet, the open spots on his calendar are far and few between. I flip through more pages and stare at the empty dates at the full-year mark and try to wrap my head around someone being so in demand that their life is planned that far in advance.

Clearly, he's talented. I mean, that much is obvious from everything I've seen today. Even without a clear view of what he's been working on, the woman's reaction gives away that she's happy with it. The photos on the walls behind me are another testament to that.

My cheeks heat as I think back to the one I know hovers above me. The design is breathtaking, but it was the woman who took me the most by surprise. Her confidence was obvious through the pose of her body, but I still had a hard time understanding.

With her knees digging into the cushion of the couch, she pressed her middle against the back of it and faced the wall, the fire-breathing dragon on her back fully displayed. The red and orange flames were the only colours in the photo, along with the red thong slung over her round hips and tucked between her cheeks.

There were more tattoos on her body, but it was clear the dragon was the focal piece, and as shocking as it was for me to see, it deserved that level of attention.

Shade must get to do many pieces like that with women of similar confidence and beauty. It's no wonder he's as cocky as he is. I won't admit it to him anytime soon, but from what I've seen, he deserves it. And it makes me even more sure of the decision I made to end our conversation early last night.

I'm nothing like the woman in that photo, and I won't ever be. Shade would eat me alive, and from what I've seen from him today, he's made the same conclusion. Why else would he not have brought up last night?

Other than his question about why I didn't let him know when I was coming today, he hasn't mentioned it, and he certainly hasn't hinted at wanting me to answer his question again.

"Okay, you're finished," Shade announces.

I keep my eyes on the pages of his appointment book, not looking up when I hear movement from his direction.

The woman groans loudly. "Thank fuck. I'm numb."

"I could do a few more touch-ups to keep you here a bit longer," he teases.

"There are worse things than your hands on my thigh, Shade."

I bite my tongue and lift my gaze to the computer screen. Shaking the mouse, I wake it up and log in.

"You flatter me." There's a clap from what sounds like a hand on skin. Her leg, maybe. "Up you go. Check it out in the mirror and decide if you actually need any touch-ups."

"I'm not sure I can afford any more of your time."

"On the house, Beck."

I press down on the mouse a bit too hard and accidentally open the wrong application. Closing out of it, I choose the calendar and scroll back to where I last left off with the appointment transfers. Having them all in a book might seem easier to Shade, but it's a surefire way to lose something important. Once I'm finished, he'll have everything available to see online, as well as inside his book.

"Unfortunately, it's perfect. No touch-ups needed, although I'm not surprised," the woman calls.

"That's what I like to hear. When you're done looking, you can sit back down, and I'll get you ready to go."

"Oh, now you're desperate to get rid of me."

Shade's chuckle is low and deep. "I've just got some dinner plans tonight. You're my last appointment of the day."

"Who's the lucky girl?"

Yeah, who?

Blinking, I fling that question out of my mind and focus on what I'm doing. I zone in to my work, disregarding their conversation. The vibration on the desk is what brings me out of it. I don't recognize the number on the screen, but it's not like anyone besides Shade and the campground knows mine.

I step outside and answer the call, pretty confident that I'll be back before the woman is ready to pay.

"Hello?"

"Millie?"

"This is she," I say cautiously.

"It's Shelly from Shimmer Lake Campground. I just wanted to call and check in as we've been trying to charge the card you left on file, but it hasn't gone through. Do you have another one we could try?"

My stomach tightens. "You're charging it already? I haven't checked out yet."

"Well, you originally only checked in for three nights, and when you didn't come into the office today to extend your stay, I was going to add a fourth night for you and go from there," she explains.

The kindness in her tone should make me feel better, but it doesn't. I'm not sure much would at this point.

"I'm so sorry. I didn't even think about coming in. You're in your right to do that. Thank you for not just kicking me out. I'll be back soon and—" And what? Beg her to let me stay for free? Oh, Millie, you're in it now. "And I'll try my other cards. We'll get it sorted."

"I'm glad to hear that. I had your cabin cleaned and restocked this morning, just in case. We'll see you soon."

"Thank you, Shelly," I whisper.

She ends the call, and I stand outside for a moment, willing myself not to cry about this. I've cried too much since coming here, and I don't want this to be yet another thing to bring me to the brink.

Turning, I head back to the studio. The sight of Shade taking payment from the woman at the desk isn't what I was expecting to see so soon. He's already looking at me when I let go of the door and start toward the desk.

"Important call?" he asks.

I swallow, trying my hardest to hide my worry. "I'm sorry. I didn't think you were so close to being done already. It won't happen again."

Shade narrows his eyes at my answer and hands the woman her receipt. She takes it from him and says something that I don't hear because of her soft tone. My emotions are too unnerved to try and dissect what it was.

"I don't think so, Beck. My dinner plans weren't a ruse," he tells her, his eyes unmoving from where they hold mine.

"What a shame. I guess I'll see you when I see you, then."

"Yeah, you will. Make sure to take care of that piece. It's going to itch real fucking bad in a bit here."

"I will."

She pats his arm, her fingers lingering on his bicep before dropping. I take a step out of the way when she passes me with a genuine smile. The door closes a moment later, leaving me and Shade alone.

"Who called you?" he asks.

"It was nothing. I'm sorry again for leaving without letting you know where I was going."

"Don't try playing it off, princess. You're clearly upset."

Ignoring him, I round the opposite side of the desk and sit in the chair. My knees are pressed flush together, the space between us not as generous as I thought it would be.

"What happens at the end of a workday? Do I need to learn how to clean up after a tattoo or anything?"

"No, you don't need to do that yet. You've done enough for today, don't you think?"

"Not really. I spent most of the day listening to Bryce's instructions and fiddling around with the calendar."

"I like my station set up and taken down a very specific way. I'm not ready to teach anyone else how to do that for me yet," he says.

"That's okay."

"Are you going to tell me what's upset you now?"

"Why do you care so much? Shouldn't you be hurrying with your cleanup so you can go to dinner?"

My eyes go wide at the attitude in my tone. Shade's eyes twinkle as he shifts closer to me, his body casting a shadow over my legs.

"Are you hungry, Millie? Is that why you're so bothered?"

"You think I'm hangry?" I ask, fighting off a laugh.

"Would you prefer I think you're jealous that I have plans tonight instead?"

"No. I have dinner plans too."

His brow lifts. "Oh? With who?"

"Myself."

"In that case, I'm the jealous one."

With a huff, I turn the chair so I face the desk. "I didn't take you for the jealous type."

I squeak when he grabs the back of the chair and pulls me right back to face him. Slowly, he lowers his hands to the armrests and bends over me, dropping his voice to a rasped murmur.

"You don't know me well enough. Let's change that."

"Why would you want to do that?"

"Is that a serious question?"

I blink, the sight of him so close to me a bit overwhelming. I've never been in this position with a man like Shade before. Someone this larger than life but who seems genuinely interested in hearing me speak and learning the things that I have a hard time sharing with other people. He has this way of getting to me so easily that it makes him dangerous.

"I would hate to keep you from your plans," I say.

"Even if they include you?"

"What do you mean?"

"My dinner plans are with you. Unless you're going to turn me down."

I ignore the heat rising up my throat. "Usually, you're supposed to ask a woman if she wants to have dinner with you instead of assuming she does."

"I was hopeful. Especially after last night."

My breath catches. "I don't—"

He drags the rough pad of his thumb over my elbow. I lose my train of thought, lowering my gaze to where he's touching me so brazenly.

"You don't what, Millie? Don't know why you stopped answering me and kept me wondering why all damn night?"

I nod jerkily, unable to speak.

"I checked my phone every hour, waiting to see if you'd answered my question. You didn't, though, did you? I want to know why."

"I fell asleep," I lie.

Humoured disbelief fills his expression. "You're something else."

"We shouldn't have spoken to each other like that."

"Why not?"

"We're not compatible, and I'm not here for all . . . of that."

Releasing the armrest, he backs up, taking his touch with him. Instead of continuing to stroke my flushed skin, he slips his hands into his pockets and eyes me casually.

"Alright."

I open and close my mouth a few times. "Alright?"

"We're still having dinner together. But alright. I'll let the rest go for now," he relents, appearing completely unbothered.

Annoyance ripples through me as I stiffen in the chair. "And if I don't want to have dinner with you?"

"Don't try it, Millie. I'm already letting you fib a bit too much already."

And with that, he leaves me at the desk, staring after him with a shiver running up my spine.

12

Before I've turned my car off, Millie's already parked and hopping out of hers. I go to follow her, but the moment I open my door, she's whipping around and shaking her head at me. The finger she's waving in my direction keeps me seated.

"No! I'll just be a minute."

"I can't come inside with you? I'll just say hi to Shelly."

"No. You're just going to distract her. I'll be quick," she rambles.

I still don't know why she needed to go to the office before her place. "As a bunny, princess. I've got an extra-large pizza on my passenger seat that's going to get cold."

Happy with that, she opens the screen door and scurries inside, letting it smack shut behind her. I inhale the smell of greasy pepperoni with extra cheese and lean into my seat, waiting.

I glance at the time after what feels like forever, seeing that it's only been three minutes. Still, that feels like long enough for her to have done whatever it was she needed to. There's nothing in the office besides a few Shimmer Lake sweatshirts, fishing rods, and life jackets. Unless she's planning on taking me on a late-night canoe ride, I don't think she'll be snapping any of those things up.

"Fuck it," I mutter before getting out.

The sun has already set, so I follow the glowing lanterns up the log steps. Camping chairs are set along both sides of the porch, but there's only one that has a stool in front of it. That's always been Shelly's spot, and it makes me feel too nostalgic to see that nothing has changed here at all.

"Are you sure you don't have any other cards we can try instead? Maybe there's been a mistake at the bank," Shelly suggests.

"Um, can you just try this one once more? There should be enough on it."

I hear Millie's voice before I see the shape of her behind the screen door. With a tug, I have it out of my way. It creaks loudly on its hinges, interrupting the two women.

Shelly glances my way and offers a brief smile before focusing back on Millie. "I can, honey."

Millie doesn't respond to my interruption the same way. Instead of smiling at me, she frowns, her lip getting sucked into her mouth. The heat on her cheeks isn't the kind I enjoy. Quite the opposite, really.

She stays silent, her heeled foot tapping the old floors as she watches Shelly swipe her card through the machine and pass it over to her. There's a shake to her hand when she pushes the buttons on the machine and waits a few seconds.

Two low beeps on the machine follow.

Millie gulps and lowers it to the counter. I watch Shelly slowly pick the machine up and put it away. There's no movement from Millie. Not even a forced laugh or straightening of her shoulders.

"What's going on?" I ask, unable to stop myself from joining them.

The lack of acknowledgment from Millie is concerning.

"Just a technical difficulty, Shade. My machine is probably just out of whack. I'll bring it home with me tonight and see if it's in need of an update," Shelly says.

Millie shakes her head, suddenly alert. "I can't afford to stay here."

"Yeah, funny joke," I say with a snort.

"I'm not joking around. This isn't funny to me."

I sober up, turning to face her completely. The way she's shrunk into herself is similar to when I first met her. Her shell is strong, but I'm stronger.

"You're working for me now. Just put her stay on my card, Shelly," I say easily.

Millie's body snaps straight, her eyes narrowing on me. "No, she's absolutely not doing that."

"Why not? Consider it a living allowance. I need a receptionist, and there's nobody in Oak Point wanting to take your place."

"That's not why you're doing this, and you know it."

The corner of my mouth twitches. "And why would I be doing it, then? What kind of guy do you think I am, princess?"

"I'm not being a freeloader. That's not who *I* want to be here," she snaps, not giving me a real answer.

"You're not being a freeloader. You work for me."

"There's no need to argue tonight. I'd never let anyone not have a place to stay at night," Shelly interrupts.

I already knew that, but I know that hearing it relaxes Millie slightly. Her anger slips for a brief moment, making room for a thankful gaze shared between them. Then, she's glaring at me, making it hard not to laugh at how unscary she is, even pissed off.

"You could also stay at the studio instead. Would that be better for you?" I ask.

Millie pauses, shock blowing across her features. "Are you really making jokes right now?"

"I'm not joking."

Fuck, I wish I were. I'm such a blabbermouth. She's not going to stay at my place, and I wouldn't want her to anyway.

"And I'm not moving in with you."

"Shit, Millie, I'm not asking you to move in. I'm offering you a room to crash if you refuse to let me help you stay here. That's all."

Shaking her head, she looks to Shelly. "I'm sorry about all of this. I'll head in here tomorrow morning so we can talk in *private*."

"Alright. Have a good night, you two," Shelly replies, eyeing me curiously.

I shrug and toss her a wink before waiting for Millie to head out. She huffs, looking at me briefly while passing by. I follow, keeping a step behind her the entire way outside.

"What cabin is yours? I'm fucking starving," I say once we've reached our parked cars.

She opens her door. "I should leave you to eat by yourself."

"But you won't."

"Don't test me."

"I like when you get pissed off, princess. You look dangerous."

"Do you have a fear kink or something?"

With a low laugh, I say, "I said you were dangerous, not that I was afraid of you."

She doesn't answer before getting into her car and starting it up. I follow her down the gravel roads through the campground and past the few cabins that I've been to during my few stays at Shimmer Lake. It's been years, but I have quite a few fun memories here.

Once she pulls into the cleared area amongst the trees surrounding cabin twelve, I wait for her to park before joining. I figure that she's still annoyed with me, so I give her space to get inside the cabin alone while grabbing our food and the six-pack in the trunk.

I'm half-surprised when I don't find the cabin door locked. I step inside and survey the space, my hands still full.

It's clean and smells like lemons from whatever products were used in here. There's a fireplace against the wall in the small living area, along with an old brown couch, a scratched coffee table, and a flannel-printed armchair. The kitchen is nothing more than a bit of counter, a white fridge, and an oven that's without a doubt older than me. The homey feel is unmatched, though. Despite this place's age or décor, it feels like what a cabin should feel like. Authentic and original.

The temperature is alarming, though. It's fucking freezing.

"I don't have plates," Millie says.

Turning toward the sound of her voice, I stare at her as she comes out of the bathroom. The lighting in here is so different from the studio—more intimate. Her posh outfit appears different here. It's still ridiculous to me for someone to wear a skirt this close to October, but I'm starting to piece together that Millie isn't the type to care about that.

"You don't need a fork and knife to eat your pizza, then?" I tease.

"No. I'm saving those for when I want to stab you in the crotch later."

My laugh is rough, unexpected as it tears its way up my throat. Millie tries not to smile, her cheeks twitching.

"You're vicious."

"I'm not usually," she admits, passing me on her way to the couch.

Without her heels on, she's got to be nearly a foot shorter than me. Staring, I join her and drop the pizza and beer on the coffee table. She watches me open the pizza box and licks her lips.

"I didn't think you were really going to split it half and half," she notes, examining the pizza.

"I don't joke about pizza."

"Noted."

Tucking her legs beneath her, she leans over the couch and snags the first slice from the ham-and-pineapple side. With the drooping corner hanging in front of her mouth, she darts a look at me.

"Don't watch me eat. It's weird."

"I'm not," I mutter, reluctantly looking away.

She lets it go, and I take a piece for myself, immediately biting into it. My stomach growls, and a soft giggle follows.

"Don't laugh at me while I eat. It's weird," I tease between bites.

"Don't be a copycat."

Spreading my legs slightly, I lean over them and look at her again. "You're going to have to figure out what you're doing here sooner rather than later. If I overstepped with my offers, I'm sorry. I've got a habit of jumping in to help my friends without thinking about whether they want it or not."

With a sigh, Millie lowers her pizza. "It's not that I don't want your help. If I accept it, I'll be no better here than I was back home."

"Explain that to me."

"No."

"Why not?"

"I like that you don't know me for who I was there. It's given me the freedom to try and find who I am without all of that," she explains tightly, avoiding my eyes.

"Unless you've changed your entire personality, I can't see that happening."

"That's the thing. I hardly know you, but I still know enough to tell that you'd have hated me if we'd met anywhere else."

"That's a bold statement," I declare, a little annoyed at her assumption.

"It's the truth. I'd never have allowed myself to sit at a bar with a stranger and spend hours speaking with him. If I'd so much as looked at you back home—a guy with tattoos from head to toe and an arrogant grin—I'd have turned away and left. Not because I wouldn't have thought you were attractive, but because it would have led to nothing but trouble."

"Was your goal for dinner tonight to stomp on my ego?"

She shrinks into herself slightly, lips tugging down. "No. I'm just . . . Things are different here, is what I'm saying. You called us friends, and I like that. Friends aren't really my thing back home. Any that I do have aren't there because they enjoy my company. It's all about status and money."

"You can't change who you are at your core by driving a few hours from your hometown, Millie. You're either a good person or you're not. That's not something you can pretend. I don't care how confident someone is on their ability to wear a mask. I'll see through it."

"I know I'm a good person. I'm just not who I want to be yet."

"So, that's why you're staying? To figure out who you really are?"

Her eyes find mine, so bright there's no mistaking her words for honesty. "Yeah, I think that's what I'm hoping for."

"Consider me a part of this mission, then."

"You don't have to do that."

"I'm intrigued by who you are already. I'd be missing out not seeing the final stages, wouldn't I?"

"That, or grateful when I learn that I'm into something really weird."

"I like a bit of weird," I poke, finishing the last bite of my pizza.

Millie gives my shoulder a bump. "So, friends?"

"Friends, but I haven't forgotten about last night either."

"What does that have to do with being friends?" she asks, her voice swooping up in pitch.

"I don't make a habit of flirting like that with my friends, princess. Either you put an end to that right now, or the label of friends is going to get a bit weighted."

Her throat pulls with a swallow. The crust of her pizza joins the rest of the untouched slices in the box, and then she's twisting her body sideways. With her knees pressing into my thigh, she inhales deeply.

"Did you mean what you said?"

"Be specific," I push gently, ignoring the quickening of my pulse.

Glancing up at the ceiling, she drops a hand to her leg, digging her fingers into the fabric of her tights. "About making exceptions to your rule?"

My groin tightens, blood pooling there and making my temperature rise. I drape an arm along the back of the couch, needing to try and loosen my tight muscles. The heat from her body makes my skin buzz with excitement.

"For you?" I ask.

Her lips part, her tongue gliding along the bottom one. "Yeah. Yes, yeah for me."

"I would have told you last night."

"Tell me now," she murmurs, gaze falling, drifting to my mouth.

I adjust my arm, letting my hand hang before looping a finger through her hair. The touch is subtle, hardly much to write home about, but her reaction to it is what makes it intoxicating. Her eyelids fan closed at the same second her body quakes with a shiver. I reach for her now, taking more of her hair and fitting it loosely in a fist.

My gaze is sharp as it runs over her face, dissecting the breaths being sucked quickly between her parted lips and the fluttering of her lashes. I give her hair a gentle tug, just enough to have her feeling it. The whimper that escapes her sends an electric charge right through my middle. I release her hair and smooth it over her shoulder.

Jesus Christ.

It takes a few moments for her to realize I've let her go. The flutter of her lashes as she opens her eyes is gentle, so unlike what I'm used to in situations like this.

"I'll make the exception for you," I decide, letting my words fall between us without knowing exactly how she'll react.

Her brows pinch together. "You . . . will?"

"Did you think I'd turn you down?"

"Don't make me answer that," she whispers.

Curling my fingers into a fist, I keep it bare of her hair and push it against the couch back. "I can't fuck you, though, Millie."

Her face blooms in a deep pink blush. "Oh! Oh, right—"

"I'd destroy you. I might be open to changing my rules, but I can't give you the kind of sex that's fit for a woman like you."

"A woman like me," she echoes, her nostrils flaring as the wheels in her mind start turning.

I reach for the hand she has still on her thigh and give it a squeeze. "I didn't mean it that way. More like I wouldn't treat you right. The romantic love shit. It's just not my thing."

"So, what, you'd only want to teach me the other things?"

My head almost falls back as my cock grows too stiff in my jeans. I clear my throat and shift my hips, trying to find a comfortable position.

"Is that what you're looking for? A teacher?"

"Why not? We could still be just friends that way."

"Spoken like someone with little experience, princess."

"Flirty friends are a thing, aren't they? You're a good guy, and I'm asking you to do this for me. We could set boundaries, rules. It would work, right?" she asks, sounding so damn hopeful that I agree without meaning to.

"Yeah, boundaries would work."

Or fuck us both over when someone inevitably tumbles over them. I know it wouldn't be me, which means that Millie would be the one getting hurt. That's not the point of her being here on this self-discovery journey of hers.

I've always known I was a bit of a jackass, but right now, it's a matter of fact. It's just too bad that still doesn't make me call this off.

13

Millie

It turns out that setting boundaries for something like this isn't exactly my specialty.

After Shade left, I stayed right here on the couch, unable to stop my mind from racing. It all seemed like a great idea at the time. An obviously experienced man being up for the challenge of teaching a much less experienced woman about sex is a dream. Especially when he's someone whom I've started to think of as a friend.

He won't let me make a fool out of myself, and I know that everything he teaches me will be useful in the future. I'll be like a sex pro by the time I head back home. Chadwick will be a guy from the past, and I'll be able to start fresh with more knowledge than I've ever had.

Still, my nerves won't settle. Neither will the guilt of feeling like I forced Shade into this.

He told me to come up with my boundary/rule list, but also a general idea of what I was wanting him to teach me. A spicy lesson plan, if you will.

Reaching up, I touch my hair. I can still feel the ghost of his fingers curling around it and pulling. My pulse flutters, the reminder having nearly the same effect now as it did then.

The low ache in my scalp shot straight down my middle to land between my legs.

While I'm terrified of what all of this could mean, I can't pretend that I'm not also excited. I've always been curious about what sex should really be like. Not the awkward first-time sex, but the real, hot, and sweaty kind where you're eager to jump somebody's bones.

I know it's partially my fault for my lack of knowledge, especially when it comes to pleasuring myself. I'm not some poor girl who had restricted access to the internet or was locked away in a castle her entire life. My castle was really a ski resort, and the lock was easily picked, so I could have just . . . tried harder. The blame for my naivety with sex is on me.

There are two bottles of beer on the coffee table, but only one is still half-full. Shade hardly took five sips of his all night, while I couldn't seem to down mine quick enough. It didn't help in the slightest. Instead, it made me all the more jittery, contemplating telling him to scratch this entire idea.

Before I could, he was standing and leaving me with instructions to come up with my boundary list and saying we'd talk at the studio tomorrow. I can only assume he'll be doing the same tonight.

The scent of his cologne lingers on the fabric of the couch, teasing me with yet another reminder of his presence. I reach for his beer and bring it to my mouth before taking a big swig. The foamy liquid goes down smooth and settles in my full stomach. I'm bloated from the greasy pizza, but while I wasn't going to tell Shade and let him get more arrogant, it was the best I've ever had.

Tapping a nail to the glass bottle, I twist my mouth and glance at my phone. It's been on the coffee table since before dinner yet hasn't lit up once. I'm unused to this kind of silence. Maybe that's one of the things I'm most grateful for being here.

I exchange the beer for my phone and settle into the

couch, fighting a shiver from the cold. With my knees pulled up and my heels under my butt, I unlock the screen and open the Notes app.

Boundaries/rules, I type. The title is there, but now what? I type the ideas that come to me first.

Don't say anything stupid

Don't act too excited

No sexual touching unless I've shaved and showered

No getting jealous

No feelings. I underline that one twice for good measure.

I doubt it would happen anyway, but it's never bad to be extra careful. Shade's made his type obvious; at least, I think he has. The woman who was at the studio the other night was very different than me, and they clearly have been together in the past. Not to mention his initial statement of not sleeping with inexperienced women.

Yeah, no feelings. Easy enough.

I move on from the boundaries and spell out another title.

Lesson Ideas.

My entire body blushes as I reread it. How exactly does one come up with ideas like that? Am I supposed to scroll through a porn site and pick the kinks I think look most interesting?

Tongue kissing.

I immediately delete that, my face scrunching in embarrassment.

"I'm so screwed here," I whisper.

Suddenly, the Notes app closes as a call flashes. I blink at the name and cautiously answer, turning it to speakerphone.

"Hi?"

"I'm starting to think that I know you too well already," Shade states.

"Why would you say that?"

"You sound anxious, Millie. This isn't supposed to be

nerve-racking. If it is, then we need to abandon the idea right now."

I jerk forward. "Being anxious is a Millie experience, Shade. Sorry to disappoint."

"So, it doesn't have anything to do with what I asked you to do tonight?"

"I didn't say that. I'm an anxious person. Don't think you're that special," I bite out.

Yeah, I'll admit to being a bit defensive. But I didn't already toss all of my self-respect out the window to ask him to do this with me only to have him turn his back on it already.

He whistles. "Okay, I'm sorry. I just don't want you working yourself up about this. It's supposed to be fun."

"You left me with the two most complicated lists to make."

"They're not supposed to be complicated."

"That's easy for you to say," I argue, relaxing bit by bit.

"Just tell me what you've got so far."

Swallowing, I go back to the Notes app. "I have the rules figured out."

"Tell them to me," he urges.

"The first one is *'don't say anything stupid.'*" Suddenly, I regret writing that. With a wince, I add, "I just don't know how I'll be acting once we . . . you know."

"Take that one off," he demands, a slight bite in the words.

"What? Why?"

"You can't say anything stupid when you're learning about what you like sexually. Don't censor yourself. I don't want that."

A few of the knots in my stomach unravel. "Okay, I'm deleting that one."

"Good girl. What's next?"

I sink my teeth into my lip and squeeze my eyes shut in response to the praise. If I ignore the pleasure I get from hearing him say it, maybe it will stop having an effect on me.

Jumping past the second rule on my list, I say, "No sexual touching unless I've shaved and showered."

There's a weighted pause that feels like it won't ever end. I shift on the couch and lie on my back, my legs kicked out and moving nervously. Worry gnaws at me, growing more painful as the seconds pass.

His voice is tense when he says, "You never told me about your first time."

"Because you didn't ask," I mumble.

"Was it bad?"

"It wasn't the best."

"Did he make you come, princess?"

My brain starts to spark and fizzle. I'm incapable of speaking as I short-circuit. My grip on my phone turns pained as I make it tighter and tighter until finally, I release it completely. I touch my cheeks and instantly feel the heat in them. They burn so badly it's uncomfortable.

"That's the mildest thing we're going to be talking about if we do this, Millie. Don't freeze up on me already," he coos, his voice like a gentle caress on my oversensitive skin.

"No," I croak, shaking my head despite being alone. "No, he didn't."

"I'm going to take a shot in the dark and say that he wasn't a fan of pubic hair either."

"No, he wasn't."

"Scratch the rule."

"I can't get rid of them all," I argue, but it's weak.

"Read me the next ones, and we'll see."

"No getting jealous, and no catching feelings."

"Those are good. They stay," he says, sounding almost relieved.

I let go of a breath I've trapped, mirroring his reaction. "They'll stay."

"What about your other list? Have you finished that one?"

"No."

"Don't overthink. Tell me what you like or what you're interested in. We won't do anything you don't want to, and even if you think you could like something but change your mind, that's that."

"How are you so good at this?" I ask, staring at the ceiling.

"I'm just no longer bothered by things like this. I know what I like and what I don't. It gets easier."

"I'm having a hard time believing that."

"You're just thinking about it too much. Close your eyes," he instructs.

I can hear him moving around on the line and grow curious. Is he at home? Is he in bed or on the couch like I am?

Letting the questions go, I follow his instructions. "They're closed."

"Stop thinking about what you think I'll approve of and focus on what would interest you. When you had sex, what about it did you enjoy?"

Easier said than done. Especially when my only sexual encounter was painful, tense, and awkward. I focus on his question, thinking past the bad and to the few good moments.

"It was quick. I wasn't anywhere close to an orgasm. He didn't touch me much before the real thing, but when he did, I wanted more than just his fingers on me."

"You mean his tongue?"

"Yes," I whisper.

"And did he put his mouth on you, Millie? Did you ask for that?"

"No."

"Put it on your list," he urges, voice raspy.

My heart nearly jumps free of my chest. "You're sure? That's intimate, Shade. You don't have to do that just because I'm curious about it."

He shushes me softly, pushing past my argument. "Would it make it easier to hear my list of rules?"

"Yes," I blurt.

"No sex."

"That's it?"

"That's it," he confirms.

"You're not worried about anything else? Or uncomfortable?"

"I'm attracted to you, Millie. If we were different people in different stages of our lives, I wouldn't have any rules at all. You're not punishing me by giving me an opportunity to do these things with you. It's the opposite."

My entire body shivers, and I'm too focused on that to stop the soft noise of pleasure from escaping my lips. The groan that follows comes from my phone's speakers, and I debate asking him to come back over so we can start now before shutting that idea down.

"I'm attracted to you too," I squeak.

I've done a terrible job of hiding that, but at least he doesn't tease me about it.

"Finish your list tonight, and I'll make one too. We'll go through them together and go from there."

"And you're sure nothing else is off limits?"

"Fucking positive," he confirms.

"I'll trust you, then."

He chuckles. "Do you feel better now?"

"I do. Thank you for calling. I didn't mean to be so obvious about how I was feeling earlier."

"You weren't."

"So, you just guessed?"

"It's like I told you. I've been paying attention."

I turn onto my side and drop my phone beside my head. "Thank you, Shade."

"No thank yous. It makes this feel fucking creepy," he says.

"You're not wrong."

"It's a friendly act."

"Friends with benefits, is what I think it's called."

"Nah, that's not accurate. We're not hooking up. I'm just your friendly neighbourhood sex coach," he teases.

I roll my lips together, trapping a laugh. "And you thought a thank you was creepy."

"I'm hanging up now. I'll see you tomorrow. *With your list.*"

"With my list," I confirm.

"Good night, Millie."

With a soft smile, I whisper, "Good night, Shade."

14

Shade

Any minute now, Millie's going to get up out of that spinning chair and say something to me.

I've been waiting for her to mention our conversation last night since I arrived this morning to find her already pacing in front of the door. She didn't spare a look at the coffee I handed over before gulping it down and rushing to that damn spot behind the desk.

The nervous energy around her is so charged it could spark if poked a bit too hard. She stares down at the paperwork in front of her, foot tapping to a quick beat. She's wearing the shoes with the fancy red bottoms today and, for the first time since I've met her, a pair of tight, black pants instead of a skirt. They're doing wonders for the legs I'm already too fucking obsessed with, as if they needed another reason to draw my eye.

Today was slow in the studio for me. I finished with my only booking an hour ago, having cut a chunk off the estimated time we'd booked for the half sleeve. My back may hurt like a bitch from sitting hunched over for six hours, but I'm nowhere near ready to head upstairs to bed yet.

Stretching out, I raise my arms above my head and stare

at her. There's no mistaking where I'm looking or who I'm looking at now that it's just us two. I release a low groan, hoping that will draw her gaze, but it doesn't.

Millie's leg starts shaking faster, her elbow digging into the desk.

Frustration urges me to try harder. Ignoring me isn't going to keep us from talking about her list or what happened this morning with Shelly. The only thing that could throw a wrench into this little plan we have going is for her to change her mind or have to go back home already. And Christ, that's not what I want in the slightest.

Yeah, I shouldn't, but I want to show her everything I know. The attraction between us is there, and I'm not the type of guy to let that pass without trying my hand at getting her beneath it. Millie isn't my usual woman, and instead of stepping foot in a puddle of complication, I'm jumping headfirst into a pool of safe exploration. We're not crossing any improper lines with this agreement.

Everything is clean-cut and simple.

"The shop is closed, princess," I say.

Her leg stills. "Already?"

"It's been empty for an hour."

"Oh, I didn't notice."

"Because you've been so busy with paperwork or because you've been focusing on ignoring me?"

Slowly, she lowers her arm, still staring down at the desk. "I wasn't ignoring you. I'm here to work, Shade. I don't want to let anyone down."

"Mm, and work you did. No disappointing happening here. Now, you're off the clock and can put an end to what you're doing. Come here," I urge gently, moving my stool back from the leather table a few inches.

"You have to promise that you really won't judge me for what I've put on my list. And I want you to go first."

When she finally glances my way, it's as she stands. Her hands collide, thumbs tapping on the backs of them.

"I won't judge you, Millie, but I'm not going first. I don't want you to just agree to everything I say because you're nervous."

"Couldn't you be a bit more selfish?" she mutters, crossing the studio.

My grin is crooked. "I could, but I'm trying to be a good guy."

"Aren't you supposed to believe that good guys are over-rated or something?"

I snort a laugh. "No, I've always rooted for the good guy. Most of the time, they deserve the girl more than guys like me do."

"I don't agree," she bites out, and that bit of fire calls to my curiosity like a moth to a flame.

"Oh? Does that tone have anything to do with why you were at Peakside in a muddy wedding dress?"

A sigh slips from her lips, and I spread my legs to make more room for her in front of me. She takes the spot, her back against the tattoo bed and hand falling to touch it.

"The only type of man I've ever known is the one who should be the hero in every story. The Prince Charming with a carriage at the ready to take me back to his castle and keep me trapped there under the ruse of protection. Sometimes, it's nothing more than a costume, Shade. I know you think I'm a princess, but that's not who I want to be. It's not even who I really think I am past the personality traits that I've been force-fed my entire life. At this point, I think I'd rather be a villain instead."

Flicking my eyes between each of hers, I find the truth in her words. She chews her lip, allowing me to look without glancing away and hiding.

"You can be whoever you want to be here, Millie."

"That's what I'm afraid of."

I frown, rejecting the impulse to reach for her hand. "Why are you afraid?"

"Because I don't know if I'll have to lose that part of me the moment I leave. I'm not sure I could be happy again without it."

There's nothing I can say yet to help her. I don't know the right answers to put her fears at ease. There's still so much time left for her to explore, and she could be right. Once she finds out who she wants to be, there might not be any way for her to pretend anymore.

I know I couldn't change who I am.

"Let's just focus on right now. Read me your list," I demand, working hard to keep my tone level.

Her breath skips as she drops her gaze to her pants. The outline of her phone is obvious in the tight material, and I poke my tongue into my cheek to keep quiet. She pulls it out and swipes at the screen before lifting her eyes again.

I roll forward on my stool and brush my knees against her legs. Her nerves are so obvious it's almost making *me* nervous.

"Do you want me to read it for you?" I offer.

"No. No, I can do it."

"Alright," I murmur.

With a clearing of her throat, she focuses on her phone. "Tongue kissing."

It takes everything in me to keep my expression blank instead of surprised. I know she said inexperienced, but I assumed she'd have done that, even if it were sloppy and disappointing.

I nod. "What's next?"

"I don't know if you'd want to, or even could help with this, but . . ." She trails off, inhaling through her nose. Her next sentence is rough, sounding as if she had to yank each word up her throat individually. "I'm never able to get myself to finish when I touch myself."

Have fucking mercy.

It's not possible to spread my legs any wider than I already am. My groin is tight, too constricted as I try to shift on the tiny-ass fucking leather stool.

"You want help making yourself come?" I ask, voice throaty and raw, as if I've scraped it with a cheese grater.

Millie glares at me. "Do you have to ask like that? It's embarrassing enough without you judging me like you said you *wouldn't*."

"I didn't mean for it to come out badly. I'm not judging. Consider it on the list, princess. Tell me what's next."

Her hesitation bothers me. Pushing forward, I box her in completely against the table and take the hand she's using to grip the leather. It's only for support. That's the only reason I hold her fingers and stroke my thumb along each one.

"What you think is judgment is excitement," I admit, risking putting that out there in hopes it helps her be more comfortable.

Blue eyes widen slightly. "You better not be placating me."

"You've had my dick hard since you came over here, Millie."

"Oh," she whispers.

It takes everything in me not to move a muscle when her stare dips, trailing down my torso to where I'm too goddamn stiff and uncomfortable. I wait for a reaction and get rewarded for my patience the second a soft exhale blows past her parted lips. Her fingers flex in my hold, clutching tightly.

"Tell me what's next," I urge, continuing to stroke her hand.

"I want to learn how to make you feel good."

She doesn't mean me, not really. But shit, right now, that's all I hear.

"How?"

"How?" she repeats, slowly pulling her eyes up from between my spread legs.

"With your hands or your mouth?"

"Both."

I tip my chin, breathing heavily. "What else?"

"There's only one more."

"That's okay. I have plenty," I announce.

Intrigue fills her gaze, but she pushes past it. "I've only ever had one thing that I've been curious about that isn't, like, base level."

"Go on."

She rolls her eyes. "I want to try touching someone when we're not alone."

"Explain not alone," I encourage, my thoughts tipping over into a place that's hot and raw, pulsating with excitement.

"Like beneath the table at a restaurant or hidden in a dark hallway somewhere. I've obviously never tried it, but the thought of doing something like that has always excited me. I know it might be too much—"

"It's not, Millie. You're interested in something, and it doesn't matter how big or small it is. If I were uncomfortable with the idea of trying, I would tell you that," I explain, hardly holding on to my head at this point.

"And you're not uncomfortable with it?"

"Far fucking from it."

Some of the tension disappears from her. There's a lightness there now that betrays how relaxed she's growing.

"What's on your list?" she asks, voice more confident now.

Instead of answering, I stand from the stool and move our joined hands to rest on the table behind her. Then, I let her fingers go. She sucks in a breath at our sudden closeness, and I tip my lips in a crooked grin while gripping the backs of her thighs and lifting her clean off the floor.

"Shade—" she gasps when her ass hits the leather table, bringing us face to face, my height no longer a hindrance.

I slide a hand through her hair and palm the back of her head. I've never felt hair this fucking soft before or smelled the soft scent that drifts from it. It's sweet yet spicy, and I'm hoping that's exactly what I'm going to find when I break into that beautiful fucking head of hers and uncover all the parts of her she didn't know existed.

"We need you to get more comfortable with me before hearing what's on my list," I rasp, gently guiding her head back.

Her lips were glossy when she arrived at the studio this morning, but that was from the makeup I caught her applying. Right now, they're wet from the pink tongue that can't seem to stop gliding across them, taunting me. And the longer I look at them, the more I'm struggling not to imagine an entirely different way to make them shine, and that's what gives me the final shove I needed.

"Follow my lead," I whisper before slanting my mouth over hers.

Millie makes a noise that gets caught in her throat. I hold back a smile at her surprise and focus on the small, soft lips that haven't moved yet. She purses them slightly, and I know she's in her head when she can't follow my lead, moving to her own beat instead of the one I'm trying to show her.

Keeping my lips on hers, I bring a hand to her waist, cupping it softly. My other one stays in her hair, pulling on it gently. She parts her lips in response, and I do it again, encouraging her to keep her mouth relaxed.

With a sweep of my hand from her waist to the small of her back, she finally falls into the kiss. Her lips chase mine, almost like they're trying to steal the lead, and while that has an immediate effect on my dick, that's not my plan.

"Slow down. Follow my lead. Make me earn it, Millie. I don't deserve it yet."

Her breath fills my mouth as she nods, a hand brushing my forearm. She slows again but doesn't fall back into the frozen state from before. Her lips cling to mine, still chasing, but slower, patient.

I pull her forward, the fabric of her pants making a rough

noise as her thighs scrape the table on her way to the edge. She drops her head further back without encouragement but then circles my wrist, clinging to it.

Our pace is still slow, but it's hot, tension clinging to the breaths we share and encouraging the slow rock of our bodies. Millie's not thinking about my tongue or worrying about when I'll use it, and that's exactly why I slide it along her bottom lip.

She jerks in my hold. I wait, testing if she's truly as ready as she thinks she is. The responsive glide of her tongue against my lip is the confirmation I needed to continue.

Palming her head a bit harder, I curl my fingers in her hair and get a squeeze of my wrist in return. She arches into my touch and presses her chest against mine before flicking out her tongue against mine. I trap a moan in my chest and nip at her mouth instead.

"That's it. Follow your instincts, Millie."

Nodding as much as she can in this position, she slips her tongue into my mouth the moment I release her lip. I'm not ready for the confident swirl of it or the shudder that ripples through me afterward. I pull on her hair and shift my hand back to her waist, holding it tightly.

She's moving with more skill than I could have expected this soon, and I'm almost disappointed to have to cut the first lesson so short.

As if reading my mind, Millie steals my tongue, sucking it sharply. There's no stopping the groan that travels from my mouth to hers. I keep my feet planted on the floor, refusing to move even an inch forward to where I know we'd press together.

I try to pull back before I get in trouble, but she doesn't release my wrist, even as our lips separate.

"Don't stop yet," she blurts out. "Tell me how to kiss you here."

Round nails run beneath my jaw and along the side of my

throat. The blood thumping beneath the skin there makes everything more sensitive, and I flex my fingers on her waist.

Tilting my head to the side, I give her the space to do what she wants. "Use your mouth, tongue, and teeth."

Her lips are slightly swollen when they move to the ridge of my jaw, scraping the shaven skin there before shifting lower. Shit, the soft pressure she's using is a tease, a fucking test of my will. By the time she places an open-mouthed kiss on my throat, I'm so twisted up I don't know where to begin to unravel myself.

The first scrape of her teeth against my skin is sharp, a bit more confident. I don't have to tell her to soothe the nip with her tongue before she's doing that on her own, leaving a wet mark behind. Suddenly, she's abandoning my wrist and using both hands to grip my shirt, tugging me closer.

She sucks on the skin beneath my jaw, and a soft noise fills the little space between us. My vision grows tinted as I tug harder on her hair. When that noise grows in volume, pleasure erupting in a way that I know can't exist in this moment, I release her.

"Millie," I murmur before taking her hands from my shirt and guiding her backward.

Blue eyes snap to mine, her pupils wide and thick. Pink lingers on her cheeks and nose, leading all the way beneath the neckline of her blouse. Her soft, panted breaths match the pace of mine, until she freezes.

"I'm so sorry!" she squeaks.

Her head shakes quickly, and a mix of bewilderment and embarrassment fills her expression before I'm taking one step back and letting her slip down from the table. Millie shifts to the side and tucks her hair behind her ears.

"I practically mauled you."

"You didn't," I argue.

Maul is a strong word. It's the wrong one. A single word

isn't accurate, although it would be easier that way. I'd go with *got lost in the pleasure of a new experience with someone willing* instead.

"I've never been like that before. I'm usually much more respectful," she rambles.

"If you want approval to disrespect me, you have it. What happened was respectful. I just don't want to rush you. This only works if you're comfortable."

"Your comfortability matters to me too, Shade. And we didn't discuss more than using tongue prior. It was just mouth kissing."

"Talking about every single thing prior to making out with someone isn't really the norm, princess," I tease, trying to lighten the mood. "A lot of the time, you play it by ear. It's alright to be spontaneous once in a while."

She exhales, staring fiercely at me. "I've never been great at that."

"Well, you did pretty alright just now," I reply with a wink.

"I did?"

From the pain in my balls right now, I'd say she did too fucking alright.

"Yeah, Millie. You're a natural."

The grin that fills her face with a pure, blissful light makes the marks on my throat feel all the more special. She claps her hands in front of her as I lean back on my foot and watch her, chuckling beneath my breath.

Yeah, this woman is dangerous in the worst way.

And I've always been attracted to a bit of danger.

15

Millie

"I don't understand."

Shelly smiles softly, her green-eyed gaze kind in the same way they were the night I checked in. "The cabin is yours for as long as you need it, Millie."

"But why? How? If I can't pay, I shouldn't get to stay here," I argue.

There's another woman wandering around the office tonight, taking in the shelves of camping supplies and sweatshirts with the Shimmer Lake Campground logo stamped on the front. It's a good logo, bright and rustic. Whoever they hired to design it did a good job. I've always been a doodler but haven't created anything that well thought out before. The way the colours work with the mountain landscape while also pulling in the rustic font is incredible.

Shelly reaches for my elbow. She tries to hide it, but I can see the curiosity in her stare. I don't blame her.

"Just consider it taken care of, doll. You're free to stay as long as you want. I've already shifted a few bookings around, so there's no point in arguing."

"Shelly . . ."

"All I ask in return is that you don't give up on finding

what you're looking for. I have a feeling you've run far enough. Stay and search now."

My throat grows sticky. I have a hard time getting my words up.

"Is it that obvious?"

"No, it's not obvious. You just remind me of the woman I was when I first got here."

"You're not from Oak Point?"

Her smile is faint. "No. But I've been here for the last twenty-five years."

"You've liked it here that much?" I ask, darting my eyes to where the other woman here has started our way.

Shelly notices the woman and asks me, "Do you like iced tea?"

"I do."

"How about you get one from the cooler over there and wait for me to finish up here. I'd love to have a bit more time to chat with you."

My heart swells with gratitude. "Yeah, so would I."

The cooler is only a few steps away. I reach it with ease as the woman steps up to the counter and sets her red sweatshirt down.

After the eventful day I've had, I wasn't expecting to come in here with the plan of sitting down with Shelly. Shade let me run out of the studio like a total wuss after kissing the daylights out of me, and the first place I came was here. I don't know what the draw was, but I couldn't go back to the cabin without figuring out what I'm going to do with my whole lack-of-funds problem.

Shelly wasn't here before I left this morning, and I'm starting to think that she did that on purpose. If this was her plan all along . . . I don't know how I'll digest that. The kindness that she's offering me right now is hard for me to understand.

I'm unsure I'll ever feel this taken care of again once I

leave.

"Have a great evening. If you need anything, please don't hesitate to come in. The office closes at nine, but my number is on the door for any emergencies," Shelly explains to the woman.

"Thank you! I'm sure I'll be just fine."

"Glad to hear it."

I open the cooler door and grab a bottle of iced tea. The brand on it isn't familiar to me.

Carrying it back to Shelly, I ask, "Do you make this stuff?"

"I do! Well, with the help of my husband. He does all of the packaging. I just make the iced tea."

"You make quite the pair."

"Thank you. He puts up with quite a lot from me, but I like to think I put up with even more from him." The wink she sends me is adorable. "Anyway, come with me and we'll chat some more."

I follow her outside and to the camping chairs on the front porch. She takes a seat on the one with the stool, and I sit beside her. It's silent out here besides the chirp of the bugs in the grass and an engine of what I think is a quad in the trees.

"The lid is a twist off. Ladies shouldn't have to struggle to open a bottle," she tells me, eyeing the iced tea I'm holding.

I give it a twist, and it comes off easily. "You're a miracle worker."

"I try. Women have to stick together. Especially in this world."

"Men are the worst."

"They are. But with a little elbow grease, you can get the right one trained just how you want him."

I choke on a laugh and try to tame it with a sip of the iced tea. It's the perfect mix of sweet and bitter, so I take another drink.

"I don't think all of them are trainable."

"Are you talking from experience there? Was he too stubborn to change or too wild to tame?"

"Yeah, and it was more like he was too arrogant to consider anyone besides himself. Let alone me."

Her nose crinkles. "It wouldn't be all that bad if you stayed here a while longer, then."

"No, I don't think so."

"Well, for the record, even the wild ones can settle a bit. And I'm speaking from experience this time."

I pause, taking in her wistful expression. "Chadwick isn't wild. I don't think he had a wild bone in his body."

"Mm. It's a good thing I'm not talking about this *Chadwick*, then," she sings.

"Shelly."

"What? I'm just putting in my two cents. Shade's a good one. I've known him since he was tiny. His parents used to bring him here for summer camp every year. Little shit-disturber, that boy, but he had manners in spades. He used to offer to scrub the kayaks for my husband and bring the clean towels to every cabin for me."

"You sound like a matchmaker."

She lifts her feet onto her stool and smiles. "I've been called far worse, doll."

"Shade's a nice guy. We're friends," I explain pointedly.

"I've been trying to get him to come back here for years, but he was always just too busy. Turns out he can make the time when it comes to driving you home."

It's impossible not to enjoy her pushing. Every attempt obviously comes from a place of kindness, and I'll take it if it means we can keep chatting for a bit longer.

"You were telling me about when you first came here. Want to continue that?" I ask, grinning.

Shelly frowns, tapping her chin. "Oh, I was? My memory is a bit spotty tonight."

"Where did you move from?"

"Fine, fine. I was born in Saskatoon and left on my thirtieth birthday. I'm not sure what it was that drew me here exactly. Not without getting all misty-eyed on you. But in what felt like a blink, I was pulling up outside of this place. I met my husband that night."

"What happened then? Did you ever go back home?"

"No. I left for a reason, and I knew I couldn't ever go back. That was my choice. Each person I hurt and betrayed has been left in my past. It's the only place we can't hurt each other anymore."

"I'm sorry, Shelly," I murmur.

She shakes her head, smiling. "Don't apologize. I'm happy where I am, and I've never regretted my choice to leave or the one I made to stay here. I met the love of my life at this place, and with our beautiful family we've raised here, how could I wish I'd done anything differently?"

"You have kids?"

"Two!" Leaning forward, she drops her feet to the porch. The sleeves of her flannel top are too long and hang to the tips of her fingers when she holds her knees. "Tilly and Ash. You'll see our son around here every once in a while. Ash lives in town, but Tilly's off in Nova Scotia with her husband."

"I've always wanted to go out East," I say.

"It is beautiful. We flew there for her wedding, and I had a hard time coming back. If it weren't for this place, maybe we would have stayed."

"You'd have been missed."

"Another good point," she teases.

"I'd love to meet your family sometime. I hope I'm still here the next time they're around."

"My husband, Kirk, is always around doing something or another, but unless you're near the dock or in the woods, you're sure to miss him. I'll call him over the next time you're around. And Ash, well, he's usually responsible for the four-wheeler noises coming from the trees. He runs the community centre in town."

I absorb that information and nod. "That's the building right by the entrance to town?"

"That's the one. Usually, the majority of sports programs run out of Cherry Peak and the school there, but Ash managed to get a softball team up and running here. He's trying to get something started for hockey, but there hasn't been enough interest."

"I'm not much for sports, honestly," I admit sheepishly.

"Oh, me neither. I don't know where the hell he got those genes from because they don't belong to either me or my husband."

I belt out a laugh, her brutal honesty refreshing. "I'm glad not to be alone, then."

"You should stop by sometime and say hi. I'll have blabbed his ear off about you by then."

"Yeah, maybe," I say, not wanting to be rude.

I can't see myself doing that, though. Not that I'll even have much time to with my job at the studio and all of the extra time Shade and I are going to be spending together . . .

Before my cheeks can go red, I change the subject.

"If you need help with anything around here that you or your husband don't want to do or don't have the time for, please just ask me. I can't stay here for free. It doesn't feel right."

"Millie, there's no changing my mind. One thing you'll learn about me is that I'm as stubborn as a mule."

"Please. Just let me help with something. I don't care if it's small or unimportant. I'm just really trying not to take advantage of anyone while I'm here. This isn't how I wanted to do things."

I'm begging now, but I don't feel shame because of it. I'm just desperate, and if I freeload my way through a stay here, I won't be able to stop feeling guilty.

Shelly stares at me for a long moment, her eyes digging into me. "What are you running from, doll?"

"A life that I know I've taken advantage of. But it's not the one I want. I'd give it to someone else if I could."

"If it makes you happy, I'll come up with a list of things you could do. But you don't need to. Truly, we have more than enough help here as it is," she says, giving in just enough for me to claim the win.

I release a relieved breath. "Thank you, Shelly."

"You'll need to get more familiar with the campground. We can't have you getting lost during one of your tasks."

"Let me guess, you know the exact person who I should ask to help show me around?"

She bats her eyes, her thin lips pursing. "What? Does that sound like me?"

"Yes, yes it does."

"I'm just thinking that you could take advantage of Shade's interest and put him to work a bit. I'd love to see him a bit more, as well. I suppose I'm just thinking about myself, really."

I take another sip from my bottle, smiling against the glass. "His only interest is in friendship."

"Oh, now you're just insulting me."

"Has anyone ever told you that you're a tad dramatic?"

"If you ask my husband, he'd tell you that being dramatic is my best characteristic."

"I don't know what I'm expecting him to be like, honestly," I say, setting my bottle down beside my chair.

"Imagine a grumpy lumberjack and then make him even grumpier."

"So, you're a grumpy/sunshine couple," I note.

"You read romance novels?"

"They're the only ones I read."

Shelly beams at me, and I can't help but laugh at her reaction. It's so pure, and honestly, I think she's the cutest woman

I've ever met. There's so much to her. More than there usually is to the ones I'm used to meeting back home.

"Have you been to the free little library that's set up by the beach? It's quite popular! There's another one on the corner of the street beside Twice Treasured, as well. I've stocked them up pretty well over the last few months. You need to take a look through," she rambles excitedly.

"I'll stop by the one here on my way back to my cabin. I've only seen them on social media before."

"Please do. And don't forget to come by and tell me if you take a book, and which one. I have a list of my favourites, but it changes so quickly."

I nod. "I haven't read in a while, honestly. I'd like to get back into it."

"This is only another sign that you're in the right place, doll."

There's no doubt in my mind that she's right.

16

I've gotten used to third-wheeling by now.

Bryce and Daisy are damn good friends, so if I've gotta watch them fawn over each other over a meal, then that's what I'm going to do. They deserve the happiness they've found, and I'm counting down the days until they get hitched. It feels like they've been together forever already, considering how long Bryce was fawning over her before finally making a move.

"You don't always have to drive out here to see me. I'm capable of heading your way," I say as we approach the door to Maggie's.

Bryce sends me a blank stare. "When you come to Cherry Peak, it's like pulling teeth to get you to leave."

"Ouch. You're fucking brutal, Bryce. And I was just thinking about how excited I am to be the best man at your wedding, and you go in for a kill shot."

"You're not my best man."

Daisy pokes Bryce in the side, shaking her head. "You know he's been trying to claim that spot, Frosty. Be gentle."

"Poppy would cut your eyes out if you took her place," Bryce says with a tug of the door.

Sure, Bryce's best friend from back home would probably be a bit upset to get snubbed from the spot, but I think I'm just as deserving as she is. I might not have known her for the same length of time that Poppy has, but we're just as close. Plus, Poppy's not my *biggest* fan, and I'd love to keep thinking that's because she feels threatened by me.

I push the door open the rest of the way and wait for the two of them to step inside before following. "She could try."

"I'll see what I can do," Daisy says, hanging back a bit so Bryce can't hear.

"Thank you, baby girl."

"You're welcome. Between Bryce and I, we have more than enough room for all of our friends to stand beside us."

"I'm just greedy and desperate."

"I wouldn't go that far, but yes, you're a bit greedy. We still love you, though."

I flash a smile and let go of the door. It swings shut, and then I'm following the two of them to the booth Bryce always claims when she's here—

Neither of them notices the women they pass, but I do. It's impossible not to grin at Millie when she feels my eyes on her and glances up from her coffee cup. My legs stop listening to my brain and keep me rooted beside their table, ignoring the question in Daisy's voice as she tries calling for my attention.

"Good morning, ladies," I say, looking at where Lacey's sitting, her expression bemused.

She greets me simply. "Hey, Shade."

"Hi." Millie palms her mug and crosses her legs beneath the table.

I'd be lying if I didn't admit to glancing down to take a look at the skirt flowing over her thighs. It's a loose one—still short—but with more movement than she usually has in those tight things she always wears.

"Have you been here for breakfast before? They've got the best french toast."

"Not yet. Breakfast isn't my meal of choice."

I frown. "Don't skip it. Try the french toast."

"And if I don't like french toast?" she counters, voice growing stronger in the way it always does when I get her riled up.

"The scrambled eggs are just as good."

"I'm going to order without you, Shade," Bryce calls from the booth on the right.

Millie drops her chin to her chest and laughs. "Good morning, Bryce!"

"Keep him at your table if you want, Millie. Just make him choose so I can eat."

I chuckle, quirking a brow in Bryce's direction. She has her back to me, but Daisy sees. The shooing motion she makes with her hand would have convinced me to leave them be if I hadn't already decided the moment I spotted Millie.

"Got room for me here? As long as I'm not ruining your plans," I say, more for their benefit than mine.

Lacey's the first to answer. "No, of course you're not. I was just telling Millie that Shelly was right about her needing to explore the campground a bit more if she's going to be helping out there."

Millie shoots daggers across the table at Lacey. I swallow a laugh and watch the interaction, waiting. A breath later, Millie's scooting further into the booth and looking up at me, some of the fire burnt out.

"I've been a bit of a hermit, I suppose."

I take the spot beside her and drop my arms to the table. Maybe I sit a bit closer than I need to, but considering what's going on between us, I think getting a bit comfortable with one another wouldn't be a bad thing. By the breath she sucks when our shoulders brush, I think I'm on the right track.

"I can show you around," I offer.

Lacey snaps her fingers. "That's a perfect idea. I was thinking that as well."

"What a coincidence. I'm also free all day," I add.

Millie's hold on her cup tightens as she brings it up and takes a sip. I smirk and spread my legs beneath the table just enough to nudge her knee. She darts her eyes toward me, the blue sharp.

I've seen a lot of that sharp blue these last couple of days. After the brief kissing lesson in the studio, I've been giving her some space. I'd rather not, but when she came in the morning after and couldn't so much as look at me without rushing off, I figured maybe she needed to figure out what she really wanted from me and the agreement we'd made.

Since then, she's become shorter-tempered with me. I've gotten a laugh or two from her fiery comebacks, but honestly, I just want her to be honest with me instead. Playing games got boring years ago. I've outgrown them.

"Are you sure you have time for something as boring as a tour?" she asks, tone strained.

I ignore the attitude. "I've always got the time for you."

"After breakfast, then."

Instead of replying right away, I reach over and pry her fingers from her mug. She blinks in surprise when I take it from her and bring it to my mouth. The coffee is still hot, and I ignore the burn on my tongue while keeping my knee pressed to the side of hers and finishing it off.

Once it's empty, I set it on the edge of the table and stretch my arm along the back of our booth. Millie whips her head to the side so fast her hair flies over her shoulder. I slip my hand from the leather booth and to her bicep, hanging it loosely there.

"I was drinking that," she pushes out.

"Consider it paying me back for the coffee you stole from me on your first day."

"I didn't steal that one. Bryce gave it to me."

"Semantics."

"I've been meaning to ask how you've been liking working

at the studio, Millie," Lacey says, butting into the conversation that I've let get a bit away from me.

Millie focuses on her friend, the corner of her mouth tipping up. "It's been good. There's certainly plenty of paperwork to keep myself busy organizing."

"You've done a great job," I add.

Better than I expected, considering her self-proclaimed faults and lack of experience.

"Really?" she asks softly.

"You're a quick learner, and you don't stop with a task until it's finished. Yeah, princess, you're doing a good job."

Her smile stretches, filling both sides of her face. "Thank you. I'm actually enjoying myself."

"You look happy," Lacey notes.

Millie leans back, either consciously or by accident, but stays in place. She doesn't shove my hand off her arm and relaxes as if she's comfortable like this. It's a confirmation that I was searching for but wasn't about to ask outright about.

"I like it here. The town and Shimmer Lake. Everyone has been really welcoming. I wasn't expecting that."

"Small towns can get a bad rep sometimes," Lacey confirms.

I run my nails over Millie's arm. "They're deserving of it most of the time."

"Should I expect something bad to happen around here, then?" Millie asks me.

"It wouldn't surprise me, but I'm hoping not. You didn't come here to get sucked back into the drama."

"It's been a while since the last scandal anyway. Maybe Oak Point has matured," Lacey suggests.

Millie scoots up in her seat, drawn into Lacey's words. "What was the last scandal?"

I shake my head, hoping Lacey can read into my lack of desire to chat about this.

She ignores me. "Have you met the Whittman kids?"

"No? Who are the Whittmans?"

"Shelly and Kirk Whittman. She's asking about their kids," I clarify, shifting uncomfortably.

Millie glances at me, picking up on the movement. It's a fleeting look, but a kind one. Like she's checking in on me.

"No. I haven't met them, but Shelly was telling me about them the other day," she explains.

Lacey nods. "Ash's best friend, Rowe, went to prison for a while for nearly killing a guy out by the campground."

I scowl at Lacey when Millie tenses. "That's a massive way of underexplaining what happened. It wasn't that simple, and everything that guy got was deserved."

"In *your* opinion. But he still lost the case and went to jail," Lacey argues.

"So it doesn't matter what happened prior to that? He's guilty because he didn't have an expensive lawyer or loaded legal team?"

"What happened before?" Millie asks, twisting in the booth and focusing on me.

"It's not our story to tell," I answer pointedly, hoping Lacey picks up on that fact. "Just don't judge Rowe for what happened, especially when Tilly isn't here to tell her side of the story."

Millie searches my face for something before asking, "Is he still in prison?"

"No. He's served his time."

Lacey keeps quiet now, and when I look at her, I see her frown for what it is: shame for gossiping. We don't know each other that well, but I do know she isn't someone to spread shit around town about anyone. Millie has a way of opening everyone up in a way they're not used to, so who am I to blame her for falling victim in the same way I have?

"Everyone whispers about it. Don't feel guilty," I tell her.

She tries for a smile, but it falls short. "You're right. Tilly isn't here to explain her side, and I'm not about to ask Rowe for his."

"Don't blame you for that. He's a cruel motherfucker now, but I can't say we should have expected any different," I say.

"Are you two friends?" Millie asks.

"Yeah, we're friends. I've known him and Ash since we were in diapers. I don't see a lot of him anymore, though. He and Ash are close. He only comes around to see me when he wants to get something inked."

Otherwise, he's held up at Painted Sky. His family ranch is along the highway leading to the campground, but I haven't stepped foot there in over a decade. Not since before Rowe got locked up. I don't know how the hell he's been living back there, considering the way his family cut ties with him. Blood doesn't turn its back on blood, but his did.

The only explanation I have is that since he's been back on the bronc-riding shit, they're looking for an extra payday. Once he gets back in the circuit, he'll be competing the way he was before everything went to hell.

"I won't judge him until I meet him," Millie declares, relaxing back into her seat. "It's only fair."

Lacey exhales. "I should do the same. It's been years."

"He'd appreciate that," I say.

There's a soft clearing of a throat from beside me that puts an end to the conversation. The waitress, wearing the typical frilly apron that Maggie loves so much, smiles at us before introducing herself. I sit back in silence while Lacey orders her breakfast and then listen closely while Millie does the same.

"I'll do the french toast with a side of scrambled eggs, please. And another coffee."

With a squeeze of her shoulder, I order the same thing. It's a struggle to keep from teasing her about her order, but I'm having too great a morning to risk pissing her off already.

Not before getting her alone again, at least. Because once I do, I'm not leaving again until we've gotten to the bottom of what's been eating her up. Hopefully, that will mean I've shared my list with her, and we can get started on it sooner rather than later.

Millie isn't going to stay here for long, and I refuse to miss any more days waiting for her to come to me.

17

Millie

"Have you been in a kayak before?" Shade asks, running his palm along the curve of a blue one hung on a wooden rack by the water.

"No. I used to paddleboard sometimes, though."

"You've got me there. I'd sink one of those."

I give him a slow up-and-down look, cocking my head. "How's your balance?"

"Shit."

"Then, yeah, you'd probably sink it," I agree.

"If it wasn't supposed to snow this week, I'd come pop your kayaking cherry. But it's too fucking cold now."

His words are a reminder of how low the temperature has gotten in the week since I've been here. Even with my coat on, there's a chill working its way into my bones. The wind scurrying over the top of the lake doesn't help.

Shade presses his fingers into my lower back and guides us away from the beach. We pass the small library that looks eerily similar to a two-storey birdhouse with a glass door on our way to the dock. I've wanted to sit on the dock since the first day I spotted it. There was a natural pull that I ignored at first.

I'm happy to be visiting it today.

"We used to compete over who could jump off the dock and hold their breath under the water the longest," he says, walking closely beside me.

"Who is 'we'?"

"Me, the Whittman twins, Rowe, Lacey. Pretty much all of us. Back then, it didn't matter what grade you were in or who your family was, we all hung out together. Especially in the summers. This place was all we had to entertain ourselves, so we made the most of it," he explains, turning to look behind us. "There used to be an ice cream shack between those trees there that would sell single scoops for fifty cents and a high five. I spent all of my chore money there for the four years it was running."

The yearning that explodes in my chest makes it hard to speak. "What happened to it?"

"The owner passed away. Shelly tried to get it up and running on her own, but they couldn't make it work without extra help."

"And there wasn't any," I finish for him.

"Bingo. It's the Oak Point special. But it's your turn now. Tell me about something you enjoyed when you were a tiny princess."

We reach the end of the dock, and I let loose a soft sigh before lowering myself onto the wood planks. I hang my legs off the edge and stare down at the dark, clear water. The weeds are low, well clipped to avoid reaching the surface. I'd bet it looks colder than it really is, even with it being mountain water.

Looking up, I watch Shade as he stares out at the lake, his smile lazy and relaxed. When he notices me watching him, he lowers his eyes and winks before joining me. Sitting closer than he needs to on this wide dock, he hangs his legs beside mine and leans back on his hands. I shove off a shiver when he adjusts his arms and strokes a finger along the lowest section of my back.

Thinking back to his question, I focus on finding an answer instead of the way I'm tempted to swing myself over onto his lap right here, right now. The last few days have wreaked havoc on my nervous system, and the only person I have to blame is myself.

After our kissing lesson, if you can even call it that, I haven't been able to stop growing aroused anytime I think of Shade or so much as catch a glimpse of him. It's downright annoying now, and I've been so frustrated with my inability to make myself come that I've been taking it out on him. It's much easier to ignore the guy at work than it is to find the courage to demand we work on the next lesson I gave him.

Not to mention, he hasn't even told me what he'd written on his list. It's like he's trying to make me explode.

"I didn't have many friends like that growing up. The ones I did have were only around because our parents knew each other. But I did use to have fun when we'd go on the boat in the summer. I like wake surfing," I say, fighting back the clog in my throat.

His brow is high when he looks at me. "You wake surf?"

"I'm starting to take offense to all of these questions."

"I just can't picture you doing it. It's not that I don't believe you."

"Well, believe it. It was one of the only sporty activities my father would indulge me in growing up. Not that I wanted to play sports, but it was fun. Wearing a bikini while getting misted with water and a cool breeze on a hot day was better than tanning in silence."

Shade shifts, leaning forward slightly. "You came here in the wrong season, Mills. I'd have loved to see you like that."

"Mills?"

"Princess," he corrects himself, smirking.

I ignore that. "I doubt you'd have noticed me if we'd stumbled upon each other on the lake."

"Wanna bet?"

"In case you forgot, I'm dirt broke right now. I've got nothing to bet with, so I'll pass this time."

"Money is the most boring thing to bet with. Be creative," he drawls.

Turning my head, I meet his waiting gaze. The cool temperature spikes at the intensity in his eyes. I swallow as quietly as possible, but he notices.

"My luck is terrible," I say, my voice quiet.

"I'd usually say the same, but it's hard to feel that way right now."

Rolling my eyes, I mutter, "You're a flirt."

"A flirt who doesn't lie. It's fucking killing me picturing you in some tiny bikini, all damp and windswept. I'm trying really hard to be a good guy here, and I've got a feeling I'm going to fail pretty damn soon."

My core tightens, growing warm. "Do you think it's only you who feels like that?"

"Like what exactly, Millie? Because as much as I want to have another go at that list of yours right here, right now, I'm also real frustrated that you've been ignoring me for days. I won't be touching you again if that's how it's going to be afterward. You've got a friend in me now, and for as long as you're here, that's what I want to continue being."

"I didn't think you cared about that. You never mentioned it upsetting you," I argue weakly, knowing that he's right.

I have been all over the place recently.

Shade rolls his jaw, his eyes clouding. "What exactly were you looking for from me? You ran out of the studio like your ass was on fire after leaving your mark all over my throat and then came into work the next day with your eyes everywhere *but* on me. I can't read your mind, Millie. When you want something from me, you need to say it. I've proven to do just about anything you ask, so this should have been no different."

"I don't know how to do that," I admit, growing tense. "What you're telling me to do, I've never been able to with the people in my life. Not without being shamed for it or guilted for having real feelings. So, I'm sorry."

It's too hard to look at him, so I focus on the water in front of us. It ripples slightly but is otherwise unmoving. Stagnant. Boring. I almost laugh before looking to the trees lining the bank instead.

"To start, I want to help you get comfortable with touch," Shade starts, drawing my attention so naturally it's almost freaky. His attempt at encouraging me to open up is appreciated, even if I keep my thanks tucked away. "You should know every inch of your skin that makes you burn up inside and release those fucking noises you were making the other day. Then, you'll start working on telling me what you want. That's an important one if you're going to be with men who aren't as attention detailed as I am."

The teasing tone helps make it less awkward for me, but I still flush, unable to help it. There's something incredibly embarrassing about being a grown woman and needing to be guided on all things intimate by a guy I've only met a week ago. Even if his intentions aren't to make me feel this way, I don't think it's possible not to.

"There's that confidence again," I reply loosely.

He chuffs a laugh, letting that light dig go. "I need to hear that you're still okay with going forward with this. If you are, I'll go back up to your cabin with you right fucking now, Millie. But if you're not, you need to tell me now so I can figure out what our dynamic is going to be for the rest of your time here."

"I'm okay with this. I never wasn't."

Fingers tap the underside of my chin before guiding my head to turn. I hold my breath when Shade's brown eyes dig into mine from only a few inches away. He darts them back and forth from my left to right, searching for any hint that I'm lying to him.

His search comes up empty the way I knew it would.

"Let's go, then." He's baiting me.

I force his touch to fall away when I push up from the dock and stand. Brushing off the back of my skirt, I palm my hips and stare down at him.

"Am I meeting you there later, or are you going to get up and come with me anytime soon?"

The quirk of his mouth incites a flurry of flutters in my stomach. Yeah, it's dangerous being around a man like Shade. Not only because of how good-looking and smooth witted he is—although that doesn't help—but because of the easy friendship he's offered me. It's too easy to be around him, and regardless of what we've agreed to do together, I feel at peace around him. Comfortable in a way I haven't been before, not once. Even if all we did was sit and talk like friends for the duration of my stay, I'd leave happy.

I offer him my hand and wait until he slaps his against it before giving him a tug. His body doesn't move in the slightest, but I feel the strain in my arm from the pull.

"These muscles are concrete, baby. Don't pull your arm out of its socket," he teases while getting to his feet.

"I've never met anyone with concrete in their muscles. How interesting."

"Luckily for you, I'm up to being groped if you want to really live up this once-in-a-lifetime experience."

I laugh, belly warming with what I've come to expect whenever I'm with Shade. An arousal that's bound to send me into a spiral when I can't diffuse it properly.

"Does that usually work on the women you meet?" I ask in hopes of playing off my reaction.

He drops an arm to my shoulders and hauls me right up against him as we walk off the dock. The arms I have hanging at my sides feel so out of place as I debate moving the one slapping his thigh behind him instead. I clench my teeth when I hesitate, continuing my awkward slapping motion instead.

"I'm not sure. Tell me if it's working on you, and I'll think about keeping it in my arsenal," he replies.

Without dropping a look down at me, he pulls his arm off my shoulder and grabs my hand instead. I hold my breath while he moves it behind him and confidently slides it into the back pocket of his jeans. Once his arm falls back onto my shoulder, I manage to speak.

"It isn't working."

We walk over a big tree root sticking up out of the ground, and Shade drops his mouth to my ear. "Liar."

The heat from his breath makes me shiver, and the laugh he lets loose a beat later tells me that he felt it. I flex my fingers in his back pocket and try to ignore that I'm cupping his butt right now. Clamping my lips together, I keep my giggle inside and focus on getting to my cabin.

Then . . . I'm sure the way I'm touching him right now won't feel so scandalous.

I can't tell if that excites me or terrifies me.

18

Shade

MILLIE'S NEARLY VIBRATING WITH NERVES.

She went from taking the lead and stepping into her cabin first to standing frozen in front of her bedroom door with a spine so straight I could probably crack it in half if I poked hard enough. I'm trying not to get a big head, but fuck, she doesn't make it easy.

Every shiver, blush, and freeze up makes it harder for me to keep from giving in to what I've wanted since I first saw her at Peakside. It's easier to pretend I don't want to fuck her four ways to Sunday when we're at the studio or when she's giving her attention to something else. But when it's on me?

I dip my eyes down her back to where her skirt brushes the backs of her upper thigh. She's rubbing them together, her tight-clad feet pressing into the floor. My fingers strain and stretch before I busy them with gripping the top of the door frame. I wet my lips and press myself flush against her.

"Duck out now, or go to the bed, Millie."

"Which lesson is this?" she asks softly, timidly.

"Which do you think?"

Her swallow is more audible than the words she whispers.

"Louder. I'm here for you. Tell me what you think we're going to do."

"You're going to watch me . . . touch myself."

I bring my hand to the side of her neck and use a finger to guide her hair behind her shoulder. Her collarbone pebbles with goosebumps that trail beneath her top. It's too easy to follow their path beneath the silky fabric until I touch a thin strap at her shoulder.

"I'm going to watch, but I'm going to help too. You should be able to make yourself come, princess. Fuck knows not every man you meet will know how to get you there. It's up to you to ease that ache whenever it gets too bad," I murmur, feeling that same goddamn discomfort between my legs.

"You think you'll be able to help? What if—"

I remove my fingers from her bra strap and smooth them down her arm instead, circling her wrist.

"I'll be able to help. Never met a woman I couldn't get screaming, Millie." With her wrist in my grasp, I move it to her stomach, pressing her palm to the waistband of her skirt. "You'll need to be vocal with me. Tell me what feels good and what doesn't."

She jerks her head in a nod and draws a sharp breath between her lips. I cover my fingers over each of hers and slowly glide two beneath the band and to where a second one rests an inch lower. It's thinner, softer.

"What are you thinking?"

"I—I'm—It's good."

"What's good?"

"This. What you're doing," she rambles breathlessly.

"What do you want to do next? Are we staying in the doorway?"

"No."

"No . . ."

She slides her fingers from beneath mine to between them, linking them. "The bed."

"Lay on it, Milie. On your back."

I pull my hand away and tap her ass. She sneaks a quick look at me, showing her pretty blue eyes as they widen before she's stumbling forward. The bed can't be bigger than a double, but it'll work for this. For now.

Millie crawls onto the mattress, pressing one knee onto it at a time. I watch in silence as she lies on her back and stares at the ceiling. Her throat jumps while her chest rises with slow breaths. The shirt she's wearing droops at the shoulders in this position, exposing the thin straps of her bra. I work to keep my own breaths the same speed as hers when she curls her toes at the end of the bed and places her hands flat on the mattress.

With her head popped on the pillows, she should have no choice but to stare at me when I move to the end of the bed, but she keeps her eyes on the ceiling. The way her body moves with a shiver doesn't escape me, and I hate that I can't tell if it's from excitement or the constant chill in here.

"Why is it so cold in here?" I ask, keeping my voice low.

"There's no thermostat. And I don't know how to light a fire."

Concern races through me as I grip the door frame. "Don't move, Millie. Wait for me just like that."

"Okay," she whispers without argument.

I turn around stiffly, bothered by more than just the chill. It's too cold in here, and I should have done something about it the first time I noticed. The older cabins don't have heat, and I doubt anyone has shown her how to start a fire before.

Grinding my teeth, I ignore the throb in my cock and stop in front of the fireplace. There are chopped logs beside it, and I get to work. There's everything you need to start a fire in a basket on top of the fireplace, but fuck, Shelly could have spent a few minutes at least giving Millie a quick rundown.

The moment the fire sparks, I feed it into a large flame and shut the heavy door, leaving it open just enough for the heat to disperse faster. I linger for a minute, waiting to see if it's going to die out before going back to the bedroom.

When I reach the doorway again, my chest constricts at the sight of her still in the same spot, unmoving. Her eyes are on the ceiling as she breathes quickly.

"Look at me," I urge, trying to keep my excitement dimmed.

She stares at me, and her chest deflates before inflating immediately. "Did you light a fire?"

"I did, and before I leave, I'm showing you how to do it yourself so you don't freeze to death."

"Thank you." The words are heavy, too heavy for this moment.

"Hitch your skirt up to your hips and ditch the tights, Millie," I command, pushing forward.

Colour floods her cheeks. Her eyes stay locked on mine as she brings her hands to the flowing hem of her skirt and flips it up. I move through the room to the small armchair in the corner. Pulling it to the end of the bed, I sit and shove my hands into my pockets.

Millie hesitates once her fingers disappear beneath the waistband of her skirt, touching the same place we were together. I nod, giving her silent encouragement to keep going.

With a flare of her nostrils, she works her tights down to her thighs before reaching in front of her to pull them the rest of the way off. I chomp down on my tongue and grow harder in my jeans when I spy her panties.

Honestly, I'd have preferred men's briefs over the baby blue silk in front of me. There's nothing innocent about these, and I'm having a hard time getting my brain to stop glitching the longer I stare at the small, damp circle over the centre of them.

"Are you okay?" she asks, her voice tight.

The beige tights fall to the floor in a ball. I unclench my

fist and press down roughly on the tip of my cock through my jeans when it twitches toward my hand. I'm too goddamn hard, and I've never been the guy to bust early, but for the first time in my life, I'm scared I could.

I nod and pull my hands from my pockets. "When you're alone, what do you do first?"

She spreads her legs wider, her knees bent, while tucking a hand down into her panties. I watch it press against the silk as she brings her touch to the part of her that I know is already slick.

"Good girl. Tell me how that feels," I murmur.

Her eyes flare, the black ring around that beautiful blue contracting. "It's nice."

"Nice? That's it?"

She nods twice, her hand moving slowly. "Should it feel different?"

I can't tell if she's being serious, and that bothers me. Unable to stay seated, I step toward the bed and blow out a loose breath.

"You tell me, Millie. It's your pussy, not mine."

Her whimper shoots through me like a fucking bullet on fire. I grit my jaw and strain to keep myself in place.

"I know you're wet, so get your finger slick and bring it to your clit. It's fucking aching by now, isn't it?"

"It is," she says, her voice breaking at the end.

"Roll it beneath the pad of your finger. *Slowly*."

Her hips jerk with the movement of her hand before falling into the bed, pressing into it. Millie's eyelids fall halfway and then open wider than before.

Every movement of her hand beneath her panties excites me further, and before I know it, my knees are digging into the wooden frame at the edge of the bed. The bite of pain doesn't register past the arousal making my blood sing.

"What do you need, Millie?"

She's moving too quickly, chasing the same feeling that's

pulsing through me. It's clunky, desperate in a way that exposes the reasons behind her every failed orgasm.

I lift one knee to the mattress and lean forward just enough to reach her ankle. With a gentle pull, I bring her leg down straight and stroke the soft, bare skin of her calf.

Her mouth gapes in surprise but then fills with a moan. I tighten my hold on her leg and breathe through my nose. She twitches in my hold, and the movement in her panties speeds up. Our eyes continue to hold, and I risk reaching between her legs to press down on her hand.

It stills, and her brows furrow. The clash of emotions in her gaze has me shaking my head, trying to silence her thoughts.

"Can I touch you?" I ask.

"Touch me . . ." she echoes, asking a question without coming outright with it.

"Over your panties. Let me show you, princess."

Her muscles relax as she breathes out. "Yes."

I crawl up the bed and kneel between her spread legs. Keeping her face in my vision instead of where my hand's moving, I wait for her to slip her fingers free of the silk and then press mine to her centre. She clamps her lips shut and tips her head back, avoiding looking at me.

That's fine. She doesn't need to look at me while I do this, as long as she listens and feels. I'm doing more than enough staring for the both of us.

I move two fingers up and down her panties, passing the wet patch and pressing the silk against her swollen skin while I explore, searching for what I need. Her reaction is more than enough confirmation that I've found her clit. She can't hide her cry beneath clamped lips this time. Not when I press my thumb harder and start to massage the spot she was focused on a beat ago.

Millie's eyes cling to mine, her plea silent but obvious. I grow fascinated with how sensitive and reactive she is. For a woman who has a hard time coming, she feels pleasure easily.

"Is that good? Talk to me, Millie," I grind out.

She gasps, but it isn't a proper answer.

"Give me words."

"Yes! It feels good. You're—you're right there," she whimpers.

Her fingers glide over the bedding as she tries to busy them. I lean over her and drop my head, giving it a shake. Reaching for her hand, I take it and bring it up beneath my shirt. She tips her head back and presses her palm against my abs, lightly scratching them.

"If you need something to touch, you touch me. We're trying to make you come, so take what you need to get there."

She nods, gulping air into her lungs. "Where?"

"Where what?"

"Where can I touch you?"

I push her hand up my chest and then to each side before lowering it to the top of my jeans. She keeps her half-lidded eyes on me, curling her fingers into one of my empty belt loops.

"Anywhere," I rasp.

Her body shudders in response. I swirl my thumb and press down harder, feeling the silk grow slicker, coating my skin. Without looking down her body, I'm relying on touch alone, and I think that makes me even fucking harder.

She blinks, keeping her eyes shut for a few moments before I swallow and slow my thumb. The sudden change forces her to look at me again. The heat that greets me this time is more than enough encouragement to continue.

"Keep your eyes on me," I whisper, releasing her hand and grabbing her other one. "I'm not looking, but I want you to slide a finger inside."

Her palm is warm when I bring it between her legs and hook her finger beneath the seam of her panties. She doesn't make a sound as we tug them out of the way just enough to make room for her to follow my instructions.

I release her and shift until I'm hovering over her, making it impossible to see what she's doing. My senses are more primed than they've ever been as I continue my thumb's slow rolling and wait for her to join me.

"Slide it inside, princess. Feel how drenched you are," I urge softly.

The rush of pleasure that fills her expression, matched with the brief brush of her wrist against mine, tells me when she's done it. She releases a tight noise from low in her throat and pulses beneath my thumb.

I start to speed up, increasing pressure. "That's it. All the way."

Her reply is broken, garbled as she's interrupted with a moan. I grind my jaw and curl my fingers into the thin blankets until I'm gripping the mattress itself. My bicep strains, wrist locked as I hold myself above her and watch every twitching muscle on her face.

"Faster, Millie. Go faster and curl your finger every time it's knuckle-deep. See if you can feel anything that brings you more pleasure. Search for what makes you see stars. Get out of your head and take what you need."

"Shade—"

I shake my head, lowering it closer to where her lips stay parted and her eyes bulge. "Don't cut yourself off. Tell me everything you're thinking."

Her pink skin deepens in colour as she holds my stare. "I don't want to jinx it."

"You're close?"

"Mmm," she whimpers.

The fingers she has digging into my chest grow frantic, darting up to where a black hoop hangs from my nipple. Her touch falters slightly, surprise lighting her eyes.

My smirk is instant. "You can tug on it if you want."

"Oh, my God."

Eyes flicking to the ceiling once again, she runs the tip of her finger across the metal, tracing the shape of it. I lean onto my hand as my groin tightens, sparks zapping down to where I've started leaking in my briefs. She doesn't notice my reaction, too busy avoiding looking at me to see how much I liked that.

Instead of teasing her, I focus on the wet, warm spot between her legs. A mewl falls into the small space behind us as she reacts to the pressure I'm applying. The second her wrist begins working faster, another noise fills the room.

I zero in on it and groan, unable to keep it in. Her gaze is still on the ceiling, and mine follows as I rub her faster, losing the ability to be slow. The time for that is done, and all I want now is to hear more of the wet gush of her pussy around the finger she's fucking herself with.

Millie's throat strains, her inhale getting trapped as she grows tenser. I pinch my brows together in concentration and curl the fingers around my thumb, refusing to let them wander to where she has to be dripping . . .

"Shade!" she cries, our eyes crashing in a collision of desperation and arousal. "Shade—I'm . . . I think—"

My nostrils flare as I nod. "Good girl, Millie."

The tight line of her body snaps. One leg kicks out while the other pulls up, her knee pressing against my hip. I hiss through my teeth when it drags across my middle and settles against my cock, pressing hard enough I buck backward to avoid coming in my pants.

"Shit!" Her voice flares out in the room, and then her neck is curving up. "Ohhhh."

I trap my voice, refusing to let the words I want to say escape. Watching her come is better than anything I could say anyway. If we weren't friends, and this was something purely sexual . . .

The quivering muscles beneath my thumb start to relax

when I ease off her and withdraw my thumb with a final stroke over her pussy. She sucks in a breath and lets it go nice and slow before removing her hand and bringing it to the blanket. The pink hue to her skin appears almost permanent as she drops her leg to the bed and rolls her lips, eyes darting over the room.

"How was that?" I ask, struggling to hide the arousal still sticking to my throat.

She chokes on a laugh, both of her brows lifting. "Is that a serious question?"

"Dead serious."

I don't sit back on my knees yet. Hovering above her, I release the mattress and lower my eyes to watch the steady rise and fall of her chest. She's calm, the tension from minutes ago completely washed away. Pride pounds at my chest.

"We can consider the whole making myself come thing checked off," she says.

I crook a grin and lean back. "I wouldn't go that far yet. You've still got to do it alone."

"I'll figure it out."

"So confident," I coo, flipping her skirt down and giving her knee a stroke. "I like it."

"Practice makes perfect, no?"

"Don't talk to me about practice right now," I beg.

Not caring whether she's watching or not, I stare down at my crotch and adjust my cock. I wince at the heartbeat that seems to have grown inside of it during the last few minutes and busy myself with getting off the bed.

"Do you need to, like, leave? Or go to the bathroom?"

My laugh is deep, rough. "Not unless you want me to. I'm just fine, princess."

"If you're sure."

"Are you trying to get rid of me? Was I a booty call?" I tease.

"Was that enough to be considered a booty call?"

"Nah, it wasn't. Not even close."

"Then, no. You're not a booty call, Shade."

"Thank fuck. I'm too old for that shit," I mutter.

Pushing up onto her elbows, she closes her legs and says, "You're not even old."

"Older than you."

She rolls her eyes, amusement glittering in the lightening blue. "Is that a warning?"

"I'd be a bit blunter with one of those. It's just a reminder."

"For what?"

"What happened this week isn't happening again. If you want to talk about something, we'll talk about it. No more running around acting like I've done something wrong. As much as I like having a beautiful woman on my mind during a slow workday, I don't want it to be because I'm wondering what I've done to upset her. Is that alright with you?"

"It's alright with me. I'm sorry."

"No apologies. I just wanted to be clear," I reassure her, running my palm up her shin and down to her ankle, squeezing once. "You hungry?"

"If you keep feeding me, I'm going to have to get more new clothes, and clearly, I'm tapped out of funds."

"Put my hoodie back on. You'll never fit into it properly."

"I was already thinking that."

And ten minutes later, she's draped in it when she steps out of the bedroom and joins me for dinner in the blazing fire's warmth, reminding me how much I fucking love that hoodie.

19

Millie

I'VE NEVER LIKED THE WORD "SLUT."

The negative connotation is not only socially damaging but also emotionally abusive and dehumanizing. Despite my lack of sex life, I've never judged others for being interested in having one. It's natural, and I'm beyond jealous of anyone who can feel so confident and excited about it that they have lots of it.

With that said, I think Shade has turned me into one. An orgasm slut, at least. It would make one hell of a bumper sticker.

After only a single fingered orgasm, I've become intensely interested in getting myself there over and over again. Maybe it was because after so long, the floodgates have opened, and for the first time, I'm able to get myself off, but holy.

I was nearly late to work this morning because I was too busy repeating Shade's instructions from last night. And it was far from the first time in the last twelve hours.

"You look horny," Bryce utters, appearing behind me.

Jerking in my chair, I whip my head to the side and swallow. "What?"

"You look horny."

"I heard you."

She drops a hand to the desk I spent all morning cleaning and organizing. "You don't have any tattoos, do you?"

"No."

"That's what I thought."

My temperature cools, going back to normal. "So why did you ask?"

"Getting a new piece can turn someone on. I was curious if you were enjoying watching Shade work."

I was, but not because of that.

"People get turned on when they get a tattoo? Why? I always assumed they hurt."

"Body modifications can be arousing to some. Or so I've heard. Shade would know more about it than me."

My skin prickles, and I'm drawn to where he sits beside the woman on the bed. He's already watching me, the needle of his gun lifted an inch above the patch of skin he's been tattooing for the last hour. It's a collarbone design that he showed off the sketch for this morning. His thick black brow curves upward when I stare back.

"He sees a lot of people get aroused while tattooing?" I ask, finally focusing back on Bryce.

She tilts her head, her mouth curling at the corners. "Oh, probably. But that's not what I meant."

"I'm confused," I admit.

With a relaxed jerk of her shoulder, she says, "You should ask him about it. I'm going for lunch now. If my one o'clock comes in before I'm back, can you ask what size they were thinking for design and print a few examples off? My iPad is hooked up to the printer."

"Yeah, sure," I mumble, my thoughts scattering.

"Thanks."

Bryce leaves, and I stay seated. The music today was Shade's choice, and as the last song rolls into the next, it's easy to tell what his preferred genre is. The raspy voice singing over a hard-rock beat flows through the studio but still can't hide the buzz of the gun. I've begun hearing that sound while I'm at home now, almost like it follows me everywhere, reminding me of where I've been spending my days.

I think I like it now, actually. Instead of annoying, it's calming.

Maybe it's because I've never modified my body in any way, but I don't know how someone could get pleasure from it. I'd expect pain and discomfort, not arousal. Then again, there are all sorts of kinks that I don't understand because I've never experienced them. Maybe this shouldn't be all that surprising after all.

Sneaking a look across the studio, I place my hand on the edge of the desk. Shade's concentrated as he brings the needle along the blue stencil on the woman's collarbone. He follows the sketch with precision, only stopping when he swipes away the ink with a paper towel or swaps out the needle he's using.

The buzzing cuts before he wheels himself toward the metal toolbox-looking set-up beneath the sign with his name and takes a packaged needle from where he has all of his supplies laid out. The cling wrap lies beneath everything, keeping it sanitary, I assume.

He swaps out the needle with ease and then presses a few buttons on the gun before wheeling back to her and dipping it into a cap of pink ink. The buzzing starts again before he gets back to work, his hand moving differently this time. Instead of short strokes, he's almost sweeping it over the skin inside the stencil.

I bounce my leg and reach for the small notepad by the keyboard. There's a pen beside it that I pick up before tapping the tip to the paper. Looking back at Shade, I increase how fast I'm moving my leg. He's so calm . . . like he feels no pressure while permanently changing this woman's appearance. If he messes up, she'll have to see his mistake forever.

Long black hairs fall against his temples, brushing his skin as he lifts off the stool slightly to lean further over her. The paper towel he was using to wipe excess ink is filthy as he dabs the edge of the design, adding pink to the black and red. He tightens his face in concentration, every move of his wrist made with purpose.

There's a soft pulse between my legs that pulls me out of my haze. I clench my core and roll my lip between my teeth. Heat builds beneath my skin, staying trapped as I drop my gaze from Shade to the notepad.

I still.

One five-letter word has been sketched on it, and as I drop the pen and lift my hand, I see the black smudges on the side of it. SHADE stares up at me from the paper, the letters thick and bold with little flicks sticking out every few strokes. Without filling them in, they look unfinished and hollow, but still cool. Interesting in a way I've never thought plain letters could appear.

It's embarrassing to be doodling your boss's name on paper stamped with the name of the business you're sitting inside. However, I never did notice the stamp there. Not until right now. It's not exactly eye-catching with its boring, thin lines and lack of visual appeal.

Why did he use this one in the first place? It doesn't match the aesthetic or the beautiful work he can create on both paper and skin.

Turning away from the sight of him working, I tuck myself into place with my legs beneath the desk and pick the pen back up. I lock in to the letters in front of me and focus on recreating them in the empty space above. One by one, I work through the rest of the studio name, skipping the *T* in THE for now.

By the time I've realized that I'm sketching the shape of a tattoo gun into the shape of that *T*, my neck pangs from deep in the muscle. I lick my dry lips and squint at it, dragging the thick tip of the pen to where I've created an ink spot beneath it.

"What's that?"

The pen goes flying into the air. My heart falls to my stomach as I push away from the desk and gawk up at Shade's face. His expression is open and curious, but that dang smirk is still there, making me more nervous that I'd be without it.

Scrambling, I reach for the notepad but can't snag it in time. Shade swipes it clean off the table and holds it in front of him, staring at it like he's either disturbed or intrigued.

"Give it back. It's—"

"If I hadn't caught you drawing it, I'd have thought you had it done by someone else online," he says before I can finish.

My eyes widen. "Like, paid someone to create it?"

"Yeah, princess. It's fucking great. Incredible, actually."

My lungs pinch, making my inhale short and nowhere near full enough. "That's nice of you to say."

"Did you just do this now?"

"I got . . . inspired? Maybe? I don't know if that was why I started doodling. It just happened."

Shade nods, seeming to understand what I'm saying despite my word vomit. "I'd say you were right to start with. Inspiration doesn't make sense most of the time. I'll see a bug on the trunk of a tree and find myself pulling a sketchbook out and drawing a riverbed. There's not always a reason for it."

"It was like my hand moved, but my mind didn't."

"Have you drawn like this before?"

"A few times. Mostly if I'm alone and haven't been out for a few days. I get restless."

He hums, shifting closer to where I'm sitting, no longer standing at the edge of the desk. "Do you have a proper sketchbook?"

"You're holding it."

"This is a notepad."

"It works good enough, doesn't it?"

His brown eyes lighten to a warm chocolate. "Use it for now, but no, Millie, you need something real."

"I'm not an artist," I argue, feeling a bit . . . sheepish. "I wouldn't even know what to do with something more real than this."

"If it's natural, it will come to you. You don't need to force anything. We'll get you one just in case."

"Okay," I whisper.

He focuses on the design again, his eyes tightening at the corners. "Can you refine this? Clean it up a bit for me?"

"Um, sure. Yeah, I can."

"I've been wanting a new logo for the studio for a couple of years now but just never found the time to get one commissioned. I want to use yours. I'll pay for it, of course. If you get me a second draft and upload it to the computer, I'd like to see a few different mock-ups."

"You want to use it for this place? Shade—"

He shakes his head and sets the pad down on the desk before tugging me out from beneath the desk. My chair is rolled back as I blink at him, swallowing the rest of my argument. Shade grips the edge of the desk and leans over me, his body creating a thick bubble around us.

"It's fucking great, Millie. Shake those doubts from your head—I can see them running wild in there. I'm not in the habit of using my business to give pity to people."

I want to accept his offer and the kindness that comes with it. He's been nothing but honest with me from the start, so it should be easy. Yet there's still that wiggle of uncertainty. Like maybe he'll pull the rug out from me the moment I do as he's asked.

"Get me the second draft, and we'll ask Bryce. She'll rip it to shreds if she doesn't like it. You can't argue with that," he adds.

"That's true."

"Just say yes. There's no harm in giving it a shot. You can make some extra cash too."

"I could use it to get some perfume. I haven't had any since I left home," I blurt before I can stop myself. My entire body burns from embarrassment as I add, "Or obviously pay Shelly for the cabin. Duh."

If I could discreetly smack myself in the face for saying something so random and weird, I'd do it right now. It would be like a scene from a cartoon.

"You smell pretty good to me, princess. Today and last night," he murmurs, his tongue tracing his bottom lip.

That forgotten pulse between my legs comes back with a fury. This time, I can't simply wish it away. It lingers, growing stronger with every second he holds my gaze, his lips quirking like he knows exactly what's happening to me.

My throat strains as I speak. "If you say so."

"It's true."

"Do you like teasing me?"

"More than I should, probably."

"Why?"

He sneaks a look over his shoulder to where the woman was earlier but isn't anymore. When he finds my eyes again, he leans further into my space and strokes his knuckles down the side of my throat, pausing with them pressed to my pulse.

His smirk stretches into a dirty grin. "You excite me."

It's almost a joke how easily he says it. As if I'm not excited in a completely different way.

"Well, that's new."

"You don't think you excite other people?" he asks, his touch sliding around to the front of my throat, a palm warm against it. "Other men?"

I swallow, and he holds my throat as it strains, locking it in his hold. "I wouldn't know."

"You should. I assume it would be obvious."

"Where's your client?" I ask, fighting the urge to look for her myself.

"Out back, taking a smoke break. We've got an hour left, and my shoulder was cramping. Bryce is on lunch."

"She told me."

I can't look at where he's continuing to hold my throat without pulling away, and I don't want to. The sensation of his hand on a place where he could so easily crush my windpipe shouldn't be as relaxing as it is. It should be intense, and I feel like I should be scared. Worried, even.

I'm none of those things. If anything, I want him to apply more pressure and squeeze lightly. My heart rate ramps up, perspiration clinging to the skin beneath my hair.

Shade scrolls his eyes down to where he's touching me, the milk-chocolate colour of them darkening a shade. He runs his thumb over my pulse one last time before pressing harder, his fingers digging slightly into the sides of my throat.

I expel a soft, breathy moan and let my eyelids droop. A shiver races through me as I sip in air through lips I can't keep pressed together.

"Millie," he says roughly once I shift, pressing my thighs together.

Without a skirt today, I feel more constricted in this position. The near-leather pants mould to my centre and the panties I can feel growing damp. My chest pulls tight, nipples beading and scraping in a way that sends zaps of pleasure down to where I'm already aching.

I force my eyes to open and let my mouth fill with saliva, unable to swallow with his tightening hold on my throat. There's a wildness in his eyes, and I'd have to be blind not to notice the dilation of his pupils. I don't need experience to know that he's eyeing me up like he's considering using this very hold on me to lift me onto the desk and—

"Alright, I think I'm good. It's cold as balls outside, so don't mind the goosebumps."

Shade's hand releases me at the same time I push myself back on the wheels of my chair. I slap my palm to the desk to stop myself from rolling to the front door and avoid looking at him as he clears his throat.

"Take a seat again," he instructs, his voice tight.

I refuse to give him the satisfaction of seeing how bright my cheeks are before he gets back to work. Instead of sparing him another glance, I keep my focus on the drawing left on the desk.

It's a reminder of something other than the touch I still feel on my throat, so I fall into it. I hunch myself over the notepad and rip off the first drawing before starting on a second draft. The buzz of the tattoo gun fills the studio again, distracting me in the same way I know it's distracting him.

Am I an orgasm slut . . . or Shade's?

20

Shade

I fucking suck at gift giving.

My family wasn't ever huge on it while I was growing up, and still to this day, we'll only do stockings at Christmas. Every few birthdays, they'll surprise me with something I've been bugging them about, but other than that, we simply don't do it.

Mom always valued time together more than she did gifts. That's the way I was raised, yet I've still tried to figure out how to properly spoil the other people in my life. With friends like Bryce and Daisy, I've had to adapt. Not bringing gifts for them on their birthdays or Christmas grew impossible pretty quickly. Now, I make sure to carve out time to go shopping for my favourite couple.

Today was the first time I've gone into a store with someone other than them on my mind. Cherry Peak was a quick drive after work, but I closed up late, and my options were limited for where to go. I could have waited until tomorrow or the weekend to grab what I needed, but I didn't want to. It was today or nothing.

Now, the sketchbook feels heavy where I've tucked it under my arm. The steps up to Millie's cabin are old and rickety, and I make a note to mention them to Shelly on my way out. With the shoes Millie wears, these stairs are an accident waiting to happen.

Blowing out a breath, I knock on the door and wait. Her car is parked in the same place it was the first time I was here, so I know she's home. But the longer I stand here without hearing a single footstep inside . . .

"Millie?" I call, knocking again.

Still, there's no answer. No movement or sound from inside. I jiggle the handle and find it locked. With a frown, I sidestep the door and look through the window, searching for her. All I see are an empty dining set and a kettle on the same stove burner as it was when I was here last.

Stepping back, I take another look at the door. Still nothing.

The stairs creak again as I clop down them and head for the path coming from the cabin. It cuts through the trees and leads to the gravel road that runs through the entire campground. I walk down the road for a few minutes, searching the day-use picnic area and calling her name through the women's showers. She'd never shower there, but shit, I don't know where else she could be.

Not unless she felt like going for a cold dip after all.

Shelly's familiar smile greets me a few feet up the road. She lifts her hand and waves.

"Shade?"

"Hey, Shelly."

"What are you doing here?" she asks, a glow in her eyes that almost makes me laugh.

"Have you seen Millie? She wasn't at her place."

"I dropped her off at the laundry cabin a half hour ago. She had quite the stack of clothes to wash."

I chuckle. "Yeah, that isn't surprising."

"You know, she could probably use some company. Those machines are so old they take hours to finish up."

"Ever thought of upgrading them?" I ask, knowing the answer already.

"The new ones aren't built to last as long as these old ones were. They'd break in a year with how often they're used, and then I'd be left figuring out how to sell pictures of my toes on the internet to snag some cash," she harumphs.

"I'm sure your feet are worth millions, Shelly."

With a pat to my shoulder, she winks. "Go on now. Bring her whatever it is you're hiding there."

"Nothing gets past you," I tease, already moving around her.

"Not much, that's for sure. It was nice to see you, sweetie."

"Hey, Shelly?" I call before she can get more than two steps away.

She pauses, glancing at me over her shoulder. "Yes?"

"Can you have Kirk come out and stabilize the porch steps at Millie's cabin? They're wobbly."

"Of course. He'll get out there today. Anything else?" she asks, smirking like she's just been told some kind of secret.

"Nah, that's it. Thanks, Shelly. Have a good rest of your day."

Chuckling, I wave at her before turning and continuing down the road.

Fuck, I haven't been to the campground this many times since I was a kid. Walking down these paths and roads and smelling the clean mountain air has me feeling a way I haven't since. It's impossible to be uptight around here, like the breeze moving through the trees carries more than just a sense of security. Freedom and peace too.

The last cabin along the road was built up on a small hill, hidden by thick trees and a few raspberry bushes. It's the most secluded one, lacking so much as a drive up to the front. The only way to reach the door is to climb up through the small path in the woods, which is why Rowe stayed there for a large chunk of time once he got out of prison. Nobody but me and

Shelly knew he was here. Not even Ash. We kept it that way because we knew he wasn't ready then to take on the town or his family. Nobody could blame him for that.

I pass the cabin and follow the curve in the road to the small lodge with the old Laundry sign hung above the door. There's a loud bang from inside it, and I pick up my pace. It rings out again, this time followed by an enraged shout. I'm completely ignoring the steps and hopping onto the small landing before tearing the door open.

The sight at the back of the cabin stops me in my tracks, one foot still in the doorway. Keeping silent, I watch a dishevelled Millie smack her palm to the edge of the washing machine. With her hair tied up on her head, she brings her knee to the front of it and growls.

The sweatpants she's wearing take me aback more than her frustration does. They drown her, making her legs look half their size. And with the black hoodie—mine—sagging down her torso, she very well might get suffocated in the weight of the fabric.

There's a beige bag resting on the floor beside her that's half slouching, half standing as clothes droop out the side. Only the washer door is open. Millie grabs the edge of the machines and heaves in a breath before dropping her head. My stomach pangs at the sight, and I go to move when she brings the toe of her shoe to the washer again, kicking it gentler this time.

"What am I doing?" she mumbles, her arms tugging wide as she pulls a pant leg out from where it's gotten stuck inside the other. "It's just laundry. Just clothes."

When she yanks hard, the pant leg makes a ripping noise. She sucks in a breath and whips the pants into the washer, her arms shooting out to the side, where she grips the sides of the machines again.

I watch her closely while shutting the screen door behind me, careful not to let her hear it. She'd run if she knew I was watching right now. I'd lose this chance to see her without her guard up.

A few coins jingle in her palm when she inhales deeply and reaches into her sweatpants, pulling them free. They fall to the top of the dryer, and then she starts sorting through them. Her laundry bag is still full, and the longer she ignores it, the more it's slouching, slipping as the sweater hanging out of it pulls it down.

Once it falls over, she abandons the coins and drops to a crouch in front of it. Too busy shovelling the clothes back inside, she doesn't notice the quarters rolling off the edge of the dryer and disappearing in the gap between the machine and the wall. Her reaction is silent. Instead of yelling again, she abandons the clothes and runs her hands over her face, pressing them against her eyes as she lets go of a long exhale.

There's a rough shake to her body that rips my feet from their place on the floor, forcing me forward. It was only one shake, barely noticeable. The kind that hints at the effort it takes to hold back a sob.

I abandon the door and go right for where she's crouched, a broken breath escaping her.

The tensing of her shoulders is the only reaction she has to learning she isn't alone anymore. I step around her and glance into the washing machine. It's full to the brim with clothes, a mishmash of colours all shoved into one load. Without looking at her for approval, I start picking out the white clothes and set them on the dryer. There aren't many, but they'd be ruined if she washed them in this load. There are too many colours in here, all of them bright.

"I can't . . . I'm not sure how to get the machine started."

Her voice is dull, caged, like she's tucked herself away and hidden it from me. I let it go, knowing that she's feeling vulnerable.

"I'll help you," I say. The pile of whites is big enough that I can scoop it up as one and hand it over to her, careful not to let the sketchbook drop from beneath my arm. "Set these back in your bag. You'll need to do a load of whites by themselves once you're done with everything else."

Pushing to her feet, she drops her hands from her face and takes the clothes. Keeping her chin tucked, she avoids my eyes. Millie drops the clothes to the rest of her laundry on the floor and then stands beside me, looking into the washer.

"Do you have any more coins? These machines take quarters or loonies."

I tug out the coin drop and eye the fading instructions on the side of it. She watches me and reaches into her sweatpants. Shifting a few steps, I make room for her to take my place and read the instructions. There's a slight tremble in her fingers as she inserts the quarters into their spot and pauses.

"Leave it like this until you're ready to turn the machine on. Is that your detergent?"

"Shelly's. She gave it to me on her way out."

"Alright. Pour a capful of it in and then shove this back inside," I instruct, tapping the metal slide that she dropped her coins into. "After that, all you have to do is choose your settings and turn it on."

Her swallow is loud, tense. "You don't have to stay and watch."

"I haven't spoken to you about what I wanted to yet. I'm fine standing here with you for a while."

She doesn't answer. Twisting the cap off the detergent bottle, she pours the thick liquid into it and then dumps it onto her clothes. The metal slide goes in next, and then she closes the lid before poking around with the settings.

I take her hand and push her index finger onto the option she should use and then let it go. She flexes her hand before dropping it to her side.

"I know what you must think."

I pause, looking at her despite the lack of eye contact she offers. "What's that, Millie?"

Her jaw works while I spot the red rim around her eyes. "That I'm a lost cause and inept at taking care of myself. That I need someone to teach me how to do absolutely everything."

She turns and walks away from the machines. I follow her. Millie's exhales are strained, wavering the way they were when I got here, so I pick up my pace.

Before she reaches the door, she sinks onto the wooden bench beneath the window. Her shoulders roll forward as she palms her forehead, hiding her face. I drop the sketchbook to the bench and sit beside her. Bracing my elbows on my knees, I keep only a couple of inches between us.

The washing machine churns across the room, humming softly. It smells like dust and laundry soap in here, but somehow, they go together in this moment.

"You know," she says after a long beat, "my mother used to say crying in public was one of the worst things a woman could do."

I glance over at her, hating that she's still hiding from me. "Because it makes you weak?"

"Or messy. Or difficult. Or dramatic. Take your pick."

I let that settle between us. With every second that passes, it pisses me off more.

"Mine used to say the opposite. That crying was proof you gave a shit. It meant you were still human in a world full of robots."

Millie turns her head to look at me, eyes wide and a little stunned. "She sounds . . . nice."

"She is." I nudge her knee with mine. "Those things you said about being inept? I don't think that."

"Why not?"

I stare at her pink cheek, noticing the single tear streak marking it. "Because you left. You ran from a life where you were safe and wouldn't have ever had to worry about doing something like this. That doesn't sound inept to me. Sounds brave as hell."

"I didn't run because I was brave."

"Maybe not. But you didn't go back. You didn't see how hard it would be on your own and drive back home. You're staying instead."

Millie looks down at her hands. They're balled in her lap, and her thumbs are running over her skin, as if she's trying to scrub them clean of something.

"This was all because of some laundry," she whispers, finally noticing the sketchbook.

I nod despite no question being asked. "It was never about the laundry."

I slide my hand onto the bench between us, palm up, offering it to her in case she wants it. She notices the gesture and flicks her lashes up, finally offering me a look at her blue eyes. Even dimmed with the heavy weight of her emotions, they're still so bright.

And after a long pause, she uncurls one hand and sets it in mine. It's small the way it always is. But as it trembles, it feels even smaller. Delicate, like if I'm not careful, I could snap it in two.

"Thank you," she says, voice low.

"For what?"

"For not laughing. And not judging. For not using this as a way to show me just how little I know of the real world."

"I'm not here to lecture you about laundry, princess."

She huffs out something between a laugh and an exhale. "Then what are you here for?"

Her eyes dig deep. The demanding gaze tugs out the truth before I can bury it.

"To make sure you don't fold in on yourself before you figure out how much more there is to you."

Her breath catches as the washing machine hums louder, kicking into a spin. And still, she doesn't let go of my hand.

21

Millie

Shade's text wasn't expected. That's my fault, honestly. After three days of no lessons, it was only a matter of time before we had another. I guess I just thought it would be me who'd have to ask for one after last time.

His interest is comforting. It's another reminder that he's genuinely interested in our agreement instead of just going along with it for my sake.

The studio is dark inside, the lights off. With the sign flipped to Closed, I know that he isn't here. The door he was talking about is the one along the side of the building that leads upstairs. My stomach rolls with nerves as I sidestep the front of the studio and head along the side.

Since the last time I was here at night, the small light hung on the brick has been replaced, no longer burnt out. It illuminates the walkway, giving me the reassurance of safety that keeps me from shaking with worry. Silence plagues Oak Point at night, even across the street from the diner. Besides a few men in cowboy hats and dirty boots sitting at a table beside the window, it's empty.

A dark space like this isn't where I'd have pictured myself ever walking at night. Months ago, I wouldn't have even entertained the idea of it. My car doors would have stayed locked as I sat outside and shook my head at the place.

So judgmental.

I smooth my hands down my skirt and shiver at the wind that scoops up beneath it, threatening to flip it up. Stifling a curse by biting my tongue, I hold my skirt down and continue toward the door.

It whips open ahead of me, the metal slamming against the brick. I pause, freezing when a man comes out from inside Shade's building. He's unfamiliar, almost terrifying. My muscles prime for a fight as I stand still in the shadowed light, gaping at him.

Standing taller and wider than anyone I've ever seen, the man snaps his head in my direction, his eyes dark and restless. I struggle to get air into my seizing lungs as he grips the side of the door and stares at me. The black cowboy hat on his head is tipped forward slightly, shielding his face from the pitiful light beside me. I open my mouth, then close it, my mind glitching.

"Careful, kitten. Looks like you're primed to run scared any minute," he grunts, voice deep and growled, like he's pissed off despite the lack of physical reaction.

He steps away from the door and lets it slam closed. I flinch at the bang that rings out in the night. It's hard to reassure myself that this guy came from Shade's place. His apartment, not just the shop. He knows him. That means he isn't a danger to me. But . . . he looks like he could be.

The curl of his fingers at his side tries to make me shrink into myself, but I refuse to run like he assumed I would. Instead, I swallow and tip my chin up, ignoring the tremble in my hands.

"Who are you?" I attack.

"How is it that I know who you are, but you don't know me? Shade's a fucking blabbermouth."

I frown, brows stitching together. The man shakes his head and reaches up to pull the heavy black hat from his head. The buzzed head isn't as surprising as the tattoos that are revealed now that there's no shadow to hide them.

Jaw to throat and down beneath the collar of his dirty button-up, he's covered in black ink. I scroll my eyes over him, trying to make sense of the number of them, but I'm not able to. There are too many to look at.

The curl of his lips tries to pass as a smile, but it's too cruel. I avoid looking at it when he sets the hat back on and continues toward me. I shuffle closer to the brick wall, and he watches me move, his nostrils flaring. I get smacked with a wave of guilt when he passes me slowly, eyes on the ground.

"Not gonna touch you, Millie," he mutters roughly.

My eyes burn at the pain in his tone. It's familiar in a way that strikes me deep, ripping open my chest. I twist, facing his back.

"I'm sorry. It's not often that I have to share a dark alley with a man I don't know," I ramble.

The man stalls, the heels of his black boots scuffing the pavement. "My name's Rowe."

"Rowe," I repeat on a loose exhale. "Shade's friend."

"So he has spoken about me."

"A few times. I just—"

"Never saw me before. Yeah, kitten. Got it. Don't blame you for scurrying away."

"I'm sorry," I push out quickly.

His throat bobs before he leaves that sharp gaze on me for a beat longer. Once he looks away, he moves, abandoning this interaction in the rearview.

I'd be lying if I said having him leave doesn't allow me the space to catch my breath. The cool wind blows over me, calming the fear that had clung to me like a second skin. Guilt comes next, punishing me for judging someone the way others have judged me. One look and I was labelled as something I never wanted to be.

Is that how Rowe feels too?

"Millie?"

Shade's voice soothes me, pulling me from my head. I turn to the door, where he's watching me, holding it open. My smile is genuine as I go to him and slip inside.

"So, that's Rowe," I say.

"You saw him?"

I let him touch my back and guide me up the stairs to his apartment. "Yeah. We ran into each other as he was leaving."

"Are you okay?" he asks, stroking my spine.

"I was cruel to him."

His touch stutters. "You?"

"Don't make it sound so hard to believe."

"It is hard to believe."

I glance at him over my shoulder once we reach the open apartment door. Stepping through the doorway, I slip out of my heels.

"He scared me," I admit.

"He scares everyone, Millie. Being fearful doesn't make you a cruel person."

"It was more than that. I judged him without even hearing him speak."

Shrugging out of my jacket, I frown. I drape the heavy fabric over the back of a dining chair and then stand awkwardly, unsure where to go next. I've only been here once before, and that was before . . .

Shade passes me and drops onto the couch. "He won't hold it against you. Rowe's a hard man. Fucking impossible to offend, really. He's got an impenetrable shell."

"What was he doing here tonight?" I ask, joining Shade.

He immediately stretches an arm behind me along the couch, his fingers curling in my hair. It's habit at this point,

I'm sure. There's only so much I can do myself to calm down before one of our lessons, and he always reads into that like an expert in all things Millie. His light, casual touches are for my benefit.

"Came to talk. I've got a piece that I've been wanting to ink for a while. I figured I'd offer it to him first," he says.

"Is there even anywhere left on his body to tattoo?"

His attention snags, eyes holding mine. "Did he give you a quick body tour or something out there?"

My laugh is loud, surprised. It punches through the apartment, making his lips quirk. "Yeah, actually. He stripped down and gave me a quick show in the alleyway. It was the most romantic experience of my life."

"I bet he fucking did," he grouses, but it's an act. His annoyance is so thin it's see-through.

"I only noticed his neck. There were . . . a lot."

Shade twirls my hair around his finger. "Yeah, he has more than I do."

"Have you done them all?"

"No. He got a good chunk of them in prison. I've been touching them up, though. Some are pretty fucking gnarly."

"I'd like to apologize to him the next time he comes to the studio. I feel really bad about behaving the way I did."

Shade tips his head in acknowledgment, eyes flicking between mine for a quick moment. They fall to my lap, clinging to the hem of my skirt. It's shorter than I usually wear, and yeah, maybe I did that on purpose. When he texted me, I was wearing sweatpants. I could have come over without changing, but I didn't. His reaction right now is exactly why.

His fingers release the chunk of my hair and drop to my shoulder, gliding along the curve of it. "Have you chosen what comes next?"

"As in?"

"You need me to spell it out, princess?" he rasps.

I reject the shiver that threatens to rock through me. "No."

"So tell me."

It shouldn't be so hard to get the words out. What I want is something that everyone does. It's natural. Nothing out of the ordinary. Yet I hesitate, feeling a thousand pairs of judgmental eyes on me from all the way in Whistler.

My exhale escapes when Shade tucks a finger beneath my chin and turns my head, forcing me to look at him. I wet my dry lips and fall into his stare, the words settled on my tongue, weighing it down.

"Tell me," he whispers.

"Teach me . . ." I trail off when he drops his hand and reaches across me to cup my thigh.

In one smooth movement, he pulls me onto his lap. I reach for his shoulders, needing balance as my legs slide to bracket his. My knees dig into the couch cushion while I lean forward and hold myself steady.

"Teach you what?" he asks, his voice deep and rough.

I gulp, thighs beginning to burn from holding myself above him. "How to pleasure a man."

His eyes darken, growing more intense than I've ever seen them, his Adam's apple bobbing. "You're sure?"

"Yes. It seems like a very important lesson."

"Men are easy, Millie. It's women who need time and effort."

"I'm not interested in learning how to please women."

His smirk is small, knowing. "I meant, it's important for you to know what it feels like with a man who knows what he's doing with his mouth between your thighs so if you're with one who doesn't, you don't have to settle."

"I'm not—I don't think I'm ready for that," I admit, gaze falling to the firm line of his torso.

Beneath his T-shirt, his abs flex, and a set of defined pectoral muscles rise and fall with his strong breaths. I remember how they felt beneath my palm and roll my lips together to hide my reaction.

He settles his hands on my hips, holding firmly. His hold allows him the ease of moving me wherever he wants me, and he does with a sharp tug. I fall against his chest, our middles pressed together, his jeans scraping the bare skin of my thighs. My inhale is sharp as I lift my eyes. Shade doesn't look annoyed with me, only curious.

"There's no rush. Just tell me when you are ready," he says.

I nod, unsure what to do with my hands now that they've fallen between us. "So, you'll teach me about men?"

"I'll teach you about me, and you can use that knowledge for others. Just remember that every guy is different. We're similar enough, but some things that work for me won't work for others."

"Like what?" I can't help but ask.

"Not yet."

I swallow my frustration with that answer and focus on our closeness. With every breath I take, my chest moves closer to his. It's like I'm leaning toward him without meaning to. It's instinct, and I know that soon enough, there won't be room for my hands between us. I'll need to move them. To use them to touch him . . .

Shade thumbs my waist, tucking his hands beneath my shirt to where I'm bare above my skirt. I shiver this time, unable to help it as goosebumps break out beneath his touch. My hips jerk forward, and he sucks in a sharp breath.

There's a bulge beneath me, rising high enough inside his jeans to scrape at my centre. It's light, a teasing brush that shoots tiny sparks up my body.

"Remember when we talked about following instincts, Millie?" he asks roughly.

I do. It pings around in my mind while I bring a hand to the back of his neck, holding it there as if waiting for approval. He leans back into my touch, his hair tickling my fingers before I curl them in it. Eyes on me, Shade tightens his grip on my waist.

He keeps his lips parted, that thicker bottom one jutting out slightly. I rise on my knees, pushing forward along his groin and hovering slightly above him. The position makes my spine straighten with confidence, power, almost. I tug lightly on his hair, urging his head back and watching the way his pupils expand.

"My instincts aren't all that sharp," I murmur, closing in on his mouth.

He pulls me forward, and our middles clash even harder, leaving me no choice but to set my other hand on the couch behind him. "Seem fine to me."

My rebuttal gets snatched from my mind when he moves his hips, rolling them slightly. I gasp, pleasure jabbing low in my belly as he rubs against me. My eyes widen and fix themselves to the twitch of his mouth. There's a fire sparking in my blood that encourages me to move this time.

There's no room for worry or doubt when I tug harder on his hair and crane his head back before dropping my lips to his.

22

Shade

My groan is strangled behind my teeth when she kisses me. I try not to squeeze her too hard, forcing my fingers to flex on her waist. She's still shy, a bit awkward as she leads us, parting my lips with hers. Her confidence is growing, though, and it's fucking hot to feel.

Millie tangles her fingers in my hair and pulls on the strands, forcing me to keep my head back. My jaw loosens in surprise, leaving my mouth open in invitation. I keep my tongue resting in place, waiting to see just how in control she wants to be right now.

Thumb gliding over the soft, pebbled skin of her waist, I rock her forward again, hinting at the continued movement I want her to make. Fuck knows there's a big enough bulge in my jeans for her to rub on if she'd just—

Her tongue traces the shape of my bottom lip before flicking at mine. She spreads her thighs over my lap and sinks onto me, lowering her centre to my groin. I grunt at the bite of lust in my middle and roll my hips up, letting her know how I'm feeling.

"Good girl," I praise gruffly when she pants, staying where she is.

She cracks her eyes open to stare at me, pink splattering over her nose. Her words are breathless, whispered.

"What now?"

"Ride it for a bit, princess. Get nice and relaxed for me."

The blue in her eyes deepens, nearly grey as she rubs her panty-clad sex over my cock. Her movements are smoother now, controlled yet still a bit frazzled. It's a goddamn mix of everything, and I'm realizing quickly that it's going to be that way for a long while. No matter how many lessons we have, she is going to have me questioning everything I've known about women. There's no fucking question about it.

Millie keeps her eyes open, watching me. I let her, holding her gaze while moving along with her, enamoured by the teeth burying themselves into her lip, pulling on it when she pulls away from my mouth. She exhales loudly before grinding harder, tipping her head forward to watch. My chin digs into her forehead as she looks at the small gap between our bodies and moans. It's soft, near silent, yet manages to roar through my ears.

"Tell me how it feels," I demand, hardly recognizing my voice.

She quivers in my hands, innocent eyes holding steady. "What?"

"How does it feel?"

Her helpless little hum isn't the response I'm looking for.

Abandoning her waist, I take her chin between my fingers, squeezing it just enough to keep her in place. "This is another lesson, Millie. You need to be open with how pleasure makes you feel. Tell me what makes you feel good, and what you need for it to feel better."

"I don't know how to do that," she whispers, continuing to move on my lap.

My chest blazes as I nod, guiding her face as close as possible to mine, our lips brushing. She whimpers. "Stop thinking so hard."

Her eyes stay locked on mine while I shift my other hand behind her to palm her ass. I slip it beneath the short hem of her skirt, feeling hot, bare skin.

"This okay?" I ask.

She tightens her hold on my hair, making the roots burn. "Yes."

I massage it, digging my fingers in before moving my palm over it. Millie's body goes still when I shift my touch lower, to the dip between her ass and thigh. Gently, I push further. The damp fabric between her legs wets the tip of my finger as I press hard enough to part her beneath it. My vision darkens as I narrow into this feeling.

Millie jerks forward, but not away, and I let go of her chin. In a blink, she's doing the opposite and pushing back into my touch, encouraging me to continue.

"What do you want me to do next?" I bite out.

Her throat bulges with a swallow. "I don't know."

"Yes, you do." I let a second finger join the first, spreading them in a way that stretches her panties tight, outlining her slick pussy. Ignoring how good she feels like this, I let my gaze grow harder, more demanding. "Tell me."

She pulls on my hair almost in punishment for my demands, and I let my lips tug up at the corner before pressing them to hers. I drag her lip into my mouth and bite down on it, making sure she feels the slight sting of it between her legs.

"This lesson isn't about making me feel good. It's about me making someone else feel like that," she argues, voice tight.

"You never touch a man's cock without making sure he gets you off first. Not ever, Millie. That's why we're starting here. With you."

I give in. Without hearing her ask me for it, I hook a finger into the side of her panties and pull it out of my way. She's exposed beneath this tiny fucking skirt of hers, and I know the moment she feels it. A tight, stifled whine escapes from her lips, filling my mouth.

"Gonna play with you bare unless you tell me otherwise," I warn, hovering my touch over where I know she's dripping.

The speed at which she nods only drives me further insane. I want to hear the words more than anything. It's important that she feels comfortable with herself enough to be vocal about what she needs, and yeah, I'm a selfish fuck who wants to hear her beg me too.

"Approval, Millie. Give it to me," I snap.

Something cracks inside of her. "Yes. Yes, you can touch me there."

I slide the tip of my finger through her slit, letting it grow slick before bringing it to the small, swollen nub. Tapping it once, I watch her shake in my lap, releasing my hair just long enough to push against my chest. She leans back, using a tight hold of my shirt to keep herself from falling completely off my lap.

Eyes wide, she watches as I move my hand between us, the shine of her arousal on my fingers. Without lifting her skirt, I reach beneath it again, using the new angle to trace circles over her clit.

"Good, Millie?" I ask lowly.

"Mmmm."

I still. "Words."

Fire flares in her eyes as they crawl up my body and burn into mine. Her single-word reply is sassy, almost annoyed. "Yes."

It turns me on more than it pisses me off.

"Good. And this?"

I glide my finger back through her pussy. The perfectly smooth feeling of her drives me so far out of my mind I could blow right here. Her entrance is tight but so damn wet that it's easy to make sure I'm lubed enough for the first push inside. She sucks in a sharp breath as I sink my finger in slowly, moving past the initial restriction.

"Ahh," she whines, falling forward against my chest. "It's —good. *Good*."

I push my tongue to the top of my mouth to keep silent. The feel of her like this is going to my head just as badly as it's going to my cock, and I'm too fucking old to be so weak-willed. I'm throbbing beneath her, leaving a pool of precum in my underwear.

The second she clenches around my finger, I speak regardless of all that, letting my mouth run wild. The need to learn every sexual thing this woman likes is a drug, and I've unknowingly already taken a hit.

"That's it, princess. You're so tight . . . it feels good, doesn't it? Do you feel full?"

Her eyes close, lashes fluttering. "So full."

"You can take more, though, right? For me? You'll let me stretch you and feel the way you grip my fingers like you're scared to let them back out?"

"Yes," she moans, pussy dripping down to my knuckle.

I give it to her, working another inside. She spreads around them, tightening painfully. I could add another . . . she'd take it. But this is good for now. For today.

"Such a good girl, Millie," I praise, nudging her head to the side so I can kiss her neck.

She tastes nearly as sweet as she looks. I run my tongue down the column of her throat before nipping at it, curious how she feels about marks.

My words strike exactly where I knew they would. Hearing my praise affects her so deeply, having damn near the same effect on her as a roll of her clit does. I've called that from our first night together. Knew she'd get off on hearing how much she pleases me. It's the good girl inside of her, branded so deep she'll never be able to shake it.

It's part of what makes her so damn intoxicating.

"You gonna come for me soon? Gonna let me feel you

gush all over my hand?" I ask, sucking at the underside of her jaw. "Make a mess of me, princess."

"Shade . . ."

"Millie," I rasp, moving faster.

Curling my fingers, I search for the part of her that will push her over the edge. I remember the way she put her focus on her clit, avoiding slipping her fingers inside the first time I felt her here. Things are different tonight. She's going to come just like this, and she'll go home knowing that it's possible so she can do it all over again when she's alone and feels the desire to let go.

Eyes flying open, she shoves a fist against my shoulder, lifting off my lap. I move my hand, following her movements and pressing harder inside of her. She cries out, the length of her body trembling as I fuck her deeper, my knuckles dragging over hot skin.

"Give it up for me," I push out, blood thumping in my ears. "Let go like a good girl, Millie. Let me have it."

She does. Like a switch has been flipped, she loses that bright glow and glimmers in darkness. I watch in awe as she transforms in front of me, a feral noise escaping her that may as well be a hot mouth around my cock. Her lips hit mine abruptly, roughly, her tongue working into my mouth to dance with mine. I groan, sucking it hard in an attempt to gain some power here.

There's no use. There's no chance of me finding any once she releases me and slips down from my lap. My fingers are wet, left lying over my crotch. Eyes blinking lazily, she moves to the floor in front of me, kneeling between my legs. Her hands palm my knees, her touch hot and claiming.

"What are you doing?" I murmur, giving my head a single shake.

"Teach me, Shade. I'm ready."

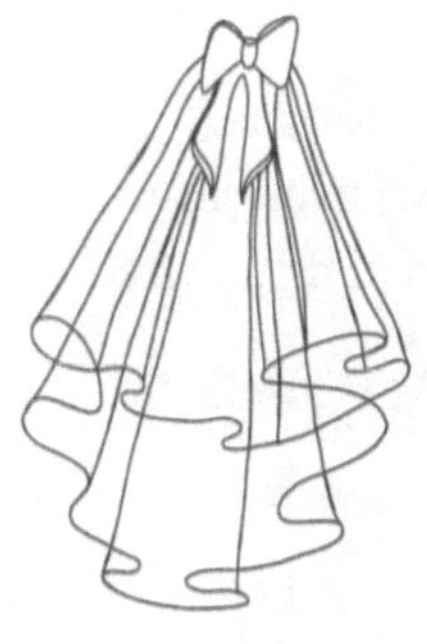

23

Millie

I FEEL LIKE I COULD THROW UP.

Sweat drips down my back as I hold Shade's knees like they're a lifeline. If I let go of them, I might fall backward.

The lingering heat between my legs is distracting enough to keep me from running. I swallow past the ball in my throat and press harder onto him, considering sinking my nails into him just so I really can't leave. My inner thighs are sticky as they rub together, a constant reminder of why I feel confident enough to get down here, pushing past every doubt in my mind.

I want this. I want it badly enough to ignore my nerves and stare boldly up at him, silently pleading for him to tell me what to do.

"You're sure?" he asks, a warning stitched into each word.

"Yes," I breathe.

Leaning forward, he drags his elbows down his thighs. His knuckle brushes the underside of my chin, his gaze dark and daring. I let him move me, struggling to calm my breathing.

"You look petrified, princess."

There's a cold drip down my spine. "No."

"Yes, you do. I don't need you to do anything for me,

Millie," he murmurs, searching my face for something. Confirmation that he's right, maybe.

I force the words out. "It's not for you. It's for me."

His expression stays the same, deep brown eyes continuing their examination. Panic squeezes me, and I tighten my hold on his knees, sinking back to sit on my heels.

"Tell me how, Shade. Show me. Please," I add, my voice a whisper.

The knuckle beneath my chin shifts to my jaw, running along the length of it before falling away. Shade leans back into the couch, wide shoulders sinking into the cushions. I watch, breath catching as he moves his hands to the button of his jeans and pops it open.

His gaze pins mine, like he's testing me with every twitch of his fingers. When he pinches the zipper and lowers it, I don't look away.

"Move closer," he says, a subtle bite of urgency there.

I obey, rising and letting my palms glide up his thighs. He brings a hand to mine, stroking my knuckles. Then he lifts it, pressing my palm against the bulge straining beneath his jeans.

My throat constricts around a breathless moan. I can't speak, my tongue numb where it lies useless in my mouth. The feel of him beneath my palm is intoxicating, and I haven't moved a muscle yet.

"Told you already that there were no limits on where you could touch me," he says, voice rough. "Squeeze it."

I do. Without thinking, my fingers squeeze around the heat and weight of him. Shade's soft grunt slithers over my skin, hot and balmy. I spread my fingers along the length of his shaft, searching for the end. My core clenches, growing slicker when I realize quickly just how long that takes to find it.

My eyes flash up at him, my lashes fluttering. I don't know why I'm searching for more approval, but it's instinct. The desire for him to tell me to continue rattles in my head, repeating until it's impossible to think about anything else.

"Good. Now, pull it out, Millie."

I suck in a breath. A shiver rolls down my body, landing low and deep.

The tremble in my fingers doesn't stop me from taking the opening of his jeans and pulling gently. Shade lifts off the couch just long enough for me to pull them to mid-thigh. I stare at the tight fabric of his briefs, realizing I didn't shed those too.

He doesn't say anything to stop me. Just lifts his shirt with tattooed fingers, baring a stretch of stomach inked in colour. I chomp down on my lip and still, taking in the sight of the black hair over the tattoos. Twin snakes coil across his torso, one poised to strike, the other watchful and still. They look alive in the dim light, each scale shimmering in blues and greens.

"Bryce?" I whisper.

"Bryce."

I slowly lower my eyes back to the fabric restraining his erection. It should be easy enough to free, but I take the waistband between my fingers and hesitate. Instead, I grow fascinated by the wet patch near the tip of him. Rubbing my thighs together, I lift my gaze.

"You shouldn't be surprised," he mutters.

It sounds ridiculous. "Well, I am."

Shade reaches his hand out and glides his fingers through my hair, gathering it all to one side. I'm not surprised when he uses his hold to move me forward, and I follow eagerly.

"Stick your tongue out."

My stomach tumbles. I do as he says.

He tugs me forward, and I flatten my tongue completely over that wet spot. My eyes shut, and I breathe through my nose before bringing my lips to him, sucking the fabric.

There's something protruding beneath my tongue that's hard
and round, and I shift to feel it more clearly—

"*Shit.*"

I flash a look at him, pulling away, worried that I've done
something wrong. He works his jaw, the muscles in his cheeks
straining. Shade presses blunt nails to my scalp and nods when
he notices me looking. I let an exhale go and swipe my tongue
over the spot again, finding it soaked through, the taste of him
gone.

The feel of his waistband between my fingers comes back
to me, and I pull back enough to give it one tug. Shade lifts his
hips again, and I work them down. His erection doesn't move,
so stiff it looks painful as I stare.

There's a round, black piercing protruding from the slit in
the tip.

"Is that . . ." I start.

Shade wets his lips, nodding. "Yeah."

"I've never seen one in person."

A slight quirk of his lips. "First impressions?"

"It looks like it hurts."

He rolls his shoulders. "Nah, princess. Feels really fucking
good when it's touched right."

"Oh."

"What I teach you today won't work for every guy. Not
unless they've got one too."

"Okay." Even if I don't understand it, I want to try. I want
to know what makes him feel good.

"Wrap your hand around me," he says, gentler this time.

I hold my breath and reach out, letting my fingertips glide
over the silklike skin before curling them around it. It's thick
and firm. Harder than I expected it to be. I've touched one
before Shade, but it wasn't like this. It wasn't nearly this size,
and I wasn't interested in seeing if I could get it this big.

"Tighter, Millie."

My hold constricts. "Okay."

"How many times have you done this before?" he asks, no judgment in his voice, only genuine curiosity.

"Once."

"Only your hand, or your mouth too?"

"Just my hand," I admit, my throat suddenly dry.

His nostrils flare, the hand in my hair nearly painful. "Spit on it. Get me wet before doing anything else."

Goosebumps rise on my arms, nerves crackling like static beneath my skin. I freeze up, my attention fixed to the sight of him in my hand, the tip slick but an angry shade of red. It's intimidating enough on its own, but to add the small black ball sticking out of it? And now he wants me to spit on it? As if that's a casual demand.

Not in the slightest.

"Can't we use lube instead?" I ask, the words tumbling out.

His brows bounce. "If that's what you want to use, yes. I'll get some right now if you tell me the reason behind wanting it."

"Spitting isn't . . . it's not attractive."

"Why not?" he counters.

I don't notice how tense I've gotten until I catch the slight wince flicking across his expression. Loosening my hold, I sigh. "What do you mean, *why*? It's not something you're supposed to do. You don't cover someone else in your spit."

Not girls like me—girls raised to be polite, to keep their knees closed and their mouths shut.

"According to who?"

"I don't want to play the guessing game."

"So don't. Do you trust me?"

It's a loaded question. On instinct, I want to say yes. I trust Shade more than I do every person I know back in Whistler. But realistically, I know I shouldn't. Not yet.

Still, I choose to be honest. "Yes."

He leans over me then, his eyes piercing into mine as his

hold on my head shifts. Inch by inch, he tips it back until my throat is arched, quick breaths slipping from my parted lips.

"Open wider," he rasps.

There's no hesitation when I follow his order. It's almost freeing to just follow his commands, letting my trust guide me.

Shade keeps our eyes locked, holding steady as his lips purse. The lust that carves straight through my centre at the sight of his spit dripping down into my mouth is ruthless. I swallow on instinct after his spit pools on my tongue, letting it run down my throat.

"Good girl," he praises, stroking my fluttering pulse. "Didn't even need to tell you to swallow."

I don't react right away. My low, desperate moan comes when he throbs in my hand.

"How do I spit on it?" I ask, gently stroking him. "Over the tip?"

He sinks back into the couch and holds himself still, the muscles in his lower stomach clenching. "Wherever you want."

Getting more comfortable on my knees, I tip my chin, hovering my mouth over his tip. It would be so easy to lick the length of it, but the piercing . . .

I exhale shakily and spit, the sound almost obscene in the quiet. The gob of clear liquid drips down the first few inches of his shaft, but it's not enough. I bring my fist up and get it wet before dragging it back up. The skin is taut, rolling beneath my palm as I stroke.

"I like it rougher," Shade grinds out from above me. "You're not going to hurt me."

My breath fans over the glistening head as I nod, swallowing thickly. I adjust my hold, moving his erection away from his groin and toward me. Closer now, it's easier to see the four sets of tiny holes along the underside of his shaft.

More piercings. Missing ones.

Pressure builds between my legs, making me so sensitive it

almost hurts not to touch myself. I can't look beneath me. Not because I don't want to grow distracted, but because I don't trust that I haven't begun to make a mess on the floor.

"Is this better?" Squeezing tightly, I spit on him again, this time aiming for the dry skin.

His hips jerk slightly. Just once. "Yes. Yes, better."

"Now what?"

"Jack me off, or put it in your mouth, princess."

There's no mistaking the arousal in his words. Hearing it affects me more than seeing it. The usual control in his voice is slipping, and I think I want him to lose it completely.

Pushing up on my knees, I try to gain as much leverage as I can. Not giving myself a chance to back out, I part my lips and slowly take him into my mouth. I stop after the tip, trying to follow instincts that I should have by now. My mind is empty, though. Blank.

Nerves threaten to undo all of the progress I've made here. I grow still, Shade's taste filling my mouth as my gaze drifts up his body.

He doesn't make me ask for help. In a blink, he has my cheek in his hand.

"Careful of the piercing. Don't let it clip your teeth or the top of your mouth on the way back. Touch it with your tongue. You can play with it that way," he directs me, all gruff confidence. "You're doing so good."

I take his instructions in stride. The tip of my tongue rolls along the black ball, swiping it side to side. Shade's reaction is instant. I whimper when both of his hands find my head, holding it in place.

"Just like that. That's what feels best for me," he moans, spreading his legs wider.

I take the words in stride and do it again, sucking gently as my tongue moves. Sneaking a breath, I open my mouth wider and lower it a few more inches. I swallow, the sensation unfamiliar. Shade doesn't push as I try and work it out.

His hands stay on my head, fingers threading through my hair.

Cautiously, I bring my tongue down the length of him. The small holes I noticed remind me of the missing piercings, and I grow fixated on them. My fingers strain around the rest of him as I try to move my mouth and fist in tandem.

"Focus on your mouth. Feels good, princess. Let it come to you naturally."

My head goes heavy for a moment before I pull off him and breathe. I try not to look at the spit connecting us as I stay close, lips still parted.

"You have more piercings," I whisper.

His brow twitches. He strokes my head. "Knew they would have been too much for you right now."

"Will you show me sometime?" I ask, my core clenching in desperation. "Please?"

"Am I supposed to be able to deny you anything right now? Because I goddamn can't."

It's a rough, almost frustrated question. I almost laugh, my lips lifting in a soft smile.

"Don't let it get to your head," he grunts, tapping my scalp before bringing me back toward his groin. "Try to smile with a mouthful of cock."

I don't bother. The moment I have him filling my mouth again, smiling is the last thing I care about. My heartbeat pounds in my ears, filling the silence as I suck in my cheeks and work my way back down his length. I don't make it very far before I cough, pulling back just enough to catch a breath before repeating the motion. Frustration blooms when I still can't make it farther than a few inches. That chafes and only encourages me to keep pushing past the invisible sensor I keep hitting.

Gagging, I open my mouth as wide as I can and pull off, scowling. My fingers are wet with saliva, but I ignore that as I try again. I pause, jaw aching, throat tight, angry at my own limits.

"Millie," Shade groans, pulling my hair. "Jesus Christ. It's okay. Deep-throating isn't a natural ability for most people."

"I want to do it," I bite out, keeping him gripped in my hand.

"You're going to kill me. I'm trying to—"

I lick across his tip, swiping away the bead of liquid there. "Tell me how to do it."

"Fucking hell. It's not that simple." His thighs clench so rigidly they quiver when I tongue his piercing, watching the way it moves inside of him.

"I'm ready," I declare.

His laugh is strangled. "I'm fucking not."

It's not the answer I want, but it turns me on anyway. Something hot spreads through my core as I work him back into my mouth. My nostrils flare as I try this again, careful of the piercing. I palm his bare thigh, feeling the strong muscles and peppering of coarse hair over butterfly tattoos. My other hand remains around him, low and tight.

He sucks in a strangled breath when I force more of him inside than the times before. The piercing grazes the back of my tongue, then my throat. I struggle to push past the reflex that's trying to shove him out of my mouth. My eyes water, and I scratch at his thigh as my body rejects this idea, too concentrated on not rearing back yet to pay much mind to anything else.

"Millie—Mill—" He cuts himself off with a raw groan, his cock growing harder in my hold. His fingers tighten in my hair almost painfully before he tries to move me away. "Stop. Pull off. *Now.*"

I furrow my brows. A hot flush of embarrassment hits me first, scolding me as I sputter off him, assuming I've done something wrong. My throat feels tight as discomfort falls over me like a wet blanket.

His release hits my cheek, sudden and hot, snapping me out of my daze as he groans.

"Fucking Christ, Millie. Too good. It's . . ." He nearly slurs the words, releasing my head and covering the hand I still have tight around him, keeping it in place. "*Shit.*"

I watch in awe, withdrawing my nails from his thigh as he comes. More of it pulses from the tip, coating my hand and his groin as he rolls his jaw and squeezes my hand just once. I'm unable to move, struck stupid on my knees, my fingers warm and wet.

Shade releases my hand, breaking eye contact first when he looks down. He uncurls my fingers one by one.

"I'm so fucking sorry," he says tightly, breathless.

That shakes me out of my haze enough for me to ask, "For what?"

"It's a douchebag move to not warn you properly first. I wasn't expecting it to hit that fast."

My spine straightens slightly. "Really?"

His eyes dig into me before he chuckles in disbelief. "You can take it as a compliment if you want to."

"I thought I did something wrong," I admit. My fingers are sticky, and I move them awkwardly to my side. "Did I?"

"Not even close. You're a risky little thing, though."

I flush, remembering the mess on my cheek. "I'm not sure where that came from."

It doesn't even matter, though. It's there, this part of me I never knew existed until I met him.

"There's a lot more to you than you think, princess."

Letting that sink in, I roll my lips and follow the movement of his hand as it moves to my face. His thumb swipes over the apple of it, and I grow hotter when he pulls back, exposing the thick liquid on his finger.

"Can I use your bathroom?" I squeak, hardly waiting for him to answer before starting that way.

If I stay, God knows what I'd ask of him. I'd embarrass myself by asking him to hold me or something . . .

"Of course you can."

My legs are weak when I stand and then scurry away without another word. Slipping into the bathroom, I flick the light on with my elbow. The water from the tap is cold, and I don't give it a chance to warm up before washing my hands. I watch his cum slide down the drain and grin like a creep as what just happened finally sinks in.

I never thought I'd have the guts to do that. To ask for it. To make him lose control.

Shade lost control because of me.

Mission accomplished.

24

DAISY TUGS ON BRYCE'S HAND WHEN SHE GLARES AT THE SIGN in front of us.

Oak Point Pumpkin Patch is scrawled across it in thick, hand-painted orange letters and sandwiched between pumpkins of all sizes. They look absolutely nothing like the real pumpkins sprawled all over the field. These ones look like they'll melt into puddles of goo before we even make it to Halloween.

"There are so many traditions we could start that don't involve this," Bryce says.

Daisy pulls her forward, and I follow. "Like? Name one."

"We already do matching costumes for Halloween."

"Only because you can't stand me dressing up as something that doesn't match you. Plus, we don't include Shade in that tradition."

I chuckle under my breath when Bryce glares at me.

"Are we in a threesome and I just haven't realized it?" she asks.

Draping my arm over Bryce's shoulder, I reach past her and tap Daisy's earlobe. "That would be impossible. You'd never forget that if it were the case."

"Exactly. Warm up, Frosty. This is what friends do. They go out and do things that don't include drinking beer at a bar or getting a tattoo," Daisy pushes.

Bryce shrugs my arm off but doesn't shove me away. I've been under her skin for a long damn time now, and there's no plucking me out. She's my friend, and I like to keep my friends. I do just about anything to ensure they don't leave, actually.

It's either my biggest character flaw or the one thing I should be most proud of. I haven't decided yet.

"If I warm up any more, I'll melt," Bryce says.

I smirk. "And we didn't even have to dump a bucket of water on you first." Her elbow finds my side, and I clutch it dramatically. "Christ, woman."

"We're staying right here and waiting for your guest," she tells me pointedly.

Brows twitching, I ask, "What guest?"

Bryce has this look in her eye now. It's too similar to smugness to have me ignoring it. I push her on this, already having a sinking suspicion about what she did when she was busy texting on the way here.

"Millie. I thought you'd enjoy not third-wheeling."

Daisy giggles, unable to help herself, while I try not to tell her fiancée off about it.

Normally, Bryce inviting Millie wouldn't piss me off, but today isn't a normal day. I'm strung tight since last night, and I thought I'd use my only real day off this week to try and clear my head. Jacking off in the shower this morning to the phantom feel of her mouth around my dick didn't do a fucking thing to help. So, I came here with them, hoping for a distraction.

Should've clarified that to Bryce.

"Why do you look like that?" she asks me, tension gathering between her brows.

"Like what?"

"Did she piss you off?"

"No. I'm not sure she'd know how to do that."

"So, you're just upset that I invited her?"

"Let him breathe, Bryce," Daisy says lightly, rubbing her arm.

This is Bryce in all her glory. From the moment I met her as a reckless teenager trying to find her footing, she's had this sharp edge. Not cruel out of anger but out of love. I've always said her love language is attitude. Right now, she's fluent.

Daisy's the only one who softens her. Instead of a cement shell, she's gooey inside.

"I'm starting to think you don't want to hang out with me anymore. You keep dropping me off in Millie's arms," I joke, trying to lighten the mood.

Daisy frowns, shaking her head. "That's not true. You're always welcome to be with us."

"I know, baby girl." I smooth a hand down her hair before staring at Bryce. She lets the fire in her eyes dim. "And I know what you're trying to do."

"What's that?" she asks bluntly.

"She's not here to stay, and I'm not getting mixed up in that."

Bryce keeps her expression blank, trying to make me crack. "Who?"

"Millie is my friend," I say firmly.

"For now."

I groan, glancing at the cloudy sky before looking back at her. "Let it go."

"The whole playboy thing is old, Shade. It's worn out. Find a different personality trait."

"You make it sound like I've been flashing my dick on Main Street. I haven't slept with anyone in months," I mutter.

And it's going to stay like that.

Bryce tilts her head, looking too closely at me. My skin tightens under the scrutiny of it.

"Spend a few hours with her outside of work. Get to know her," she encourages mildly.

The dick she thinks causes all of my problems kicks in my jeans at the mention of just how much time we have spent together outside of the studio. I roll my jaw and nod stiffly, ready for the conversation to end.

"She's coming right now?"

"Yep. Pretty sure that's her fancy fucking car pulling in right now."

Daisy hums, following our stares. "It's dirty. Someone should take it to the car wash for her."

"No better place than the campground. A handwash would have it sparkling," Bryce joins in.

I fight not to laugh. They don't need to know that I'm enjoying their attempt at matchmaking. Honestly, as annoying as it is, it's cute.

"I think she's capable of washing her own car," I reply.

Millie climbs out, and the first thing I notice is her goddamn heels. They dig into the ground but don't pierce through. Not now that the ground has started to harden. We haven't had the first frost of the year yet, but it's coming soon. That's why Daisy insisted that today was our last chance to pick a pumpkin.

"You need to get her out of those things," Bryce tells me, focused on the same thing I am. "She's one hole in the ground away from a broken ankle and a lawsuit."

"You try it and tell me how it goes," I mutter.

Head turning left and right, Millie starts toward where we're waiting, not noticing us yet. She's in a light pink, lace-sleeved dress today, this one brushing the tops of her knees instead of her mid-thigh, along with a matching jacket. The sheer socks she has on have lace and a slight ruffle around the ankle and somehow don't look as fucking ridiculous as I'd have thought they would. Somehow, they look right in place inside her white high heels.

I force myself not to go to her first and help lead her over to the women beside me. It's not my place to help her with small shit like this. That's a job for someone else.

"Millie!" Daisy calls, waving wildly. "Over here!"

Bryce watches Daisy, taking in her excitement with a subtle—damn near impossible to catch—hint of a pout. Fuck me, that never gets old.

"She looks like she pisses money," Bryce says, almost to herself once she removes her eyes from Daisy.

"You did once upon a time too," I remind her.

She bares her teeth at me. "Don't remind me."

Millie waves back at Daisy and makes her way over to us. I feel the moment she notices me. Like the universe pinched my chin and held it in place so I can't look away. She smiles softly, nervously, and I swallow.

Her eyes scan the crowd, posture perfect, but her fingers twist around the strap of her purse. Even from here, I can tell she's unsure. Still walking like she's got eyes on her, still trying not to show the crack beneath the polish. It's a trained behaviour. The kind that gets beaten into your head every day of your life. Suddenly, I want to bump against her just to ruin the perfection of it, but I'd never risk that.

"Hi," she says once she stops only a few steps away from the three of us. "Thank you for inviting me. I've never been to a pumpkin patch before."

Bryce still stares at her feet. "You need a pair of boots."

"Boots?" Millie glances down, frowning. "Oh. I know these aren't very ideal for this kind of thing."

Something in my chest cracks at the nerves in her voice. The obvious embarrassment.

"They're fine," I snap, glaring at Bryce before I realize it. Her expression shifts, revealing her surprise. I ignore it, focusing on Millie and the way she's looking up at me like she's hoping I don't keep pushing on that wound. "If your feet get sore, I'll carry you around on my back like a fucking horse. Got it?"

I expect the sudden choking noise to be from Bryce, but it's Daisy who bends over with a fist knocking her chest. Bryce's *nicer* half gawks at me while trying to catch her breath. Millie presses her knuckles to her mouth to hide a giggle that I know is trapped in her throat. I watch her boldly, debating whether or not I should just haul her away from everyone without a word.

"I'm going to get Daisy something to drink," Bryce says, doing a shit job of not staring at me like she doesn't recognize me.

I roll my eyes and let her haul her fiancée away. Millie turns slightly, drawing my attention back easily.

"A horse, huh?"

"You got a better animal to use?"

"No."

"I doubt you'll need me to carry you anyway. I've never met someone who can walk as well in those shoes as you can," I say, my voice softening.

"I could get boots. It's probably more fitting for this town. Wearing heels here was silly anyway."

I shake my head, my hands deep in my hoodie pocket. "You don't need to fit into this town. You couldn't if you tried."

"I am trying to," she admits softly.

"Stop. You not being like everyone else here is part of what makes you so fucking special. Don't change that, especially not because of what Bryce said. She's giving you a hard time because that's her way of getting to know you, not because she really thinks you need to change anything."

Millie blinks, her lips parting. She looks like she's trying not to believe me.

"Don't overthink it," I add, stopping her mind in its tracks.

Her voice is softer than it's been in days when she asks, "You meant it?"

"I'm not in the habit of saying things I don't."

"I know."

She doesn't look away, not even when I give her the smallest grin I've got.

"If I say something nice, you don't have to dig around for the catch."

"Easier said than done. There's always a catch somewhere, even if it's not obvious."

"The only one I have is that I'll keep saying it 'til you start believing it."

Her lips twitch, like she's not sure whether to laugh or cry. There's a shift in her then, like she feels more *seen* than a minute ago. Like what I've said means something to her. Then her fingers brush mine. It's barely a touch, as if she's testing the weight of what I just said.

It's enough to pull all the air out of my chest. I don't grab her hand. Don't push either of us. But I let my knuckles stay there, grazing hers until she looks away with the faintest smile.

And that's how I know I've got her believing me—at least a little.

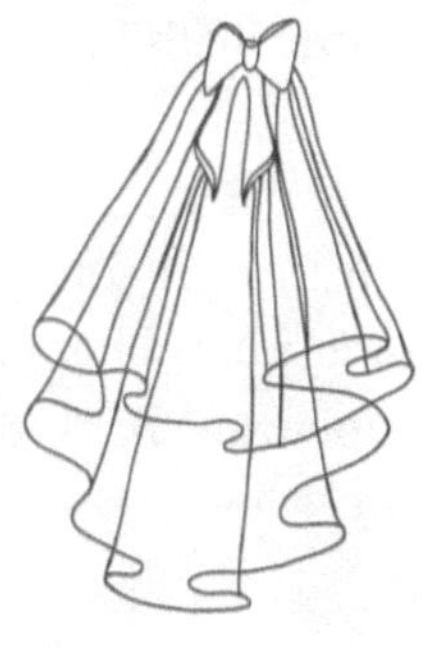

25

Millie

SHADE BLOWS CASUALLY INTO THE CUP OF APPLE CIDER IN HIS right hand a few times before handing it over. He falls back to my side, and we continue through the rows of pumpkins.

I take a cautious sip to make sure it isn't going to burn my tongue, but it's the perfect temperature. My pulse flutters slightly at the easy way he thought to blow on my drink like that. He doesn't so much as look at me for any sort of reaction to the sweet gesture, as if he truly doesn't think it was a big deal.

It was.

"Do you always carve pumpkins for Halloween?" I ask, trying to distract myself.

"Fuck no. Not since I was a kid. But Daisy's got this new fixation with starting traditions, and I guess we drew the short straw with this one."

"Traditions aren't your thing?"

"I don't mind traditions. If *I* get to choose them," he says.

"I've never had any. I don't think this one would be all that bad."

I feel his attention fall over me. "Not even one? How is that possible?"

"My parents weren't much for family time. That's what traditions are about, aren't they? Spending time with those you love?"

"In a way, yeah, I guess they are."

"You should enjoy having people who want to start something like that with you, even if it is just carving pumpkins in the fall," I encourage softly, this dull ache appearing behind my ribs.

"Alright, so join us, then."

My heel catches slightly in the dying grass, and I stumble forward just enough for Shade to reach for me, a steadying hand around my elbow. "I think Daisy just invited me to be nice."

"And now that you're here, I'm telling you to join our tradition."

It's impossible to hide my smile as it takes over my face. Even as my cheeks pulse with a blush, I look up at him and nod just once. He winks, releasing my elbow to palm my back. His hold is firm, as if he's nervous I'll trip again.

"Alright. I'll join. But if Bryce kicks me out of the group, I'm going to kick *you* right back."

"You got it, princess. She won't do that, though. I think she likes you more than she's let on."

"Because she hasn't made me run for the hills yet?"

He chuckles under his breath. "No. Because she didn't veto Daisy's invite for you to come today."

I let that settle, thinking it through as a giggling little girl comes tearing past us. She bumps into my arm as she avoids being caught by the boy chasing after her. He's a bit more aware of his surroundings and leaves a gap between us and him.

"Jenny! Get back here, please," a woman calls weakly from behind us.

I twist, catching who I assume to be the girl's mother rolling her shoulders forward and shaking her head. Yet despite the obvious exhaustion she's showing with her daughter's antics, she has this twinkle in her eye still. Adoration, maybe. Gratefulness.

My heart twists violently.

Sipping on the cider, I try to school my expression and turn in the opposite direction. My heels nearly dig into the ground with every step I take away from the scene. There's more open space on this side of the field anyway. More room to breathe.

Shade's spiced cologne gets picked up on the chilled breeze as he follows me, his steps heavy but even. I avoid looking to see how close he is behind me and how much time I have before—

"You want to talk about whatever it is that upset you just now?" he asks, his voice kind enough to encourage me to open up.

I sigh, flicking a gaze over my shoulder, finding him only a couple of inches away. "That depends on how much of my childhood trauma you want dumped on you today."

"Well, am I allowed to talk shit about your parents afterward?"

"I've never been asked that before," I admit, almost smiling at the bluntness of the question.

"I'm not going to overstep, but I know already I'll have a few choice words to say after you tell me what's going through that pretty head right now."

"There isn't really much I'm thinking about, Shade. It's more just a mess of feelings."

"Which ones?"

We turn down a path between two patches of fat, misshapen pumpkins. Their bottoms are flat, and their stems are long and thick, curled slightly at the tip. I almost like them better than the perfect ones that are displayed at the entrance to the patch.

"Resentment, jealousy, anger. The trifecta," I say.

He snorts a deep laugh. "What about that girl back there brought those feelings out?"

"Do you ever miss anything?"

"Not when it comes to you," he says bluntly, dropping that like it means nothing. I'm starting to realize that's the Shade specialty. "So, tell me."

There are a couple of worn benches at the end of this patch, along with a photo booth and a few bare apple trees with an excess of rotten apples littering the ground. It's a shame they weren't picked while they were fresh. Now, I guarantee a few are home to worms and food for the animals that must stalk these fields at night.

Shade follows my gaze, pressing his palm steadily to my back and heading to the bench beneath a few overhanging branches. We sit, not bothering to leave distance between us. His thigh presses to mine, offering me some of the limitless strength he has leaking from his every pore.

"I've never experienced the type of relationship with a parent where they can be frustrated with you but still let you see how much they love you. Honestly, I don't know what the latter feels like at all," I explain, letting the words fall from my lips without trying to shove them back in. "I was raised in a dynamic that feeds off of power. My entire existence has always been about how I can give my parents more of it. The friends I had were selected for me and had to be from families of equal success as mine. My entire dating life has been planned for me since I was an infant, I'm sure."

"Which explains the shitty fiancé," Shade mutters.

"Chadwick is from a family with almost more money in the bank than mine has. His father owns the biggest investment firm in Western Canada. Our families have been shoving us together for as long as I can remember."

Shade's thigh tenses. "That's a lot of power for one man."

"You'd hate mine, then," I say with a bitter laugh. "I'm

pretty sure he was born with his chin already pointed at the sky."

"You've never told me that your father does. What makes him think he deserves the world served up on a silver platter."

"He owns nineteen ski resorts spanning through British Columbia and Alberta. Name one and it's his."

"Christ."

I lean against the back of the bench, nodding. "My first few nights here, I thought I'd wake up and he'd be at the door to my cabin, ready to haul me home. But he hasn't, and the longer I stay, the more I'm realizing he's waiting for me to break and return on my own."

"Do you think he knows where you are?" Shade asks tightly, the gruffness in his voice drawing my eyes.

"Without a doubt."

He clenches his jaw, and I watch closely as the muscles flex and pull. "How badly do you want to stay here?"

"Bad enough that I'm tempted to ask Shelly to swap me cabins every few days just in case he's been having someone watch me."

"Stay with me instead."

I pinch my brows together, blinking slowly. "What?"

"Is it that surprising?" he teases, releasing the tension in his thigh.

"Honestly? A little."

"Well, don't let it be. I have an extra room that I've already offered to you before."

"You can't honestly want to share your place with a woman. It's so . . ." I trail off.

His smirk is feline, dangerous on so many levels. "So what, princess? Out with it."

"It's a bachelor pad. You're okay with sharing a bathroom with me?"

"Do you think I'm scared of tampons or something?" he asks with a low laugh.

I knock my knee against his, rolling my eyes. "Maybe! I don't know. Have you ever lived with a woman before?"

"Only my mother for eighteen years."

"That's so not the same."

"Tell me what it'll be like with you, then. I'll decide after you've tried to scare me away."

It's a ridiculous push. I know that once I get past my initial surprise, I'll find the real reason behind my doubt. Even now, it's obvious it isn't because his place has a weight rack in his living room or posters of beer models on the walls.

"For starters, I take twenty-minute-long showers every day," I say.

He quirks a brow. "Any particular reason why?"

"Nope," I half lie. His soft laugh makes it clear he doesn't believe me, but I push to my next point without giving his curiosity any more attention. "I burnt Kraft Dinner the other day, so I can't guarantee I won't burn the place down by accident."

"Fuck, you're something else," he muses, draping an arm along the back of the bench. I don't move away when he strokes my shoulder. Not when it warms me on a level I refuse to analyze right now. "So, I'll keep you away from the kitchen. Problem solved."

"Shade."

"Millie," he drawls. "I don't care what you do to the place. We've already established that I'm more than comfortable sharing my space with you. Stop trying to make me take the offer back. I don't give a shit about the faults you believe are bad enough to have me changing my mind."

"That's not what I'm doing."

"It is, and I'm sorry you've been treated so poorly in the past that you've learned to second-guess the validity of kindness when it's offered to you."

I suck in a sharp breath. An invisible hand squeezes my throat. Suddenly, it's too hard to look at him.

"Your parents sound like pieces of work, princess. I'm glad you got away from them," he adds, his tone gentler now. "Let's forget about them for a bit. How do you feel about a distraction?"

I follow his line of sight to the photo booth between the trees. It looks worse for wear, old enough that it leans slightly to one side. There are scuffs on the side where the generic samples of different photo layouts are, and I can only imagine what the inside looks like.

"Is that thing even safe?" I ask, nose crinkling.

Shade drops his arm from the bench to my shoulders, tapping his fingers to the fabric of my jacket. "Let's find out."

"Fuck it," I mutter.

His laugh is rough with surprise. "That's the spirit."

We stand together, and Shade keeps me anchored beneath his arm. I rub my palms against my thighs before remembering where he brought my hand the last time we walked this closely together. My heart gallops when I shift one to the back pocket of his jeans. His chest shakes with a low chuckle that I use as encouragement. This time, when I slip my fingers into the pocket, I let them spread wide and mould to the shape of his ass.

He waits until he tugs the photo booth curtain open before speaking, his gaze heating my cheek.

"You can squeeze." That sinful half smile of his returns. "See if you like it."

"You're shameless."

With a shift of his body, he lets his arm fall and reaches behind him to cover my hand over his pocket. I bite back a laugh when he squeezes it for me, his eyes bright.

"See? That was easy," he says before removing my hand entirely and using it to tug me with him into the booth.

I let myself fall forward into it. The space is immediately cramped with him in it, but with the both of us, the air grows warm and sticky. Hands palm my hips, and then I'm being tugged backward. Shade's lap catches me.

"How risky are you feeling today?" he asks lowly, the hint of something dangerous twirled around the words. The heat of his breath fans the back of my ear, and I shiver. "Close the curtain."

The change in me is so sudden it should be terrifying. I feel the flicker of arousal in my toes first. They curl of their own accord, and then I'm leaning against Shade's chest, lust creating a buzz beneath my skin.

Letting my head roll back onto his shoulder, I reach over and close the curtain. The screen in front of us moves, and suddenly, there we are. It's jarring. I part my lips and stare at myself in the camera. The loose hair, wide-blown eyes, and relaxed posture have me almost unrecognizable.

Then, there's Shade. The man behind me keeps his hands out of view, running them down my sides and over to palm my stomach. His head is tipped down, our jaws rubbing. He's staring at where he's touching me, ignoring the camera, before suddenly flicking his eyes up.

I trap a moan in my throat at the flames in his intense brown gaze. Even like this, I can feel how *deep* he can see me. How he's managed to slip past the guards and through the maze I've constructed to keep people out of my mind.

"Choose the kind of photos you want," he instructs softly, fingers slipping to my thigh and beneath the hem of my dress.

I don't move. Not until I part my thighs.

Shade's tongue wets his lips, and I watch the screen as he dips that branding stare lower to where I'm spread. Then, he's slipping a hand beneath my thigh and pulling it up to drape over his. The heat in the booth cranks to sweltering.

"Concentrate, Millie. Choose the photos."

How?

The only thing I can concentrate on is the slow drag of his fingers beneath my skirt to where I'm damp. I have to bite the inside of my cheek to keep from crying out at the ghost of a touch he gives me over my panties.

He waits until I've forced myself to slide the options on the screen one single time before grunting, "It's not as public as I think you meant when you came up with your list, but it's a good starting point. We're not alone out here. The only thing keeping us from getting caught is a flimsy curtain."

My teeth sink deeper into my cheek.

With his chin, Shade moves my hair from my shoulder to behind me, leaving my neck bare. He runs his finger up my centre, applying a bit more pressure while his mouth falls to my pulse point, parting his lips over it.

"If you want to stop, just say so. One word and we'll stop and finish this somewhere more private."

I shake my head, releasing my cheek long enough to refuse. "Don't stop."

He sucks lightly on my neck, dragging his teeth over the skin. The hand between my legs shifts, and then my panties are out of the way. My exhale is shaky, nearly a moan.

"You can be as loud or quiet as you want, princess. It's your choice, but if you let those pretty sounds of yours out in the open, you have to be okay with what could happen."

My thigh shakes where it's draped over his, and I gasp, something about that threat tightening me up. I reach behind him to hold his shirt, trying to ground myself in case I start floating.

"Shit, you like the idea of that, don't you?" he bites out, exhaling over the skin still wet from his mouth. "The idea of getting caught like this with your legs spread and wet pussy bared for anyone to see."

His fingers glide through me, parting me where I ache and groaning lightly, finding the mess I've made already. There's no point in wasting time denying what he said. It's the truth.

My belly turns iron hot as I pull in long, heavy breaths and find myself on the screen again. It's dirty, watching the flutter of my lashes and slack of my jaw as he touches me in here. I'm watching myself through someone else's eyes right now, and I like what I see.

I whine when he sinks a finger inside of me. It takes everything in me to try and trap down the end of it, trying to keep quiet. Shade nips at my jaw and swipes his tongue over where it stings.

"You're soaked," he hisses, gliding another digit alongside the first. "That for me or this?"

There's no right answer. I'm not sure which I'd choose if not both.

"Doesn't matter. You'll come for *me*, not the people walking past us."

I nod without thinking, pressing back into him, my eyes drooping shut when I feel the stiff bulge beneath me. His groan grates in my ear, trying to draw one of my own out of my chest.

"You're so fucking sexy, Millie," he curses, dragging his teeth over my throat almost in punishment. "So unaware of what turns you on until I'm knuckle-deep in your cunt and you're quivering in my arms, trying not to beg me for more."

Our eyes meet on the screen, the camera picking up on every ounce of pleasure we're feeling. I hold his gaze, willingly letting this window open between us. He'll be gentle as he prods his way through my brain. I know he will.

It becomes impossible to keep quiet when he quickens how fast he's moving between my thighs. I tighten my grip on his shirt and buck my hips, eyes flaring with panic in the camera. The balloon expanding in my belly is getting too full, the elastic stretching too far.

"Shade," I warn on a wavering exhale.

"I know. Can feel you tightening around my fingers like you don't want them to slip out. Let me get you there, Millie. Be a good girl and let me have another one of your firsts."

I can't look away from the screen. Shade's expression shifts as his other hand disappears but doesn't join the one under my dress. His fingers curl, prodding deep inside of me as I stare at us, watching as the screen suddenly brightens and a countdown starts flickering in the middle of it.

His head turns then, and instead of watching the screen, he watches me. The sight of his teeth sinking into his lip pops my balloon.

"That's my good girl," he grates out, spreading his fingers enough that I question whether there's a third one alongside them. "*Jesus fucking Christ.*"

I let a raw sound of pleasure fill the booth before he pinches my chin and turns my head. His mouth swallows the rest of the noise, swallowing it eagerly. My body jerks as my climax tears through me, emptying my mind for long enough that I stop caring about who could have heard me.

Shade removes his fingers and brings his hand to my stomach, rubbing it soothingly as I tremble, trying to stitch the scattered pieces of me back together.

"Relax," he murmurs, another arm curling around my first, holding me tight against his chest. "You're here with me."

His voice drifts through my subconscious, soothing me. It takes longer than usual for me to calm myself long enough to speak. Even then, my voice is ragged.

"What was that?"

"That was you discovering something else about yourself, Millie."

"It was intense," I blurt.

There's almost awe in his voice when he says, "I know."

Neither of us talks for a moment. Shade continues rubbing my stomach, and then my thighs and arms, until I'm no longer unsure if I'd be able to walk if I stood up. He makes no move to leave the booth, though.

"Are you ready to go?" I ask quietly.

"Just waiting on you, Millie."

I nod. "I'm ready."

He hesitates for half a breath before bringing his lips to my jaw and kissing me softly there. I don't have a chance to react before he's guiding me off him and pulling open the curtain. The sun streaks into my eyes, another reminder of where we are.

I quickly adjust my skirt and pull my hair over my shoulders while Shade drops to a crouch in front of the booth and reaches inside a small cut-out. When he pulls his hand back, I spin away, running hot from head to toe.

His laugh is so blunt and honest I can't decide whether I should join him or cry.

"Look at you, Millie," he says.

"Not a chance."

"Do it for me."

Letting go of a heavy exhale, I turn just enough to snag the strip of photos from him. The woman in them doesn't even look like me. The camera caught everything, from the pink on my cheeks to the sag of my head as I got lost in the throes of pleasure. Every muscle in my face is relaxed, and my eyes—it feels dirty to be looking at them. Like I'm witnessing an intimate moment I shouldn't be.

"Take them," Shade urges, staring down at the strip.

I shake my head and hand it back. Reluctantly, he slips the strip into his pocket. He doesn't have to ask why I won't take them. I answer his silent question regardless.

"I'm not ready to see myself like that."

"Alright. I'll hold on to this until you are."

"Thank you."

Shade winks, breaking the tension. "Come on, princess. We still have to choose pumpkins."

"We're actually doing this?"

"Does Bryce seem like the type of woman to let us skip on something her woman wants us to do?"

"This sounds like something that should be a you problem," I poke.

His hand comes up to squeeze the back of my neck, staying there for a beat. "Don't you know? One roommate's problem is the other one's too."

"Maybe I'll just go back home instead . . ." I start, a high-pitched laugh following when he lowers his hand and swats at my backside. Spinning around, I push his hand away. "Okay! You win. We'll pick pumpkins."

And when we finally call it a day, I have a misshapen, flat-bottomed one in my passenger seat, its stem fat and curled. Its twin is on Shade's lap in the back seat of Bryce's car.

A perfect pair.

26

Shade

THERE'S A LOW ACHE IN MY NECK AS I HEAVE THE SECOND garbage bag of clothes into my arms and haul it out of the cabin. Lacey's van is parked in front of the stairs, the sliding door open for us to continue filling it with all of Millie's things.

There's not too much in there yet, and it won't be anywhere near full by the time we clear the cabin out. The only things Millie has here are clothes, shoes, makeup, and hair products. Still, there's more than enough of each to worry me that I won't have room for it all at my place.

She warned me.

I set the bag down beside the first and turn back to the cabin. Lacey's stepping outside with a suitcase rolling behind her. Then, Millie appears, holding a small box.

"For someone who came here with nothing, you aren't leaving the same way," I muse.

Millie follows Lacey, glancing at me as she passes. "Some of us need more than a stick of deodorant and the same outfit to wear every day."

"Hey, I use soap too."

"I stand corrected," she teases, her tone light tonight. Happy.

"Is that everything?" Lacey asks once she's slid the suitcase inside the van. She takes the box from Millie and adds it.

Millie nods, palming her hips. "I just want to say bye to Shelly before I go. You guys can head out."

"Alright. I'll see you in a few, then," Lacey says, rounding the van.

She slips into the driver's seat and starts the engine. It rattles, showing its age as the dark smoke plumes from the tailpipe. I clear my throat, waiting until she's pulled away to speak.

"I'll wait here for you."

Millie turns from the gravel drive. "You can go. I'm not going to crash on the short drive there."

"That's not why I'm going to stay, but thank you. I'll add that to my list of concerns."

"I don't need you to watch over me, Shade," she argues.

"Alright, but I want to anyway."

And that's the fucking truth right there. The reason behind the restlessness that's been prowling beneath my skin these past few days. It's why I asked her to stay with me at my place and why I've been doing everything in my fucking power to keep her from leaving town.

I've become *attached*.

She's my friend, and I've started seeing her as someone I want to keep in my life instead of a visitor free to come and go as she pleases.

Pushing past my frustration with that revelation, I add roughly, "Go see Shelly, Millie. I'm waiting."

"Alright. If you're sure," she mumbles, eyeing me curiously.

I scowl, immediately closing up. Instead of answering, I act like a downright asshole and pull out my phone, trying to busy myself with something other than her. Her shoes crunch in the gravel as she leaves, heading in the opposite direction of where I'm silently telling myself off.

Only once the sound of her footsteps has all but disappeared do I look in the direction of the office. It's cold as shit today, and I know she's wearing those goddamn high heels despite the rocks in the gravel. She's a walking hazard, and it's driving me insane.

Tipping my head back, I shove my phone back in my pocket and groan so loud I'm sure I scare the birds from the trees. I don't give myself a chance to change my mind before heading after her, following the trail of sweet perfume.

She hasn't made it that far yet. Not with the shoes on her feet. As talented as she is with walking in those death traps, there's only so good you can be while dragging them through rocks and dirt.

The moment she hears me following, she looks over her shoulder, and her brow climbs up her forehead. I inhale and call for her.

"Hop on."

"Hop on what?" she asks, starting to spin around.

Before she can, I'm dropping to my haunches in front of her and pulling her onto my back. Her shocked squeal is music to my ears. She grabs onto my shoulders, her hands clasping against my sternum. I shift my hands to her thighs and encourage her to wrap them around me.

"You could have driven," I grunt.

"And waste the gas?"

"It's a minute drive."

"Did you follow me just to scold me?"

Tightening my jaw, I squeeze her thighs. "No."

"So, it was to apologize, then?"

"Apologize?" I almost choke.

She hums boldly. "For getting so grumpy for no reason."

"Grown men don't get grumpy."

"That's a lie, and you know it. If I said or did something

to bother you, I want you to tell me. Wasn't it you who made a whole show of needing honesty?"

"You know, I don't remember you being so goddamn sassy the night we met," I grunt.

She grows quiet for a moment, and I almost blurt out an apology before she says, "I wasn't myself that night."

"And now you are?"

"Yes, I think so. Or at least more than I was then."

Well, fuck.

Loosening my hold on her thighs, I stroke my thumbs across them and force up a rough "I'm sorry."

"It's okay."

She leans her head against mine, her cheek to my ear. The office appears in front of us, and I slow my pace, hoping she doesn't notice. The slight rub of her cheek to the side of my head has me debating turning us right back around.

"Shelly suggested we start a book club the other day," she says suddenly.

My brain lags. "A book club? The two of you?"

"Yep! I think it would be fun. But I'm not sure if there are enough readers in town."

"What type of book club?"

"Romance."

I chuckle, readjusting her when she starts to slip. "Stupid question."

"Don't even try it, Shade."

"Try what?" I ask innocently.

"I know you're just itching to make a bad joke. Something about how I shouldn't need sex lessons when I've got books, right?"

"Absolutely not."

She shakes her head as much as she can without pulling it away from mine. "Right."

"Watching a shit ton of porn doesn't mean you'll actually

know how to do the things you saw, princess. I'm not thinking any of that shit right now. I promise."

"Do you read?" she asks after a beat.

"Not at all. Last time I did was in high school, and I can't say I took pleasure in it."

Her clasped hands tighten against me. "So we can mark you off the list of people to ask to join the club, then."

"That's probably a smart idea."

"Do you think we should do it?"

I pause at the edge of the cabin stairs. The screen door is shut, but there's a low hum of music inside, where I know Shelly's singing along under her breath. Lowering myself back to a crouch, I wait for Millie to slide off me before turning to face her. She adjusts the knee of her tights, drawing my eyes to her legs.

With a swallow, I force them to meet hers. "I think you should do whatever the hell you want to do. If starting a book club will make you feel more at home here, then yeah, princess. I'll put up goddamn posters for it around town if it helps."

There's a warmth in her eyes that closes my throat. I watch as it spreads to her entire expression, brightening the edges of her soft smile. It's too fucking much, honestly. The raw openness she's showing me right now. Yet, I can't look away. Can't shut it down before the sight of her like this tucks itself into the achingly empty space in my chest.

Millie rolls her lips, but the twitch at the corner of them is anything but secretive. I stare at it with an intensity that I don't care if she can feel at this moment. If she runs . . .

Her tiny hand reaches out and strokes my knuckles the same way she did that day in the laundry room. The only difference this time is that I do the same back. Then, I slip my fingers through hers. I squeeze them and then let go, nodding toward the cabin.

"Go say goodbye, Millie."

"Right," she whispers, hesitating. "Are you going to walk back with me or head off now?"

I almost laugh at how obvious the answer to that question is. "I'll be right here when you're done. Who else is going to carry you to the car?"

"I've gone twenty-six years without being carried around, you know."

"Sounds like things have changed."

In more ways than one. And shit, I don't think I'm hating how different they already are.

"YOU CAN DO whatever you want with this room, but I draw the line at putting up fancy-ass wallpaper."

Millie sighs dramatically, tossing me a pleading look over her shoulder. "So I'll need to return the pink one with the poodles and cupcakes I ordered?"

"Smartass."

Lacey took off a few minutes ago after receiving a call to go to the shop, and I know Millie's a bit disappointed in that. It's why I already placed an order for pizza, making sure to cover the entire thing in pineapple instead of just half.

"The room is perfect the way it is," she says, already reaching for the two bags of clothes we've dropped in here. "And I can use the entire closet?"

"I doubt I have enough hangers in there for all of your clothes, but yeah, go for it."

She nods, attention snapping to the box on the dresser against the wall. Abandoning the bags of clothes, she scoops up the box and looks into the hallway.

"And the bathroom? Is there a certain shelf or drawer for me to use?"

"Wherever you can find room. Just try not to leave your

tampons out. You know how much they *terrify* me," I tease, stepping out of the room and toward the door opposite hers. "It's small as fuck, though. I'm not sure how many things you'll fit."

Following close behind, Millie makes a noise of agreement. She moves past me and ducks into the bathroom, sweeping her eyes over it. Then, she sets the box on the counter and starts to pull things out.

Moisturizer, under-eye serum, dry shampoo, and leave-in conditioner are all names I read on the first few bottles she unpacks. For a woman who has only a single paycheque to her name, I wasn't expecting this much. Then again, I've never asked how much money she brought with her.

Without hesitation, she starts opening drawers and the cupboard beneath the sink, examining the space. I hold back a laugh and lean against the door frame, crossing my arms as I watch. She slides the bigger bottles beneath the sink and organizes the smaller ones in the first drawer. When she opens the second, she glances at me, curious.

"What? Did you think I just couldn't grow facial hair at all?" I ask.

She cracks a smile. "I wasn't expecting a literal blade. Most men use electric shavers or those stick ones."

"A real blade gets a closer shave."

She tightens her gaze, dragging it over my jaw and up to where a mustache would grow if I weren't so diligent in shaving it off. I tilt my mouth in response to her staring, biting back a taunt.

"You'll have to show me how you use it one day," she says.

It's too hard not to tease her. Not when I enjoy doing it so much.

"Curious? If you need help shaving, I could just lend you a hand instead."

Her cheeks flush. "You're not getting anywhere close to me with a blade like that."

"Are you planning on using my lesson to shave the face of your future husband, then?" It comes out harsher than I mean it to.

I grind my teeth slightly, frustrated at myself. Curling my fingers into my biceps, I press my side harder into the door frame.

Millie watches my every move as if she's categorizing them in her head. There's got to be a spreadsheet up there by now with every one of her reactions linked to what causes them so she knows exactly where to push to get the one she wants out of me.

"I wasn't thinking that exactly. But it's not a bad idea," she answers, lips pursing around the words like she's trying not to smile as she says them. "For now, I'll stick with just watching you."

"Great," I mutter, cock twitching in my jeans. "I'll leave you to unpack."

She tips her chin, her gaze still flickering with light. "Try not to imagine the poodle wallpaper on the kitchen walls while you're out there."

I almost laugh. Of all the things I'll be imagining, it won't be fucking poodles.

27

Millie

I DIDN'T ANTICIPATE MY FIRST TIME LIVING WITH A MAN TO BE so . . . normal.

It's only been two days, but they've flown by with no issues. I can't tell if Shade's truly this easygoing or if he's putting on a front for me so that I don't run screaming. The worst part so far has been the occasional grunts from the living room every night while he works out.

I make sure to be in my room with the door shut during that time. I'm positive that I'd take one look at his shirtless, sweaty torso and drop to my knees right then and there. The only time I should do that has already passed. Doing it again outside of a lesson would be unwise.

That doesn't mean I don't still bury my head beneath my pillow and imagine that every grunt he makes isn't because I'm pleasuring him, though. But that's a secret I'm taking with me to the grave.

I drag my finger over the screen of the iPad Bryce dropped on the desk for me earlier and squint. The logo is still rougher than I'd like, but I've cleaned up the edges and gotten the drop of ink beneath the gun needle as perfect as it'll get.

For my first time using this kind of set-up, I think I did pretty good.

But is it good enough to show Shade? I don't know.

With the tip of the pencil, I finish up the lettering a bit more, stalling. He's already done with his client today, and I can hear him putting everything he used away. I've gotten pretty familiar with his set-up now, so I'm also aware he'll be done in about . . . five minutes. Then, I won't be able to stall any longer.

There's a calmness to the studio today. I noticed it from the moment we came down from the apartment together and he got started without me having to ask what I should do. It's become habit to start up the computer, turn the built-in speakers on, and double-check his appointments before confirming with him. Bryce comes in an hour later, a frown on her face as she grumbles about missing her fiancée. It's adorable, but I don't tell her that.

She never needs me to tell her the appointments she has for the day, but I do anyway, and she's stopped telling me that it's a waste of time. I think she's warming up to me the way Shade said she was, and I'm trying not to get ahead of myself with hopes of us being best friends.

Shade's taking up more than enough of my time here anyway. Between him and Lacey, I'm never alone for too long. I'm still trying to get used to that.

"Princess," Shade grunts, drawing my attention from the iPad. "Come here."

My stomach flutters despite my efforts to act unbothered. "For what?"

"Just come here. And bring the iPad."

I push away from the desk and cross the studio, clutching the tablet like it's going to be some sort of shield. Spoiler alert: it's not.

Shade spreads out on his stool and takes the tablet. He stares down at the design I've been working on for what feels like forever and smirks. It's not a dirty look, but almost proud, in a devious way.

"This is what I was waiting for. It looks finished, Millie."

"Finished? It's not. I've still got to smooth out the edges of the letters and add more, I don't know, dimension maybe?" I ramble, cheeks burning.

"No you don't. This is perfect. It's better like this than it would be if you spent more time trying to make it more clean-cut. I want to try a few different colours, though. What are you thinking?"

"You don't have one you want already?"

"I want to hear what you think," he says bluntly.

Pressing my lips together, I look around the studio, hoping I'll find a hint as to which direction to take. It's too dark, though. Besides the lights around the mirrors and the neon ones around the signs both he and Bryce have hung over their stations, there isn't much colour at all. I've never really noticed before.

Shade strokes his fingers along the back of my knee, staring up at me. I swallow, not giving in to the distraction, regardless of whether he meant it to be something other than that. His touch is always a distraction. My body can't handle it, especially when it's so soft and honest. I short-circuit instead.

"It doesn't have to match the inside of this place," he says lowly, cupping my leg firmly now. "When you think of me and this place, what colour do you see?"

"Red." It explodes out of me.

"Red it is, then."

I cinch my brows. "You don't have any other ideas? Just red?"

"Just red. And now that that's decided, I want to show you something."

"Alright . . ." I trail off.

He stands, returning to his towering height before pointing

at the table by Bryce's station. I follow as he goes to it and touches a small black printer.

"I'm going to teach you how to print stencils," he announces, already reaching for something in a drawer beside us. "It's not hard, but it'll probably take you a few times to get the hang of it."

I nod, my attention snagging on the confident way his hands move. He's obviously done this a million times, but it's still new to me—watching him do this side of the job. I'm used to only catching the actual tattooing part from the front desk, not what leads up to that.

"This fucking iPad that Bryce is so obsessed with does make it easier for this, but don't tell her I said that," he adds.

I crook a smile. "She does love it, doesn't she?"

"I've always been a pencil-and-paper guy. Not sure why, but I just feel like I have more control that way. It's not as easy to get everything printed off and stencilled, though, as much as I hate to admit it." He sets the iPad on the desk, a new design replacing the Into The Shade logo that was just there. "When a design is on here, it's easy to just print it off through the regular printer. This one here is a thermal printer, and we have to feed the regular paper through it with the tattoo paper to get the stencil."

Leaning close to him, I take mental pictures of the black gloves he slips on and the label on the paper he's grabbing. He slides it onto the table beside the printer and peels up the yellow sheet before ripping it off completely. The blue one that was hidden beneath it appears now, over top of a thin white one.

"We can't just print off the design through one or the other?" I ask.

There's not a fleck of judgment in his voice when he answers, "Nah, princess. In a perfect world, yeah. But for now, this is the way we do it."

"Alright. So, we print the design off with the regular printer and then use it for this one."

The black thermal printer doesn't look any more complicated to use than an office one, so that's a plus.

"That's right. Can you print that design off?"

I grab the iPad and send it to the printer. It comes to life instantly with a clunk before starting to push the design out.

"I always thought you were just printing off the stencils when you did this," I admit sheepishly.

Shade smooths a hand across my back as he reaches around me for the design. A breath slips from me, sounding too close to a moan for my liking.

"Not quite," he murmurs. With the design in his hand, he clicks a few buttons on the thermal printer. The drawing is small on the paper, and he doesn't hesitate before ripping the empty portion of the paper off and discarding it. "Now, we have to feed the tattoo paper and the design through the printer at the same time."

"Okay."

"The tattoo paper goes in like this, and the design like this with the black side down. Watch me."

He moves steadily, showing me how to set the tattoo paper into the machine the proper way, and then slides the design into the upper part. I let the heat of his body roll over me as I watch eagerly, almost excited by the promise of learning more about this line of work. Of learning more about him.

"Alright, now, you just have to hold the tattoo paper as it moves through. Don't pull too hard, but keep your grip firm," he instructs, guiding the paper through.

Once it's done, he takes the paper out and separates the blue sheet from the thin one. The small crown has been transferred onto the thin paper.

"That wasn't that bad," I say, still staring at the design.

Shade winks at me before carefully ripping the thin paper and taking the transferred design.

"Hop up on my table, Millie."

I freeze. "What?"

"Who did you think this was for? Me?" he purrs, suddenly right in front of me.

"I thought you were going to throw it out or something! Not put it on me. I don't know if I want a tattoo," I blurt out.

But if that were the case, why am I getting excited?

"Tell me not to do it, then." It's almost a dare.

I glance toward his station, expecting to find it empty, but it's not. He's left his things out, and the table has been rewrapped. My heartbeat ramps up when I look back at him and our eyes clash.

"Where would it go?" I ask.

A gloved hand takes my wrist, lifting it between us. Then, his thumb sweeps over the inner portion of my wrist.

"Right here."

"Is it going to hurt?"

"A bit. This part of the body isn't bad," he answers honestly.

With a nip to my inner cheek, I start toward the leather bed. Shade's eyes follow me, clinging to my body. The excitement in my belly only grows, now mixed with the unmissable sensation of confidence.

"Is that a yes?"

I roll my eyes. "Obviously."

When I hop onto the leather, I throw him a taunting look that says *come on, then.* His mouth curls in a half-cocked grin that should have me running scared but instead keeps me seated, anticipating what he's about to show me.

This isn't a lesson, exactly, but it feels the same as every other one has. I'm coiled tight, my breath trying to saw out of my chest so desperately it's like it wants to be in his instead. Every scuff of his heavy footsteps on the floor as he makes his way to me is another number my temperature rises to.

There isn't anyone else I'd trust to give me a tattoo, and

it's almost . . . flattering to know that a man as sought after as Shade is offering to give me my first and maybe only one.

But then again, maybe that's how I've felt from the night we met. Grateful that he was there at the bar and that, for some reason, he decided to stick around when others wouldn't have. And now he's my friend, and I don't remember another time in my life where I've felt so free to be myself.

That's the Shade effect, I think. And I'm content living in it for as long as I can.

28

Shade

MILLIE'S LEGS SWING BENEATH THE TABLE AS I FINISH APPLYING the small stencil to her wrist and linger a beat longer than necessary. I run the tip of my finger along the curve of her knuckles, hesitating to roll away from her.

Maybe it's the atmosphere, or some emotion that I don't want to touch with a ten-foot pole. I can't decide yet.

"Can you promise that it's not going to hurt?"

I take her question as an opportunity to force myself back, grabbing my tattoo machine and adjusting the settings just right. The black gloves on my hands are tight as I flex them and then scoot toward her again.

"I could, but I'd break it if you just have a really low pain tolerance," I say gently before patting her bare knee. "Lay on the bed with your legs all the way out, and then rest your hand here on this table."

It's a small black one, already wrapped and ready for me to move it into position. I shove it to rest beside her and guide her hand onto it. She doesn't fight me as I roll her hand into the position I need and stroke the bone in her wrist.

The blush-pink dress she's wearing has ridden up her thighs, exposing more of her soft, pale skin. I tighten my jaw and ignore that, turning the machine on and getting started. She doesn't flinch when I make the first line, and I snap my eyes up, curious to see if she's trying to hide her pain.

Vibrant blue eyes are already on me, no sign of pain for me to see. "That's not so bad."

"That's my girl," I coo.

She smiles coyly. "Proud?"

"Very. Next time, we'll have to do something bigger. Maybe right here," I murmur, reaching up to palm her warm thigh, right above her knee.

"A thigh tattoo?"

"Mmhmm," I hum.

"What would I even get there?"

I swipe away some extra ink and continue around the right side of the crown. "There are plenty of options for a '*slutty little thigh tattoo*,' as Daisy calls them. I've got both my knees done, so mine are a bit higher on the thigh, but I've got butterflies."

"I remember seeing them when I was . . . you know." She tries to hide her smile, but the humour in her eyes gives her away.

"Go on, laugh it up, princess. I'm not ashamed of them."

Millie rolls her lips, the corners twitching. "Why butterflies?"

"Why not?"

She lets that answer sink in before saying, "I'd get butterflies too, maybe."

"Bryce did mine. She'd do yours if you asked."

Idiot.

I don't want Bryce to do them. If Millie chose to get another tattoo, I'd be the one to do it. I would fight with Bryce for the honour, and that's fucked up.

Millie purses her lips slightly, head tilting as she looks at me. I focus on the tattoo for the next several silent minutes, swiping the red skin gently to remove the ink every few strokes before turning the machine off and setting it down. Grabbing the bottle of alcohol, I spray the crown and wipe it again, cleaning it well enough I can do a final look for imperfections.

There aren't any, but I tell her to check anyway, just in case. When she lifts her hand, I watch eagerly, my leg bouncing. For the first time in years, I'm nervous for someone's reaction to a tattoo I've given them.

"It's so cute. Dainty. I love it," she murmurs.

"If you choose to later, I can add something else to it. Some pink would look good."

"I wonder where you got that colour suggestion from," she teases, setting her hand back onto the table.

I spray it with alcohol again and use a clean wipe to make sure all of the ink is gone. Before I reach for the healing balm, I gently lift her wrist and take a final look at the design.

"If the colour pink was a person, it would be you, Millie."

"Does that mean you'd be grey?"

"Grey? That feels like an insult." I wink and slather some balm on the crown before cutting a piece of second skin and applying it. "Don't take this off for at least two days. I'll be checking tomorrow to make sure it's still on."

"Okay, bossy," she drawls.

My brow slides up. "You're not getting an infection, Millie. I'll be bossy about that any damn day."

"And I'm sure you keep all of your new tattoos covered, right?"

I lean forward on my stool and brace my arms on the edge of the table she's still stretched out on. Her eyes follow the shift in my stance, and I trace the edge of her skirt, my groin tightening.

"Give me one and we'll see how well I follow your aftercare rules," I rasp, enamoured by the sight of her thigh breaking out in goosebumps, the short, thin blonde hairs rising.

"Give you . . . a tattoo?"

I sweep my gaze up her body. "Yeah, princess. Give me a tattoo."

"That's not a good idea. I'd probably hurt you. I'm not—"

"The first time Bryce came into my shop, she was eighteen and had never tattooed anyone or anything before. But I saw something in her. I saw the clutter in her head and the desire to dump it out into the world in a way that wouldn't land her in prison or completely isolated from the people who loved her. Tattooing gave her that, and it did the same for me. And maybe I'm reading you all fucking wrong, Millie, and if I am, you can tell me to shut up, and I'll listen. But I've got a feeling that if I put this machine in your hand right now and offered you a bare piece of skin anywhere on my body, you'd feel the same way Bryce and I do."

Palming her thigh now, I knead my fingers into the muscle. She doesn't reply for a few long moments, her eyes drifting as she sinks into their thoughts. There's still music playing, although it's quiet and doing nothing to drown out the tension swirling around us right now.

The worst case here is that she tells me off for assuming things about her like a jackass, and I apologize because I'm too much of a suck for this woman to let her stay mad at me for anything. Especially not something like this.

Her hand shifts, covering mine. The gentle weight of it smothers my fingers, squeezing just enough for me to feel it.

"I don't have a bubbling rage inside of me. That's not what I feel," she whispers.

My swallow is audible. "So what *do* you feel?"

"Helpless," she admits, gripping my hand tighter. Her mouth flattens, eyes dulling. "And guilty. Guilty for feeling helpless in the first place when I come from a place of privilege. Being anything less than grateful for that is wrong."

"You don't owe anyone anything. Growing up with money doesn't mean your feelings mean any less than mine do. I didn't have shit when I was a kid, but I don't believe that you deserve to be miserable because you grew up differently."

"My resentment comes from being so sheltered. I feel like I've missed out on so much. So many years that I should have been, I don't know, making stupid mistakes and getting my heart broken."

"You yearn for the wrong things," I muse, touching her in a way that reeks of . . . possession.

Her voice drops when she asks, "What should I yearn for, then?"

"This."

"And what is this?"

I drag my palms over the tops of her thighs and to the inside, where she's hot and so sensitive that her exhale morphs into a low moan. Wetting my dry lips, I roll forward further and let my pinky drag beneath the hem of her dress.

"Lust, Millie. The kind that turns your breath shallow and makes your muscles quiver," I breathe out, pushing my hand up further until I'm wrist-deep up her dress. She wiggles down the table, pressing against my fingers. Her gaze glitters with mischief when I feel the slickness on the centre of her panties and pull in a quick breath. "You should experience a sexual chemistry that pulses like a living thing at least once in your life."

"I've already done that," she admits before sinking her teeth into her lip.

"And?"

"And I'm afraid nothing will compare to it."

To you.

It hangs on to the tip of her tongue, refusing to fall. The clarity in her eyes is so pure and honest that I nearly combust.

My heart pounds against my ribs. I let go of the groan I've been holding in and press my thumb against her panties while standing so quickly my stool shoots backward. Millie doesn't do anything but lie and wait, staring at me as I lean over her and pant like a man seeing a fucking steak after being starved for a decade.

Her head rolls on the table, her neck arching in invitation before I'm taking it and burying my face in her hair. Lips dragging up the side of her throat, I shift her panties out of my way and rub my finger between her slit, finding her drenched and so hot I might have burn marks on my fingertips after this. She writhes on the table, her hips lifting and falling as she tries to get me to touch her harder or faster, or I don't fucking know. All I do know is that I'm not going to stop touching her until she comes for me.

"Shade," she whines, slapping a hand to my shoulder and trying to pull me closer.

I suck under her jaw, my teeth dragging over the mark I hope I left before bringing my lips to hers. She kisses me hard, demanding and controlling. My balls ache as I let her lead the kiss and slide a finger inside her. There's no resistance now, just a smooth, wet glide that has me spitting a curse into her mouth.

"Next lesson."

I back up just enough to flick my eyes between hers, searching for any hint of fear. She runs her nose along mine and licks my bottom lip, the hand pressing to my shoulder trailing up to my neck, gripping me there.

"You're sure?"

She nods rapidly, and I jerk in surprise when she brings her other hand to my chest, palming it so low she's nearly at my jeans. "Yes."

Without thinking, I lift her into my arms and haul her out of the studio. She squeaks and tightens her grip on me, as if I'd ever fucking drop her. I swallow my tongue when she pushes my shirt up and starts running her nails up and around my stomach. She follows the path of tattoos, and shit—I'm going to lose it any minute.

"Not tasting your pussy for the first time on a tattoo table,"

I answer her curious stare before shoving the side door open and hitting the stairs.

Her cheeks explode in pinks and reds. "Why, are you shy now?"

"Not shy," I grunt, taking the steps two at a time. *Possessive.*

When we reach the top, I shoulder the door open and carry her through the apartment to her room. She dips her thumb beneath the band of my jeans and drags it side to side, those big blue eyes looking up at me through thick lashes. It's filthy in a way only Millie can pull off.

"Keep looking at me like that." It's a warning and a plea.

I take wide strides down the hall and turn into her room. She unbuttons my jeans and then pulls the zipper down. My head falls forward, hanging there as I groan and say a silent prayer.

"Like what?" she purrs.

At the edge of her bed, I pull her close and let my words fall across her parted lips.

"Like you want more than my tongue, princess."

29
Millie

SHADE DROPS ME ONTO THE MATTRESS AT THE SAME TIME HIS words hit me.

I blink softly at him as he stands at the end of the bed, his huge frame hovering. I crawl back toward the headboard and claw at the blankets beneath me. The pressure between my legs is taunting me as I fight the urge to spread them in an invitation.

There's desperate, and then there's *desperate*. I don't want to be the latter, and if I let him see how badly I really do want him—*this*—right now, I can't guarantee that he'll want to stay in here with me. Coming on too strong feels like the one thing that will have a man like him slipping away.

Instead, I try to slow my racing heart and watch him with a calm expression. His jeans are already open, his black underwear showing where the zipper's undone. One tug on his belt loops and he'd be stripped of the jeans completely, but he keeps them on. He keeps his eyes fixed on me, pupils expanding quickly.

It feels like minutes pass before I finally crack. "What are you doing?"

"Waiting for you to let me know you're sure about this

before I keep you pinned beneath my mouth for the next several hours."

My lips part, a surprised breath escaping me. "Hours?"

His body lurches forward as he glares, but not at me. Shade curls his hands into fists before bending to push them into the mattress. My blood sings when I let my thighs relax and part slightly. He snaps his narrowed eyes to where I wanted them, and I bite my cheek, spreading my legs another inch.

"Millie," he warns, voice garbled.

I shake my head, leaning up on my hands. "Teach me. Show me how to be comfortable enough to share this type of intimacy with someone."

"*Christ.* That's what I'm going to do, princess. Just need to try and not lose it in my pants first."

My skin flushes worse than it already was. "You always say that."

"Because you're constantly pushing me there."

"I'm not doing anything," I say, lowering my voice.

"You do *everything.* Just don't know it."

"What if I want to watch you . . . lose it?"

Shade tips his head back and stares at the ceiling for a minute before tugging his shirt over his head and tossing it away. The ring in his nipple becomes obvious now, and I fixate on it. Then, I force my eyes away to the tattoos running up and down his torso before disappearing around his back and out to his arms. Blue, green, yellow, orange. I wouldn't be surprised if he bleeds colours.

There's a blank chunk of skin over his sternum, though. An empty canvas amongst a lifetime of artwork. I stare at it as he settles his knees onto the bed and moves toward me.

"Why is it empty?" I ask, unable to help myself.

He hovers above me now, bulging biceps bracketing my head. "Haven't found the right design yet."

I touch his side, letting my nails follow the curl of the

snake's body from his hip to his back and then his middle. Shade tenses as I trace the tattoo, his jaw working as he stares down at me. His hips lower, pinning me into the bed.

Eyes flaring wide, I look up at him and hold still. The entire length of him is obvious, pressing between my legs and pushing my dress up my body. The corner of his mouth lifts as he leans to the side and brings a hand down to grab my dress, yanking it higher. It clings to my waist, leaving my panties bared.

"Tell me what you want," he says, gripping my thigh and guiding it around his hip. "This? Or something else?"

I choke on a reply when he presses against my panties, rolling against me. My eyes shut, my body starting to grow so tight I shake. Fingertips brush my jaw, then beneath my chin, before he's pinching it.

His voice is airy, loose. "Eyes open as you tell me what you need."

"Shade," I whine, the sound so unfamiliar I force my eyelids open to make sure it didn't come from someone else. "You know."

"I do. But you still need to say it. Give me permission."

Instead of speaking, I slide a finger through his belt loop and pull him harder against me, brows knitted together. I rub against the bulge he's still grinding against me and exhale heavily.

"Words," he asks, a bite to the word.

Frustration burns through me at my inability to ask for this. "How?"

"Tell me to get between your thighs and make you feel good, princess. Tell me how bad you want my tongue sliding through your pussy, licking up the mess you've made for me."

"Please," I whisper, my voice filling with embarrassment. "I can't."

He presses harder between my legs, gritting his teeth when

I grab his side. "You can. The only thing stopping you is your fear of saying something wrong."

I lose the ability to breathe for a few seconds when he takes my hand from his side and brings it to his crotch, pressing it hard against his erection. My fingers flex around the thickness, involuntarily squeezing.

"That's for you. I want to taste you so fucking bad, Millie, that I'm going to need to get myself off while I do it so I don't lose my goddamn mind and end up doing something I shouldn't. Nothing you say could change that or make me hesitate once I hear you tell me I can. You'll need to pull me away from you when you've had enough because I won't want to stop," he declares, eyes so dark they're almost black.

"Oh, my God," I breathe out, my core pulsing.

"Almost, but not quite."

I focus on the heat of him beneath my palm and hold his stare. The need in his eyes is almost violent as he jerks in my hold, grinding into my hand.

"Please . . . please taste me, Shade. Lick my pussy," I whisper, every muscle in my body locking up.

A rough, desperate groan floods from his lips before he's pushing himself down my body. My panties don't last longer than a second before he has them ripped from me and on the floor beside his shirt. I gasp and cry out as he takes both of my legs and shoves them up my stomach. He keeps them there with a forearm tucked beneath them both and brings his mouth to my centre.

Hot breath fans across my sensitive skin, and then he hisses, "Prettiest pussy I've ever fucking seen, Millie. It's perfect."

The first swipe of his tongue through my flesh is electrifying, but the next—

"Shade!"

My hands move on their own. I slap at the mattress and tug the blankets viciously. He spits on me, and every muscle in my body starts to quiver. I can only see the mess of black hair from where he's buried his face between my legs, and my legs block the rest of the view. He doesn't let them go, though.

The first breach of his finger comes as he sucks on my clit, finding it without hesitation. I know he's trying to make it easier to fill me, and it's working. The pleasure is so strong it's nearly too much.

"Taste even better than you look," he grunts, swirling his tongue around my clit. "This is princess pussy, Millie. It's too fucking rich for me, but I'm going to ruin it anyway."

I moan low and long, nodding despite knowing he can't see. It's better this way. I can't see his expression as I clench around his finger, needing more. Just . . . *more*.

Shade teases me with his teeth, the new sensation forcing my body to jerk against the bed, my legs straining where they're pressed to my front. He growls against my core and wiggles a second finger in along the first. The stretch is what I was looking for.

"Want you to come like this before I fuck you with my tongue." The demand scrapes up his throat, sounding painful. "Get my fingers wet before I let you gush all over my face."

His dirty words ripple through me, pressing down on sensitive places that I didn't know existed before right now. I'm moving my hips now, rolling and jerking as I try and force his fingers deeper, wider, and his tongue faster. He doesn't make me beg. Reading me as if he's inside my head, he gives me what I need without hesitation.

"Shade," I warn, teeth tearing into my lip.

He moves his hand faster and taps the top of my walls. I open my mouth, but no sound comes out. Pleasure snaps at me with a ferocity that doesn't leave me any time to prepare. It's savage, all teeth and brutal strength as it attacks me, ripping me open with an orgasm and leaving me scattered on the bed in pieces.

Shade moans against me, continuing to keep my clit

trapped between his lips before finally releasing me. He lets go of my legs, and they fall instantly. Running his tongue over my swollen skin, he gently spreads my thighs and brings his second hand between them.

His dark eyes watch me over my stomach, the shine of my arousal on his nose and cheeks so obvious even with his tongue running over my slit. He pulls his fingers from where they've become wedged inside of me and sucks them off before lowering his mouth. I hold my breath, watching his every move.

"Do that again," he pleads, his body shifting.

My core tightens viciously when his jeans slide down his thighs and settle at his knees. His boxers stay on, but he pulls his shaft out from inside of them. I gasp when I see the four black barbells along the underside where the empty holes used to be.

I tremble into the mattress, my thighs lifting slightly as I feel myself growing wetter. "What . . ."

Shade shuts his eyes for a moment, his hand gripping around his length, covering the piercings before gliding up once. Without answering me, he releases himself and swipes his fingers through my pussy, covering them in my arousal. Then . . . then he's spreading it along his shaft, making it glisten.

When he opens his eyes, they snap to mine, dark and greedy. Desire leaks from his expression, and I know I look the same. By the time I let my breath go, it's nothing more than a low noise of need.

"Give me one more, Millie. Then, I'll let you run that pretty tongue of yours all over these piercings. Make you taste them so you don't fucking forget this cock," he grits out, stroking himself again, this time not stopping.

I don't bother telling him there's no way I could, even without the piercings. He already knows.

Lowering himself to his front, he blows on my pussy and

uses his free hand to spread me. The first swipe of his tongue over my entrance is intense. I'm already so sensitive after one, but it's not possible to turn down the promise of another.

Slowly, he digs his tongue inside of me and spears it deep. I keep my eyes fixed down my body, to where he has his shut, his mouth busy and arm jerking with his firm strokes. In this position, I can't watch as he pleasures himself, but the noises he makes . . . I'm going to come too fast. Too soon.

His nose bumps my clit when he sucks at me and groans, lapping at my entrance with a vengeance. Like he's desperate this will be the only time I let him do this.

My stomach burns at the reminder that he's right.

"Millie," he spits against me, eyes flashing up. "Need it. Need you to give it to me before I blow on my fucking sheets."

A sharp lash of desperation and fear of losing my chance has me moving. I bury my fingers in his hair and give it a brutal tug. Shade curses and has no choice but to abandon my pussy and crawl up my body. He keeps himself hovered above me, his fist still gripping his cock. Adrenaline forces my demand up my throat, the threat of only getting one chance at this with him controlling me.

"Let me feel the piercings. Rub them over me," I ramble.

His jaw looks rigid enough it could snap as he pries it open. "Jesus, Millie. *Fuck*, I can't."

"Yes you can. I trust you." I curl my thigh around the back of his thigh and pull him forward. "Please."

"Don't. Move," he demands sharply, already moving between our bodies.

His hand falls from his shaft. Hips together, he slides the length of him through my slit, getting it wet before retreating and doing it again. I scrunch my face together and let my mouth fall open as I feel the piercings running along my pussy, each one bringing with it a new sensation. My clit pulses, getting the perfect amount of pressure with his every glide.

"I'm—Shade . . ." I moan, tasting another orgasm on the tip of my tongue.

His eyes flash, mouth lowering until our lips brush, touching but not pressing. "Give it to me. Let me feel it like this."

"Kiss me first," I whisper.

He doesn't hesitate. It's brutal, another reminder of what we're doing. There's anger there, frustration too. I don't know who it's coming from, and right now, I don't care. My core tightens, and then I'm coming, my hips lurching down violently.

Shade's feral curse steals my breath as I feel the pierced tip of him press against my entrance. It doesn't go inside. He brings his hips back, and before I can blubber an apology, there's a new wet sensation against me. I roll my lips and watch as he comes, coating me in it.

"Shit. *Shit*," he grunts, falling back onto his heels.

I can't look away as he strokes himself a few times, more milky liquid spilling out the tip and down his knuckles. His hips jerk every few moments, and then he's stilling.

I'm unable to think, let alone speak. He focuses on me, his chest heaving.

"You gonna punch me, princess?" he asks lowly.

My frown is immediate. "For what?"

"Getting too close."

"That was my fault. No punching necessary," I murmur.

He shakes his head, hair drooping over his forehead. "That was fucking reckless. Both of us were."

My chest flushes as I push myself up the bed and close my legs. He watches me move, too freaking tuned in to me to miss a thing.

"It was only once. We won't do that again."

A muscle in his jaw ticks before he slowly gets off the bed. "Only once."

"Right?" I ask before I can stop myself.

Idiot. Colossal idiot.

Shade freezes, turning his head to look at me. The coolness in his expression is all wrong. It's a warning, and I hate the way I want to push right past it.

"Right, Millie. Your list is finished. That's it. We're done with the lessons."

I don't have anything to say. And when he realizes that, he heads for the bedroom door.

"I'll clean up and bring you a towel."

"Sure."

Then he's gone, and I'm alone, left to reel in silence. What could go wrong with that?

30

Shade

"I've got the tablecloth!" Daisy announces, diving over the folding table in my living room.

She slides an orange-and-black, Halloween-themed table-cloth over it and then nods at me. I drop the two heavy-as-fuck pumpkins on one end of the table while Bryce leaves another two on the opposite end. Hers and Daisy's are smaller, more aesthetically pleasing, while mine and Millie's are *ugly*. There's no way around that.

Millie hasn't minded. She's fawned over them this past week like they're her fucking babies or something. She spent an hour last night researching the best way to make a pumpkin last outside in the cold, and I swear I saw her reading the ingredient list on my body spray after.

"Do you think there's a difference between these, or is it just the brands?" she asks the group, holding four sets of carving tools.

Bryce deadpans, staring at the packages. "They're all blades, aren't they?"

"Yes, but do you think one set works better than the other? I don't want to use bad carving tools."

I take one of the sets from her and place it on the table.

"Just sit and start carving, princess. If your set sucks, I'll trade you."

"Fine." With a sigh, she tosses the other two packs to where Bryce and Daisy are sitting. "I'll be watching."

There's a stubborn warmth in my chest as I pop open both of our packages and set Millie's on the table in front of her. Then, I shuffle her giant pumpkin over and grab mine.

"Did you print out stencils or something?" Bryce asks roughly, glaring at her pumpkin.

I laugh under my breath. "Me?"

"Yeah, you. This is your place."

"It wasn't my idea to carve pumpkins."

"So why are you so eager to do it?" she rebuts.

I narrow my eyes at her. "You're an artist. Go without a stencil."

"You're the one person I know who can fucking freehand —as if you need anything else to be arrogant about. This feels like your attempt at cheating," she mutters.

"Freehand?" Millie asks, rolling two black markers down the table for the other couple. "Like for tattoos?"

Bryce hands the first marker to Daisy, who takes it eagerly and bites the cap off before starting to draw on her pumpkin. Millie's gaze sinks into the side of my head as I take the last marker.

"I don't do it often. And not on regular clients. Family and friends only so I know I can ignore their moaning and groaning if I fuck up," I answer.

"That sounds ridiculously stupid," Millie says bluntly.

I watch as she takes the cap off her marker and starts drawing a pair of triangle-shaped eyes on the lumpy front of her pumpkin. Strands of blonde hair curve around her face, not tied back in the low, messy bun the rest of it's in, and I squeeze my marker before I do something stupid and tuck them behind her ear or something.

Bryce's snort cuts across the table, and I let my eyes linger on Millie for a beat longer before glaring at the dark-haired devil again. She makes a show of smirking before Daisy jabs the rounded edge of her marker into the back of her hand.

"I bet you fifty bucks my pumpkin will look better than yours," I say.

"You're fucking on," Bryce tosses back before zoning in.

She scoots her chair closer to the table and brings her face a few inches from the pumpkin before lifting her marker and starting to draw on it. I stifle a laugh and glance at Millie. The pumpkin's eyes have been drawn uneven, with the right settling at least an inch below where the left is.

"I can see why you focus on logo designs," I murmur, subtly dragging my chair closer to hers.

Millie snaps her head to the side, our eyes meeting instantly. "Is that an insult or a compliment?"

"Both, I think."

"Well, you keep stalling, so maybe you're an even worse pumpkin carver than the rest of us."

"Impossible."

Her laugh is soft, nothing more than a fast push of air. "You *are* arrogant."

"You're just learning that now? It's been weeks."

"Oh, I've known it since the night we met. I'm just reminding you in case you've forgotten in the last two minutes."

"It's a wonder I have an ego at all with you and Bryce in my life," I mutter, finally bringing the marker to my pumpkin.

The bumpy shell of it makes drawing anything difficult. My lines are squiggly, and there's no goddamn chance of making a real shape. Millie's pumpkin might have mismatched eyes, but the grin she sketches is big enough that I nearly ask her why she chose that size.

"We keep you humble," she confirms, flicking her wrist to add what I think are dimples to the pumpkin.

"Amongst other things."

Her attention shifts slightly, falling on my terrible fucking drawing. "Are those its eyes?"

"Maybe," I grunt.

"Maybe? They so are. And you were giving *mine* a weird look."

"I was not."

"You were," Daisy pipes in without looking away from her pumpkin.

I point my marker at her. "And how do you know? You haven't looked away from that thing once since you started."

"That's what you think."

"You're all trying to distract me so I'll mess up," I grumble.

Bryce lets loose a laugh that's far too amused. "That's not necessary when you're doing that all on your own."

"You're going to eat your words," I warn.

The competitive streak in me flares, heating my chest as I try to tune out the rest of the table and get to work. I use the opportunity to show off, sensing the curiosity beating into me from the woman in the chair next to mine. It's shameless, but I can't help it. I'm unable to control myself half the time around Millie. Every day this week has been a reminder of that.

My hand slips when I get another flash of a memory from when I was above her, my cock pressing—

The black line that drags across the middle of my pumpkin draws an almost animalistic sound up my throat. I slowly lower my marker and look beside me, unable to ignore the impulse this time. Millie's watching me already, her brows furrowed and lip pinned beneath her fucking teeth again. I have half a mind to use my thumb to pull it free and rub the imprint that'll be left behind.

My groin tightens for the thousandth time today alone as I shift on the chair and bite my tongue to keep from telling her to drop her marker and go to the bedroom. I've been a tense motherfucker since that day in her room, and my entire body is taking the lack of further sexual encounters as a punishment rather than what it is: *the end of our lessons.*

I'm not even going to acknowledge the restlessness that's starting to plague me goddamn everywhere I go. In the studio while I'm working, or in my apartment while I'm trying to work out, where instead of seeing the pin-up posters on the wall, I have to stare at the shirtless firefighter calendar that she put up in their place.

Without having to ask, I know Shelly gave that to her.

I've debated taking it down, but I haven't been able to. It's one of the small changes she's made to this place, and discarding it feels like I'm discarding her. That's the last thing I want to do.

"Are you okay?" she asks, her voice dropping so the question is just for me.

I tap the back of my teeth with my tongue before replying, "Yeah. Just peachy."

"You look like you want to punch the pumpkin."

"I'm just ready to carve it."

"Already?" Her doubt is obvious. "Like that?"

A laugh explodes from me. "Yeah, Millie. I'm going to freehand it. Have a bit of faith, eh?"

"Alright, alright." She hands me the carving tool and takes a long look at my sketch.

"It's too bumpy," I explain.

"It gives them some originality."

"Sure it does."

"Don't hate on them. They're just children," she scolds lightly, a smirk toying with her mouth.

"You have the eye of a mother who believes their newborn is the cutest one in the history of newborns when it's absolutely not."

Her head falls forward as she giggles, setting her marker

down in exchange for her carving tool. "Fine. If you want to freehand, then so will I."

"You've already drawn almost all of his face."

"We both know it's ugly as hell," she says, lifting her head to stare at her pumpkin with a grimace. "I'll restart."

"Alright. We'll start from scratch."

She points her orange-handled carver at me and smiles. "May the best pumpkin carver win."

"Good luck," I drawl, all fake confidence.

"You'll need it."

And then she's turning away from me and stabbing the blade into the top of her pumpkin.

I STAND BACK and stand at the pumpkins we've placed at the front of the studio and crack, my laugh booming through the snowy night.

Daisy follows suit, dropping to a crouch and poking the goopy eye socket on Bryce's pumpkin before shaking her head. I hover close to Millie, staring at the heavy black jacket draped over her shoulders and the way she's grinning so damn wide before looking back to the pumpkins.

"They're so fucking bad," Bryce states.

I grunt in agreement. "Nobody won here."

"At least we can only get better from here," Daisy suggests.

Bryce palms her waist and pulls her close. "There's no silver lining here, baby. These are god-awful. We can't keep them here. We'll turn customers away."

It sounds dramatic, but . . . they're really that bad. Millie's still has guts hanging out of the top that's been cut somewhere too small for the hole and sinks an inch inside. Its eyes are so wide they take up three-quarters of the entire pumpkin, and its smile looks like something out of a horror film.

Bryce's is worse, somehow. While the top was cut perfectly, the rest of it looks like she just plowed her fist right through it. Mine started good but somehow morphed from an intricate skull design to a lopsided dick with balls the size of my hands.

Daisy's is the best, and even saying that doesn't carry the same meaning as it should. It's the most pumpkin-looking, with triangle eyes and a small nose. But its mouth is jagged yet somehow so thin you can tell she didn't push the blade the entire way through the pumpkin.

"I think it gives the place personality," Millie says, tilting her head at the pumpkin display. "Plus, it's snowing. It's only a matter of time before they get covered."

Bryce chews on that. "They're going to get covered in snow or go rotten and look even worse."

"We'll keep an eye on them, then." Millie turns to look up at me with a wide, pleading gaze. "I'll watch them. Let's just leave them out here for as long as we can."

I ignore Bryce's huff of defeat and focus on the bright blue eyes in front of me. Millie doesn't risk me looking away. She reaches out and takes my hand, pulling it beneath the side of my jacket she's wearing and squeezing my fingers. My decision was made from the moment she looked at me, but this? *This is dirty work.* She could ask me to sleep naked out here in the snow tonight, and I'd agree when she's touching me like it's all she wants to do. Like she doesn't have to think twice about it.

"They'll stay," I mutter, brushing my thumb across her knuckles.

Her lips curl around a bright smile, and that's fucking that. *Maybe sleeping out in the snow is exactly what I need after all.*

31

Millie

"Everyone's nearly finished the book. You just have to convince Shade to let us hold the meeting at his place."

Lacey's voice carries through my cheap phone's speaker, slightly muffled. I cross my legs at the end of my bed and try not to let her hear how nervous I am.

When I first entertained the idea of a book club, I didn't actually think it would happen. It was just a toss-away conversation filler, but Shelly didn't let it stay that way. I either looked really eager to find some sort of group of friends in Oak Point, or she could just tell how deeply I enjoyed books because she took it upon herself to make it happen.

Then, Lacey was talking my ear off about it, and we were making all sorts of plans. From how we'd choose our first book and what we wanted our options to be, to whether we wanted to have a theme for the meeting. Location wasn't really ever a factor in our excitement, and now we're rushing to find somewhere to host it. We're only a few days from our first meeting, and I've been dragging my feet on asking Shade if we can host it here.

Things have been going so well for us that the thought of unintentionally annoying him has kept my mouth shut about this. Sure, he usually says yes to the things I suggest we do, but this isn't the same as sliding an extra tub of ice cream into the grocery cart or swapping the old black towels in the bathroom to soft pink ones.

I'd be asking him to invite half a dozen women into his place to talk about smut and the acts of service love language.

"Do we have a backup in case he says no? What about one of the cabins?" I ask, chewing my lip.

"Already asked. They're fully booked with tourists now that the snow's fallen. Shelly said the November rush is going to be even worse if we decide to wait."

"What about the back room of the shop?"

"Sure, if we want to all sit on each other's laps," Lacey says with a sigh. "Just ask him, Millie. The worst he can say is no."

"I feel bad," I admit, shifting to let my legs hang over the edge of the bed.

"Why? No offense, sweetie, but I think your crush is making you overthink this."

I laugh roughly, my stomach tightening. "Crush?"

"Yes, crush. The one you have on Shade. It's obvious."

"Have you been drinking your grandmother's moonshine?"

Her scoff is deep, pointed. "No, I haven't. Don't try and act confused. You're into him. And that's *okay*. I'm just saying that maybe your feelings for him are making you hesitate to ask."

"We're friends, Lacey."

I think he's my best friend, actually. The kind I've always wanted to have.

"Okay, so you're friends who want to bone. That's fine too. But you still need to ask him."

"Boning isn't going to happen." My cheeks flush, heat crawling up my spine before I add, "I'll ask him."

She ignores my acceptance and focuses on the first part of my statement. *Of course.*

"Why not?"

"Because we're just not, Lace. Can we just leave it?" I ask, exasperated and way too embarrassed to continue.

She huffs into the speaker. "Fine. But that doesn't change that you're into him. I'd make a move before it's too late and you're driving your pretty ass back home. At least take that man for a test drive. See if you'd entertain the idea of putting an offer down."

"He's not a car," I groan.

"Just think about it."

"I'll ask about the book club," I push firmly. "And you're going to leave the other topic alone."

"You're no fun, Millie."

I stand, taking a quick look at myself in the mirror above the dresser before saying, "I'll text you what he says."

"Fine. Hurry."

Hanging up, I stare at my reflection for a moment longer. I'm still in my pyjamas, and I haven't brushed my hair yet. Lacey's call woke me before my alarm, and with her blabbering tendencies, I probably have next to no time to get ready before work.

Usually, I'd stay in my room until I was sure Shade was in the kitchen or hidden in his room before rushing into the bathroom, but today . . .

I don't bother changing out of my PJs before pulling my door open and leaving the room. The scent of coffee fills the apartment, drawing me toward the kitchen. Shade makes a full pot of coffee every single morning, even though we only ever drink half before work.

He brings the rest down to the studio for Bryce. She doesn't really communicate with anyone until she's finished the cup of whatever she orders from Maggie's and then downed the rest of Shade's pot.

At first, I didn't drink the coffee because he only ever used milk as creamer, but then I started finding a fancy mocha-flavoured one in the fridge both upstairs and in the studio. Now, I can't start the day without a cup. My body almost craves it. Espresso shots are a thing of the past.

The bathroom door swings open, and I jump backward in surprise. Shade's low, dark chuckle finds me next, and I whip my head to the side, staring into the thick clouds of steam. The at *least* six-foot-four man blocks the entire doorway as he leans against it and crosses his arms over his very wet, very naked chest.

There's a tension in his jaw that wasn't there last night. And now that I notice it, I follow it all the way down to where his pink towel is tied low on his hips. Not only does he have muscles that I know took years to get that defined, but a dark trail of hair perfectly centred between two lines leading down, down . . .

My middle heats as I stare at the outline of him beneath the towel, the upward positioning of it—

"You're running late," I ramble, my voice cracking like a boy going through puberty.

"Yeah. My alarm didn't go off," he says, avoiding my eyes.

"That explains the towel, then. Unless you're planning on going to work like that."

He lifts a brow, eyes gliding down my body and stalling at my thighs, his lips pulling down into a scowl. "I'm not the one with bed-head and wearing whatever the fuck those shorts are. I know damn well you aren't going down looking like that."

Glancing down at myself, I frown, confused. Yeah, the shorts are short, but they're PJs. Who wants to sleep in pants? Going downstairs dressed like this wasn't ever a possibility to me, though. It's odd that he'd mention that at all. He's never mentioned my clothing before.

"They're just shorts."

"Not fucking shorts. Those things are glorified panties, Millie."

"Are you trying to lay down some house rules, daddy?" I tease, holding my waist.

There's a dark gleam to his eyes when they finally lift from my bare legs. The intensity in that blunt gaze makes my skin pepper with bumps. There's far more than just attraction there.

"I'm not your fucking dad. But if you're going to walk around my place in those itty-bitty shorts, you can at least let me look at you," he grinds out.

I tear my teeth into my lip to hold in a squeal when he replaces my hands with his and hauls me into the bathroom with him. The steam clings to my skin as we squish ourselves into the small space together, and he spins me. My hips hit the edge of the counter when he bends me over it and keeps me there with a firm hand against my spine.

"If you want to look, then look," I whisper, finding a voice deep in my chest that doesn't waver with nerves. There's a confidence to it now that wasn't there when I first got here.

After weeks of nothing, no lessons or sneaky touches, I'm coiled tight. I'd gotten used to what we were doing together, and stopping so abruptly has felt wrong. Like we're making a mistake.

Shade's hands are so wide they swallow my curves, making them—me—feel tiny. *Fragile.* Yet despite their size, he's gentle. His grip is strong but careful in a way that has no right meaning as much to me as it does.

He shifts behind me, moving closer. The shorts are pulled tight between my cheeks in this position, and I'm too close to letting a giggle escape. With the fog around us, the mirror isn't clear enough for me to catch a glance at his reflection, so I glance over my shoulder. He doesn't miss the shiver that rolls through me when I meet his narrowed, dark eyes.

"I don't want to just look, princess. That's the fucking problem," he grunts, wetting his lips.

The palm of his right hand leaves my hip and curves down over the shape of my ass before gripping the cheek tightly. His left traces the shape of my shorts, following them to where they get bunched, the lace all that's left. He tucks a finger beneath the bottom and runs it along the lace until it disappears completely.

I suck in a tight breath and watch, enthralled with the focus he's giving my ass, staring at it like it's a dang work of art. Like I'm not bent over his bathroom counter in a pair of cheap PJ shorts, but wearing an expensive, silk lingerie set imported from Paris and splayed out on a California king somewhere with a view.

"What do you want to do, then?" I ask, forcing the question up on a panted exhale.

Shade swallows, his throat working hard. I don't dare move a muscle as he follows the lace between my cheeks and down to where it's pressed up against my centre, damp and slick. The press of his finger as it wedges beneath the fabric and spreads the lips of my sex yanks a garbled moan from my throat.

"Tell me you want another lesson," he spits, sounding angry with me as he stops moving.

I don't hesitate, my hips moving back toward him on their own. "I want another lesson."

"I'm gonna turn your ass red, Millie. And then, I'll pull you up on this counter and teach you something else so you can feel the burn of my handprint while you sit."

"Okay," I moan, nodding frantically. "Yes."

"So *fucking* eager. I'm going to go insane. You're driving me out of my goddamn mind," he hisses before his palm hits my ass. "I want to do a million more things with you. Knowing I can't has me exactly like this. Feral."

I suck in a sharp breath at the contact, feeling the slight

sting in the skin but continuing to press backward, toward him.

"You can. You can do anything," I whisper brokenly, the admission flying out as if I've had it on the tip of my tongue for weeks.

"Such a good girl. You're so willing to let me have my way with you, princess." His hand swings again, hitting harder this time. "But we can't go there."

My whimper has less to do with the pleasure sparking between my legs as he rubs my clit than it does with his rejection. There's more than friendship here, and I've known that long before Lacey brought it up. It's been that way for weeks. But I'm the only one feeling it.

I clutch the side of the counter and try to steady my breathing. The stretch of two fingers pushing inside of me makes that an impossible task. I lean heavier against the counter to support myself as I force my eyes to stay focused over my shoulder.

"Wanna sink my teeth into this ass," he groans, his head falling forward as his hips jerk, so close to pressing us together. "Could tattoo the mark onto it so you'll be branded with me forever."

Heat goes off like a sparkler inside of my belly. My hold on the counter makes my knuckles white as I grow light-headed. I hear the soft smack of his palm to my ass before I feel it, the slight sting growing fiercer with every swat that follows.

"Do it," I gasp, my hard nipples scraping the fabric of my top. "Bite me, Shade."

"Millie." It's almost a growl.

"Please."

He drops to his knees then. I moan, both in relief and pleasure, when he peels my shorts out of the way and brings his mouth to my pussy, licking a hot stripe through it. The room tilts on its side as he grabs my thighs and lifts me off the ground, holding me up above him. The sounds he makes are filthy—wet and desperate.

"Missed this pussy," he breathes out, sucking hard on my clit. "So. Fucking. Good."

No words come out of my open mouth. I can only feel as he ravages me, bringing me to the edge and then shoving me over it with a devilish grin. My throat tightens around a cry as I come, making it stick before he brings his mouth to the middle of my ass cheek and bites down on it.

"Shade!"

He sets me onto my feet and palms my sore ass, making it burn as he removes his teeth and then sucks on the mark he's left. It's primal and raw, and I fall into it like it's the most perfect thing I've ever experienced. With him, it might be.

His body moves to cover my back, the heat from his chest beating into my chest. He grips the counter on either side of me and sets his chin on my shoulder, exhaling.

"Does it hurt badly?"

"Wasn't that the point?" I ask, still breathless.

"I don't know what the point of that was."

I stare down at his hand, watching as it slides closer to mine, whether he means it to or not.

"Why does it have to only be lessons?"

He pauses, tensing behind me. "Because you're going to leave someday."

It's a punch to the chest, leaving me winded. I want to look at him but know that if I do, I risk him putting an end to this conversation. Shade might be open about almost every-thing in his life, but when it comes to this, to emotional inti-macy, there's a wall there that I haven't been able to sneak around yet.

"You say that like I've already made that decision."

"Have you made one to stay?" he asks, tone dropping in temperature.

I frown, staring up at the mirror as the fog clears. Shade's looking at the shower, avoiding me despite how close we are.

"Not yet," I whisper.

The answer shakes him out of his head. When his eyes meet mine in the mirror, they're guarded.

"I told you I'd teach you how to shave a man's face with a blade."

Before I can ask why he's bringing that up right now, he's bringing his hands back to my waist and lifting me onto the counter. I swallow my frustration and push it back, searching for the comfort of our friendship instead. It's safer on that side of the boundary anyway.

Even if the safest alternative would have been to leave this room and take a few minutes to gather ourselves instead. Yet here we are, still close, and pretending that when it comes time for me to choose where to go, I'm not going to be begging him to tell me to stay.

32

Shade

I can't stop looking at her.

It's taking everything in me not to storm across the studio, bend her over that desk she keeps hiding behind, and take her the way I've been thinking about for the last week straight. Soft to start, careful as I work my cock inside before grinding deep. She'd moan my name, and I'd curse hers against her throat, her shoulders, or her mouth.

I'm so far past losing my mind. It's already gone, and now she's chipping away at my rib cage, determined to rip my heart clean out of my chest and shove it into her tiny pink purse. I grind my teeth and continue flicking through this week's photos on my camera, not paying attention to a single one of them.

They're a blur, a distraction.

"Can I ask you something?"

My entire body tenses at the sound of her voice. She hasn't spoken since the last client of the day left, and *fuck*! How could I have missed it after only an hour?

"Go for it," I grunt.

A tense pause. "Could I host the first book club meeting upstairs? And don't feel pressured to say yes. It's your place. I know I'm just a guest here, and I'd never want to put you out or make you feel uncomfortable—"

"Yes," I blurt, my voice rough. Clearing my throat, I add, "You can have it upstairs."

"We can? You're sure?"

The happiness in those four words shoots through me like adrenaline, lighting me up on the inside. It's painful to hide how pleased it makes me to know I've made her feel that way.

"You're not just a guest. Make your plans without worrying about my approval, Millie."

Just one look. I can take just *one* damn look at her without . . . My heart hammers viciously when she stares right back. The soft gleam in those pools of blue keeps me locked in place, something so raw and desperate gnawing at the walls of my stomach.

"Thank you, Shade. I just wasn't sure you'd be okay with a half-dozen women filling your apartment with sparkling wine and finger foods. If that spread around town, you could lose your 'playboy' reputation," she teases, smirking.

I swallow to wet my dry throat. "I'm not a playboy."

"What are you, then?"

There's a beat of silence before I force myself to speak, dropping my gaze back to my camera. "I've never wanted a relationship. They're complicated. There's no time for complicated in my life."

"Relationships are only complicated if you want them to be."

"Is that your professional opinion?" I ask, attempting to hide the frustration that keeps bleeding into my voice. "You have less relationship experience than I do."

"I've read about plenty."

"The whole point of fiction is that it isn't reality."

The wheels of her chair roll across the floor as I keep clicking through photos. "Maybe you should take part in the book club meeting. You could learn a thing or two."

"I'm not going to turn into a romance novel fan, Mills."

"Have you ever even had a girlfriend?"

It's a struggle not to groan when she doesn't let it go. "How did we get on this topic?"

"It doesn't matter. I'm genuinely curious."

"I've had a few. And like I said, they were too complicated."

Millie hums, and I debate looking at her before turning the idea down. "When was the last time?"

"Jesus, you're like a hound with a scent."

"I'm curious!"

"Yeah, I know you are."

"Just tell me."

"Seven years ago. When the shop had just started to get really big," I grit out, abandoning the camera on the metal cart.

"So, that's why it was complicated, then."

I let loose a low laugh before turning on my stool. Millie's got this know-it-all look on her face that should piss me off more than it turns me on, but today's been so ass backward I just accept the latter.

"You think you know everything, hmm?"

"I know more than you think I do."

"All because of your books?"

"Are you familiar with early 2000s rom-coms?"

I let my head fall forward and blow out a breath. "So it's not just books, then."

"Of course it isn't. I grew up sneaking DVDs into my room and staying up at night watching the classics. By the time I was sixteen, I knew all the ways I wanted a guy to prove how much I meant to him. How I wanted him to fight for me when he did what all men do and put his foot in his mouth. I combatted my lack of real-life dating experience with movies that made me forget about *reality*."

I lean forward, spreading my knees. Millie watches me

shift around, clearly trying to get comfortable beneath the weight of her supposed expectations. Knowing she has standards when it comes to men is as admirable as it is intimidating. My confidence takes a blow when I wonder to myself whether I'd be able to ever meet them. But it wouldn't matter.

She's. Leaving.

"There are things a fictional man from one of your books or movies would never think to give you."

Her eyes sparkle. Fucking sparkle like sapphires. "Like what?"

"You need examples?"

"I want them. Prove your point to me, Mr. Arrogant."

My laugh is scared, cracking in the middle. Standing from my stool, I let myself take a risk. I don't bother looking at Millie before walking toward the leather chair seated in front of the studio's big window, pulling my rolling cart of supplies behind me. Her eyes pierce into my side as she watches me, staying quiet.

"Print your logo out on a stencil," I order softly.

"My logo?"

"The one you've drawn for me. Print it out and bring it over."

She doesn't move. "Am I getting a tattoo?"

"No."

By the time her footsteps finally hit the floor, I'm wrapping the tattoo machine. The printer kicks up soon after, and I don't need to look toward the back of the studio to know she's doing it correctly. She's been printing a dozen stencils a day for the last week.

"Now what?" she asks on her way back.

"Now, I'm going to sit on the chair, and you're going to tattoo that fucking logo of ours on my chest."

Her heels scuff the floor. "You're joking."

I pour the ink into the caps, set the needle, and dispose of my gloves before taking a seat. Once I'm facing her, she stops moving altogether. Her eyes are round, full of nerves as they cling to me, a battle of wills taking place within them.

"Tell me which of your fictional men have done this," I say, the possessive demand obvious.

She shakes her head, slowly coming closer. "It's not a competition. When they make a gesture, there's a meaning behind it. They don't do it to be better than someone else. That's what makes them gestures in the first place."

"What if this was always my plan?"

"What was?" she whispers, her fingers bunching her plaid skirt in two fists, lifting it up her thighs slightly. "I'm not trained in how to do this."

I skip her first question, not ready to say it out loud. "I always planned on teaching you. We're just skipping a few steps now."

"A few? We're skipping all of them. I'll hurt you."

"Maybe."

It goes far beyond wanting to outdo the men she fantasizes about. It's about proving that I could if I wanted to. That I could be worthy of her if I ever gave myself the chance. I'm not the guy to go out and stand in the rain shouting my feelings for everyone in a ten-block radius to hear. But I am the one who'll show it in private. Just like this.

"I can't," she argues on a heavy exhale.

"Yeah, you can. It's not as hard as it seems. And I'll help you."

Her lip slips beneath her teeth. I smooth a hand down my thigh and lift my hand for her to take. She eyes it before slipping her fingers through mine and letting me pull her between my legs.

"You can't possibly want this logo on you forever. Not by someone who will mess it up."

"It's the only tattoo I want right now. It's perfect for this place, and I'm so fucking proud of what you created."

"Where?" she croaks, blinking quickly.

My heart twists as I bring our hands to my chest. Where the only blank space of skin on my torso hides beneath my shirt. "Right here."

"Stop."

She tries to pull her hand free, but I keep it trapped in mine. The unshed tears glistening in her eyes are enough to send me to my knees on the ground in front of her, but I stay seated. I squeeze her fingers and tug, forcing her close enough that I can palm desperately at her waist.

"I'm proud of you," I repeat slowly, so quietly a slight breeze could blow it away.

Her chin tucks as she drops her head, inhaling a shaky breath. "You'll guide me as I do this? So that I don't hurt you?"

"Yeah, princess. I'll be here."

"What if I hate doing this?"

"Then you hate it. You'll never have to do it again," I declare.

When she looks up at me again, there's clarity in an endless sea of blue. "Okay."

I hold her firmly, not ready to release her yet. My palm is hot, searing into her waist before I let it slide beneath the ruffled hem of her shirt. She shivers against me, lips parting around silent words. I release her hand just long enough to tug my shirt over my head before taking it again, clutching onto it. Her cheeks fill with a blush that matches her skirt.

"Sit on my lap, princess," I instruct, already reaching beneath her thigh to lift her. "It'll be easier this way."

She doesn't hesitate. And once she's seated on me, I hand her a pair of the smallest gloves we have here.

"I'll prep everything. You just need to watch."

"Okay," she whispers.

I get to work while she keeps her eyes fixed on me, taking note of the way I shave the area, apply pre-stencil lotion, and the technique I use to put her design to my skin. She absorbs it all like an eager student, betraying her initial worry of hating this.

"I've got the proper needle in already, and the settings are chosen. The only thing I need you to focus on is feeling how deep you're pressing into me. You need to go deep enough that the ink will stay, but not too deep that you damage the skin."

She nods once, staring at the blue replica of the studio's logo on my sternum. Flanked by colour and designs I haven't thought about since I got them years ago, hers is front and centre, taking the spot I wasn't sure why was so goddamn special to me. Keeping it blank was habit as I waited for something of importance to find its way there.

Today, Millie is going to fill it with something that will never only represent this studio.

Putting the gloves on, she adjusts her position on my lap. "Will you tell me if I'm doing it wrong?"

"Yeah, Millie. I'll tell you," I promise.

When she lifts the tattoo machine, I tense beneath her. She hesitates, eyes flashing to check on me.

"What?"

I almost laugh. "Grab it. I'm fine."

"Why the tension, then?"

She takes the machine in her grip, and I tug the metal cart right up beside us.

"I'll tell you once you've started."

Her eyes roll, but there's no real annoyance there. "Fine."

"When you turn it on, you'll put the needle into the ink and wait for the cap to fill before starting. Try and always keep it full."

"Okay."

"Pull my skin taut, and slowly let the needle press into the skin as you follow the stencil. Don't jab it in right away. I'll tell you when you're deep enough," I explain, tightening my grip on her waist. "There's paper towel on the cart. You'll use it to wipe away the ink every time you stop. Just like I did when I put that crown on you."

"This is way more complicated than a crown."

"Do you trust me, Millie?"

The question looks like it rocks her. Her lashes flutter as she blinks quickly before answering, "Yes."

"You can handle this. But if you decide to stop once you start, I'll go over to the mirror and finish it myself, okay?"

She lets some of her fear go, relaxing her hold on the machine. "Don't judge me for this."

"I'd never fucking judge you for anything. Especially not this."

It's enough for her. I feel her move, reaching to where the ink is before a familiar buzz fills the room. It's impossible to look away from the determination tightening her expression, transforming her into the confident badass that I knew has been inside of her all this time.

I fill my other hand with the curve of her ass, keeping her locked onto my lap. She faces me now, my tattoo machine in her hand. It spits ink as she leans into my chest and stretches my skin. My groin tightens in preparation for the first jab of the needle, and I hiss a breath when it comes.

"Deeper."

She nods, pressing slightly harder. The initial drag of the needle hurts as she figures out the right angle, and once she does, the pain becomes what it always is. A nuisance more than something that could make me howl from its bite.

"That's it," I praise, dragging my thumb over her stomach. "Go slow. Stop when you need to wipe the ink."

"Does it hurt?" she asks, pulling the needle away to clean the lines she's made.

"No."

Her lips twist. "Are you lying?"

I reach beneath her skirt to squeeze her bare ass. There are no panties to be found until I extend my fingers and find the thong tucked beneath her cheeks. My cock stiffens against my groin, growing too fucking hard.

"Got a distraction right here if it starts to," I muse.

"You'll distract me more than yourself. Then, you'll really wind up with a botched tattoo."

"Is that what I'm doing, Millie?"

She stretches to the side and pokes the needle into the ink before returning it to my chest. "Wasn't that your plan?"

"That's not an answer."

"I'm working."

My chuckle is deep and loud. "Multitask, then."

She scoots further up my lap then, the needle hovering over my chest as she looks at me. There's heat in her gaze, a vibrant want that she's trying to trap behind blunt words. I feel it too, though. Feel it so intensely that I'm wondering how easy it would be to pull my dick out of my jeans and push her panties aside long enough to get a single inch inside of her.

"Careful," I warn roughly.

The quirk of her lips is anything but.

33

Millie

My movements are automatic. Comforting, almost, despite how new they are.

The feel of the vibrating machine in my hands freaked me out at first, but with every stroke of it along Shade's skin, I grow more comfortable with it. My work is terrible despite the movements becoming easier. The lines are crooked, and the curves are slightly squiggled.

I stare at the black portion of the design and focus on not jerking my hips forward hard enough that I send the needle piercing through his chest. The tension radiating off him is doing more to distract me than his handful of my backside or the steady stroke of his thumb over my bare stomach. I'm too few moments away from discarding the tattoo gun and begging to mark him in an entirely different way.

"Millie," he says, my name sounding like a curse.

What I want to say is already twirling around my tongue, tasting like a bad decision. If I let myself speak, it'll escape, and I don't see how we could ever move past it. He'd either reject me outright or accept me and then regret it after.

I keep it to myself and start on another section of the design. The chunky letters are the easiest part to tattoo. I've avoided the pool of ink, knowing that's going to be the hardest.

His large hand follows the upward curve of my ass until he can stick his fingers beneath the string of my thong and loop it around one of them. I hardly get the needle off his skin before bucking forward, my other gloved hand smearing the excess ink on his chest.

"Bryce told me something a few weeks ago," I ramble, breathless.

He loosens his pull on the string but doesn't release it. "What's that?"

"She said some people get turned on while getting tattoos. And that I should ask you about that."

"Fucking Bryce."

"It's true, then?"

Because I'm not the one getting a tattoo right now, but I'm having a hard time not thinking about the tightness between my legs. And if the colour to his throat and the rigid feeling of his thighs beneath me isn't a betrayal of him feeling the same way . . .

"How badly I want you right now has nothing to do with the tattoo you're giving me, but yeah, it's true."

"How badly is that?" I whisper, holding the tattoo machine like I'm one moment from chucking it across the studio.

His eyes tighten at the corners, head shaking in refusal. "Finish the tattoo, Millie. Before I don't let you."

"Just answer my question," I plead, my pulse skipping too many times. "Please."

The way he's touching me changes then. Caution turns to possession, making my arousal flame higher, singeing the both of us. I let a moan slip free when he follows the band of my thong to the front and dips below it, into the gusset. He finds how badly I want him and leans his forehead against my chest, cursing.

It's euphoric watching a man like Shade lose control. To see the break in his controlled expressions and feel the slight tremble in his confident touch. I'm helpless to the words clawing their way up my throat, too desperate to be spoken.

"One last lesson."

"There's nothing left to teach you," he grinds out, eyes flashing.

"Yes there is. And I want you to."

I push the gun away from me, and he's quick to take it before I drop it, putting an end to the buzzing. Once it's set on the cart, I don't bother taking the gloves off before pinching the hem of my shirt and pulling it over my head. It falls to the ground as I kick off my heels, letting them join the fabric.

His expression turns pained when he says, "You already know how to have sex."

"Not in this position, and not the way you'd show me," I argue, trying not to preen when his focus snags on my breasts. "You'd make it good. Better than I've ever had it."

"Don't say that shit." It's a broken groan. His fingers part me, running through my arousal as he pulls a long breath into his lungs. "I'm not a saint."

"I don't want you to be."

His touch grows more pointed, quicker. I drop a hand to his groin, finally feeling the way he's responding to me, finding the obvious answer. Closing my eyes, I let pleasure ripple through me and palm his erection harder.

"All you have to say is yes or no," I add, keeping perfectly still.

The ragged groan that kisses the lace cup of my breast tells me his answer before his mouth finds my collarbone, teeth nipping. "You want something, you can take the tip. *Just* the fucking tip, Millie, or I'll take you too hard, too fast. I've got all my piercings in."

That doesn't help stifle my desire.

"Just the tip," I repeat, but it's thick with a disappointed whine.

The gloves on my hands disappear quickly as I peel them off and drop them on the floor. Staring straight ahead, I'm met with an open view into the street in front of the studio. The blinds for the window are still up, and from this position, it would be obvious to anyone who walked past that I was shirtless. But I don't think they would be able to see what we were doing past my torso. Not with the back of the chair shielding us.

My pussy pulses in anticipation, dripping down Shade's fingers as he continues to rub me. He's teasing me or himself, I'm not sure. But when he fills my aching core with two fingers, it doesn't matter. I exhale into the small space between us and work the button of his jeans, then the zipper. The moment I can push my hand into his underwear, I'm burying my face in his hair and moaning.

"So hard," I murmur, stroking him softly as his piercings press against my skin. "For me."

"Fucking right I'm hard for you, Millie. I'm *always* hard."

His fingertips dig into my side as he brings them to the band of my bra. I arch into his touch, pushing my breasts forward. He leans back against the chair and traces the lace cup with a blunt nail, letting it make a pass over my stiff nipple without stopping. I rock into the slow, stretching movements between my legs, nodding rapidly.

"Tell me what you need, princess. Need to hear you be crystal clear when you tell me that this is what you want," he orders.

I set my hand on his shoulder, rolling my entire body forward. My thighs part further over his, bringing us close enough I can feel the heat from his cock against me when he slowly removes his fingers. I'm still gripping onto his shaft, refusing to release it as though it belongs to me.

"I need to feel . . . need to feel you inside of me. Even just the tip," I beg, so far past caring about appearing desperate at this point.

It's a miracle I can even speak without every word being an unrecognizable whimper.

"Take it, then, but don't be surprised when it hurts us both to stop."

The risk doesn't matter. With a sharp inhale, I guide him toward my entrance and roll my hips. He palms my hip with one hand while bringing the other to my throat, holding me there firmly. He glides through my slit before we connect, the pierced tip bumping my clit repeatedly.

"Shade." I whine this time, losing myself here.

He forces my head to stay up with his grip on my throat, his dark gaze snaring mine as he pants, "Gonna kill me, baby. Gonna kill me."

It's the encouragement I need before I'm notching him where I'm clenching painfully and slowly taking the tip inside. I dig my nails into his shoulder and force myself to stay still. My walls tighten around that initial few inches, making it harder not to sink deeper.

"Need—"

He cuts me off with his lips, kissing me with a savage hunger that betrays how badly he feels the same way that I do. I grab his nape, tugging him away from the chair and closer to me, my thighs burning from keeping myself held in my current position. Still, I don't pull away.

Our tongues slide together, the kiss turning desperate. He sucks on mine, and I pop my eyes open in warning when my knees start to shake.

"Need to get off before I take more," I murmur into his mouth, chasing the taste of him.

His hold on me tightens instantly, refusing to let me, regardless of my lack of trying. "Another inch. Just one. Slowly."

My thighs ache worse as I lower myself what I hope is an

inch. But it's not enough. The stretch feels too good for us to stop like this. I have to bite my cheek to keep from crying out in frustration.

"Tell me you can take it."

His voice is rougher than I've ever heard it as his breath fans my face. I don't hesitate to answer.

"I can take it."

There's no more burn in my thighs when he thrusts up, driving the rest of his length inside of me. I collapse onto his lap, our bodies flush now as I stare at the ceiling, unsure of when my head fell back. The fullness is sharp, almost too much.

"Jesus Christ," he hisses, guiding my hips forward and adjusting the angle. "Set the pace before I do."

"How do I do this?"

His throat works through a swallow as he moves me again, bringing our middles together and then away in slow, fluid motions. I take over after a few seconds, keeping the same pace. His piercings press against my walls, intensifying the pleasure that's filling me before I push closer, and the one through the tip—

"Shade!" I cry, my jaw slack.

He thrusts up again, deeper this time. The angle steals the breath from my lungs, and I gasp when he drags along that same spot inside of me. I cling onto his shoulders for some semblance of balance before I topple over.

"Take it, Millie. Nice and deep just like that. Feel it in your belly. Right here," he spits, pressing a palm to my lower stomach. "You wanted it, and it's yours now."

My ears fill with his filthy words, shooting straight to where I'm clenching around him like I'm trying to keep him buried inside of me for the next fifty years. I rock against his thrusts, meeting them eagerly while an endless chant of moans and pleas spills from my lips.

"It wasn't enough you got to mark my body. You needed

your claws deeper. Greedy princess," he breathes out, smashing our chests together. His lips part over my cheek and then my mouth, resting there. "Where do I get to mark you?"

He knows the answer already. We both do.

I tighten around him, my entire body starting to shake from exertion. My release is imminent, but there's something primal inside of me that demands we get there together. I don't have the strength to fight that pull.

"Inside."

"Inside where?" he rasps, moving faster beneath me.

I curl my fingers in his hair, pulling harder than I should as I struggle to hold on. "Of me."

"Inside your wet, perfect pussy," he corrects me, licking my lips.

Falling against him, I let go. I'm still holding on to his hair, and his head tilts as I come, getting pulled with me. My teeth sink into his shoulder, leaving indents. I squeeze his shaft, pulsing with every shake of my body.

His following groans are loud enough to pierce through the white noise in my ears, letting me hear the way he falls apart beneath me. Heat floods my core, flames warring against flames as he jerks and holds me tighter than I've ever been held before.

"Good girl, princess. Good girl letting me fill you up like this," he praises, continuing to move inside of me with shallow, soft thrusts. "Stay right where you are."

I nod, unwilling to move anyway. Moments pass before he stills, and I've caught my breath enough to speak, guilt baring its teeth at me.

"I'm sorry."

"For what?" he asks, sounding offended, his muscles growing rigid.

"That wasn't just the tip."

His laugh explodes from his chest. It's a warm sound, yet unexpected. "There's nothing for you to apologize for."

"It crossed a line," I whisper.

"We've crossed every goddamn line there is. I'm not focusing on them right now. I'll do that later. After you finish the tattoo. And spray it with alcohol before I get an infection and die."

I jerk back, feeling his still-hard length rubbing inside of me again. "Will that happen?"

"Just clean it before getting back to work," he says, gentling his voice as he runs fingers through my hair.

"Like this?"

Looking down at where we're still connected, I try not to break out in a bright red blush. The longer we stay like this, the more intimate it feels, and I'm not sure if that's something he's okay with.

The way his pupils dilate when I ask the question, though . . .

"Yeah, like this. Just a few more minutes."

I press my lips together—not because I want to argue, but because I don't want him to know just how okay I am with staying connected.

Keeping my mouth shut, I lean over to the cart and then put another pair of gloves on before following his directions. Doing that feels like the only way I'll manage to get through the rest of this tattoo without making a mistake that could cost me everything.

34

"What was your favourite trope?" Millie asks the room.

Standing in front of six women, she confidentially holds her list of questions in her hands and demands everyone's attention. The meeting has gone slow for me, but I could have left at any time. I didn't read the book they're all here to discuss, yet I'm still sitting on a beanbag chair Shelly brought with her, just so I don't miss seeing this side of Millie.

It's clear from the way she holds herself up there that this is comfortable for her. Speaking in front of this crowd—regardless of its small size—she keeps her chin up and shoulders back, her voice strong. The soft-spoken, blushing woman who I know from our quiet moments is the opposite of this one. And I know why that is and where it stems from without needing it explained to me.

This is what she's used to. Back home, she's always this person. The one with impenetrable armour and a smile that could send a grown man tripping over his feet. It's how she was raised. And before she came here, this is the only version of herself anyone saw.

It's unfair for the world to miss the other side of her when I know how beautiful it is.

"I liked that she fell first, but he fell harder," Maggie announces to the room. "That's how it should be. Give me a simp any day."

Shelly barks a laugh while Millie just stares at both of the older women with wide eyes.

Maggie's silver hair isn't tied back today, and she's not wearing her diner apron, which almost had me choking on my tongue when I saw her get here earlier. I still don't know how the girls convinced her to leave the diner long enough to join the meeting, but it made Millie happy, so I didn't bother asking questions.

"That's exactly what he was," Lacey howls, pointing at Millie. "What was it you said to me? That she could have made him drop to his knees and bark, and he would have?"

My brows shoot up to my hairline as I stare at Millie, her hands hiding her face now. Lacey laughs like a goddamn hyena, loving pulling this reaction from her. I chuckle lightly, crossing my arms over my chest.

"That's good, actually! Maybe that should be a trope," Shelly states, snapping her fingers and pointing at Millie.

The other women in the room laugh in agreement, bringing up the idea of choosing a book for next month based around that entirely. It's odd, sitting here and listening to this conversation, knowing that next month isn't even guaranteed with Millie.

The thought is enough to sour my stomach, turning my smile into a deep scowl.

"It was a late-night thought!" Millie defends herself, dropping her hands.

Shelly simply shakes her head. "Don't take it back now. It's a hit. What do you think, Shade?"

Everyone turns to me expectantly. A pair of curious, soft blue eyes are the ones I fixate on.

"What do I think about what?"

"About a man who is so down bad for his girl that he'd drop to his knees and bark like a dog if she asked him to," Lacey says, slightly exasperated.

"Is that supposed to be the ultimate test of how much a guy is willing to do for someone?"

"Careful with your answer, Shade. I would hate to have to ban you from the diner," Maggie warns.

"This is my house, you know?"

Millie's lips twitch before she butts in. "Shade isn't the type of guy to bark."

"But he gets on his knees?" Shelly asks, and I can hear the smirk in her voice.

The red creeping up Millie's throat and to the tips of her ears has me putting an end to this conversation. If she gets any more embarrassed, I'll have to bark just to distract her, and I don't know if my pride could handle that right now.

"Wouldn't you like to know, Shelly," I drawl, patting the beanbag. "Ask your husband to act like a dog, and then come back to me to share how it went."

Millie clears her throat, the red softening as she smiles at me with a silent thank you.

"Let's get back on track. Is there a specific part of the book that was your favourite? Anyone?"

One of the women who I don't know all that well—Katie, maybe—blurts out something about a cowboy dropping his hat on the head of the woman he'd been chasing all book. An array of sighs and high-pitched praises fills the living room.

I bite my tongue, letting them have this moment of swooning. It's a real rule, as far as I know. The whole *wear the hat, ride the cowboy* thing. Rowe made that a whole thing when we were teenagers. He used it to his advantage a few too many times.

"Is that the epitome of romance for you all, then? Barking men and cowboy hats?" I ask.

Millie stares at me, the corner of her mouth twitching just

enough to give her away. "Go ahead and find out. You don't have a hat, but that doesn't mean you couldn't try your hand at barking."

"Not gonna happen, princess."

She shrugs her shoulder, blowing me off. "Fine."

"What a disappointment," Maggie sighs dramatically.

"Don't you all have your own husbands to make do these things?"

Shelly shakes her head. "It's not the same."

"Plus, I don't have a husband. Millie and I are single and now miserable on top of it," Lacey adds.

My chest heats as I stare bluntly at Millie. I wait for her to feel the weight of my gaze before slowly looking back at me. She rolls her lips, her posture softening slightly. I spread my legs, smoothing two palms down them in invitation. Then, I wait to see if she'll take the bait despite the audience.

It's reckless sitting with her on my lap like this, but the beast pounding at my rib cage doesn't give a shit what any of these people think. Not now that it's heard the words "single" and "Millie" in the same sentence.

She hesitates to move, doubt flickering across her expression. Worry too. Still, I don't back down. Having these women leave my place and spreading what happened here tonight around town doesn't seem like a nuisance. It's the opposite, actually. At least I wouldn't have to worry about a fucking cowboy from the stables planting his stupid hat on her head the next time she's at the diner alone.

"Just take the seat already before someone else does," Shelly mumbles under her breath.

Lacey giggles before Millie's finally coming right to me. My princess glares across the room at where the owner of Shimmer Lake sits and grins at her. There's no real heat behind it. There's no chance for her to find any before I'm gripping her hips and pulling her down onto my lap.

She falls onto me, exhaling softly before leaning against

me like it's the most natural thing for her to do. I palm her thigh, trying to anchor her to my body before hovering my lips at her ear.

"Sit here first next time," I murmur.

It's been too many days since she's been right here. She's made it her mission to stay off my lap ever since she finished my tattoo and scurried into the bathroom the other day. I wouldn't say she's been hiding, but there's been some tension between us that I'm chomping at the bit to erase.

She lowers her chin in a small nod. "Okay."

Her list of questions is crumpled in her hands now, so I help her straighten it again before clearing my throat and asking the next one.

"How much would you say a found family dynamic adds to a good romance story?"

"You're a doll for letting us have the meeting here," Shelly says, patting my arm.

I lean my hip against the kitchen counter and cover her hand with mine. "Anything for you."

"However, I am still a bit bitter that you took Millie from me. The camp has been too quiet without our morning visits."

"I didn't take her from you," I argue lightly.

"Oh, don't try it. She's not staying at Shimmer Lake anymore, is she?"

"Don't start complaining now. You wouldn't have had this place for your meeting if it wasn't for that."

And even I'll admit that it worked just fine. There was enough space, and I didn't hear any complaints. Before the majority of women left, I even heard one of them ask if they'd be coming back here next time.

Shelly huffs. "Fine."

"You could always ask her to stop by the grounds more," I suggest, winking. "She'd do it if she knew you wanted her to."

Fidgeting with the stack of sangria-stained, pink wine glasses beside the sink, Shelly says, "You're right. Somehow, you've gotten wiser in the last few weeks."

"I've always been wise."

"Mm, but this is a different kind."

"It's all of the plants in here now. The air is cleaner," I joke.

"I did notice the plants. And not the easy-to-care-for ones either. There's not a single cactus to be found."

"Millie's got a green thumb. She likes to water them all every morning before work."

There's a scary twinkle in Shelly's eyes when she smirks. "Is that so?"

I immediately wish I hadn't said anything. I've made a grave, rookie mistake opening that floodgate. Especially after all but forcing Millie to sit on my lap for the last half of the book club meeting.

"Don't make me dip on our conversation, Shelly."

Her nails press into my arm when she tugs on me, keeping me in place. She narrows her eyes, scrolling them over every inch of my face.

"Are you serious about her?" she asks lowly, a fierce streak of protectiveness there.

"It's hard to be serious about a woman who's bound to leave."

"Cut the shit with me. You've got feelings for her, right?"

I stiffen with discomfort. With a quick check for Millie, I force an answer up my throat when I don't see her close enough to hear.

"Yeah, I do."

"Give her a reason not to leave, then. Encourage her to stay."

"You're kidding me, right? Be serious, Shelly. If you want

her to stay, then ask her yourself." I clench my jaw in response to the shitty attitude I'm giving her. Forcing myself to soften as much as I can, I add, "I'm not going to force her to do anything."

"I wouldn't ever force someone to stay somewhere they don't want to be, Shade. I've just grown to care for her and would hate to see her go back to the life she felt the need to run from in the first place."

"I'd hate it more than you would. That doesn't mean she'd be happy staying here forever either. This place is small. It's got nothing to offer her."

And there it is. The fear that's been cramping my stomach for weeks.

If she chose to stay, this place might not keep her happy forever.

Shelly loosens her hold on my arm, patting it softly again. "It's worth a conversation. You'll regret it if you don't and run out of time instead."

The hair on my arms lifts when I hear Millie's laugh. I turn away from Shelly instantly, needing to see for myself why she's laughing like that. Lacey appears first, her arm linked through Millie's as they sway down the hallway to a song playing from one of their phones.

Millie points at me, beaming so wide it's got to hurt. "Dance with me!"

Before I answer, I steal a look at the four empty wine bottles on the countertop, confirming my suspicions. "I'm not a dancer, princess."

"Not even for me?" Her lip juts out, and I curse.

Lacey lets go of her, skipping to Shelly and leaving me my opening. I swallow, accepting that I'll never be the barking kind of guy, but if she wants dancing, I can figure it out.

I cross the room to her, keeping her pinned under the weight of my gaze. She doesn't stop smiling, not even slightly. And when I take her into my arms and follow her lead, I think it even grows.

35

Millie

I don't remember the last time I had more than one glass of champagne at a party.

Or rather, even attended one that wasn't thrown by my mother or one of her colleagues. Last night wasn't even truly a party. Not in the true definition. Yet, I had more fun in those few hours than at any real party I've ever been to.

That's why I can't get frustrated when it was a headache that woke me this morning. I assume it's due to the sangria that never stopped flowing and my plateful of Shelly's lemon squares that I don't think helped suck any of the wine up before I fell asleep.

I expect there to be sun already coming through my sheer curtains, but as I pop one eye open, I'm met with darkness instead. Stretching my legs, I point my toes and turn my head. The man beside me is absolutely never usually in my bed, which means only one thing . . .

Holding my breath, I turn fully onto my side and slide my hand beneath my pillow. Shade doesn't stir at all when I move. He continues to sleep, snoring so softly it could pass as heavy breathing. The same blanket I've got tucked beneath my armpits is heavy, black, and draped around his waist. The bare expanse of his chest is right there beside me, practically begging me to stare at it.

I'm generous with myself this morning and let my eyes wander, soaking up the sight of him so at peace and unaware of how much I'm enjoying the view. There's no chance for him to get a big head about my attention like this. I can just enjoy right now.

My fingers twitch beneath my pillow and at my hip as I refuse myself a quick touch, not wanting to risk waking him yet. Instead, I push myself up on my elbow and look down at where his chest rises and falls, the pace peaceful. The small black loop is still through his nipple, and it's a bit over-whelming to try and spend an appropriate amount of time on each tattoo around it. Looking too quickly feels like a disser-vice to the detail in the designs.

Or that's what I think before I can no longer avoid the one still healing over his sternum. I inhale through my nose and lean closer, focused on the red that's visible even in the dark and the look of the raised skin.

It's so bad.

The crown on my wrist isn't even itchy anymore. I don't feel it at all usually, but that? He's got to feel pain where I've ruined his skin.

I finished the entire design on his lap after we . . . had sex, despite how challenging that was for me, both emotionally and physically. He refused to let me separate us, so I stayed on his lap for another hour, still impaled on the erection that wouldn't soften, tattooing him. I'd love to say my work got better as the minutes ticked by, but I'm pretty sure it got worse. At one point, I thought he was going to have to take over for me out of pure disappointment.

But he didn't. He never said one negative thing about what I was doing. I was waiting for him to snap at me because I pressed too hard with the paper towel or strayed from the stencil despite how hard I tried to focus, even when I knew deep down he wouldn't. This man did the exact opposite. He just stroked my back and told me about the first time he let Bryce tattoo him, letting me learn without being smothered.

I've held myself back from asking him to let me try again on the fake skin I saw in the back room instead. It wasn't until I sat back just far enough to look at his tattoo completely finished that I stopped caring about how terrible it looked. Pride and excitement swelled too high inside of me.

Now, though? Staring at the painful-looking tattoo, I'm wishing I'd stopped and let him take over after all.

"Might as well just shove me, princess. I could feel you staring at me in my sleep."

I hesitate to speak, unsure of what to say. Especially when he turns his head and looks right at me, all tired eyes and a drowsy smirk that might be sexier than his dirty one.

"What are you thinking about so hard?" he rasps, his voice thick with sleep.

"Does your tattoo hurt?"

He blinks three times, reaching up to run fingers through his messy hair. The bunching of his arm muscles as he does so is one of the filthiest things I've ever seen.

"Which one?"

"Your new one."

He looks down at his chest. "No. It's normal for it to look like that."

"Are you lying?"

"No, Millie. I'm not lying," he drawls, dropping his arm as he rolls toward me. It curls around my waist over the heavy blanket. "Is that why you look so worried?"

"Why else would I be worried?"

"Other than the fact you're in my bed this morning?"

I flip onto my back, staring wide-eyed at the ceiling. "Oh! I didn't even think—"

"We didn't," he soothes, voice still rough. "I wouldn't have done that. You were drunk."

"I know. I just don't really know how *I* am after more than one drink," I admit, relaxing into the mattress.

Shade tightens his hold on me, letting his heavy arm drape across my stomach. "You're the same you always are around me. Bright and bubbly."

"Okay, cocky," I say with a snort.

"Am I wrong?"

The question is a heavier hitter than I think either of us anticipated, because no, he isn't wrong.

"Did I crawl into your bed on my own, or did you bring me here?" I ask, trying to get even.

He rubs my stomach over the blanket. "Is there a right answer to that question?"

"Yep."

"You know damn well you didn't crawl into my bed, Millie."

I smile, trying to trap it down but failing. "So, you brought me here all on your own."

"I needed to make sure you didn't choke on throw up in your sleep," he drawls, studying my expression as it twists.

"Right. I'm sure that was the entire reason."

Leaning up, he hovers over me slightly, raising his hand to run his knuckles along my jaw. "Do you need another one?"

"I'd like one," I admit, forcing my confidence not to falter.

"And if I told you that it was because I just wanted to have you here? In my bed next to me when I woke up?"

I release a breath and tilt my chin, bringing our mouths so, so close. "Well, then I would tell you to kiss me so it was a morning to remember."

He doesn't hesitate to do just that. The first press of our mouths is soft, a warm caress that grows hotter, firmer. I grab his wrist, holding it tightly as if I'm scared he'll let me go already. The thought alone has my heart clunking against my rib cage.

In one smooth motion, he rolls over my body, using one

arm to keep himself from crushing me beneath his weight. I let him separate our lips long enough to chuckle, shifting his hold from my jaw to my waist, squeezing me there.

Opening my eyes, I watch him glance down my body to where the blanket has been pulled down, revealing my lack of usual pyjamas. I almost laugh when I realize what I'm wearing.

"I suppose dressing me in your clothes was also your idea?"

His smirk is straight sin. "Fucking right it was."

"And here I thought you secretly loved my silk sets."

"You're going to get more than you bargained for this morning if you keep teasing me."

I laugh loudly, freely. "What time is it?"

"Early enough we don't need to go downstairs yet," he nearly growls against my mouth. "Let me keep you here for a bit longer."

I splay a hand on his bare back and run it up the taut muscles along his spine. "You're more possessive than I expected you to be."

"Not possessive," he denies with a nip at my lip. Then, his tongue glides across the wounded skin. "Just pathetically clingy."

"That's no better."

Lowering his hips, he grinds down on me, and I immediately lose the ability to tease him further. The blankets are pooled beneath him, keeping us from getting closer. He doesn't seem to mind, though. His forehead presses to mine, his long lashes lowering as he kisses me again.

I part my lips against his, letting his tongue slip between them. He rolls his lower body again, dragging a moan up from the bottom of my chest. I wiggle beneath the blankets, wanting them off but remaining pinned in place.

He grins into the kiss, letting me know that he knows exactly what I'm thinking and still refuses to give it to me. It's as aggravating as it is enticing. With Shade, I want to prove myself as badly as I want to please him, and that's a heady combination.

Suddenly, I'm back in the studio, sitting on his lap as he bucks up into me, leaving an imprint deep inside that I'm not sure will ever go away. I fall into his kiss, sinking into the sheets and feeling every flex of his muscles and shift of his hips like it could be the last time. My stomach burns with dread as I realize that it's a real possibility.

"Millie," he rasps, pulling back just enough to stare down at me. "Where did you go?"

The nightstand starts to rattle as a phone buzzes. I try to look whose it is when he pinches my chin and tugs it forward, not allowing me to take my eyes off him.

"Answer me."

I nip at my cheek once. "Would you let me tattoo you again?"

The question comes out of nowhere. It's not at all what I'm thinking, but I guess it works well enough to distract him from trying to dig into my mind any further.

"Any day, princess. Wanted to talk to you about that, actually. I just didn't expect to do it right now."

My pulse quickens. "Really?"

"If I offered you an apprenticeship, would you accept?"

"Like, with you?" I ask, almost stumbling over the words.

His laugh is rough against my lips. "Yeah, with me."

"At the studio?"

"Millie," he says tightly, like he's taking everything in him to keep it together. "Yes, here. At Into The Shade, with me, *Shade*. Unless you'd prefer Bryce. But in that case, I would absolutely get possessive."

The buzzing continues on the nightstand, stopping only briefly before starting up again. I watch as Shade's eyes tighten at the corners, his mouth curling into a scowl.

"You should answer that," I ramble.

He looks at me for a moment longer, unspoken words clear in the intensity of that stare, before he rolls over to grab the phone. His voice is strangled when he answers the call.

"What?"

The voice coming through the speaker sounds like Bryce, but I can't make out the words she's saying. From Shade's bristling posture, it isn't anything good.

"Who?" he snaps, already getting out of bed. "Tell them to wait outside. They're not allowed through the door."

Without looking back at me, he goes to the dresser across the room and starts opening drawers and pulling clothes out. A pair of black jeans goes on first, then a tank top cut high on his shoulders. He doesn't reach for socks, and I sit up on the bed when he freezes, casting me a tense look.

"Yeah, I'm coming down now."

His phone flies toward the bed the moment he hangs up, and I hold my breath, waiting for him to speak. There's a raw sensation in my gut, like a premonition or something.

"Stay here," he commands, leaving little room for argument.

I make some anyway. "Why? What's wrong?"

"Just a couple of guys downstairs. I don't want Bryce dealing with them on her own."

"I'll come too, then."

I shove the blankets off my thighs and swing them off—

"No, you're staying up here. Get dressed, and I'll come get you after they're gone."

Brow lifting, I pause with my feet on the floor. "Are these guys dangerous or something?"

"No," he grunts, and I believe him. "I just want you to stay up here."

Something twists in my stomach, intensifying the lingering burn. There's a desperation in his voice when he speaks this time that forces me to obey him. At least for right now.

"Please."

I palm my knees, finding them damp with sweat. "Fine."

"Thank you," he blows out on a heavy exhale. "I'll be fast."

With a tip of my chin toward the door, I stay glued to the bed. He tenses his jaw for half a second before coming over to me and cupping my nape. My head gets guided back at the same time he kisses me, not holding back in the slightest. I fill my hands with his shirt and pull him close, hating this sick feeling that's rolling through me like some sort of sign.

His fingers press harder into my neck, keeping me held firmly against him before he releases me, swallowing audibly. When he lets go and steps back, I frown despite my better judgment, letting him see how badly I wish he'd just stay and continue our soft morning.

"Come down when you usually would. Don't rush," he mutters, keeping our eyes tangled as he walks backward to the door.

I keep my voice even as I lie, "Alright."

If he doesn't buy the lie, he doesn't show it. In a blink, he's disappearing into the hallway, leaving me alone, my muscles tightening as I prepare to follow after him. It's almost comical to think that for even one minute, he'd believe that *I'm* going to sit and wait for him to take care of this without me.

Especially when I would be a complete fool not to already have an idea of what I'm going to find when I get downstairs. And shit, I'm not ready for it. Not by a long shot.

36

Shade

I have always had an unnatural ability to keep my cool.

Egg my place? I'm going to turn away from the mess and count to twenty before cleaning it up. Insult my family? We're pushing the bounds of my patience, but I can give someone another chance to correct themselves before I get really pissed off.

Out of everything I could have expected to trigger me to the point of experiencing a hot flash and a tinted red gaze, seeing Millie's father standing on the sidewalk outside of the studio wasn't it.

Rage like I've never known transforms me into a version of myself that I've never seen before.

"They're not leaving," Bryce says, following after me as I move through the studio.

"They will."

"Is that Millie's—"

I cut her off, my chest heaving like I'm a fucking bull ready to buck my rider off. "If I had to guess, yeah."

I'd bet everything I own on nobody having ever driven through this town in a Rolls-Royce before right this moment. Someone sane wouldn't risk bringing it here and having it stolen unless they didn't plan on staying long enough for that to happen. And the old prick standing against the passenger door, wearing a perfectly tailored suit with cufflinks that shimmer in the sun? He doesn't appear to be staying longer than he thinks it'll take to get what he came here for.

My throat tightens to the point of pain. I clench my fists and stare at him through the window, trying desperately to get myself together enough that I can go outside and speak with him without winding up in jail.

"There's someone else here with him too. He went into Maggie's."

"You're fucking kidding me," I say bitterly, scrubbing a hand down my face.

"Yeah, that's what I thought too. Does Millie know? I can go upstairs and tell her."

I shake my head, dropping my hand. "Don't bother."

"You want her to come down?" Bryce asks slowly, confused.

"She was beside me when you called."

A pause as my best friend soaks that in. When she starts blinking, I nearly laugh.

"Beside you . . . as in . . . *beside* you?"

"She was in my goddamn bed, Bryce. And she's too stubborn to stay upstairs for long, so I need to go out and talk to this guy before—"

I cut myself off, unable to admit it out loud.

"Millie isn't going to go home with those fuckers," she declares, more confident than I am.

"I'm going outside. If you see me close to doing something that's going to get me hauled away in a cop car, please intervene."

"How about you just don't do anything stupid? Men like that don't play fair, Shade. Trust me."

The warning falls on deaf ears once I turn for the door. I keep my spine straight as I shove it open and join the man on the sidewalk, ignoring the bitter chill of the morning on my bare arms.

Who I assume to be Millie's father regards me with a blank, emotionless expression that I'm sure as shit not going to fall for. It's all a façade. I know for a fact he's planning at least ten different ways to make me disappear before I so much as open my mouth.

A man like that doesn't look at me and see a worthy opponent. He sees a man so far below him that it's a wonder I don't automatically bow at his feet.

"Are you the owner of this place?" he asks, voice cold and detached.

"That depends on who's asking."

"Sterling Harrington."

I eye the hands tucked into the pockets of his slacks and swallow a laugh when he doesn't pull one free to offer it to me. Making a show of crossing my arms, I arch a brow.

"And why are you here asking, Sterling?"

His eyes are so similar in colour to Millie's, but instead of warm, they're blizzard cold. "You're harbouring someone who doesn't belong to you."

"I don't know who you mean," I state, glancing past him at the door to Maggie's.

Sterling turns long enough to stare at where Millie's car has been parked along the curb for the past couple of weeks. I've moved it a few times so the RCMP don't tag it when they do their routine sweeps through town, but other than that, it hasn't moved.

"Stop playing coy."

I narrow my eyes. "You're going to have to be more specific, then. I expected someone with your business experience to at least know when to be straightforward."

"Alright." He clears his throat. Pulling his right hand from his pocket, he points lazily at Millie's car. "That belongs to my daughter. Now, unless she spent the night at the fire station or the shop down the street, I can only expect that she's somewhere in the business behind you. I would like if you went inside and got her for me."

I hum lowly, pretending to think it over before grinding out a single word. "No."

"No?"

"That's right. I'd appreciate it if you left now." I take a step back toward the door, wanting to be done with this before it gets a hell of a lot more complicated.

The muscles in Sterling's jaw twitch when he tracks my movements. "If you don't go get her for me, I'll do it myself."

"Like fucking hell you will," I spit, my patience fraying. "You so much as touch the door to my studio and I'll break your hand."

"Threatening me isn't wise."

I do laugh this time. It's dark, vibrating with the anger that I'm trapping down. The thought of letting Millie leave with this guy—of losing her already—is enough to have me so far out of my body I'm not sure how I'll get back inside of it.

"The only threat here is you. She's here for a reason, and it isn't because I've stolen her away from the life she had with you."

Past his shoulder, the diner door swings open.

My nails dig into my forearms when I spot the man stepping outside. I don't need verbal confirmation as to who he is. One look at his blond combover and teal-coloured golf shirt, and I know exactly who the man Sterling brought with him today is. Who he is to Millie.

My patience is so close to snapping, I should go inside before it's too late.

"Mr. Harrington? Why haven't we gone in yet? She wasn't at the diner. Although I can't say I'm surprised. It's rather filthy."

I stay right where I am, fleeing no longer an option.

When Chadwick reaches Sterling, he glances at me,

blinking a few times. The slight curl of his lip as he runs a judgmental gaze down my body doesn't exactly help my desire to decorate the street with his white teeth.

"Are you the owner?" he asks me, much more open with his emotions than Millie's father.

I can hear every vibration of disgust in his voice.

"Is your name really Chadwick, or is that just a joke? A playground tease that just stuck?" I ask with a fake sense of calm.

He glares at me then, brown eyes deepening. "Excuse me?"

"Don't fall into his games, Chadwick. Millicent is inside, and we need to get her," Sterling chastises.

"Millicent?" I ask, stumbling slightly.

Her father simply stares at me in genuine shock. "Did you think Millie was her full name?"

"It is to me."

He scoffs under his breath, and then his features smooth out. His attention drifts behind me to the window. My entire body tenses when I twist as much as I can manage and find Millie at the door. She pushes it open quickly, rushing outside before coming to a sudden stop.

"Millicent," her father snaps, his cool expression twisting into annoyance in the blink of an eye. "How could you do this? Are you living here?"

The lash of his words hits the mark. In one moment, all of the work she's put into herself these last few months crumbles. I lurch toward her, making myself a shield between her and the two men who had her running here in the first place. Softly, I grasp her shoulders and rub my palms down her arms.

She stares at me, her eyes wide and so unbelievably sad. Her hands rise between us before settling against my chest.

"Don't let him do this to you," I murmur, keeping the words soft, just for her. "He doesn't have a say anymore."

"Millie—who is this man?"

Chadwick's voice bounces off my back, and I exhale through my nose. Millie taps my chest over the fresh tattoo she gave me before dropping her hands. The smile she gives me isn't real. It's the same plastic one she wears when she feels like she can't be herself. The sight of it twists my stomach.

She moves from my hold, and I let her go, refusing to trap her like everyone else has done.

"How are you here?" she asks the men.

Her father looks at her then. *Really* looks, as if he's seeing her for the first time. She may have dressed in her usual armour—a pink dress with her high heels—but that's the only thing about her that's stayed the same all these weeks.

There's a natural glow to her cheeks now, and her hair is longer, the ends split slightly. She's lost the tights she used to make herself wear beneath her skirts and dresses, and only a blind man would miss the crown on her wrist as she lifts her hand and tucks her hair behind her ear.

All of these small changes that I've noticed . . . ones I know Chadwick never would have.

My hands hang at my sides as I watch her stand in front of both of these men, knowing I can't choose anything for her. As sour as it tastes to hold my refusals in, I refuse to be another person in Millie's life who forces her to do something or uses a bribe like an apprenticeship to keep her.

If she wants to stay, she'll decide that on her own.

"Your car," her father says, tearing his gaze from her tattoo. "It has a tag for safety reasons. We simply followed it to this . . . *town*."

I trap a growl in my throat, two seconds away from going to tear the car apart until I've found the tag they've put inside of it.

"I should have guessed that," Millie says, sounding completely unsurprised by that.

"Yes, you should have. But it doesn't matter. You had more

than enough time to throw your little tantrum. It's time to go back home. We can still salvage what happened at the wedding once we get you home. A full ceremony isn't even necessary anymore. You can get married at the house if you're too scared to stand in front of a crowd again. As long as there are photos to share, it won't matter."

Chadwick wastes no time joining in. "Put this back on, Millie. I can't believe you didn't bring it with you in the first place."

The sparkle of an engagement ring shakes the ground beneath my feet. It's a showpiece, the diamond so big it has to hurt to wear for all hours of the day. I can't comprehend how much it must have cost.

"Your mother has been going out of her mind while you've been out here, doing God knows what with God knows who and risking the family name. We don't have more time to stand here talking about this. The plane leaves soon. We need to get on the road," her father demands, already moving toward the car. "*Come.* You're finished here."

"I haven't even packed my things," she croaks, standing frozen.

Unable to stop myself, I inch toward her, needing to help her. *Soothe her.*

"What things? You don't need to take whatever you've collected from this place. Leave it all," Chadwick says, stretching his hand out for her to take.

I can feel the panic ringing inside of her. The tremble in her hands cuts me from the stomach up to my throat.

Say it, Shade. Tell her to stay with you.

She looks up at me now, seeking the same words I'm repeating in my mind. The hope shining there is cruel. It's a fucking joke from the universe. A punishment for the number of times I've told it to kiss my ass.

We stand like this for what feels like ever, her begging me with her eyes to tell her to stay, while I grow angrier with myself for my inability to do it. But *fuck*, can't she choose to stay on her own?

After all this time watching her grow more confident in herself and find the person that had been suppressed her entire life, I want her to look at Sterling and tell him to go back without her. That she's happy here and thinks she could stay that way forever.

But she doesn't.

Her bottom lip quivers when she looks away from me and goes to her father. It's confirmation of the biggest fear I had when it came to this woman.

Oak Point was supposed to be a place for her to stay just long enough to catch her breath. It was never supposed to be her home. Not even if I wanted it to be.

37

Shade

I suck in a sharp breath but keep walking, needing out of this fucking studio before I destroy it. She doesn't let me go without pushing again, this time spitting fire under her breath.

"You're a fucking idiot."

"Tell me what I should have done instead!" I snap, the words punching out of me.

When I whirl around, my best friend is looking at me as if she doesn't even know who the hell I am. It stings, but I hardly feel it. I'm too torn up already.

"You should have made her stay! Or told her that you wanted her to stay here with you. Instead, you watched her leave while she believed you didn't care!" she shouts, eyes wild.

"So I could have just been another person who made decisions for her? It wouldn't have been that easy."

"Gah!" She brings her hands to her hair, nearly ripping at it. "You're dumber than you look, Shade. I thought I was bad, but you take the cake."

I scowl, scratching roughly at my unshaven jaw. "Insulting me won't bring her back."

"No, but maybe it will encourage you to go do it yourself.

Because honestly? I'm disappointed in you for rolling over like this."

"Don't, Bryce."

"Don't what? Slap you with the truth? Jesus, you've fallen for that girl, and instead of telling her that, you let her leave!" she yells, exasperated.

I step forward, my chest heaving. "She needs to make her own decisions. If I told her that I loved her, she could have stayed because of that and not because it's what she truly wanted. Millie has lived for other people her entire life, Bryce. I want her to choose herself again."

Bryce pauses, her throat pulling taut with a swallow. I lift my brows, waiting for her to speak.

"Did you just hear yourself?" she asks cautiously.

It hits me then. I let my chest absorb the impact of those words. It settles, feeling right in a way I couldn't have ever expected. A chuckle slips from me, one heavy with disbelief and lingering frustration. Shoving a hand through my hair, I meet Bryce's fiery stare.

"Tell me what that changes because I still need her to be the person I know she can be and choose what's best for her," I declare, stubborn to the core.

Inch by inch, Bryce's ice melts. "She deserves to know and have all of her options laid in front of her before she chooses, Shade. I'd bet the only reason she went with her dad was because she didn't know staying here and being with you was an option."

"How wouldn't she have known that? Would telling her I loved her have made that much of a difference? I've already moved her into my place, and fuck—I offered to apprentice her this morning."

"Those are things any of us would have given her, Shade. They don't necessarily declare love."

"Fuck."

"You can't let her stay away. She's . . . it's not right to let her go without trying," Bryce mutters, staring me dead in the eyes. "And that guy with the god-awful ring? He's not her future. Don't let him be."

"Shelly's going to tie me up and set me out on the lake in a canoe when she finds out Millie's gone."

"Maybe. But only if you stay and let her find out."

"What are suggesting I do, then, Ice?"

Bryce lifts her chin, smirking. "First, we get your head out of your ass and back where it belongs, and then we come up with a plan."

MY MOTHER HAS HARDLY LET me out of her sight since I got back home yesterday.

She's taken my bedroom door off its hinges and has Chadwick staying in the room across the hall. Despite the fact that he owns his own home, he's been unofficially moved into mine. I shouldn't have expected much else, considering the way I left things.

The wedding has been the topic of discussion since the moment I sat on the private plane. First, it was the fallout I caused that took weeks for my father to resolve, then the clear guilting of how my actions forced the legal team to rework all of the paperwork that was set to be signed after the ceremony that day. They're all things I don't care about, but I sat and listened anyway, too lost in my own thoughts to begin to think of what I should say in defense of my actions.

There's no real excuse, though. Not one that neither my

parents nor Chadwick would consider relevant in this situation.

I stare at my ceiling, lying in a coffin disguised as a bed. The clock showed that it was past ten in the morning the last time I checked. My freedom is a mirage, but at least I'm alone right now.

Beneath my pillow, I hold my phone, keeping it hidden. The few texts I've received since leaving Oak Point yesterday have come from Lacey, and it's clear she doesn't know I'm gone yet. Shelly doesn't text, really. I've debated sending one to her anyway so she hears it from me and not someone else in town.

I haven't, though.

My chest feels tight, pained. The sharp pain in my belly with every memory of Oak Point brings tears to my eyes that I let fall, unable to help myself. Being here is wrong. This house feels like a tomb instead of a home now that I've felt the warmth of a real one.

He hasn't texted or called.

I keep holding out hope that he will. That Shade will be the one to reach out and tell me to come back. It's unfair to expect that of him, though. He doesn't owe me a life with him, even if I'm sure that's what I want.

All he had to do was tell me to stay. Or showed me that it's what he wanted before I got into that car. I know we didn't agree to have a future together, but I thought . . . or hoped, that he felt the same way I did. That he'd fallen in love with me back, because shit, do I ever love him.

From his flirty grins to his unwavering support and blunt personality, I've grown to appreciate everything about him. The way he isn't afraid to try something new and has never judged me for a single thing, past or present. He's offered me the type of kindness that doesn't come naturally to some. It's the purest form of it that never fails to bring me out of my shell and give me the courage to follow what I want.

There's more that I haven't even begun to find yet, but I want to. We didn't have enough time together, yet the time we did have was more than enough for me to realize that I could be happy there, with him.

But I couldn't risk my heart so soon after healing it. Not when he didn't tell me how he felt.

"Why are you still in bed? Get up! Chadwick has been waiting for hours alone."

Mom stalks through my bedroom and rips my curtains open, forcing the sun to flood through. I blink my tears away and stay lying beneath the blankets, unmoving.

"Millicent, this isn't a joke."

"I don't hear myself laughing."

A pause. The air grows thick with tension. "Watch your attitude."

"Do you remember how many birthdays I've had?"

"Is that another one of your jokes?" she bites.

I roll my head along my pillow to stare at her. "Twenty-six, Mom. I've had twenty-six birthdays. That officially makes me no longer a child to be bossed around."

The rage that rips through her should be studied. I'm not sure anyone is supposed to get *that* red.

"Millicent," she snaps, eyes so narrowed I can hardly see the brown colour of them. "What happened to you?"

"I grew a backbone."

"No, you learned how to disrespect your mother." She grips the bottom of my duvet and rips it clean off the bed. I grind my teeth, only a thin sheet covering me now. "Get. Up. You're going to get in the shower and wash away that town and the way it clings to you like a bad smell."

Pulling my legs up, I sit against the headboard and shake my head. "I don't feel up to being flaunted around the property today."

"Millicent," she hisses.

"*Millie.* I prefer Millie."

Without another word, she spins on heeled feet and struts out of my room, not bothering to acknowledge my statement at all.

I cross my legs and exhale, a few of the chains that were wrapped back around me slipping free. The lack of bedroom door doesn't allow me any privacy, so I pull the sheet up to my chin and stare into the hall. When a set of low, muffled voices sounds from where my mother disappeared to, I clutch the sheet tighter, knowing who's going to appear next.

And like a bad dream, Chadwick appears.

He frowns at me from the doorway, his eyes betraying how unimpressed he is with all of this.

"It's past eleven," he states.

"I wasn't aware there was a wake-up call scheduled."

His jaw twitches. "Your mother mentioned you being upset about leaving that town."

"She did? How'd she figure that out when she never asked?"

It's like I can't help myself. The serrated edge of my words continues to strike before I even realize it. This tiny bit of freedom is all I have in this place, and now that I've tasted it, I can't go back to how I used to be. Not when everything around me is all wrong.

"What happened there, Millie? Why are you behaving like this?"

I glance out the window, taking in the dark clouds in the gloomy sky that I know are heavy with snow. It's warmer here than Oak Point, even being up on a mountain.

"What am I behaving like, Chadwick? Other than someone who finally doesn't feel a loyalty to this family the way I convinced myself I needed to for the last two decades?" I ask bluntly.

"Family is all any of us have."

"You're wrong. I had a real family back where I was."

"They didn't even know you. Not the real you. Even now,

you don't look like yourself. You're all wrong," he says with a huff.

I blow out a silent laugh. "Wow, that's exactly what you should be saying to the woman you're supposed to be marrying. Maybe that's why you're not."

"What does that mean?" His words are sharper now.

"We're not getting married, Chadwick."

Shoving the sheet away, I slide off the bed. My hair is a mess, all tangled and dry as I pull it up and grab a clip from my nightstand, holding it out of my face. The silk on my body feels wrong, scratchy as I cross the room to my closet.

I look over the endless racks of clothes, from dresses to matching sets and jackets, and realize there isn't a single thing that I want to wear. Months ago, I would spend hours in here trying everything on and doing spins in the mirror, but things have changed. My love for nice clothes and shoes hasn't swayed, but where I've gotten them has. The expectations that line the insides of each piece weigh them down to the point that I'd rather wear a garbage bag and wool socks instead.

"We are getting married. It's already been decided," Chadwick argues, following me into the closet.

Opting for a skirt short enough to scar my mother and a matching blouse, I fill my arms and turn to him. "Have you ever thought about how unfair it is that our parents get to decide who we spend the rest of our lives with? Do you really not care about that?"

"I care about my future, and if my future at my father's company relies on me marrying someone chosen, then I'll do it. It's not about me, Millie. It's not about you either. This is bigger than us."

"That's a pathetic excuse for you being a spineless pussy, Chadwick."

I toss my clothes onto a nearby shelf and then reach for the biggest suitcase I have in the corner of the closet. Shoving it onto the floor, I crouch to unzip it.

"That hick town turned you into a cunt."

My eyes fly up to where Chadwick stands over me, his hands clenched at his sides. "Maybe it did. Or maybe I always was deep down beneath the quiet woman I was always taught I had to be."

"You're going to ruin everything for our families," he warns.

"I wish I cared."

"Millie, this isn't a joke. You need to think about the consequences here. If you fight this any harder, you'll be thrown out. The Harrington name will be stripped away and given to someone else if that's what they decide to do."

Ripping clothes off the racks, I drop them into the suitcase. My stomach clenches at the threat of what it really could mean to leave for good this time. To not have this place to fall back on in case everything goes to shit. There's so much fear inside of me, but I don't allow myself to change my mind. If Shade doesn't feel the same way I do, then we'll have to make it work because I'm going back home, and I'm not leaving again.

"If my choices are to stay here and live a life like this, then I'll take my chances somewhere else. The Harrington name is nothing more than a brand only recognized by those of high enough status to know who we are. It doesn't mean anything in the real world. I've done just fine without the money and influence that name has, Chadwick. There's far more to life than what you've seen in the bubble everyone here seems to be afraid to pop."

I finish with the clothes and move on to shoes. Each pair has its own shelf lit by white lights, and as I stare at the wall, I laugh. I almost can't believe how much money is in this room or how little I cared about that before.

Pair by pair, I drop them into the other side of my suitcase, focusing on the ones with the red bottoms or jewels that I know were imported specially for me. They fall to the suitcase with loud clunks.

"That guy has ruined you," Chadwick sneers, not valuing a damn thing I've said.

"No, he hasn't. He helped me find the person this place tried to make disappear."

Without another look at him, I take my chosen outfit and exit the closet. I can feel him following me, hovering like maybe his breath on my neck will make me give in.

"If I speak with your mother right now, she'll come in here in a far worse mood than she was earlier," he warns.

"Let her. It won't change anything. Now, get the fuck out so I can get dressed."

He doesn't have time to argue before I take a single step into my ensuite and slam the door in his face.

38

Shade

"Shit," I mutter when I pull up outside the towering castle of a house.

It's closer to a mansion than anything else, but I'm still not sure if this is actually where Millie lives or if this is a resort. Surely, she didn't grow up in a resort, but I can't comprehend living somewhere like this.

It's three stories high with a wide, curling driveway in front and dual balconies attached to both sides. The exterior is a dark stone with a white-and-black double-sided door, because obviously, one wasn't enough. The longer I look at the place, the more I hate it. This type of flashy wealth has never appealed to me. When someone bleeds money like this, they always make a show of making sure everyone who stumbles upon them knows it.

I don't need to look inside the separate eight-car garage to the left of the main house to know it's crammed full of luxury cars that never get driven and every toy imaginable. Side-by-sides, dirt bikes, maybe even a boat with a giant ski tower on it. They'll never get dirty or feel the rock of a wave, but when it comes to giving a house tour, they sure will draw a few surprised approvals.

Shelly knew exactly where she was sending me when I asked for the address. When Millie filled out all of the paperwork to stay at the campground, she didn't know she was giving Shelly permission to Google stalk her house. The nosey woman probably looked that first night and kept her opinions on the place to herself this entire time.

Pulling up beside the giant water fountain in the middle of the driveway, I try to ignore my discomfort. It doesn't matter what these people say to me or about me. I'm here for Millie, and I'm not leaving without her.

There must be people trapped in the goddamn shrubs because I can feel myself being watched the moment I step out of the car. I can't spot anyone lingering out here, but they're around somewhere. It's enough to have my skin crawling.

I don't bother locking my car before heading for the front door. Nobody here is going to try to steal it. The closest they'd get is having it towed so it didn't sit like a shit stain on their driveway for too long. Fuck, I don't know how Millie lived here for so long. I've been here for three minutes and can already feel the poison in the air start to affect me.

Skipping both of the stone steps, I knock on the door and ring the doorbell twice. It's not snowing here the way it was the first half of my drive, but the ski hill I had to pass on my way up here was still busy, thick with it. The fake kind of snow that sticks beneath your boots and gets as slick as ice after a wet freeze.

The door opens after a minute. I hold myself steady when a woman appears in front of me, somehow glaring down her nose at me despite being far shorter. Dark hair is swept tightly behind her head as she taps her hip impatiently.

"Who are you?"

Jesus, she reminds me of Bryce's mother. From the smug expressions to their hoity-toity voices, I have to do a double take to make sure this isn't actually her. The solidifying difference is that not even Bryce's mother could afford earrings with diamonds that big. They damn near look painful as her lobes droop.

I skip her question entirely, my gut telling me she already knows. "I'm here to see Millie."

"Oh, I bet you are," she snips, giving me a brutal up-and-down look. Her disgust seems to triple by the time she's done. "You can leave now."

"Nah, not yet. Let me see her."

"Do I need to call my husband?"

I chuckle, flattening a hand to the door when she tries to shut it in my face. "Yeah, you go do that."

"This is breaking and entering!"

"Call it in and I'll report you for kidnapping."

Her gasp is dramatic as hell, nude-painted lips spreading wide. "That's outrageous. You don't have the nerve."

"Try me," I dare, voice low.

She doesn't hesitate to jump out of my way when I push past her and enter the house. It's worse inside than outside, all high ceilings and chandeliers that glimmer from the exuberant number of crystals on them. I fight a cringe and continue walking, not stopping until I'm at the bottom of a rounded staircase that looks up onto a balcony.

"Millie!" I shout, caging my mouth with my hands. "Millie!"

I can hear high heels clipping on the floor behind me. "You need to leave."

"Not without your daughter."

Her mother grabs my wrist and tries to pull me. "Now!"

One tug and she's releasing me, leaving red marks from her nails. I step away from her and go to the stairs, glancing back for half a second.

"Is she upstairs?"

Her lips clamp shut, eyes glowing with silent rage. It's the only answer I need.

I take the stairs two at a time, shouting when I get halfway up. "Millie, it's me!"

There's a loud clang from behind me as I pick up my pace and tear down the hall. Passing door after door, I move quickly, knowing it's only a matter of time before her father pops out like a fucking ghoul and tries to push me back down the stairs.

We've been apart for two goddamn days, and if I don't get to her soon, I'm going to—

It's got to be a joke from the universe when the fucker she was supposed to marry butts into me instead of her. The sight of him in her house is bad enough, but throw in the curl of his lip when he notices who it is he just ran into and I'm on a hair trigger.

"Get out of my way," I grit out.

Chadwick pushes his gelled hair back and tries to stand off against me. "You're not welcome in the Harringtons' home."

"Are you a long-lost brother or something? Why the fuck are you speaking on their behalf?"

"You're the reason she's not the same," he spits, smashing a hand to my chest. "You changed her, and now everything has gone to shit."

Alarm blasts through me. "What do you mean?"

"You and those drawings all over your skin! She was perfect. A sweet, quiet girl meant to be my wife. Now, she won't keep her mouth shut and let things be the way they were supposed to!"

"You need to shut yours before you say anything worse than what you already have," I warn softly, meeting his glare with one far worse.

Chadwick doesn't stop while he's even marginally ahead. He pushes me harder, further, until I'm positive I'm going to smash his face into a thousand unsalvageable pieces.

"She's worthless to this family now that you've soiled her.

If she chooses you again, she'll be nothing worse than a degenerate like you."

I don't think. In a blink, I have my arm pulled back and fist raised. It's not me who punches him, though.

I'm shoved to the side a mere second before a much smaller fist is flying through the air and smashing into his nose. He goes stumbling backward, shock and pain registering in his eyes before he falls onto his ass.

"Shit!"

A familiar curse snaps me into action. Whipping my head to the side, I find Millie clutching her hand, bent over at the waist. My body focuses on her as I turn away from the whimpering, bleeding idiot on the floor and scoop her into my arms.

My chest loosens while my heart ramps up, filling my ears with a quick *thump, thump, thump*. Millie's blue eyes are wide when they meet mine. I laugh without meaning to, letting it fill the gap between us before I'm pressing her to the wall, filling my hands with her thighs.

"Is it broken?" she asks, reminding me of her knuckles.

While a little red, they're fine. "No, princess. His nose must have been made of rubber."

Her smile is bright, so pure it makes my knees shake. I use my body to pin her to the wall and bring a hand up to cup her cheek, stroking the soft, warm skin.

"Two days have never felt so long to me, Millie. Not once in my entire fucking life have I missed anyone the way I missed you."

"What took so long?"

I quirk a brow. "What?"

"I've been ready to go back since the moment I got here. Before that, even. I should have never gotten in that car," she declares, bringing both her hands to rest on my shoulders. "I was waiting for you to tell me to stay so I didn't have to make the decision on my own, when that's what I've always needed to do."

"I should have told you I love you weeks ago when I started realizing I couldn't shake you. The moment you started infiltrating my thoughts at all hours of the day, I should have known something was going on. When I couldn't help but ask you to live with me—to share my place and rearrange my things without giving a shit what you replaced them with. That's never been me, Millie. But then I woke up one day, and suddenly, it was.

"I don't know how you did it so effortlessly, but you've become so engrained in my life that I don't want to spend another day, let alone two, without you beside me again. It doesn't matter if I'm sitting in another one of your book clubs or watching you across the studio as you sketch away at your desk. The only thing I want is to be close to you. All I need you to do is decide that you want that too."

Her eyes shine as she exhales a near-silent breath and nods, her thighs tightening around my waist. "I love you, Shade. Every coloured, cocky, yet patient and talented inch of you. You helped me find who I am, and I don't think I'll ever be able to thank you enough for that. But you also encouraged me to take that person and grow into a version of myself that I didn't think even existed. I've never been as happy as I was with you in Oak Point. Not once, and I know I won't be until I'm back. So, all I need is for you to take us home now."

I drop my chin and claim her lips, kissing her the way I wish I had two days ago. She meets me with equal strength and loops an arm around my nape, pulling me closer. I squeeze her thighs, reacquainting my palms with the lack of tights on her bare legs. My smirk forces our lips apart when I run my hands higher beneath her short skirt, opening my eyes to see her trying not to laugh.

"Jesus," Chadwick grunts.

I roll my forehead across hers and look at him on the floor, still clutching his nose. Millie doesn't let go of me, so I keep her right where she is.

"Problem?" I ask him.

"This is her parents' house," he hisses in disgust.

Millie wiggles then, so I let her down. She's wearing her heels inside the house here when she never did back home. It's such a small thing to notice, but it doesn't slip past me.

"It was you who said the minute I chose Shade, I wouldn't be a Harrington anymore, so why should I care whether it's their house or not?"

My groin tightens at her attitude before I tug her waist and bring her back to my side. "You're not leaving without your things this time, princess."

"Right. My room is down the hall."

She takes my hand and leads me past Chadwick. I keep him beneath my stare until I'm positive he isn't going to follow. And once we're slipping into a pink room, he's the last thing on my mind.

"I've already packed," she reveals, heading for a giant sliding door.

With a tug, it starts to glide on a track, revealing a deep walk-in closet. I blink a few times, trying to get used to the sight of it before she's no longer in sight. Waiting in the middle of the room, I slip my hands into my pockets and stare at the empty spot where she just was.

"I came here with a whole plan," I start, hoping my voice carries to where she is.

"Are you going to tell me what it was or keep it a secret?"

"Come out here first."

Peeking her head out, she tries and fails to hide a grin. "Well?"

"I wasn't exactly anticipating you coming to my rescue and punching someone in the face for me today, so you threw a wrench into everything."

"Well, *sorry* for trying to show off for you."

I roll my eyes, taking a handful of steps in her direction. "Never apologize for that. All it means is that I get to beg for forgiveness without the fear of you rejecting me after all."

"So, technically, I did you two favours," she teases.

"Christ, baby. Stop picking on me for a minute." With a low laugh, I reach into the back pocket of my jeans and pull out what I brought with me.

She freezes, staring at the hot pink leather collar like she doesn't know whether to chuck it out the window or ask me to put it on her. Heat flares in my stomach at her second reaction before I clear my throat.

"Is that supposed to be a gift for me?" she asks, pitch rising.

I almost whip it across the room. "No. Fuck no. It's more of a figurative thing."

"I'm so confused."

"Just remember you're responsible for me doing this, okay? You're not allowed to get the ick and leave my ass after I'm done."

Her brows pinch together as I drop to my knees and throw away my ego for as long as it takes to do this.

Without hesitating any longer, I drop my head back and start barking like a fucking dog. The instant alarm in her eyes is quickly overcome with amusement. Her hand presses to her mouth, hiding her loud, carefree laugh.

I grin as I howl, soaking up the bright sound of her happiness. It feels like it goes on forever until she drops to a crouch in front of me and shuts me up with a kiss. I palm her back, holding her in place before letting her pull back, shaking her head at me.

"I thought you said you'd never bark for a woman."

"I said a lot of shit that isn't true anymore, Millie. Turns out I just hadn't let myself accept that I'd do anything you asked, as long as it meant I got to keep you."

"The collar was a nice touch," she says, taking it from me.

Twisting it around, she pinches the single charm hanging from the leather. "A cowboy hat?"

"I don't have one to put on your head, but I was hoping it would still count."

"You're ridiculous."

"You don't seem to mind too much," I drawl.

"I'll suck it up, I guess."

And then she's kissing me again, making it true.

39

Millie

SHADE LIFTS MY SUITCASE INTO THE TRUNK OF HIS CAR LIKE IT weighs nothing. It slides in quickly, and then he's reaching for the smaller one, treating it carefully after having watched me fill it with expensive skincare and makeup.

I hover close to him, palming the side of the car. "This is your last chance to make me take my own car. You can't decide three hours into the drive that you regret coming here to get me and dump me on the side of the road, you know?"

"I can't?" he asks, straightening and shutting the trunk. "Damn."

"I'm being serious! If I go back with you like this now, we may as well be husband and wife."

"That was easy," he rasps, dipping down to kiss me just once before smacking my ass. "Get in, princess. We're going home now."

I watch him round the hood with the confidence of a man who doesn't have a single doubt in his head, and that's more than enough for me.

"Millicent! If you leave right now, that's it," Mom calls, stomping down the driveway.

While I feel a small wiggle of fear in my stomach, I know it'll go away eventually. Today, I'm deciding what the rest of my life is going to look like. I believe her when she says that this is it. Unlike when I fled from the wedding, this is permanent. I'm making a conscious choice to leave. There's no running this time.

I'm going to do it with my head high, knowing that I'm doing what's best for me.

Shifting, I face her. "I *am* leaving, Mom. We both know this place isn't ever going to make me happy the way I deserve to be, even if you refuse to believe it."

"You're a Harrington," she argues, stopping a few feet away from where I stand.

"That's not a reason for me to stay."

"There are obligations—"

I cut her off, frowning. "You're not getting it. I don't care about the obligations that you've forced on me. They're not my weight to bear, and I'm choosing an alternative. If you love me at all, you'll accept that and let me go without giving me more reason to never consider coming back to visit."

"Being a Harrington isn't a part-time position. You don't get to throw it away and only come back when you feel like it."

"Why does it have to be all or nothing?"

My question is followed by the slow roll of tires on pavement. Then, a door slamming shut. My entire body clenches at the heavy sound of footsteps approaching from behind me.

"What's going on?" Dad doesn't wait for me to reply before speaking again. "Millicent?"

"I'm leaving," I answer firmly before twisting and meeting his hard gaze.

He looks to where Shade's standing back on my side of the car, having moved without me noticing.

"You have the nerve to disrespect me by coming onto my property and taking my daughter?"

It's embarrassing having your father scold your grown boyfriend like this. Almost as embarrassing as this has all been hurtful. Instead of one of my parents caring enough about me to try and understand where I'm coming from, they're too stubborn.

Shade keeps his focus on my father, not backing down even as I try to will the ground to open up beneath me.

"I'm not taking her."

"Like hell you aren't!"

"I'm going on my own, Dad. And you can either accept that or refuse to. Either way, I'm going. It's up to you whether this is the end of our relationship or if we can speak again someday."

That finally gets a reaction out of him that isn't lined with rage. "Someday?"

"I don't think any of us are going to be making amends in the near future."

"You're offering us an ultimatum," he barks, but there's something in the way he does it that gives him away.

The smallest tinge of fear.

"There's no ultimatum. I'm just offering the potential to speak again once things have settled down. Trying right now isn't going to do any good. You refuse to see my side of things," I say.

Mom scoffs coldly. "You're making a mistake. This is the move of a teenager who doesn't know better."

"I do know better, though," I murmur, glancing beside me. Shade's already looking at me, his hands twitching at his sides. "It's where I'm going."

There's no need to wait for more arguments. I watch Shade open the door for me and go to him without looking back. He keeps dark eyes on my face as I move, and I smile, reassuring him that I'm okay.

Once I'm in the car, he shuts the door and stands outside for a moment. His body is facing my parents, and in the side mirror, I catch the loosening of my father's features following the low rumble of his voice. The tight line of Dad's mouth parts as he speaks, the words too quiet for me to hear inside the car.

They don't speak further. At least, not from what I can tell when Shade pulls open the driver's door and slides into the car beside me. I sigh at the relief of having him beside me again and snag his hand before he so much as has the chance to turn the ignition.

He flips it and slides his fingers between mine, clasping them tight. "Ready?"

"Ready."

Snow falls in thick flakes as Shade grips my bag and ushers me into the motel.

My heels slip on the ice, and I flail around, leaning into him for balance. He grunts when my elbow digs into his ribs, stopping the both of us.

"I'm buying you winter boots," he declares.

I scrunch my nose, ready to complain before he's suddenly tossing my bag over his shoulder and crouching beside me. In one smooth motion, he tucks a single arm beneath my legs and sweeps me off the ground. My feet swing in the air, and I curl my toes in my heels to keep them from flying off.

Curling an arm around his neck, I stare up at him and groan dramatically. "Really?"

"Really what?"

"You make it utterly impossible not to want to climb you all the freaking time."

His laugh is rough and deep as he pulls open the lobby door and stalks right past the front desk, already having checked us in. He eyes the sign with a section of room numbers that's hung on the wall for a second before turning right, his hold on me strong.

"I didn't know that was a bad thing," he says.

"Oh, you didn't? God, you know exactly how hot you are and love to use it to your advantage."

"Don't pout, princess."

"I'm not pouting."

In reality, I'm so turned on it's criminal. For the entire six-hour drive here, he kept his hand on my thigh, massaging and stroking it in a way that didn't look overly sexual but still had that effect. I know better than to think for even a second that he didn't plan on that either. Shade knows my body too well, and he knew exactly what that would do to me.

"Yes, you are."

"I'm going to make you sleep in the snow," I threaten weakly.

"Nah, you're not."

I look away from him long enough to check what room we're in when he stops. "You don't know that."

"I know everything about you, Millicent," he purrs, setting me down on my feet.

My jaw slacks slightly as she uses my full name. It's the first time he's ever said it, and while I don't hate the way it sounds coming from him, it's not right. Not me anymore, if it ever was.

He keeps his eyes on me as he uses the room key to unlock the door and then pushes it open. Each backward step he takes draws me to follow him, matching his pace.

"I'm not Millicent when I'm with you," I say, breathless.

Shade's exhale saw out of him as he reaches for me, taking hold of my waist. He pulls me toward him, and the door swings shut, sealing us in the room. My bag falls from his shoulder before he picks me up again, this time so I'm strad-dling his middle and our mouths hover an inch apart.

I don't look where we're going when he moves through the room. The only thing I want to see is him.

"My Millie girl," he says, voice low and tight. "Need you to teach me something for a change."

I fist the hair at the back of his head, craning it back so I can bring my lips to his neck, inhaling as I kiss the warm skin. He shudders against me, the hardness of his body pressing so firmly against me that we may as well be moulding into one person.

"What lesson?" I whisper.

Shade grips my ass, using the new hold to keep me in place when he lowers us to the bed. I pull back just enough to meet his gaze. It's blazing, his need on display for me to see while he presses between my legs, letting me feel it, too.

"I don't want to fuck you tonight."

My throat closes up, my eyes flicking between his in search of a reason why. "Did I do something wrong?"

He dips his head, kissing me softly, his lips barely ghosting across mine. I loosen my hold on his hair, stroking fingers through it instead as I wait for him to speak.

"I've never made love before, Millie. Not once."

My lungs constrict. Words fail me. All I can do is tighten my legs around his waist, keeping him against me in case he tries to run away.

"Me neither," I admit softly.

"No, but you know how. You know what it should feel like and how to get there. I want you to show me so I can give you that."

"Shade . . ." I bring his face closer, kissing him now, making sure it's more than just a brush of lips.

"Don't argue. I trust you. Just tell me what to do."

This side of him is new. It's raw and vulnerable in a way I knew he could be but wasn't expecting to see tonight.

With a gentle touch, I stroke up his side and shift beneath

him. Our middles brush, and my breath disappears at the spark of pleasure that follows.

"We need to move further up the bed," I croak.

He doesn't reply before moving us. With a steady arm beneath my body, he pulls me up until my head sinks into the pillow, hovering above me.

"Clothes." I pinch the fabric of his shirt and let my legs fall to the bed.

Backing up, he reaches for my shoes, slipping them off one by one. I watch him carefully set them on the floor before bringing his hands back to my feet and drawing a firm line up each arch with his thumbs. The sound that escapes me is rough, a mix between a whine and a moan.

"I'll do this more often." It's a promise. "As long as you wear those pretty things, I'll make sure your feet never hurt."

My lips quirk. "You think they're pretty?"

"I think everything you wear is. You could wear a garbage bag and I'd pant after you."

I grow serious fast, my smile slipping as my belly tightens, pressure building between my legs. "I need you to touch somewhere other than my feet right now, Shade."

He groans around a laugh, releasing my feet to cup my knees and push his hands higher. Inch by inch, his rough palms run along my legs, feeling the goosebumps that I know are covering them. I bite my lip, trying not to fill the room with my moans when he reaches my panties.

Instead of pulling them off, he pulls his hands out from beneath my skirt and pinches the sleeves of my blouse. I shiver, arching toward him.

"Where do you want me to touch you?" he asks lowly.

"Everywhere."

His eyes flick up my body, glittering with a thousand dirty promises. "Don't let me choose, or we'll never leave this bed."

"Would that be the worst thing?"

"Millie." He says it like a curse.

I tug at the top button of my blouse, forcing his attention to follow. "Start here."

He doesn't hesitate. His fingers are so long that they make the buttons look tiny as he works them out of their loops with care. And once he's finished, we both watch as my blouse slips to the bed, exposing my stomach and the lace cups of my bra.

I swallow the emotion in my throat and guide his hand to my breast, enamoured with the way his palm covers the entirety of it. The letters on his fingers stake their own claim to my body, marking me as his.

"Gonna take this off," he rasps, squeezing me.

Leaning up, I make room for him to slip both my shirt and bra off. Left in only my skirt and panties, I lie back down as he studies me.

My nipples bead under his attention, and I wiggle against the mattress, feeling damp between my legs. I itch to bring him closer again, until he's hovering above me with his mouth and hands all over me, but I wait.

"I want to be selfish with you. I want to cover you in my work. From here—" He palms my throat, thumb drifting over my pulse before dropping it to grip the inside of my thigh. "—to here. Just so I can look at you and know you're mine. I want everyone who looks at you to know that you're spoken for."

I twitch beneath that possessive touch. "And if I wanted you to do that?"

His hand returns to my throat, holding a bit tighter now as his eyes flare. "Don't placate me. I don't need that to be happy."

Covering his hand with mine, I encourage him to stay there. His throat strains in response, jaw feathering.

"Start with the butterflies," I murmur, bending my knee and sliding my leg toward me along the duvet. "I want them where yours are."

He pulls in a long inhale before pulling his shirt off and

dropping it to the floor. My eyes drop to his stomach, still not used to the sight of him like this. His muscles flex when he undoes the button on his jeans and slides the zipper down.

"Show me where," he demands.

I tap my inner thigh, just below the bunched hem of my skirt. His nostrils flare as he nods once, bending to drag his lips across the area. My body tenses in response as I pulse with arousal.

"No teasing," I rush out, shaking my head. "I need you now."

"Don't say that."

"I do. I just want to feel you, Shade. That's all I need."

He breaks. There's no need to argue further before he's working both my skirt and panties down my legs and adding them to the growing pile on the floor. He undresses himself next and moves up my body, fitting himself between my legs.

I mewl at the tease of pressure when he rubs through my pussy and kisses me, letting our bodies touch just like this for a few moments. It's enough to steal my breath, desperately trying to steal his in return.

"Gonna be a tight fit without stretching you," he warns, the warning a garbled mess of tension and want.

I take his face into my hands and nod, snaring his eyes. "I don't care."

"*Fuck.*"

With a shift of his body, he lines us up and slowly presses inside. I force myself not to look away from him as my mouth gapes in pleasure. Every inch is accompanied by the cold touch of a piercing, and I hold him tighter, curling my ankle around his thigh.

"That's it, baby. You're doing so good for me," he breathes out, letting his forehead fall onto mine. "Almost there. You're such a good girl, taking my entire cock like this."

It's impossible to stifle my moan this time. It rips through me, hitting his mouth before he swallows it. He finally stops moving, fully buried inside of me.

"Are you okay?"

"Yes," I choke, swarmed with a million sensations.

"Can I move?"

I kiss him in answer, writhing beneath the firm press of his body. The movement forces him somehow deeper, and the metal piercings rub my inner walls.

"Yes!" I demand with a rough noise of pleasure.

He lowers himself over me completely, his heaving chest meeting mine. I turn my head and kiss his bicep as it strains when he starts to pull out. The glide is easy with how wet I am, making the barbells rub in the best way. He stalls once I'm nearly empty before rolling forward, pushing back inside.

"*Princess*," he hisses, closing his eyes. "Tell me you're closer than I am, or I'll stop right now and eat your pussy first. I'm not going to last long like this."

"Don't." I cling tighter, keeping him trapped in place as I wrap my legs around him. "Don't stop."

He grinds his teeth before punching out his next words. "*Tell me.*"

"I'm close already," I whimper.

His body moves faster then, his thrusts growing deeper, harder. Still, he doesn't rush. Each time he fills me, it's a new sensation. We move together, sharing the pleasure erupting inside of us. There's something so different about the way we touch this time.

It's impossible not to recognize that this is what love should feel like. Raw and open, terrifying but comforting. He pushes me with a steady hand, and I tug him with an excited one. There's a friendship at the core of us, and those ties are permanent. What we've built around them is unbreakable.

"Trevor," he mutters, opening his eyes to stare at me.

"What?"

His pelvis grinds against my clit as he stays seated inside of me. "My real name. It's Trevor."

My eyes burn with hot tears. I nod, letting the name echo in my mind before my body shakes, the feel of him so deep growing to be too much—

His deep, vibrating groan follows when I tighten around him and come. I bury my face in his throat and let the bone-deep pleasure in my voice coat his skin, creating a permanent mark of my own. He thrusts into me a few more times, growing more clunky in his movements before stilling.

I almost laugh at how in sync we are and that the last thing to push me over the edge was hearing him tell me the secret I've been waiting to hear since the night we met. My limbs are weak when I let them fall, my body sensitive from the intensity of my orgasm.

Shade lets out a strained laugh before kissing my flushed cheeks. "You're going to kill me one of these days."

"Me?" I snort before moaning when he pulls free of me. "This was all your fault."

"I don't know if I should be offended or flattered that all it took was the sound of my name to get you to come."

I pinch his side, rolling my eyes. "It was more than that, and you know it."

"Mm, maybe."

He rolls onto his back beside me, and I push myself up to follow him, flushing a deeper shade of red when I feel warmth leaking between my legs. Glancing down my body, I stare at the mess he left behind.

"You know, I'm tempted to push that back in," he says, drawing my attention again.

His stare is focused exactly where mine just was, but instead of embarrassment, there's a hunger there that nearly makes me beg him to do exactly what he's threatening. I don't want him to move, though. Not yet.

Turning onto my side, I bring my finger to the healing

tattoo on his sternum. He looks at where I'm touching him now, filling me with a softer kind of heat. Slowly, I lower my hand.

"You know, Trevor and Millicent never would have had a chance," I tease, resting my head on his chest.

His arm automatically curls around me, keeping me pressed against him. "No, princess. But we do."

EPILOGUE

TWO MONTHS LATER

Shelly shoves a mug of hot chocolate into Millie's hands and then drapes a blanket over her thighs, muttering under her breath about her bare legs looking frozen. I smirk in response, squeezing my girl's thigh beneath the heavy fabric of the blanket.

It's the first time I've been invited over to celebrate Christmas like this, and I know that all has to do with Millie. She's become like a second daughter to Shelly, and that means she's automatically invited to all of the family events. Thanksgiving was the same, and I think I still have frozen turkey in my deep-freeze from how much she sent us home with afterward.

I know Millie loves every minute of these nights, though. With the raw wound left behind from her broken relationship with her parents, the one she has with Shelly has kept her too busy to focus on missing them. They're not worth missing, if I'm being honest, but whether they deserve it or not, they'll always be her parents.

Maybe they'll realize that one day.

"She's going full mother hen on you today," I drawl, exhaling across the back of Millie's ear.

The happiness in her words threatens to choke me. "I don't mind."

"She'll get used to it eventually."

"Get used to what?"

"How little you take the weather into consideration with your outfit choices."

She leans her head against my shoulder, snuggling into my side. "If I did that, I'd never wear anything I want to in this town. It's been freezing for months now."

"I'm not complaining."

"Yeah, I know you're not. You like my clothes too much."

"I could do without you wearing heels in the snow and having so many close calls, but yeah, you've got me there," I agree easily.

"How much do you want to bet my gift under the tree is my own pair of those clunky boots she tried to make me wear last week?"

I chuckle. "I'm not taking that bet."

"Are you two talking about me?" Shelly asks, a sassy hand on her hip as she stands in front of the fireplace.

Millie's such a shitty liar that she doesn't even try to answer before tucking her face into my shoulder, hiding. I kiss the top of her head and wink at the older woman.

"Never, Shelly. We were talking about how much we like this blanket. Did you knit it yourself?"

Her scoffed laugh is immediate. "Not a chance. It was a gift from Tilly. She sent a box of them over last week."

"And you already opened them? It's only Christmas Eve." I cluck my tongue.

"She chose not to come again this year. So, you're damn right I opened them early."

The mood in the room dips slightly as we pick up on the tension in Shelly's voice. I had a feeling it could get like this today when I bugged Ash about his coming back for Christmas and he said she wasn't.

Millie's been here for long enough for no one to censor themselves around her anymore, but there are still things she doesn't know. The dark hue of Tilly's past here in Oak Point is one of those secrets. Her recent divorce, however, isn't.

Ash, who's been in the kitchen with his dad for the last few minutes, sticks his head into the room and says, "Don't start, Mom."

"I'm not starting anything!"

Her son huffs, not buying it as he runs a hand over his shaggy blond hair. "You know why she's not here. We're not going to get into it today of all days."

Millie slips her hand beneath the blanket on her lap and takes my hand, threading our fingers. I let her, squeezing with the silent promise of explaining things to her tonight once we're home.

"Did you invite Rowe?" I ask Ash.

He frowns, nodding. "He couldn't make it."

Shelly's husband, Kirk, walks past Ash and takes a seat on the armchair by the fireplace. His dark features have grown weathered, giving away his age. His eyes are still as sharp as they were the day I met him as a kid, though. It's impossible to keep anything from him.

His son struggles beneath the weight of that stare, knowing better than I know the way it can break down even the strongest-willed man. If I had to guess, I'd say that's the reason Rowe isn't here today.

"We'll save him a plate. You can bring it to him later," Kirk says firmly.

"He'd appreciate that, Dad."

Kirk tips his chin in agreement. His wife stares at him, her brows knitting together for a blink before she claps, her expression transforming.

She announces, "It's time for presents."

"We haven't even had dessert yet," Ash argues, patting his stomach.

Millie swings her gaze to him, the corner of her mouth twitching. "Don't act like you weren't in the kitchen eating all the mini cheesecakes I brought. There's some on your collar."

"You know, when you and Tilly meet, you're going to get along great." Ash stares down at his shirt, thumbing away some filling and licking it off. "It's like I have a sign on my back, begging to be teased."

"It's more like a tattoo on your forehead."

Ash looks at me like I'll help him out here. When I shake my head, leaning closer to Millie, he mouths "*traitor*" at me.

Shelly ignores their bickering and moves to the Christmas tree, starting to sort the presents beneath it. Her husband watches with a soft, fond expression, looking so unlike the man he shows the rest of the world.

Millie moves the blanket over my lap, covering the both of us. My smile is instant as I look over at her, soaking up the warmth in her eyes and on her cheeks.

"I couldn't exactly bring your present here with me," I tell her, keeping my voice low so only she can hear.

"That's okay. I'm saving yours for tomorrow."

"Is it you in a sexy Santa outfit?"

A choked noise escapes her. "No. But I should have just saved my money and thought of that."

"It's like you don't know me at all," I scold lightly, nipping at the tip of her ear.

"Shut up."

I pull back with a soft tease. "Such a sore loser, princess."

When she pinches the back of my hand, I laugh, squeezing her fingers tighter. Shelly brings the two of us a present and sets it on our laps, waiting expectantly. It's wrapped to perfection in pastel pink paper and a ribbon a few shades darker.

"Well, what are you waiting for? Open it," she says, nearly squealing with excitement.

"Already? Nobody else has anything yet—"

Cutting off Millie with a pat to the head, Shelly rushes out, "I know you won't stay for much longer before heading home, so please just indulge me and open one before you go."

"You got it, Shelly," I say, looking to Millie. "You do it."

Her fingers fly over the ribbon, untying it before her nails are cutting through the paper. As the wrapping falls away, I narrow my eyes on what looks a lot like a photo album.

"It's a memory book. Every couple should have one. Plus, now you'll have somewhere besides your wallet to keep those photos of you two, Shade," Shelly explains, eyes glittering.

That pulls Millie's attention from the book. "What photos?"

"The ones from the photo booth," I say, unashamed.

"You keep them in your wallet?"

Shelly sighs. "Oh, he does. I saw them a few weeks ago when he insisted on paying for my breakfast at Maggie's. They're quite . . . scandalous."

"Mom, don't snoop through people's personal belongings," Ash groans.

"What? I wasn't snooping. They were clearly very intense photos, and—"

"Thank you for the gift, Shelly. It's perfect," Millie says, her cheeks so red they look painted.

I clear my throat to hide a laugh. "Yeah, thank you."

"You're welcome. I hope I didn't overstep with including a couple's gift, but I just couldn't help it."

"No, this was really thoughtful," Millie whispers, her heart exposed in the way she always seems to do around those she cares for.

I keep an eye on it, knowing there isn't any boundary I wouldn't cross to protect her. Even here, where I know nobody would so much as think anything that could hurt her.

Shelly beams down at her, a beat of silence passing between them. Once their silent conversation is over, Millie clutches my arm and watches our host move back to the tree and start grabbing more presents.

"Is it okay if we stay until all the presents are open?" she asks me softly, bright eyes lifting.

I press a kiss to her temple. "You don't even have to ask. My only plans involve you, Millie. And if this is what you want to do, then we'll stay."

Fuck, I don't remember ever being this happy.

Millie taps her bare feet on the floor, fidgeting.

"You're so impatient," I muse.

"For good reason! You can't tell me that I'm going to love my present the entire drive home and not expect me to be antsy when I finally get to see it."

"Were you doubting my gift-giving abilities prior to the drive, then? Because I don't remember you being like this when we left for Shelly's this morning."

She blows out a dramatic breath. "You're such a snake."

Running my hands down her arms, I start guiding her down the hall, staring at the pink sleep mask I slipped over her eyes a few minutes ago.

"Careful. You know how much I love your insults."

Her mouth twists into a sly smile. "My apologies."

"Good girl," I drawl, my grin rivalling hers.

"Shade."

"Sorry, dear. No more talking until it's time to take the mask off."

"Thank you," she mutters sarcastically.

It's a quick journey to the spare bedroom. I shuffle her into position and then open the door.

"Okay, are you ready?" I ask, flicking the new light on.

"*So* ready."

Once I'm standing behind her, I pinch the mask and carefully remove it. Her gasp is immediate, and I think I'm fucking blushing when she speaks, awestruck.

"A closet? You—you built me a closet? You got rid of the spare room for me?"

"The only person who ever spent any time in here was you, and now that you've moved into my room, it was just sitting empty."

She spins to look at me, then glances back into the room. Her head moves on a swivel, like she can't choose where she should be looking right now.

I swat her ass and give it a push into the room. "You can thank me after."

Her eyes glisten when she nods and reaches for my hand. I give it to her before she pulls me in behind her. The pink room is incredibly bright, and I don't know if that's just because of the new fancy gold light in the ceiling or the pastel paint. Either way, she doesn't seem to mind. She does a slow sweep of the new space, focusing on the custom shelving units Rowe and I put up last night.

They took so fucking long to build that I had to ask Lacey to keep her out at Peakside long enough that by the time she finally got home, she was apologizing to Rowe for the thousandth time about the night they met the entire way out to his truck.

The sangria in her blood was the only reason she didn't get snoopy and pop a look into the closed room, though. Plus, she's the cutest goddamn drunk I've ever met.

"There are lights for all of the shelves and the mirror too," I say.

"This is incredible."

"I know you'll probably want to move things around, but I didn't want to show it to you without any clothes hung up and shoes on the ground. Nothing has to stay the way it is now."

I'm rambling now, heat clinging to my neck and cheeks.

After another long moment, she turns to face me. The full weight of her attention is a welcome pressure as I use our joint hands to pull her close. She slides a hand up my chest to rest on my shoulder. Her fingers twirl a few strands of my hair curling behind my ear.

"This is the most thoughtful gift I've ever received," she declares, her eyes bright and clear.

"Yeah?"

"Hands down."

I palm her cheek, keeping her head tilted back. "You deserve it. All of it."

"I love you," she murmurs.

They're my favourite words she's ever said to me, and they'll remain that way forever.

With my mouth hovering over hers, I say, "I love you, princess."

Then, she's kissing me, and I'm responding in the only fitting way.

Like I'll die if she stops.

Thank you for reading Show Me How! If you enjoyed it, please leave a review on Amazon and Goodreads.

Join my newsletter to receive a bonus spicy chapter with a few inked surprises . . .

I hope you enjoyed your first trip to Oak Point. This is already one of my all-time favourite small towns, and there is so much more of it coming your way.
Book 2 in the Oak Point series is coming in December, and yes, it will be Rowe's story. (Brother's best friend, bronc rider, enemies to lovers with a few darker themes)
You can preorder it now!

While you're waiting for more of these characters, jump into my backlist! Want to learn a bit more about Bryce and Daisy or their friends in Cherry Peak? Jump into my newly COMPLETED Cherry Peak series, starting with Strung Along on KU and Audible.

Strung Along – Brody + Anna (Text pals, country singer x new girl in town)
Catching Sparks – Poppy + Garrison (FWB, one night stand, billionaire)
Chasing Home – Johnny + Rory (Love at first sight for him, golden retriever x black cat)
Stealing Sunshine – Bryce + Daisy (Secret crush, fake dating, roommates)
Choosing Forever – Darren + Delaney (Second chance, single dad, daughter's teacher)

To be kept up to date on all my releases, check out my website! www.hannahcowanauthor.com
Subscribe to my newsletter now!

Acknowledgements

I've written nineteen books now. NINETEEN!

I remember most of them in great detail, with my favourites being the ones that stay with me the most. Show Me How will be one of the novels I never forget.

Millie and Shade healed something in me that I didn't know needed any fixing. They were a breath of fresh air for me while writing, and I flew through their book like I've only done a handful of times in the past. They allowed me to just write something I love with no pressure, and god, I needed that.

As always, I owe a very big thank you to the women in my life who never stop supporting me. Nicole and Becci, y'all know the drill by now. Thank you for the hour-long voice memos, the late-night brainstorming sessions, and for not being afraid to tell me when I've written something that sounds like ass.

To my husband, thank you for everything you do for me. From following me around the world while I share my love of books with thousands of people to helping raise our son like the most perfect stay-at-home man, you make my job possible. I love you.

To Sierra, I love you endlessly. Thank you for being only a text away and for being here on this journey with me. Your ideas never fail to make me giggle and question how I never thought of them myself. You're an icon.

To Lauren-Brooke, thank you for telling me when I'm an idiot, a mastermind, and a pain in the ass. I love you.

To my team of creative masterminds, Sandra, Julie, Mary, and Cassie. Thank you for the thousands of things you do for me. These beautiful book covers, designs, and social posts are all because of you.

And a huge thank you to my influencer team, my arc readers, and to every single reader who shouts about my books. I've been doing this for almost five years now, and that's because of you.